A Man of His Time

ALAN SILLITOE

HARPER PERENNIAL

Harper Perennial
An imprint of HarperCollins*Publishers*
77–85 Fulham Palace Road
Hammersmith
London W6 8JB

www.harpercollins.co.uk/harperperennial

This edition published by Harper Perennial 2005

9 8 7 6 5 4 3 2 1

First published by Flamingo 2004

A catalogue record for this book is available from the British Library

ISBN 0 00 717328 8

Typeset in Galliard by
Palimpsest Book Production Limited, Polmont, Stirlingshire

Printed and bound in Great Britain by Clays Ltd, St Ives plc

Part One

1887–1889

Alan Sillitoe left school at fourteen to work in various
factories until becoming an air traffic control assistant with
t̶ an
rs
zy
g
or
ks

Also by Alan Sillitoe

ONE

A tin alarm clock shattering the first glimpse of daylight broke into Ernest Burton's dreamless sleep. At half-past five on May 2nd 1887 he strode to the mantelshelf in his nightshirt and turned the noise off so as not to wake his brother Edward in the same bed. The ironed striped shirt pulled over his head was followed by his second-best suit. Travelling in working clothes wasn't for him. Finished at the end of the day with the world of fire and iron in the forge, you threw off the leather apron and washed sweat away with strong carbolic to spruce up for the alehouse. Or you walked into the garden to get a whiff of fresh air and bent your back to do some weeding. But on a journey you must look your best.

He arranged the watch and chain into his waistcoat, synchronized to the minute by the church clock. Time meant little to a blacksmith. You started work at six and if trade was good didn't notice the hours till it got dark, but every minute away from the forge was for you to enjoy, not caring what the next hour would bring.

A sluice of the head from a bucket filled at the garden pump sharpened him further after last night in the White Hart supping a pint while talking to his mates and saying goodbye to the barmaid Mary Ann. He trawled fingers through short wet hair and, drying off, opened the curtains to let in light. At twenty-one, with his lines as a journeyman blacksmith, he was off to work for his brother George in South Wales, to get experience and earn his bread – as their father had said.

He'd been to Derby and Matlock, but now he was going to an unfamiliar place, and George who was eighteen years older had drilled him on how not to reach the wrong town by mistake.

3

You had to go where the work was, blacksmiths being as common around here as houseflies in summer, but if the pay wasn't good where he was going he'd come back even if he had to walk, though if all went well, which he expected, it would be better than putting up with the snipe-nosed lot in this area whose horses he shoed, like that preachifying lickspittle Bayley who spent all his spare hours on church business. Once when I fixed his nag he threw sixpence at me for a tip, so I looked him straight in the eye and left it for the striker. I don't take tips, and only touch my cap to a personable woman.

In Wales I'll be working for George, and he doesn't stand for any cap-touching either. People who want their horses shod spout all the penny-pinching notions to save a farthing or two but make no bigger mistake because it isn't economy in the end. They'd come back a lot sooner if I didn't tackle the job my way. A badly shod horse is like a house with rotten foundations.

He took sticks from the warm oven to lay over last night's embers and, when flames stopped chasing each other up the chimney, put the kettle on. Stropping his razor till the water turned hot, he filled a mug for as careful a shave as could be without leaving nicks of blood. You never knew what handsome woman might be met with on your travels.

A slice of pork fat over the piece of bread turned crisp at the heat. Normally it was a crust and a drop of water, before a proper breakfast in the forge at eight, but he was setting out on a journey, and didn't want to get famished.

He checked his bag of tools by the door: hammer, buffer, rasp, drawing-knife, long pliers – everything in place. George told him he didn't need to bring any. They were there already, he said, and they were a weight to carry. Well, George could think what he liked. You worked best with your own tools. You knew their balance. You kept them sharpened to your taste. They were always clean. And as for carrying them, what did you have arms for?

Ernest, at six-feet-five the tallest in the family, overlooked his father's balding head when he came down dressed for work. 'You must have been through those tools a dozen times already. They won't run away.'

Ernest tied the string. 'They wouldn't get far if they did.'

'Tell George when you see him he ought to send Sarah a bit more money.'

Ernest ignored him. You couldn't tell George anything.

'Did you hear me?'

He went through the other cloth bag to make sure of his best suit, spare shirts, razor, boots for walking out, a couple of ironed handkerchiefs, socks, a piece of towel, and some soap in an old tobacco tin. 'I did.'

'Tell him, then,' but knowing he would get no more words from such a stiffnecked son.

His mother came in, a shawl over her nightgown, long grey hair not yet pinned. 'You're off, Ernest?'

'I might as well be.'

He was her tenth child, and the youngest. 'I've put bread and cheese in your bag, and some eggs.'

'So I noticed.'

'You'll spoil him,' his father said.

'No, I won't. He'll not go hungry. It's a long way.'

'A couple of hundred miles, bar an inch or two, so George said.' Ernest smiled. 'I'll be all right, Mother. I expect I'll be back in six months.'

He might meet a girl and marry, stay away for good. Or there'd be an accident and he'd get killed. Or he'd catch a disease and die. Things happened to a young man of twenty-one. You could tell what she was thinking. 'If you meet a nice girl who can write, ask her to send a letter and let me know how you are.'

A cold idea: if he found a girl it wouldn't matter whether or not she could read and write. That wasn't what he'd want her for.

'Do you have enough handkerchiefs and shirts?'

'All I'm likely to.'

She poured tea for his father, then for herself. 'We should have sent you to the Board School. I always knew you'd have to go away.'

'I don't care about such things.' He could tell time, and reckon the numbers for cash. When he was ten George saw him playing by the forge, and decided that nobody was too young to learn the trade. He would have started him earlier if his arms had been long enough and strong enough, and if their father had agreed. 'Don't worry about me, Mother. I can look after myself. And I'm not going to the other side of the world.'

His father, on a second cup of tea, looked up at Ernest. 'It's time you were off. You'll need every bit of daylight to get there. The earlier the better.'

He took his jacket from the back of the door, put on his cap, folded the light raincoat over his arm, picked up both bags with one hand, and said nothing as he walked out.

Air fresh and pleasing, the birds whistled their hot little hearts out after a wormy breakfast. He lifted his cap to the windows of the White Hart hoping Mary Ann would wave back, but she'd be laying fires in the kitchen so couldn't.

Long strides took him towards the hooting train and grey-black smoke over Lenton station. He could have saved a penny or two by walking to Beeston, more in the Derby direction, but the tool bag wasn't light so he would put wheels under him as soon as possible. A young brewer, Harry Hughes, set out on foot last year to a promised job in Sunderland. Men did that, but no Burton was such a pauper he couldn't afford twenty-one shillings for the workman's fare. He'd put a bob or two by for a few months, denying himself the odd pint at times, to avoid the indignity of walking. He could have borrowed the money from his father, but wouldn't owe anything to anybody.

Some come by good fortune easily. A bloke in the pub the other night said that a gang of labourers knocking a house down in the middle of town found what looked like pieces of tin or bottletops. They pelted each other till realizing they were ancient coins, when they ran to get a good price at the silversmith's.

The five-minute ride into Nottingham took him by the castle, squat and bleak on its high rock, thunderclouds piling above he hoped wouldn't follow him to Wales. Fifty or so years ago it was set on fire, an old codger told him who'd seen it as a youth, one of thousands cheering the rioters, the sky all flame when not blotted out by smoke. 'I watched the fire till it started to rain, then walked home. Some of those who stayed were caught, and hanged.' The Duke of Newcastle got twenty-one thousand pounds to have it built up again, so the poor paid for the bonfire out of their own pockets. All the same, it must have been a treat to see it go up.

Smoke in his throat at Derby station, he asked a porter which platform to stand on for Worcester. 'You've got half an hour yet, sir, time for a cup of tea in the refreshment room.'

No reply to that. Time to go outside to the Midland Hotel as well, but he wasn't thirsty, boots clattering on the ironwork of the footbridge, light in the head at belonging to nobody for a day, everything he owned on his back or in his hands, and not caring who was left behind – not even Mary Ann, if it came to that – or what he would find on getting where he had never been.

Tea urns steamed in the refreshment room but he stood outside watching engines and wagons shunting through, footplate men shovelling coal to keep the pistons moving, all the doing of that clever chap Stephenson who'd invented the things, though they'd taken some of the blacksmith's trade.

Two young women went by – he'd bet a guinea they were sisters – the handsome one a year or two older but with the same small nose, pale high forehead, and cherry-rich lips a man would give a fortune to kiss, or stake his life to do even more. The older one wore a tall hat with embroidered flowers along the brim, but the other had a swathe of fair hair roped into a coil and pinned under a sort of yachting cap. Near the edge of the platform, halfway facing him, he fixed them with his eyes so that one or the other would sooner or later turn, and once they became aware of him they might want to make sure of what they had seen, and look again.

A goods train went to the shunting yards, another belched from the engine sheds. When the women moved from getting splashed at sudden rain the younger caught the fire of his grey-blue eyes, took in his tallness, and stare – firm but without being offensive – the trim moustache, and thin features. Premature speech was the mark of someone unsure of himself, though he didn't want to lose an opportunity by such an attitude. If they got on a train before his at least he'd had the pleasure of being noticed. He could afford a look yet keep his dignity as a black-smith.

Her smile was the best present he could wish for. If they were going in the Birmingham direction he would find himself by chance in the same carriage. 'Are you travelling far?'

She must have liked the way he touched his cap, not to know he only ever did so for a woman. 'We're waiting to meet someone.'

It should have been obvious they weren't going anywhere, without hatboxes and portmanteaux. 'You live in Derby, I suppose?'

The glare from her sister deserved a smack in the mouth, but he touched his cap to her as well. She buttoned her mauve gloves, as if he might try to shake her hand. 'Maud!'

'We live at Spondon,' Maud told him, ignoring her sister.

'Do you ever go into Nottingham?'

'Sometimes, to the shops.'

With such a smile the other would have trouble keeping her on the rein. 'We might cross each other's path, then.'

Most unlikely, her look said, nor had he thought so, but you never got anywhere unless you tried it on. He recalled delivering a piece of iron grating to a house in Nottingham, a bit of fancy work his father had done. The woman was a parson's wife, but after a bit of joshing he'd had her on a couch in the summer-house.

The elder girl tilted her head. 'Here's the train, Maud. And they'll be coming first-class.'

Pleased at the encounter, he hoped for better luck in Wales. A crowd along the platform, he pushed through before the train stopped, to find a seat.

Blossom from the trees came down like confetti at a wedding, as if earth and sky thought a meeting might do some good. The Trent flashed steely water now and again, meandered its merry way through the meadows. If the girls at Derby had got on the train he would have helped them into the carriage, a bit of a climb for such dainties, and if they hadn't wanted to talk to him – though he couldn't see why not – he'd have kept an eye on Maud for a mile or two. With the glint in her eyes she looked as if she'd spend marvellously, though he didn't doubt that the one with the sour face would bring the house down as well when she came.

Forgetting them for a moment, he pictured Mary Ann at the White Hart, a well-built girl the same age as himself, worth twenty of them. The blue and white striped high-necked shirt with a lapis lazuli brooch at the throat told him she was no common sort of barmaid, as she assiduously filled the pint pots, or dispensed stronger stuff from a high façade of bottles behind the bar, responding with a flick of her auburn hair if anyone made the kind of remark she didn't care to hear. He wasn't daft enough to talk like that to any young woman.

On first seeing her and asking where she came from her soft though decisive voice had a different twang to the neighbourhood accent. She stood back to answer. 'I was born at St Neots.'

'Where might that be?'

'In Huntingdonshire. I was a milliner's apprentice' – which showed in the neat dress fitting the slim waist so nicely, noticed as she walked into another room at the call of her mistress.

'How did you come to find this situation?' he asked another time.

'My father saw an advertisement in the newspaper, and thought I'd be better off in service than looking for work as a milliner.'

She could read and write, so belonged to a decent family. 'Are there many girls at home like you?'

'I'm the fourteenth child out of fifteen,' she told him, 'but seven died when they were babies.'

'That was a shame. I'm the youngest of ten, and we're all still alive. Will you come out with me on Sunday afternoon? We can walk to the Trent. It's pretty in the meadows.'

'I only have one day off a month.'

He already knew, but the more words from her the better. 'Come on that day.'

'I can't. I go to church. Mrs Lewin sees me there, and fetches me after the service. Then I have other things to do.'

He disliked being denied. 'Such as what?'

'I must write to let my parents know how I am. And then I have to see to my clothes.'

'If that's the way it is.' Men at his elbow were calling for ale. 'Pump me another before you go back to your work.'

He ignored her for a few weeks, though noticed her look in his direction when he asked Ada the other barmaid to fill his tankard. He could have had *her* for tuppence. Her mouth always open, he called her the Flycatcher, not that he had ever seen a fly go in, and she wasn't bad-looking, but would have been prettier if she closed her mouth. Mrs Lewin the landlady told her about it once, but it didn't get through. Even when she smiled her lips barely met but, gormless or not, she'd have done all right under a bush, though to try and get her there would have spoiled his chances with Mary Ann.

Hard to keep his glance from whatever part of the bar she was in, and enjoy the modest way she served, wondering how she could favour anybody more than him as she went quietly about her work. When not at the bar it was because Mrs Lewin had her attending to household matters in the back, or busy on a millinery job. She'd be a useful wife, though he wouldn't tackle wedlock yet, there being so many willing girls in Nottingham.

He had gone home a few weeks ago with a woman called Leah who worked in a lace factory, her husband doing shifts as a railway shunter, and had the sort of time that showed no need to marry for what he wanted. A lovely robust woman ten years older, he seasoned her till she was greedy for all he could give, asking him to call any time he liked, as long as nobody else was in the house.

The only way of getting Mary Ann into bed, and he wouldn't think anything of her otherwise, was with a marriage certificate pinned on the wall behind. So maybe he should ask her hand before anybody else did, though if she turned him down there were plenty of others to keep him busy.

He smiled when his name was called, on realizing it was that of the place they were stopping at, a smell of beer and hops wafting in from the breweries. The train went puffing its way by foundries and forges, workshops and coalpits, wholesome beer fumes replaced by a sulphurous stink. Laden drays trundled up to their axles in mud along lanes and tracks, but even if he got off here he would find work as a trained blacksmith, though he couldn't because George was expecting him in Wales, and George didn't wait for any man, brother or not.

It was George who had tutored him in the basics of the trade from the day he could swing bellows, shoulder pieces of iron, hump bags of coke to the fire, or hold a hammer with a firm hand, and any mishap on the uptake, or slowness in obedience, he got a blow across the shoulder with a bar of iron. George had a temper when it came to doing your work properly.

Filling the unfamiliar idleness Ernest recalled George's fury after setting him to polish a pile of horse brasses. At eleven Ernest hadn't brought out a sufficient shine so George held him against the wall and banged his head until stars prettier than any from the anvil followed him into blackness.

A few moments later Ernest ran into the street, George shouting him back, but Ernest was ashamed at having failed in his work, though knew he hadn't deserved such a knocking-about either.

Thinking it better to do himself in rather than go back, he walked and ran through the streets and across fields, bitterness and anger holding the pain down, no one wondering why he moved with such speed and purpose. Beyond Old Engine Cottages and into the scrubland of the Cherry Orchard, he slowed down but kept on.

In Robin's Wood he pushed through the undergrowth and stopped on seeing an older boy on his belly drinking from the brook. Ernest drew some into his stomach as well, splashed his head to cool the pain.

'What's up, surry?' He was a farm youth, smart in his smock and leggings.

'Nothing.'

'Somebody been knocking you about, have they? Lost your tongue, eh? Well, next time somebody hits you, hit the devil back.'

The wood was peaceful, but he couldn't stay, walked on, along a bridlepath to the canal, not much caring where he was going, ran across the lock gates for fear he would fall if he went too slowly. Maybe someone on the puffballs of cloud looked down at him running in his working clothes, exhausted, scruffy, his heart breaking.

Darkness chased him home, everyone gathering for supper.

George was washed, and smoking his pipe, silent on their mother asking Ernest how he had got his bruises. He said nothing, so was told to wash himself and sit at the table to eat. It wouldn't happen again. But it did, often enough, till he was fourteen when, as tall as George, he picked up a hammer and told him to do no more.

Now he could more than hold his own with George, who had turned him into as hard a man as himself, which was something to thank him for. George could still be surly and distant, but believed you had to help one another in the same family, it was human nature, if you didn't you went under, like many who trod the smooth cobbles to the workhouse with their wives and children, too downhearted to look back.

Passengers getting on and off looked as if they had clinker sandwiches for their dinners every day. Dirty cottages, as dreary as he'd ever seen, squatted between heaps of slag and refuse, and if this was what people called the Black Country, he thought, they could shove it up their backsides; he was glad when the last of Birmingham went, and green fields turned up again.

A middle-aged grey-bearded titchbum of a chap came on board with two workmen in their aprons. Titchbum, who wore a pepper-and-salt suit, waistcoat, cravat, and watch chain with two sovereigns dangling, stabbed the air with opinionated snuff-stained fingers, pontificating thick and fast to the others about some poor bloke called Disraeli, for reasons Ernest couldn't fathom. Then he went on about the price he could get for a bag of nails at his workshop, the other two men nodding like a couple of donkeys at the Goose Fair.

Titchbum ran out of topics, and turned to Ernest. 'Where are *you* going, then?'

Ernest waited till asked again, Titchbum adding 'sir' as politeness called for, hardly a gold-plated sir, but Ernest told him: 'Wales,' and resumed his looking out of the window.

'I expect you heard the first time.' Titchbum's finger came towards him. 'Some people don't know their place,' he said to his companions. 'Not like when I was young. And why might you be going to Wales?'

A word not spoken was a word saved, which might later be used with more effect on somebody else, if you were in the mood to let it. One of the few luxuries in life was the right to be silent, and you couldn't let anybody take it away.

Titchbum's friends looked at Ernest as if, since they had to truckle to their gaffer, so ought he. 'I suppose he's lost his tongue.' Titchbum had a dry annoying I'm-the-cock-of-the-walk laugh. 'Like a lot of young men who don't have one to lose.'

Titchbum's finger came too close. Words could be stopped from invading the mind, but the finger in his direction was different. Titchbum, as a 'self-made man' too much like Ernest's father to tolerate for long, made him wonder why the fool had taken against him.

'He must be a country bumpkin.' Titchbum couldn't leave well alone, as if he'd got worms, or a canker was eating his stomach. Maybe he'd drunk too much whisky with his breakfast, in which case Ernest would have understood, and ignored him.

'I'd be quiet, if I was you.' One of his men had caught Ernest's stare. 'He doesn't work at our place.'

'Neither will you, for much longer, if you don't keep your opinion to yourself. Somebody like him doesn't know when one of his betters is talking to him. I only asked a civil question.'

Ernest got up, fingers spread against the ceiling to steady himself. Titchbum couldn't have realized his height, and remained sitting as a graven fist came close to his face. 'Leave me alone, or I'll throw you off the train.'

He sat to look at a pair of fine cavalry mounts running across a field – a tall trooper standing with a saddle over his arm.

'It's Droitwich in a minute,' Titchbum said. 'We get off there.'

At least one of them deserved a pasting, though none was worth hanging for. He laid a red-spotted handkerchief across his knees, opened a clasp knife, took cheese, bread, and two hard-boiled eggs from a paper bag, thanking his mother for a hungry man's banquet, while the train rattled, and puffed its constant whistle. He could talk to other men in the pub for hours and not feel hungry, but on his own he ate as if reluctant to waste time, however much there was to spare in a train. A man who came in at Droitwich tipped his cap and wished him good morning. He received a nod in response; and then silence to Shrub Hill station in Worcester.

TWO

George had drilled in the procedure to get to the Great Western depot on Foregate Street. 'You should be able to keep everything in your noddle and find the way, but be careful not to get drunk on Lea and Perrins Sauce! If you do, and you're lost, don't be too proud to ask. I know what you're like. You're a stuck-up young bogger. People enjoy it if you ask directions. Gives 'em a chance to do a good turn. So if you aren't sure, open your haybox.'

Every landmark stood out as clear as the items of steel his father sent him to get from the wholesale merchants as a boy, and woe betide him if he came back with measurements that didn't tally. He scoffed at George doubting his ability to keep all instructions in mind. George said that Ernest, being so tall, found it hard to see the ground when walking, yet always avoided treading in horse and dog muck. 'I can't think how you do it.' Ernest did, had trained himself to notice what was everywhere with little or no swivel of the eyes.

After the church his usual striding walk carried him up Shrub Hill, across the canal, and forking left into a road called Lowesmoor. No station was hard to find, coal in the nose and smoke above the sheds, always a flow of traffic towards it, shunting noises to pull you the right way, a jumble of carriages and carts on getting there. The smile wasn't entirely hidden by his moustache: George didn't know everything, was a bit of an old man at times, too set at forty in the path of their father, something to pity him for.

His throat was as dry as the day, so he ordered a fourpenny pint in the crowded taproom of the Star Hotel, an elbow at ninety degrees so as not to be put off his drink by a nudge from the dinnertime riff-raff who, he supposed, were common labourers from some building job. Near enough to the wall clock, he took out his watch and reminded himself not to be late for the half-past two to Pontypool. The taste of his ale was swill compared to the Nottingham stuff, but he pushed his tankard forward for refilling, which would last him until Wales, where George had promised a very fine bitter – though we'll see how right he is.

He settled himself into a window seat looking left, as know-all George had advised. When a woman who was sixty if she was a day pushed into the crowded carriage carrying a large basket with a lid, he stood to put it on the rack for her. 'Are you going far?'

The train was crossing the Severn. 'Only to Ledbury.'

The poor drab looked worn out, a bonnet lopsided on her grey hair. Must have been in Worcester selling her wares, for the basket was almost empty. 'How far's that?'

'About forty minutes.' A toothless smile told him she must live on gristle and baby food. 'I've done it twice a week for the last twenty years, my son.'

'Take my seat, then.' Nobody else looked like getting up, as if she was beneath them because of whisky on her breath. 'I've got legs to stand on,' bending his head only to see more fields.

The train stopped at what looked like the side of a mountain, heavy cloud almost hiding big houses on the lower slopes. Trees and bushes shrouded a summit half-hidden by rainy mist, scenery reminding him of Derbyshire. The air was close, though he only ever sweated in the forge, where it ran off you like drink.

Most of the people got out, and a tunnel later the sky was blue. He seemed to have been travelling days instead of hours, Lenton far behind, glad to be away from working under the grudging eye of a father never satisfied with anything he did, though what Master Blacksmith would be?

Nothing to think about, he fancied another drink sooner than expected. Travelling put salt in your windpipe, and then he was diverted by a youngish woman in all-mourning black getting on at Hereford. He couldn't show breeding by giving up his seat, because the carriage was empty, but the leather portmanteau he lifted onto the rack for her strained his arms as if filled with lead. Observing it, she told him it contained her devotional books.

Bibles and hymnals, it serves me right, but I couldn't let her break such pretty little hands – rewarded in any case by the lift and fall of her bosom as she settled herself.

She didn't thank him, not strictly needed, a good sign because if he talked to her later she might recall her lapse of courtesy and make it easier for him than otherwise. He took in everything without seeming to stare.

She wore a mantle and muffs, pale lips sighing as she took off her bonnet and laid it on her knees. The lifted veil showed a face so porcelain-fine he knew he wouldn't deny himself a word or two later. Auburn hair, roping down her back to contrast with deep mourning, recalled Mary Ann's at home, though he saw good reason to put her out of mind for a while.

Boots buttoned to the hem of her skirt shone black like his own, but a maid hadn't buffed them up or she wouldn't have been on the same class of train. She absorbed the landscape as if to draw out colour that might lighten her blackest of garbs. One hand lapped over the other didn't hide her wedding ring, yet he thought it time to divert her from whatever tragedy soaked her through and through, and who better than himself to give such a service?

With the flicker of a smile he said: 'I started out from Nottingham this morning' – a remark which could bring no response, as he well knew, but you had to begin somewhere, though she didn't even turn her head from a family of sheep on the hillside. Words he hadn't used that day welled up for spending, could now let her know that someone in the world had worse troubles than her own. 'A couple of miles before we got to Derby a chap threw himself out of the train.'

She was as much disturbed at being spoken to as by his shocking revelation. 'Oh dear!'

'It nearly made me late for the change to Worcester.' Time to keep quiet, even if she said no more, and look at birds on telegraph wires, blocked by a cutting. He wondered what the label on her portmanteau said, but the wheels of her curiosity turned sooner: 'Why did he commit such a terrible act?'

George had given an imitation of the Welsh lilt one night after a few pints in the White Hart. 'Now you have me. I can't think

16

why. He was sitting next to me one minute, then the handle rattled and out he went. He was too quick for anybody to save.'

Her mouth showed small white teeth. 'What a terrible sin,' she repeated.

He wanted to hear more from her, so went on: 'He wore a good suit, so it wasn't poverty or debt that drove him to it, though you can't always tell. Perhaps he'd got himself up specially this morning knowing what he was going to do. Some people only do a thing like that when they're smartly dressed, as if they like to look formal as they float into hell. Or maybe he thought to do himself in only at that moment.'

'But why?' Not much colour came into her cheek, but it was a start. 'My goodness, why?'

He wondered whether he hadn't overdone it, though her question called for an answer. 'Perhaps something in the newspaper upset him. Just before he jumped he'd been reading one, and when he went out it was still in his hand, as if he might want to finish what was in it when he got to where he thought he was going. You can never tell much about a chap like that.'

Her lips parted again, as if a smile was somewhere in her after all, though it was far too early. 'Was the poor man dead?'

'He could have been. He wasn't moving when he was on the ground among the nettles.' He liked the nettles part, amazed at what his lips came out with when he got going. 'But just as the train was starting two constables lifted him on a cart and took him away to the infirmary. Unless the morgue was the place they had in mind.'

It was wrong to tell lies, but a plain tale to console was something else, and he waited for more words from her, though if they didn't come it would be no loss to him. George always said there was a time to speak and a time to keep quiet, and you should always know when. If you let others speak it saved you bothering, and you might get to know something. Only talk when you knew what you wanted to say before opening your mouth. Then close it when you'd finished. On the other hand words could be like tadpoles. You might have them by the tail but they often slipped out.

Land rose mountainously to either side, the train spindling a river whose name he didn't know, fields and rivers much the same everywhere. The lovely woman was so shy he forgot his intention not to speak till she did. In any case he wondered about the wedding ring. 'Are you travelling far, miss?'

She stared numbly. 'I'm a married woman.' A young and handsome man was only trying to be kind. 'Not very far. I shall be alighting at Newbridge.'

George had mentioned it as two stops before his, so she would need his help at Pontypool on changing to the Swansea line. 'My name's Ernest Burton,' he said, now that the waters of her speech had been broken. 'But call me plain Burton. Everybody does. I'm going a bit beyond Newbridge, where my brother has a smithy. He tells me it's a dirty little hole, though good for business.'

'You could say the same about most settlements in the coalfields.' She flushed, as if not sure her judgement was reasonable.

'You're in black, I see.' Hardly possible not to, but what could you say? Her ability to speak seemed an accomplishment, so he had to come out with something. 'You have my condolences,' hoping that whatever happened had been long enough ago.

'Thank you.' Tears shone like pearls on her pale cheeks, and the ironed handkerchief from his pocket was there before she could pull hers from the muff, which she accepted as one was entitled to do in the land of mourning, so that if nothing else happened he'd kiss the memory of her cheeks on soft cotton as long as the imprint lasted.

'My husband died three weeks ago.' She looked towards the luggage rack, as if his image might appear by Ernest's shoulder or as if, he thought, his body might be in the portmanteau.

Killed by a horse? Sunk with delirium tremens? Bludgeoned to death by a footpad? Got consumption and coughed himself to death? Suffered a growth? Had a seizure? He tried to guess. 'That's a terrible thing to have happened.'

The young man was as if sent by Our Lord to comfort her. 'He was an engineer at a coalmine in Staffordshire.'

'Such places are dangerous. I've never been down one.'

Another dab at her left eye. 'I wish my husband hadn't. It

took all day to find his body under the coal, but the undertaker did a beautiful job.'

And so he should. Every man must know his trade. One of them would already be working on the chap who had jumped from the train near Derby – if it had happened – which he was about to mention but was glad he didn't, because she said: 'I'm going to live with my sister. My other possessions will go on by carrier.'

Church books in the portmanteau were too precious to be trusted to the road. Her grief was tempered by an air of tenderness in a compartment growing smaller by the minute, a loosening in her, as if she didn't know where she was, or what she was doing or, what was better, wasn't able to know – like the effect of a tot of whisky.

He felt as if alone with a woman in a meadow on a warm spring day, knowing there was only one thing to do before dusk came on. The unexpected sense of levity and opportunity was more than welcome, though he wondered whether it was only in him, at the same time sure a good measure came from her, pious as a dormouse or not.

He held her cold hands to give comfort, as a man should, his as ever hot, large compared to hers, a sheltering stove she couldn't refuse. 'What about your children?'

'There aren't any, which I suppose has turned out for the best, though I'm sorry the Good Lord didn't bless me with some.'

Her husband's spunk had been no good. 'Was he a great age?'

'He was twenty years older, a good and upright man.'

He would be, at that age. 'I'm sure he was.' Breath and body heat thickened the air between them. If this goes on we'll need to be prised apart with a chisel. Time to get going, though not sure how she would take it. Moving to her side was a better place to console, seeing as how she needed him, but the goodness of his heart brought on more weeping, which wasn't the ticket at all.

A passenger looked in for a seat but, unwilling to intrude on mutual and private grief, stepped down. A chink in the blind showed the train steaming along a valley, its whistle permitting them to do what they would, his only hope that no one else would try to get into the carriage.

He secured the blinds, and put his lips to her warm forehead. Hers were moist with a kiss no man could resist, or care what was behind it. A hand around her neck, the other at her well-covered bosom, he took in the rich clean odour of hair, yet held back from going like a bull at a gate, the urge to be fast a sure sign that you must go slowly.

She turned away, but a kiss at the nape of the neck always got them on the melt, Bible books in the portmanteau no defence for a woman's flesh whose gander was up. A sudden leaning forward told him she knew it was too late to hold back, though any sign and he would have stepped up and asked her pardon. Men were rightly prosecuted for bothering women in trains, and the treadmill wasn't for him.

A sudden jerk and she crushed herself to him, saying softly: 'Oh, do take me, then.'

Not to accept her would be unmanly. He lifted her, a free hand drawing his raincoat from the rack to lay on the seat, using all his strength to let her down as if onto a bed of feathers. Clothed arms rustled around his neck, till the seat vibrated under her, carmine features contrasting with the black of mourning as she held out her arms.

No more waiting, he bundled up the complication of skirts, and she drew him through smells of lavender and sweat to the greed of that vital place. All control was given up as if only now able to allow it after her husband's death. He held back to match her eagerness but she was determined not to let him (which couldn't be held against her) and spent more quickly even than Leah.

An hour ago they hadn't known each other, but she must have been half in death for it, the stars fixed that he would be the one to be drawn by her so completely. Glad that she had reason to be pleased with taking him as much as he had taken her, he was also amazed at a coupling of so few words, when with others he'd used many in his persuasions, Nottingham girls brazenly expecting them so as to save, he supposed, what they thought of as their modesty.

Her smile could only be for the ironic twist to his lips while she went back to her status of bereaved woman. The handkerchief that had dried her tears was used to wipe between her legs, as he stood away to fix his buttons. She held out her hand when he moved to put the soiled handkerchief into his bag of tools, demanding it for her reticule, then arranged her dress and sat down. He fetched out a clean one, blessing his mother who had ironed it so well. He looked into her eyes to let her know she deserved more than had been given. Flicking up the blind he was surprised that the world was still the same, yet thinking that if this was travelling by train he wouldn't mind doing a bit more.

She shaded her eyes as if daylight was too much for them. 'We're close to Pontypool.'

Needing to smoke, he took out a packet of Robins, lit one, and dropped the spent match on the floor. He moved to touch her, at the flush knew she wanted him to, but there was only time for a press of hands. 'I'll see you walking the street at Newbridge, if I can get out a bit from my work.'

'My sister's husband is a Methodist minister, which iş why I came third-class. The Good Lord doesn't like waste.'

'They'll keep you locked up, I shouldn't wonder.'

She arranged her mantle. 'I'm a widow, so I can walk out on my own.'

'I shall look for you.' I could marry her, if I wanted the bother of courting, take an armful of blooms to meet her in-laws, and make them think I'm somebody I'm not. 'What's your name?'

She tied the strings of her bonnet. 'I'm Mrs Dyslin.'

That wasn't good enough. 'And who's she when she's at table?'

'Minnie.'

A pretty name. He had given his already, but didn't want her to forget. 'I'm Ernest Burton, blacksmith. My brother has a forge near Tredegar Junction.'

'That's close to my sister's.'

'So I might see you.'

She sat as if never wanting to leave. 'I feel better than I did an hour ago.'

'I'm glad. And I'm sorry for your loss, but you've got to go on living, whatever happens, that's all I know.' He was surprised at offering so many words of consolation. Well, he could talk when he wanted to.

'You're a young man.'

'I'm twenty-one, and that's not young. Not in my line it isn't.' She must be a few years older, but it wasn't right to ask a woman's age. Not that it mattered, as long as you gave her what she wanted.

'I'm going to be the housekeeper at my sister's, because she's ailing much of the time. That's all I can do with my life from now on, though there is a small annuity in my name. My sister has been married ten years, and has four children. Two are young, so I can teach them their letters, make myself useful in whatever way I can. Frank, he's the minister, will be grateful if I arrange everything to do with the household, I know, which will help me forget my troubles.'

Maybe she'd have a child after what they had done, people thinking that the last act of a dutiful husband had been to lie with her, the timing more or less right. His smile brought one back, a rose opening under the warmth of summer, happiness that would need concealing once she got to where she was going.

The train squeaked alongside the platform at Pontypool Road station, and he reached for her bag, noting how much livelier and more attractive she was after what they had done, back in the world of the much desired where he hoped she would stay, because a woman can look beautiful at any age as long as loving spunk is pumped into her which goes straight to the eyes and makes them glitter with the come-on of a peahen everybody likes to see. There's only one way to please a woman, and if another woman guesses what it is, I'll please her as well. Minnie's brother-in-law expects her to look sad in her black, so I hope he doesn't wonder what she's been up to.

He set their bags on the platform, held a hand for her to step down. George would twit him half to death if he could see him acting the cavalier.

'The platform's over there,' she said on seeing him hesitate. 'The notice says so.'

'Ah, so it does.' He kept a footstep behind, something against his habit, since a woman's place was to walk after the man. When the train set off she was blawting again. Her husband had died three weeks ago, and she was crying because things would seem strange at her sister's, till she got used to it. Women often cried for less, so he spared another handkerchief to mop the salty waters, feeling in some way responsible for her.

Two long pools flashed by, furnaces and collieries scattered over the valley. A train puffed and billied up a hillside among scarves of smoke. 'At least you've got a sister to go to, and you'll be all right once you get there. A family is all a person needs.'

She stopped crying. 'It's not that.'

He leaned forward to touch her warm cheek. 'If her husband gets on to you, and makes your life miserable, I'll have a word with him.' He showed his fist, hard and worn with work. 'I'll look after you.'

She was shocked. Didn't all women want protection from bullies? 'It's not that,' she said. 'It's that I would like to see you again sometime.'

'And so you shall.' He was gratified, though not sure it would be possible because George would have him slaving all the hours God sent. 'Write your address so that I shall know where to find you.'

She took a silver pencil and small pad of paper from her reticule.

'And if you want to find me, send a note to the post office at Pontllanfraith,' where George called for his letters. 'That'll find me.'

He slipped the note into his lapel pocket, looked at woods to either side of the track. 'It'll be the second stop after this,' she said. 'My brother-in-law told me in his letter that he would meet me with his pony and trap.'

The departure kiss was as if they were married, or at any rate as if he ought to marry her, though he scoffed at the notion. Her embrace was so passionate because of the loss of her husband, and maybe even of him. It could not be prolonged, though the look of tenderness pleased him. 'I'll put your bag on the platform.'

His tall figure leaned from the carriage window watching the brother-in-law greet her with uplifted hat, a slender middle-aged man whose smile was nowhere close to his face, a Stephen Meagrim in a Bible-black garb almost as deep as her own.

Glad to be by himself, he sat opposite a man and woman who fixed him as if knowing he couldn't be of the area. The man was probably a farmer, and the bedraggled woman one you might see on a winter's day trudging towards the workhouse. But they smiled, and wished him good afternoon.

Another cutting of green and shale, and the train stopped. The first thought as he stepped down was to slake the windpipe, but he must let George know he had arrived. He looked north, east, south and west and along the lane wondering where the forge could be, feeling more alone than he liked now that Minnie had gone. Seeing a ragged man covered in coal dust, as if he had just crawled out of the earth, he asked the way to the forge.

Teeth showed white when he smiled, Ernest barely understanding the singsong response, but waving hands gave the direction, and he walked towards houses on the main road.

The sky was cloudless, air sweet, a sun still high enough to warm the ripening hedges, a couple of larks arguing as if their wings were lips. It was good to be alive and on his own in a foreign country. Coal smoke tangled faintly at a change of wind as he put down his bags to light a cigarette. He would have plenty of work from now on, knowing George.

THREE

The forge was a small building of neat red brick and slate roof on its own at the end of a lane. A field behind sloped up to a line of trees that marked the track of a railway, lifting beyond to a skyline of villa-type houses.

George, leather-aproned and fire tongs in hand, stood at the door, looked more surprised than welcoming at his brother's appearance. Willie, the bearded shortarsed striker holding a shoeing hammer, called in a squeaky voice: 'I could tell it was you a mile off. Master Burton asked me to keep an eye open. You walk just like him, as if you owned the world!'

'Shut up, you daft old bogger.' No blacksmith suffered fools gladly.

'You've come, then,' George said.

Ernest didn't suffer fools at all, so made no answer. None was needed. Everybody could see that here he was.

'I'll shut the place up in a bit,' George said, 'then we'll wet our whistles at the Mason's Arms. I expect you're ready for one. I know I am.'

'What about my tool bag?'

'Keep it here. It'll be safe.'

'Let's hope so.'

'You don't trust anybody, do you?'

No answer was needed to that, either. Not even his brother, if it came to that.

'Anyway,' George swung the big doors to, after Ernest had taken the bags inside, 'there's plenty of work for both of us. I'll set you on straightaway in the morning. There's a chain to make, and a few scythes to sharpen, for a start.'

The bar room was full, men at their pipes and pots before

going home, such a gabble Ernest couldn't pick out a word, a pint sliding down like an eggtimer with the bottom ripped out, which stayed his hunger. 'You can sleep on the floor tonight,' George bawled, 'and tomorrow we'll fix you up with Mrs Jones. She'll lodge you for twelve-and-six a week. And her husband's a miner, so don't think you can get away with anything. They're God-fearing people who go to chapel every Sunday.'

'Can't we share your room, and I'll pay half? What do I need one for myself for?'

'You can for me.'

The floor was better than a bed too short to stretch on. He suffered now and again with twinges of cramp, as did many black-smiths because of too much sweating, and even large intakes of salt didn't help. 'We'll go, after this,' George said, on his second jar. 'I've got to save the pence so's I can send a florin or two back to Sarah. Six young 'uns are a lot to feed. Did you see 'em before you left?'

'They were in bed when I called. Except Sarah. She was at the washtub.' At forty she looked an old woman. No man should leave his wife after they were married. 'She wondered when you'd be coming home.'

'I'll send another money order, then she can stop wondering.'

'It's a hard life for her.'

George's Adam's apple worked down the last drop of ale. 'It is for me, as well.'

Nothing more to be said, Ernest followed him to the door. Clouds rushed from somewhere and brought a drift of rain, but the air was fresh and sweet, a few stars showing as they tramped along the rough clinker-covered road, potholed and worn from the traffic of drays and wagons. You had to take care where you put your feet. Ernest filled one of the holes with a long piss. Pictures closed in from the day's trip and his encounter with Minnie, her forlorn goodlooking features less clear now than those he had left her with, the memory of her warm arms such that cheeky John Thomas chafed at his trousers.

Lights showed faintly from farms and cottages on the hillsides, trains whistling from all directions. Dimly-lamped drovers' carts trundled towards the red and coppery sky.

'It's always busy round here.' George didn't find it easy to keep up with Ernest who, descending to a crossroads, noted the post office. A left turn beyond a narrow river took them by another public house into a street of raw houses, and faint odours of iron and sulphur.

George's room was small but neat, his best suit covered in brown paper on the back of the door, shaving materials laid out on the fireplace shelf before an oval mirror with a brown stain in the middle. Seeing the single bed, Ernest didn't have to wonder where he would sleep, though unsure that any man could do so with the clink of bottles, shrieks, and breaks into song from next door. 'Is somebody getting married? Or are they just back from a funeral?'

'It's like that often.' George put a match to the fire laid before setting out for work that morning, and took off his jacket and belt. 'But you can't tell 'em to be quiet. They're Bible-backed Taffies, and like a drink now and again. It's live and let live around here.' He took a loaf and two plates from a cupboard on the wall. 'The bread's a bit hard, but it'll have to do. The bacon's good, though, and there's a bottle of ale each. A Hebrew pedlar comes from Newport, so I got a couple of penny bloaters. He's an obliging chap. Anything else you want and he'll bring it up on his cart.'

They sat on the bed and, with the remains of what their mother had packed, ate fish, meat, and cheese by the light of a candle in front of the mirror. An argument from next door, as if the walls were made of cardboard, caused Ernest to look up. 'People have got to sleep after their work.'

'It's nothing to do with us,' George told him. 'Work is what I want to talk to you about. If you're lucky you'll earn a guinea a week, maybe more at times. We get farmers' trade, and the odd thing or two from the pit or railway. If you aren't lucky you might draw less than a quid, but you'll be better off than at home. Our work's got a good reputation, and people know where to come.'

Ernest was willing to work if he could put the odd shilling by for when he got back to Nottingham. 'Everything's arranged, then?'

'As much as I can make it. I'm not God. Anyway, we'd better look to our sleep. We need to be up by five.'

Ernest took the suit from his bag and smoothed out the creases, hanging it behind George's on the door. The inability to hear his brother's words may have been no bad thing at times, but was not to be tolerated now.

George noted the direction of his gaze. 'You might have the key to the door at home, but you don't have it here, so leave them alone. They'll be done in an hour. It don't bother me. I can sleep through anything.'

A man's head slamming against the party wall was followed by a cascade of cheering. 'Doesn't the landlady put in a word?'

'She daren't, I think.'

He took off his neckcloth and, before George could tell him not to be such a fool, set off across the landing. His shins caught a large iron bucket which, going by the stink, was for use should anyone feel a call in the night. Punching the door open, he bent slightly to get through.

Such a pack of scruffy dwarfs he had never seen. He with the banged head sat on a box, pressing his temples as if to hold in whatever bit of brain lay between. Another man with uptilted bottle was getting rid of the beer quite nicely, while a third who was lighting his pipe by the fireplace asked what Ernest interpreted to be: 'What might *you* want?'

'I'm from next door.' He spoke in as reasonable a voice as could be mustered. 'We've got to be up before five, and want to get some sleep.' He stood a moment, to be sure his message was understood. 'So I'd be obliged if you'd make less noise.'

Thinking he could safely turn, a bottle hit the lintel by his head with the force of a shotgun. Thanking God they were half-drunk, he faced them again. 'Any more of that, and I'll lay you all out.' He was ready, but no one came for him. 'All I ask is that you keep a bit quieter.'

'You'd better sleep in your clothes,' George said when he closed the door. 'It gets cold around here, even in May. There's a bit of blood on your cheek.'

'It'll dry.'

'I'm glad you didn't have it all your own way.' George

sometimes disliked the sort of person his brother had turned into, who at times seemed reckless and needed watching. He was young, and just didn't think, though whether he would ever be capable of that he wouldn't like to prophesy. 'It's all right threatening violence but you've got to think well beforehand, and not do it out of temper.'

Ernest lay on the floor, a blanket over him, and his folded bag for a pillow. 'I did think about it, but I think quick.'

George didn't want to feel responsible for what scrapes Ernest got into in Wales, but knew that brothers must never stop caring for each other.

They traipsed through a deep and ghostly mist between hedgerows. 'I forgot to tell you,' George said. 'I've got a chap coming from the village today who's going to take a photograph of me at the forge. I fancy getting something back to Sarah showing me earning my bread. Otherwise she might think I'm living the life of Riley.'

'How much will it cost?'

'Only six-and-a-tanner, because he's glad to do it for that price. He likes taking photos of blacksmiths. Don't ask why. He wanted to know if there was a tree outside, and when I told him there wasn't he looked a bit put out, but then said he'd do it, just the same. He only hopes it won't rain, in case his camera gets wet.'

A thin man of middle height, a cigarette under his clipped moustache, ash flaking into the greying Vandyke beard, Ashton gaffered them into place like a sergeant-major. Ernest was surprised at the latitude allowed to such a shortarse, till the picture began to compose around George as the star. Then Ashton had to wait till a placid carthorse was brought to be shod, and George took the hoof firmly between his legs. Sleeves rolled up, he was told to look towards the camera, as was everyone in the scene, head tilted uncomfortably to show full face.

Thick hair was combed forward to a line along his forehead, moustache sloping to either side from under the nose. He gripped the hammer a third of the way down the haft, poised to nail on the shoe held with a pair of long pliers by the striker, a small bearded dogsbody George employed by the day. He steadied the horse's head.

Leaning against the wall was a man with a curving pipe in his mouth, not in working clothes but wearing a collar and tie because the horse belonged to him. Two little pinafored girls on their way to school were collared by Ashton to stand by his side and complete the scene. Ernest and George were the only men not wearing caps.

Ernest didn't want to be part of it, yet chose not to upset his brother by looking on from the open door, unmistakably himself, a tall thin young man with a well-shaped head whose thatch of short hair made a line halfway down his brow much like his brother's. He wore a highnecked collarless shirt, a working waistcoat, but no jacket, a self-aware youth who wanted after all to be somewhere in view. He looked towards the camera, speculating on the mechanism when the black cloth went over Ashton's head.

The photograph came a week later with, printed on the back in an ornate scroll: 'Ashton of Pontllanfraith, Monmouthshire.' George was happy with the scene. 'Do you want a copy?'

'Not likely.' Ernest didn't care for anything to do with the picture, since he wasn't the gaffer in it, but he would keep it in his memory as something he hadn't had to pay for.

Rasp in hand, Ernest faced the dray horse's quarter, the front left hoof between his lower thighs. Willie, a tool bag convenient to his feet, waited to put on the new shoe. Ernest told the horse to keep still, though there was little need with such a quiet animal.

All through youth he had talked more to horses than he did or wanted to to people, not only because horses couldn't answer back – the worse thing, he reckoned, that either human or animal could do – but because they liked to hear your voice even if you only nattered about the weather. It also calmed those horses that baulked at being pushed between the shafts when the work was finished.

He talked in silence but as if he'd be heard and understood. I'll do the thing so well you won't tell whether you're walking at all, especially as the tracks around here are fit for neither man nor beast.

To get the old shoe off was a job in itself, because you never tear the nails out by force, as I've known some blokes do. Raise the clenches carefully and keep them straight, so that you don't make the holes wider, or injure the hoof, or leave in stubs that make the horse limp, or go lame after a while. A horse who's had that done to it feels pain just like a person, so it's harder for other smiths to shoe and the horse might injure them in its distress. You get the job done as quickly as you can or you won't make any money, but you still have to do everything well.

He rasped down the cusp at the edges, careful not to take off too much, for if you did the hoof would become too thin. Sometimes the horn of the sole was so hard and thick it needed softening with heat, though not in this case, which saved a bit of trouble. A flat iron drawn over the sole and held close for a few moments did no harm, and made it easy for the horse after a little paring here and there.

'Let's have the shoe, Willie.' Some daft ha'porths who were as mean as hell with their pennies arranged for a smith to make so many shoes a year, but they got taken in, because the smith might put heavier shoes on the horse hoping they'd last longer and save him making so many, which wasn't good for the horse.

An almost perfect fit – nothing could be perfect, however you tried – but he went to work with the file. The cold fitting needed a good eye to get all surfaces flush. He'd made shoes for anything from a pony to a lame Clydesdale, and every hoof was different, as every shoe had to be.

George and his father had taught him that you could always tell if a horse was happy after you had shod it, and if some never were it was the fault of their owners for not treating them right, who think all you need do for a horse is feed it and pat it on the backside now and again, and then it'll do whatever you want and not need any other looking after, but a horse is a living thing and knows more than you think. As for beasts born with pebbles in their belly, you talk them into keeping still, avoiding wounds in the fleshy parts when putting the shoe on so as not to cause presses or binds. Horn's thicker at the toenails than elsewhere, so you begin there and work back till you've done the seven new nails, guiding the shoe into position by sound and feel, and calculating the angle of each cleat to give a firm hold.

That's that. Now you won't have gravel or dirt getting underneath and chafing you to hell and back. The farmer whose horse it was leaned by the wall. 'You've done a good job, I see.'

Ernest ignored the remark. What does he expect, a bad one? He smoked a cigarette, and after the horse had been led away George said: 'I like to keep that old chap happy. He's a good stick and a fair customer. I shall want you back inside now though.'

Work never stopped. They were lucky. He placed a length of bar iron in the fire till it took the heat. Skill and instinct were like man and wife, George often said, no one knowing where one ended and the other began. He watched the metal in the fire, and at the right moment swung it to get rid of cinders and loose flakes. With the striker beating time on the anvil to keep him in tune, he manipulated the metal with his hard hammer into the form of a shoe, shaping the heels to a proper slope.

Turning it over, he pressed out the fullering, and began to stamp the nail holes, slightly marking them at first, then with heavier blows driving them well in and finally right through, all at the same heat and no time to lose. The rhythm controlled time itself and, as his father had always said, when you had grasped the notion of timing you were more than halfway to becoming a master of the trade.

George stood at his shoulder. 'There'll be a few more to do after this.' To which there was no reply but to get on with it.

On the way home, calling at the post and money order office for tobacco, Ernest was handed a small envelope which could only come from Minnie. George had picked up the ability to read but Ernest didn't want him nosing into his business, so had no option but to knock on next door at their lodgings after supper and ask Owen the bottle-thrower for his services, setting a jar of good Welsh bitter on the table. All three men stopped what they were doing. 'One of you knows your letters, I hear,' Ernest said.

The man with the battered head stared at the embers between the bars while setting a kettle on, and the pipe-smoker at the table was about to tackle a large round loaf with a carving knife, saying: 'Read his letter, Owen, then we can drink his beer.'

'I lost my temper last time,' Ernest said. 'I'd had a long day.' He never apologized, but came close to it now, hoping he would never have to do so again, though knowing that Minnie was worth it.

The room wasn't clean, but everyone could live as they wanted. Favour for favour, he would do one for them if he could. The man turned from the kettle. 'I don't want to read it if it's bad news, man.'

'There's no such thing, as long as your wife and children are safe. And I've got neither. So come on, I hear you read the Bible often enough.'

'Keeps it under the bed so I won't light my pipe with the pages. They flare up a treat!'

Owen unfolded the note and held it high, as if proud of being able to recite in a singsong half-mocking tone: 'I shall meet you on my walk in the wooded place near Newbridge, across from the tramway. I stroll there on most days, and pray you will do so as well.'

'What name?'

'No name. Only MD,' Owen said. 'But I'm sure you know who it is.'

Gratified at Minnie's sense, Ernest thanked him, and held out a hand for the letter, but without meeting Ernest's eyes, Owen smiled, and slowly tore the paper into pieces. Ernest had intended putting it into the forge in the morning, so the fool had saved him the trouble.

A man in collar and tie huffed and puffed uphill on his penny-farthing, alighting at the top to look at a sheet of paper to find where in the world he was. Ernest passed, and walked as far as the tramway, coal drays rattling in the opposite direction. Work never stopped, but had to for him, wanting to keep his tryst with Minnie.

He followed a hedge as far as the wood rather than going through the village where his conspicuous figure might be remarked on, not wanting to get her talked about. Sheep stared from a field, ran towards the middle chased by crying lambs. Cornflowers thrived on the windless bank, a flash of rosebay by fully-leafed trees bordering the scrag of woodland. The day was hot and dry, but he didn't suppose the clouds would stay high for long because the wind was changing.

Last year's twigs cracked under his boots, and he used all-round vision so as not to miss her, though in an area of such sparse trees she'd easily be seen. A rabbit panicked towards a patch of ferns, and when another followed he picked up a stone, but the thing was too fast. To get a rabbit on the hop was difficult without a shotgun, though you couldn't use one in a wood for fear of hitting a person. If you did you'd be for Dartmoor or the rope. All the same, a rabbit would make a fine stew when caught and skinned.

She walked through a patch of sunlight on green, in the deepest of mourning still. Coal trucks had to pass before he could cross, so many glimpses of her through the gaps she looked a different woman every time. She took a hand from her muff, which he held for a moment, her fingers more those of a working woman. 'The day's warm, but the wind's got a chill in it,' he said.

'I hurried. I was so hoping to see you.'

The same for him, though he didn't say. 'I'd been wondering how you were getting on.' She stood a few feet away, but he went forward to kiss a face no longer pale. She had been eating well, at any rate. 'They're looking after you, I see.'

'I'm very happy there.'

Memories of the train journey reminded him that he was only here for one thing. He gripped her hand, drew her towards denser vegetation. 'We'll walk over there for a bit.'

Her eyes half-closed, tears about to run. 'Ernest, I must tell you. I'm with child.'

'Are you, then?' His exclamation indicated that the matter need have little to do with him. 'You mean it's mine?'

Her look of entreaty was mixed with some pleasure. 'We fornicated on the train.'

Such a plain statement brought a flush of wanting that day over again. 'Does the parson know?'

'I told my sister, and she informed him.'

'What did he say?'

'He told me it was God's final blessing on me and my husband. He was very happy. We sat around the table and read the Bible so that he could give thanks to the Lord.'

A few moments went by. 'I suppose it could be your husband's. It's as well the parson thinks so.'

Pale eyes fixed him while she crushed an elderberry leaf. 'It can only be from you.'

He hadn't thought to send a child into the world just yet, though it was no shock to know that he could do so. It wasn't a feat for any man, though the story was a good one to tell George, except that it would stay a secret forever. Her eyes and lips formed such a smile that he yearned to get her into bed, and have the delight of ploughing babies into her for the rest of his days. All cares swept away, she would have it in her to give both a lifetime of spending. 'When it comes we'll have to talk about what to call him.'

'What if it's a girl?'

'It will be a boy. It's got to be. Now come with me.'

'I can't delay. They're expecting me for tea.'

'They'll keep it on the hob for you.' He stepped back and took hold of her. 'I love you. You know that, don't you?'

She put her arms around his neck with a sweeter passion than he could recall from any woman. 'We ought to marry, Ernest.'

'A woman waits for a man to propose. Only I can't. I'm promised.' He might or might not be, though going by the glances he had got from Mary Ann he could claim to be. Lying was against his pride, but he wondered whether he would get the warmth from Mary Ann as now came from Minnie Dyslin.

'If you're promised, there's nothing I can say.'

'It can't be that bad,' he said at her tears. 'What would your parson think of you marrying a blacksmith? I'm a journeyman still, and go everywhere to find work. I never know where I'll be from one year's end to the next.' The space in her would have to be filled by the child.

She pulled him close. 'See me as often as you can while you're here. That's all I ask.'

'I'll do that.' It wouldn't put him out. 'You're the finest woman I've known. There's never been anyone I wanted more.'

She followed his long back into the bracken, noting where he trod. He turned: 'Come on, Minnie. And don't lose your muff.'

He sometimes wondered when he would go back to Nottingham, though homesickness was no part of him. Sooner or later he would go because that was what you did after a stint in a strange place. You did what mattered, not what you thought. He would be sorry to leave a girl in Tredegar Town, as well as Minnie, whose child he'd see into the world and get a look at, feeling such curiosity about the matter it was necessary to fix on his work with more than ordinary attention: hammer and tongs weren't playmates, nor the anvil a silent partner. A blow at the glowing iron with the wrong weight behind might cause a spark and blind you. They mostly went wide, and looked pretty enough in their angles, but the odd little murderous fly, all metal and fire, could stop your sight forever before you even saw it, the one-eyed blacksmith not such a rare bird in the trade.

It didn't do to think and work at the same time, no matter what pleasant features flashed to mind, best to save it for when the beer was going down your throat, or on your way to Pontllanfraith in the evening.

'You've got something on your mind,' George said while they were eating their bread and polony in the forge.

Ernest wouldn't sit outside for his dinner, not wanting strangers to gawp while he ate. Anyway, it was raining. 'That's nothing to do with you.'

'Your head's full of it. Not that you'll say much.'

Ernest grunted in the way of their father. 'Not more than usual I wouldn't.' When the boy came back with their beer jug from the Mason's Arms he fixed him with a gaze. 'You've had a swallow or two out of this.'

The boy was shoeless, stunted and half-starved, barely worth the half-crown a week George paid him for fetching and carrying. He reared at the accusation, an arm over his face to hold off blows, not so rare when he irritated George, who only took him on to have a body for knocking around. 'I didn't,' he cried. 'I would never do such a thing, Mr Burton.'

He'd be daft if he didn't. Ernest had always taken a good sup as a child when sent to get ale. He passed the boy a large part of his sandwich, saw it find a good home in his mouth, then drank his share of the pot.

Standing at the door, warm and gentle rain giving a smell he had grown to like, he wondered how much higher Minnie's belly would be on next seeing her, nobody able to tell what was in his mind, and whoever stared trying to find out would come up against a wall no nosiness could break.

Let George tap all he liked, he'd get no answers, though you had to watch it. The less somebody knew about your business the better for them but most of all for you, the only trouble being that you had no control over what people said about you between themselves.

The weather was too bleak to go in the wood so they stayed outside, such December cold as if blankets of snow were on their way. He wore his suit and light raincoat, since it was Saturday afternoon and he had a young woman to see at Tredegar in the evening.

Close to her confinement, Minnie said that their last meeting had been spoken about in the village, and if one person knew, they all did. Luckily it was a day when she hadn't cared to be touched in the way he wanted, being too far gone with the baby, but her brother-in-law asked who the man was. 'So I told him about you.'

Such tongue-wagging was an attack on his inviolability which he could well have done without. Even Leah the shunter's wife hadn't blabbed, and maybe he'd got her in the pod as well, though she was a more knowing piece than Minnie, who seemed less familiar with the ways of the world. 'Couldn't you have made up another story?'

'I'm not capable of telling a falsehood,' she said firmly. 'All lies are wicked. The Lord never forgives a liar.'

She'd certainly been got at. 'You told him everything?'

His annoyance was hard to understand. 'There was no other way.'

She might be a few years older, but age had made her no wiser. 'I'm surprised he didn't chuck you on the street.'

'He's a Christian man.'

'One of them, is he?' – an ironic turn of the lips.

'He would never do such a thing.'

'Did he torment you?'

'He asked, so I had to tell him. He said God would forgive my transgressions, as he hoped God would forgive yours.'

'That's cold.'

'We prayed together. Then he said he would forget what I had told him. And he will. He's a man of his word.'

He stiffened to his full height. 'What else did he say?'

'That I wasn't to think of marrying you.'

'Not the right sort for you, I suppose.'

'He would never say that.'

'No, but he would think it.' As far as he was concerned he was too good to be related to a preacher's family.

'He said I must stay the rest of my life with him and my sister, who would see that the child had a Christian upbringing, and a good education.'

His laugh was dry, at not too outlandish a notion that the child would get on in a world of hypocrites. 'He's got some sense. But I'll never forget you, Minnie.'

'Nor I you.'

He kissed her lips in haste, aware that every tree had eyes and ears, not caring to get her into more trouble. 'What shall we call it?'

She smiled. 'David, if it's a boy.'

He'd wanted Ernest, but the choice had to be hers, or her brother-in-law's. 'It could well be a boy.'

'But a girl I'll call Abigail, though my sister would prefer Martha.'

'Abigail's prettier.'

The trees darkened and a mist was forming, bleak country compared to that on the outskirts of Nottingham. 'I'm happy talking to you,' she said, 'even if only for a few minutes.'

'It's the same for me, my darling.' He wondered what she was thinking, and whether there was any good in it for him, but didn't care because he couldn't be bothered to find out whether she was saying what she really thought. None of it mattered. You only knew what was in someone's mind by the words that came from their mouths, and had to be satisfied with that, believing it if you cared to. 'When the child's grown up will you tell him how he came to be born?'

'That will be for me to decide, if the Lord spares me to live that long. Nobody knows the future. When I found out I was going to have a baby I was in despair, but now I'm glad.'

Her stiffening tone made him indifferent to what she would do. All that mattered with women was that you didn't catch the pox, and that they didn't get it from you. If they became pregnant it was their lookout, though if that happened to Mary Ann he would marry her and no mistake. You couldn't do any such thing to a girl who lived across the street, and she was too closely looked after by Mrs Lewin – who seemed to know all the tricks – and he was glad she was, because when he got home, all dressed up and gold jingling in his pockets, he would go into the White Hart and ask her to marry him, before he got into any more scrapes.

'I shall never forget you,' she said, which he liked to hear.

'And I'll remember you for the rest of my life. When I look over the wall of the parson's house in a couple of months, perhaps you'll give me a glance at the child before I go back to Nottingham.'

'It's your right,' she said. 'I don't think my brother-in-law will disagree.'

'I must be going.' Sleet blew against his cap. 'You'd better put your umbrella up. I don't want you getting your death of cold.'

The picture card was of Nottingham Castle. 'Must be from a woman,' George said, before Ernest could snatch it away. 'I can almost smell the perfume.'

He wondered who had sent it. His parents had no cause to write. They'd have to get someone to do it for them. Leah the shunter's wife had no call on him, either. She might be able to write but didn't know where he was. Hard to think who it could be, people had no right to pester him, till the thought shot to mind that it could only be from Mary Ann.

Outside the post office George read his letter from Sarah. 'She wants me to come home.'

'Shall you go?'

'I've been thinking about packing it in down here.'

'It'll be soon enough for me.' He wants to see Sarah, Ernest assumed, and give her another child, providing she was still up to it. He put the postcard into his pocket, went on with his walk and forgot about it sufficiently to stop George's curiosity by saying: 'I've got my life. You've got yours. They're nothing to do with each other.'

He bought a quart of ale, and before going in for supper went to see Owen-the-Bible, whom he had grown to respect if not like. Two months ago Owen had written a ha'penny postcard to Mary Ann showing a Welsh woman in a tall hat, the briefest of missives but in the finest Board School copperplate which Ernest hoped she would think was his.

Owen sat at the table, a plate of bread and cheese and half an onion before him. 'Now here's the tall stranger again. You must be wanting something of me.'

Ernest set the bottle by his knife. 'Drink some of this first.'

Talk cost breath, due to work in the mine which did nobody any good. 'Is it poison?'

'No. It would cost more than ale. But you need a brew like this for the dry stuff you're eating.'

Upending the spout, Owen downed a third, and Ernest showed the postcard. 'Read me this,' ready to use a fist should he damage it. 'All right, take another drop, then read it.'

Owen drank to make his breathing easier. He looked at the picture and turned it over. 'Do you know that when I go to sleep I don't close my eyes.'

'How do you know, if you're asleep?'

He finished the beer before replying. 'The others tell me. I sleep as deep as any man, but my eyes stay wide open. All night. What do you think of that, then?'

'Very rum,' Ernest conceded. 'Now read that card.'

Owen's knife shivered into the table, and stayed upright. 'It's excellent Welsh bitter you've brought me.'

'Make as it's your birthday.'

'I don't know when that is. My mother never told me, though I did ask her often enough. But I'm feeling happy from your drink, so this is what the card says. The handwriting is small, but very clear: "Thank you for your postcard. I'm glad you are getting on all right. I am, as well. People ask about you, and now I can tell them. We wonder when you are coming back. A lot of people would like to see you. Mary Ann." She's even put the commas right.'

Ernest told himself how pleasing he found Owen's singsong voice, and knew that in many ways he would regret leaving an area whose people had been so honest and straight.

Minnie passed a cloth package. 'It's food for your journey. My sister and I put it together.'

Taking the bundle, he leaned over the wall to see the baby; felt as if leaving home again. 'He looks healthy,' noting that the closed eyes gave a stern expression, the features more his than Minnie's. 'Pretty, too. What did you christen him?'

'David Ernest. Does that make you satisfied?'

'It'll have to.' Minute fingers uncurled from the swaddling, reached for him, eyes open to look. 'What a blue-eyed beauty. He smiled at me.'

'He has a human soul,' she said, 'and a fine name from the Bible. My brother-in-law says he will sing the psalms of King David.'

The pang of wanting to stay with him forever came and went. 'He's a marvel.'

'I'm happy. My life changed after meeting you.'

He was glad for her, though couldn't say the same for himself. To see a child of his own was miraculous enough, but happiness was for those who didn't know themselves, and who would be one of them?

A tear came onto her cheek, and he passed a white handkerchief freshly laundered by Mrs Jones. When she had wiped it away, and other tears threatened, he told her to keep it, all he had for her to remember him by. She tucked it into the baby's clothes. 'I have everything I want. I'm settled and content. My sister and brother-in-law adore him.'

David's fingers curled strongly around one of his. 'I'm sorry to go. And I shall always love you.'

'We mustn't linger. People will comment. So go now.'

'I shan't forget you both. When I come back I'll see you and the baby again.'

'You won't come back.' Then she was gone, and he went with a heaviness he didn't know how to understand, but was more than glad to feel.

'More pints go into your trap,' George said, after they had changed trains in Worcester, 'than words come out. Something in Wales must have struck you dumber than usual. I can't get a word out of you.'

'Nor will you.' George was wrong if he thought anything was worrying him. On the other hand he was right, because the vision of Minnie and David stayed in his mind. Even thinking of Mary Ann wouldn't drive it away, though the more he thought of her the more vivid her face became, and the more he knew he would have to marry her, settle down and have a family, no woman more suitable, unless somebody had made off with her during his time in Wales.

'You ought to have been a deaf mute instead of a blacksmith.' George arranged his tranklements for the third time on the rack. 'I can just see you with a coffin on your back.'

Ernest took out his clasp knife. 'You can kiss my backside. Just shut up.' Opening the cloth bag Minnie had given him, he found a compact meat and potatoe pie, a lump of cheese, an onion, and a loaf of bread.

'Who made that up for you?' George asked in wonder.

He cut the pie neatly, and passed the other half across. 'Put it in your mouth, and don't ask any more questions.'

FOUR

Young Burton was back – a year away, but time had altered him. Watch and chain looped across his waistcoat with a sovereign attached; a nick of white handkerchief in the lapel pocket like the wingtip of a bird attempting to hide there. Crossing the road so as not to tread in dog or horse droppings, he was aware of looking his best – a flick at the red rose snapped from a bush in the garden. The May evening was warm, but cap and waistcoat were part of his renown as a neat and formal dresser. He would have smiled to know that never again in his life would he appear in more impressive aspect – while in no way believing it.

Saturday night in the taproom was the busiest night of the week, an ant heap turned upside-down in the clamour for pots and jars, so he couldn't get close enough to Mary Ann and put the question. Back straight and head high, he overlooked everyone in the bar, and saw what he wanted to see. The whiff of home ale dominating the odour of gaslights made it seem as if supping a different brew all last year had been a dream.

Fred the barman drew his tankard, Mary Ann busy at the far end pulling the smooth white-handled pumps with her lovely young arms. Nakedness through the shirt came with a clarity that made his peg stir, and her smile in his direction gave no need to wonder who it was for.

You couldn't ask a woman to marry you among so much riff-raff, so he enjoyed slaking a thirst for home ale built up during the time in Wales, knowing it better to put the question at dinner-time, in the middle of the day, when less people would be around to nudge your elbow and drown private business with their clatter.

A question that had to wait wouldn't spoil any the less for

43

that, and while he was nodding to those who knew him, or thought they did, or passing a few words with those he considered had a right to acknowledgement, he stayed by the bar to observe Mary Ann at a distance, satisfied by glances which he thought buttered by a smile. He disliked the notion of being back at his father's forge on Monday and lucky to see sixteen shillings a week counted out of the leather bag for his labour, but it would have to do till something better was found.

In the morning Mary Ann would be chaperoned to church by Mrs Lewin, and if he went he could glimpse her and maybe flash a wink during the sermon or between hymns, but he'd prefer to fry in hell than enter such a place, though when he and Mary Ann were married it would be a forceput, because there was no other way of getting such a woman into bed for life.

She wouldn't go to church after they were married because there'd be too much caring for him and bringing up a family, such a responsibility on his part as well that he called dilatory Eli for another pint, his last of the evening since he was watching the coins he would surely need for the time when every bun cost tuppence, and a bit more than that with a lot of little buns running about on two legs.

Tomorrow he would work in the garden to please his father, but in any case he liked attending to the rows of beans and peas and potatoes while the church bells rang, knowing he would never jump to their musical summons and join in the prayers and hear the parson spout about what could have nothing to do with him. His mother went once a month but what could you expect from a woman, though there were plenty of men there as well, hypocrites to the bone.

Outside it was almost dark, the windows a protective sheen through which nothing could be seen. If he was to be up at five he would need sleep, though garden work or not he left his bed at that hour every day, always had and always would, not like those who said they couldn't do without a lie-in on Sunday, not realizing that you would get sleep enough in the cosy box of the grave when the time came, and that if you craved it while still alive you were already more than halfway there.

* * *

He had asked her twice, and at twenty-one she ought to know her own mind. 'I'm happy here,' she said. 'It's a good situation, and I don't know what Mrs Lewin would do without me.'

'It's me I want you to marry, not Mrs Lewin.'

'I know, and if I marry anybody it will be you.'

Such uncertainty wasn't good enough. He only wanted a plain yes. 'I've chosen you.'

'I can tell you have. But you can't choose me like you would a horse, or a piece of iron you work with.'

'I know what I'm doing.'

'You haven't said you love me yet.'

'I wouldn't be talking to you like this if I didn't.'

'But you've got to say it.'

'I'm saying it now. I've never loved anybody but you, so you can give me a yes as soon as you like.'

Mrs Lewin came into the bar; Ernest was attracted by the high forehead, dark hair pulled back, the interesting mould of her lips, and middling bust under a striped shirt fastened at the neck with a brooch of amber. He wouldn't have minded sliding into her, widow or not, though she must be nearing forty. Her luscious brown eyes looked at them. 'Mary Ann, I'd like you to go to the kitchen and make some bread – that is, if Mr Burton will allow you.'

The 'mister' and her smile softened his annoyance, and he wondered whether he wouldn't do better with her, except she wouldn't have him in a million years, and he didn't fancy running a pub.

'I still can't make up my mind,' Mary Ann told him.

'Let me know when you can, then,' he said off-handedly, and noted the lift of Emma Lewin's eyebrows before walking away, telling himself *she* can think what she likes, as well.

'He's a bit of a devil,' she said to Mary Ann as he closed the door. 'But I suppose every woman likes a devil.'

A state of uncertainty wasn't for him. He'd never lived like that, and didn't see why he should. When the hammer hit the anvil it always bounced up for another blow. He wanted her, and would have her, so the only solution was to go on asking, though he let a fortnight go by in case she thought him in too much of a hurry.

She haunted his waking dreams, which could be dangerous in his sort of work. Auburn hair flowed over naked shoulders, her eyes enchanting him, a lovely young woman in season, with outstretched arms and saying come to me, there's no other man I want. Her face would shock its way before his eyes, taunting with a prospect to last a lifetime.

He left his pie and hot tea at the forge, hungry only for what had to be done. George and his father wouldn't mind. They would eat the lot. There were fewer people in the pub at midday, though had it been packed he wouldn't have cared. The usual greetings were followed by a call for ale, not so much to swamp his thirst as to see the working of her arms, which would be better employed in a house they'd one day live in. He was at a disadvantage in his smithing clothes, but couldn't help that. She must take him as she found him. Her finger traced the small print of a newspaper. 'I've come to ask you again,' he said, not waiting for her to look up.

She glanced from the advertisement sketch. 'I still don't know.'

Her tone sent a spark of hope, the uncertain smile telling him that a favourable decision might be close, so he ought not to be sharp with her, better to stand quietly and give her space to think, the opportunity to make up her mind, and talk, even if only to ask something. He stayed away from the bar, never one to put his elbows on the wood.

She showed him the illustration. 'I've been looking at these gloves. They'd go halfway up my arm, and look very fine.'

He admired their style, having an eye for clothes that went smartly on himself, but also those which adorned a woman. 'Why don't you get them?'

'I'd like to, but it's three weeks till my day off, and I only saw them in the paper today. They're on sale at a shop in town, for one-and-eleven-pence three-farthings.'

'That's not a sight.'

'I know, so they might be sold out in three weeks.'

'I shouldn't wonder.'

'Shall you go and get them for me, after you've finished your work this evening?'

He pushed his half-finished ale aside, having sensed what was coming. 'I'll do it now.'

Her delight convinced him he had said the right thing. She took a florin from her pinafore as if, he thought – and he was to think so for the rest of his life – she'd had it there all the time and knew what he would offer. 'You don't have to go this minute.'

'That's true.'

She tore out the pattern so that he could show it and make no mistake, and wrote down the size she wanted. 'It's at that big millinery shop on Exchange Walk. You can't miss it.'

He put her coin in a pocket that held no money of his. 'I'll be back when I can. If you're not at the bar I'll ask Mrs Lewin for you.'

He could walk the couple of miles into town and back, but the less time taken the higher he might go in her esteem, so he caught the first train, and if the shopkeeper looked down his nose at working clothes he could jump up his rear end, because he loved Mary Ann, and by God he would have her, and go through fire and flood to do this little errand. Even if she said no to him again he wouldn't stop thinking about her, and never stop asking either. He felt a letch at seeing any pretty woman, but it was more than that with Mary Ann, and he only knew that after their marriage she would adorn him as much as he would dignify her.

It was a quick ten minutes from the station to Exchange Walk, between St Peter's church and Old Market Square. He had to wait while a woman was being served, but it didn't seem too long on thinking about married life with Mary Ann. The sallow assistant climbed three steps of a wooden ladder and took the white cotton gloves from behind glass. She laid them into paper, and he paid at the till with two one-shilling pieces from his own money, and put the farthing change into his pocket.

On Lister Gate he knelt to retie a bootlace, and standing up saw Leah in his way, too close for his liking. 'Don't you know me?' A basket overarm, her hair was untidy, and she wore rouge. 'Why haven't you been to see me?' she smiled. 'It's over a year, and I've been hoping all the time that you would.'

He knew her, such a handsome woman it was easy to see why

he'd had a fling, but you never answered anyone who accosted you on the street. Yet he wondered why he had meddled with someone who did it on her husband and had the cheek to greet him with people going by.

'What do you want?' he had to say.

'What do I want?' she cried. 'How can you ask me what I want?'

He ought to have been pleasant, even promised to see her again, but with Mary Ann's face before him such a response was less than reasonable. 'Is your husband still shunting then? I haven't seen him hurrying to work lately.'

'What a rotten thing to say,' she hissed. 'After what we've done together, this is how you treat me.'

'Get away from me.'

'Don't you want to see me anymore?'

He pushed her aside. 'God will pay you out.' If only she hadn't shouted. He wanted to turn back and knock her down, which was what she deserved. A slut with no pride. Tackling him on the street was the last thing she should have done. It was true enough that he'd had his way with her, but so had she with him. It was over a year ago, all fair and square, and now she pestered him, people beginning to stare, though what could you expect from a woman like that?

He wondered what the world was coming to, as the train jangled out of the station, though with Mary Ann back in mind and the vital package in his large hands he became calmer. The Castle glared less severely from its rock now that his errand was done. Then it was gone, leaving Mary Ann's face so present in the glass that Lenton station was being called.

She looked as fresh and tempting as when he had left an hour ago. If his father ranted at his staying out so long from work he would tell the old so-and-so what to do with himself. He laid the packet on the bar, with the florin given to pay for it in the centre.

'Are they in there?'

'They were when I last saw the young woman pack them up. Nobody's tampered with them since.'

'What's that florin for?'

'Put it back in your pinafore.'

She looked at the Queen's image in her palm, then held up the gloves so clean and neat and, above all, fashionable. 'Thank you, Ernest.'

'You'll look a treat in them when you're dressed up.'

'I don't know what to say.'

'You haven't got to say anything. I did it because my heart wanted to.' After a moment's silence: 'I'm putting the same old question.'

A blush covered her face as the folded gloves went back into their paper, aware of the words he wanted to hear. 'What sort of question?'

'Shall you marry me?' To ask before requesting a pint of ale showed how strong his mind was on the matter. The world spun before her, as if she would faint, though she reached across with a smile and touched his hand.

'I will.'

His forename on the certificate was spelled as 'Earnest', in the script of an elderly absent-minded man who had stood to write it. Ernest signified his agreement to the event by the mark of a cross, as did his father Thomas, both down as 'blacksmiths', on 25 January 1889, while Mary Ann's father, Charles Tokins, was described as 'engineer'.

The bride's signature was fair and steady, as was Emma Lewin's as witness, who on that occasion consented to go into the Holy Trinity Church of the Parish of Lenton and see her friend and servant through the formality of marriage. She gave twenty pounds towards a trousseau, and allowed the saloon of her public house to be used for the reception, generosity Mary Ann remembered for the rest of her life.

The saloon was filled with the relations of both families, and with friends of Ernest's father who, thinking of trade, felt justified in inviting some of his customers after paying so much towards the celebrations.

Ernest stood beside his bride, a single whisky to last the evening, not caring to drink more, because tonight would be the most important of his life, not the day that had seen the knot tied in church, but what was to come in their cottage across the road, where a room had been prepared for them before setting off for Matlock in the morning.

Fully turned-up gas mantles gave a whitened aspect to the room – or as much as tobacco allowed – every face and figure clear, which Ernest liked because the only god he halfway respected was that of fire and illumination. He allowed Mary Ann to hold his hand surreptitiously, while observing the mob gathered at their splicing. She said she had been in love with him from the moment he first walked into the pub, that she had never loved any other man, nor ever would.

Her father Charles Tokins had come from St Neots on the train. Tall and soundly built, and looking young for his age, with a well-shaped black beard, he had started work in an iron foundry as a boy. The family had left County Mayo in the 1840s to escape hunger and destitution caused, Mary Ann said – and Ernest saw no reason to disbelieve her – by the wickedness of the government in London.

Ernest went through the crowd, to hear what Tokins was saying to his father. 'I'd had enough of getting myself dirty working in the foundry, so I rented a workshop to repair penny-farthings and tricycles. I'd had a tricycle a few years, and knew others who had them. There's plenty of flat land around where we live, but the roads aren't in good repair, and a lot of people don't know how to look after their machines. When one breaks down they can't get it mended properly, so not only do I do it, but I've started buying and selling as well. I get new ones at a fair discount from the manufacturers at Coventry, and do enough trade to keep us quite nicely. We prosper, in other words.' He drank his whisky, as if to get breath. 'You can't beat the bicycle for getting from place to place. I read in the newspaper the other day that somebody rode on a Humber from London to York in twenty-four hours.'

'They make Humbers near here.' Thomas at last got a word in. 'At Beeston, a couple of miles away.'

Tokins looked at the ash on his cigar, and gave it permission to fall. 'He even beat Dick Turpin on Black Bess. The machine didn't die when it got there, either.'

'I wonder if he could have done the same distance the day after,' Ernest said. 'His legs wouldn't have been much good by then.'

'I'm making money out of the trade.' Tokins was annoyed at the interruption. 'That's all I know. If you want to come and live in St Neots, Ernest, I'll set you on. Your father tells me you're a fine blacksmith. You'd soon pick up the trade, and be an asset to us. I'd guarantee a better wage than if you stay here. Times are changing.'

There must have been talk between Tokins and his father, but Ernest would jump for no man. 'They always were.'

Tokins saw him as too opinionated ever to get anywhere. 'If you want to make the move, let me know. Mary Ann wouldn't be unhappy, living close to us.'

Tokins wanted his daughter back where he could keep an eye on her, and would be interfering in their lives in no time, so it was a cold idea as far as Ernest was concerned. In any case what man would want to work for his wife's father? It was bad enough sweating for your own. 'I'll think about it,' he said, not caring to make things difficult for Mary Ann.

He went back to his wife, as if to be sure nobody had run her away after it had taken him so long to win her. Her dignity and calm beauty were dreamlike when she came to him from laughing with her bridesmaids. The step she had taken would never lead back to the happier days of her youth, Mrs Lewin thought as she too looked at her.

Part Two
1914

FIVE

Youngsters looked in the open door to see what he did, and they're welcome to, Burton thought. They stand all clean in a row like so many sparrows on a wall, staring as if I deal with magic, and when I look up they've gone to a place that'll teach them how to read and write, which they'll learn if they're sharp enough, though I've managed well without it, sometimes better than a lot of fools who think they've learned all there is to teach.

Still, children might end up with more magic than I did, who never went to school because my father needed me, young as I was, two more hands making a difference, so he can't be blamed for me not knowing my letters. There weren't as many schools built then as there are now, but you can never blame your parents for anything, and those I've heard in the pub who whine against them have no pride, no backbone to stand on their own feet and blame themselves.

My father gave me a trade that's like gold, you can go anywhere with it, turn your hand to anything. There are smithies all over the place, at every pit and a lot of factories, wherever you go you'll find one. Each village has enough work to keep more than one family, so nobody owes me anything and I owe not a penny to them.

He took a bar of iron from the mound of heat, shook and tapped the sparks away. Like Vulcan or Tubal-Cain, his arms were bare, his eyes alert and, lean and agile as he had always been, and still was at forty-eight, battered the iron to his will. The world did not exist while he made the first bend of the shoe, saw that it was clean, and brought the two prongs to the right distance apart. He drove the holes fully through, and when the shoe came steaming bright blue from the bucket and the job was finished he looked up at the ever-familiar thin smoke lanced by light and fighting its way through the solitary square window.

The forge, on a lane leading to the church at Lenton, was similar in size and structure to the one in Wales. Work never done, he set to making another, Oliver his eldest son of twenty-three standing by as his striker, a man as well trained as Burton at that age, and much like him in physique, though a trace of sensibility had blended into his features from Mary Ann, and given a more vulnerable aspect.

Oswald, the second son, tackled the bellows with the dignified attentive face of a Norman warrior at the Battle of Hastings. Talk was impossible in the swinging of arms, the clatter of hammers, and the stench of coke, explaining the taciturnity of smiths who worked for hours without speaking.

Burton took a silver snuff box from his apron pocket and tapped a small khaki mound of dust onto the back of his hand, held it under his nose, drew it sharply into one nostril and then the other. A moment's stillness was followed by a twitch at the face signifying a violent inward sneeze rocking the system as the drug took effect, clearing his head so that for a few seconds the world showed in greater detail and more vivid colouring. At the sound of a customer leading a horse to be shod he went outside.

Oswald put the hammer his brother had used on a bench by the wall, then took tobacco from his pouch to roll a cigarette. He and Oliver had been at school till they were thirteen, so could read and write, but they feared Burton, who would be sure to remind them with his fists if a mistake was made in their work. On the other hand, should a good job be turned out, he would give no sign of satisfaction.

Glad to see the back of him, Oliver wiped his face with a rag, but went out to forestall any shout that he would be needed. A locomotive hauling coal wagons through a nearby cutting shrieked like a glutted kitehawk sighting more offal, so frightening the horse being shod that it broke free and scattered a couple of bystanders.

Burton pushed the shoeing smith aside, took the reins and brought the head close, and looked in the eyes shimmering with panic. He stroked down the grain and, drawing breath, exhaled a warmth of intimate snuff-smelling reassurance up the nostrils to calm its heart, in the way his father had shown him even as a child, who had been drilled in how to do it by *his* father. How many generations such knowledge had come through he didn't think to wonder. The worst time was when lightning flashed and a horse imagined that the head of fiery light was meant for it alone. Then you had to take care and, if you could, persuade it that lightning was unavailing against animals close to Thor's heart. Lightning might go for men, if they got in its way, but never horses, those who cared for them also immune. A higher power looked after horse and farrier, and Burton supposed that even the first blacksmith on earth didn't know where such protection came from, though they believed in it, and that the only friend of a horse was the blacksmith who fitted its shoes and sent it well-shod to work in comfort.

No blacksmith ever harmed a horse, let alone killed one, and no horse wantonly killed a man, though many a man had been killed or injured while riding because he had done something daft, or hadn't understood the animal. You had a feeling for horses other people didn't have. You were born with it, and picked the rest up along the way, no horse impossible to tame, though he wouldn't ride one, because no horse would trust him again, would smell the breath of the other horse, and think the blacksmith was sharing his favours. A horse, which will do what you want if you know how and what to tell it, would never stand for bad treatment.

Oliver knew all that was in his father's mind as he watched him still the horse. He had often seen him do it, but the thought now came, and he felt a spurt of triumph at the knowledge, that Burton, in spite of all his experience, had an inborn ancestral fear of horses that would never leave him. He had spotted his father's one weakness, and wondered why it had taken him so long; because he himself had never been frightened of horses, but was glad at having found a slit in Burton's armoured covering so small it could only become apparent to a son of his in the same trade.

'Always get the shoe off slowly,' Burton told the shoeing smith. 'They think you're going to hurt them if you don't make them think you're doing it in their time.'

'The train frightened it. It wasn't my fault.'

'It's always the farrier's fault. Learn to take care of them.'

'I do take care.'

He stood at the door before going inside. 'Don't answer back. Wait till you've got eight young 'uns to feed like I have, then you'll hold the horses still.'

'Old Burton's a hard one,' said the drayman whose horse it was. 'I wouldn't like to work for him.'

The shoeing smith looked towards the noise of hammering. 'I'm fed up with the way he treats me.'

'Pack it in. Go somewhere else.'

'I'd like to, but you work where you can. And every day there's more motors on the road.'

'Yeh, one day horses won't be needed anymore.'

'We get enough trade here,' the shoeing smith said, 'because Burton makes sure the work's good. People know where to come. But he's a hard man to be under.'

'That's because of the way he was brought up,' the carter said. 'I wouldn't like to be one of his sons. He must have taken some stick from his own father to make him the man he is.'

'It was his brother George who put him through the hoops. Or so I heard Burton say the other day when he was telling one of his lads off.'

'I wonder what Burton was like when he was young?'

'He never was young, if you ask me.' The shoeing smith stood erect to rub his pained back. 'Here you are. That should keep your nag going for a while.'

'I hope so,' the drayman said. 'Two bob a time's getting a bit expensive.'

Burton had so much sweat on him as he stood in the doorway it looked as if he had dipped his head in the waterbutt. He held a hand over one eye where a spark had chipped the flesh below. 'If you can find somebody to do it for less go and trade with them. But if you do, God help your horse.'

'Times are hard, Burton.'

'They always were.' Two of his daughters came along the lane. 'What do you want?'

Oval-faced Sabina, ten years old, shook her chestnut hair, and flushed at his sour greeting. He knew very well why they were there, because couldn't he see the billy-cans of tea in her hand? 'We've brought you your dinners.'

'Put them down there.'

Emily set the snap tins on the bench and stepped back as if he might hit her should she get too close. Eight years old and Burton's youngest, everyone in the family regarded her as a bit touched, being slow-witted and more unpredictable than the others, with too much willingness in her smile to please whoever she met that she was never allowed out of the house on her own. Mary Ann told Burton that while it was his right to treat the children as he thought they deserved, he was never to strike Emily since, when she misbehaved, she didn't altogether know what she was doing. He found it easy to do as Mary Ann wished because a mere look was enough to scare Emily. He picked up the cans with no word of thanks. 'I thought you two were at school?'

'We're just going,' Sabina said.

'Don't be late. I've told you never to miss any of it. See that you don't.' His glare at their backs seemed to force them into the right turning. Inside the forge, his eyes roamed over the tools, materials, state of the fire. He missed nothing, but looked again as if he might have done, ever on the lookout for discrepancy, damage or misplacement. 'Where's the hammer you were using?'

Oliver stood. 'It's over there.'

'Where's there?'

'On the bench.'

'Don't I always tell you to put the tools back in their right place when you've finished with them?'

'I didn't have time to do it.' The veins jumped on his father's temples, and he knew that what was coming couldn't be avoided, the blow at his head too quick. 'Don't answer back,' Burton said. 'I don't want to have to tell you again.'

Oliver balanced the weighty hammer as if to swing in for the kill, but didn't much relish the vision of his body hanging from a gallows. He had long regretted having the misfortune to be Burton's firstborn and prime competitor.

'Put it in its proper place, and be quick about it. How shall I be able to find it if it's not where I think it is?'

'There won't be anymore of that.' But he did as he was told. 'I'm telling you now. You aren't going to hit me again.'

A smile shaped Burton's lips, much of himself in Oliver from almost too long ago to be remembered, except at moments like this. He admitted that the time had come to stop the punches but, even so, he had made him one of the best young men at the trade, who in a few years would be as good a blacksmith as himself, though all you got for such effort was the insolence of being answered back. 'I hear a horse coming along the lane, so get outside to see to it. And send Oswald in to me.'

'We haven't had our dinners yet.'

He softened a little, which for Oliver was far too late. 'If you're thirsty drink some tea from one of the cans. You can eat when things get slack. Never delay a customer longer than you have to. So do it now.' Hunger could wait. Burton only felt thirst, a fire inside always there to be put out. He wiped sweat from his face with a large red spotted handkerchief, took a scoop of water from a bucket covered by a wooden lid, and carried it outside.

Oliver sat on the stool to get the shoe off, the lame horse's hoof between his knees. He stroked the horse's poll, knowing when to keep quiet as Burton held the bucket for it to drink, Oliver thinking you had to be a horse to get any kindness out of Burton.

He walked well ahead of his sons on the mile home, went into the long tunnel which carried railway lines to Ilkeston, the way narrowing between brick walls, a muddy pestilence in days of rain, hardly ever drying in summer weather, and dark enough at all times to make the girls timorous of going through on their way to Woodhouse. Beyond, the sunken lane was resplendent with elderflowers. He moved tall and upright, with the slightly swinging gait of a man on his own.

His sons were careful not to follow too close – Burton would never allow it – and came on in silence, until Oliver said: 'One of these days I'm going to push his head into the fire.'

'He'd have yours in first.'

He stroked the bruise on his face. 'Not if you help me. I'm fed up with it. Ever since I was born I've been kicked from arse-hole to breakfasttime by him. As soon as I can, I'm off. I hate the sight of him. He's always been like that, and always will be. He makes everybody pay for the fact that he's alive. He's dead ignorant. He can't even read and write.'

'That's not done him much harm. Anyway, people like him live forever.'

He shredded a leaf of privet with a fingernail. 'There's too many of his sort around, and it's time things changed. When he dies they'll have to put nine padlocks on hell's door to keep him out, for fear he'd give the place a bad name.'

Burton left them to close the latched gate, walked up the path and paused to inspect two fat porkers in their sty, poking each with a stick till they squealed through the slush out of range. Satisfied that they were lively enough for his mood, he passed the brick storehouse with its copper inside for boiling the weekly wash, and on by a smaller outbuilding divided between coal store and earth closet by whose wooden holes was a large tin of creosote to splash down and diminish the stench. The yard extended to the lane, and behind the cottage a long garden provided the family with vegetables. The first of three proper-ties, each was brickbuilt and tile-roofed, with three bedrooms, a living room, kitchen and larder leading off, and a parlour. The cottages were well fenced and separated, which suited Burton, who never gave more than a nod to his neighbours. He left the door open, again to be closed by those behind.

The warm living room smelled comfortingly of meat, baking bread, and potatoes steaming on the wood fire. After greeting Mary Ann he washed his hands and face in the pantry. Oswald and Oliver stood not too close to do the same. 'You'll need to fill the buckets after you've had your dinners.' He spoke as if to no one in particular, but those who would have to do it knew who was meant.

A large brass oil lamp hung by a chain above the table, taken down for cleaning once a fortnight. No one allowed to help, he and Mary Ann polished the brass till their faces could be clearly seen, and washed the shade sufficient to make the glass almost invisible, the only task of their married life performed together.

Oliver combed his hair at a mirror by the door, the trade name 'Sandeman Sherry' blazoned in gold letters along the bottom. To the right was a glass-fronted showcase of Burton's prize horse-shoes, and often when Oliver looked at them he recalled how at fourteen Burton had taken him to a county show near Tollerton: 'Put your suit on tomorrow,' he was told. 'You'll see a few other blacksmiths where I'm taking you.'

On their way through the city Burton allowed him half a pint at the Trip to Jerusalem, in a cool room hewn from the sandstone rock of the castle. By the time they'd done the seven miles to Tollerton he wondered whether his father had only asked him along to test his walking prowess, having trouble at times keeping up with the long stride while maintaining his respectful distance behind. But Oliver adjusted his pace and enjoyed a good day of his life, for it was the middle of May, blossom on the trees and birds happy in their heaven, and he thought how much he could love his father if only it had been allowed.

Burton stood outside the competition marquee, wilful pride preventing him going in to find out who was the winner of the Grand Horseshoe Competition. Oliver wasn't able to understand his hanging back, but when he came close Burton said, after someone had announced him as the winner, and aware of what was puzzling his son: 'They can come and talk to me if they want. If you've learned nothing else today you've learned that a blacksmith never goes up to others in a case like this. Now go to that table and bring me a pint of what they're dishing out, and get yourself a cup of tea from the tent over there.'

Oliver watched his father accept the prize and handshake from the Duke of Something-or-other, merely nodding at the grandee's words, and walking away with the five-pound note in his waist-coat pocket, and the prize horseshoe in his hand.

Mary Ann lifted the half-finished rug from her knees, gathered the coloured unused clippings into a cotton bag to get everything away from the fire. Idleness was the only sin, Burton knew, and he had never seen her idle for a moment. He felt justified in scorning others who indulged themselves, because he too had never been idle.

He sat at the large oval table, every muscle aching from his day's work, though nobody could know and they would never be told, certainly not his sons, because he did his best to make sure they wouldn't become as tired as himself. Still young, they would strengthen in a year or two, but it was unnecessary even to think such things, though you couldn't stop what jumped into mind.

Mary Ann drew a pan of Yorkshire pudding and a sauceboat of gravy from the oven by the side of the grate. 'Where's my ale?' Burton asked.

She brought a bottle and glass up the few steps of the pantry, one small task of the number necessary to remember, almost without thought. The potatoes she strained, new from the garden, gave off a pleasing smell of mint, as she served slices of roast lamb.

Burton looked at Oswald. 'Use a fork with your bread to mop the gravy, not your fingers. You aren't starving, are you?'

'We're hungry,' Oliver said.

'So am I. But it looks bad. When you've finished, fetch some water from the well.'

'Do we need it?'

'We always do.' He turned back to Oswald. 'Some wood wants chopping, and that'll be your job.'

Mary Ann served herself last and, sitting on Burton's left, saw the darkening bruise on Oliver's cheek. 'What happened to you?'

He smiled, always careful not to upset his mother. When Burton struck, all his strength was in it. 'I banged into a brick wall.'

'You'd better put some witch-hazel on it.' She said to Burton: 'It's not right, hitting a grown man.'

'He should do his work properly.'

'But he doesn't deserve that.'

'It won't happen again,' Oliver said.

Burton's grunt was as profound a statement as could be made at his son's defiance. Having heard such an expressive monosyllable so many times they always knew what lay behind it, on this occasion wondering if he was about to strike out, but Oliver was ready, and decided he would be from now on.

The meal went peacefully, Burton eating to live rather than living to eat, knowing that Mary Ann's cooking was in any case the best. The first to finish, he pulled the door open and called into the yard: 'Thomas!'

Thomas was thirteen, none of the children allowed to call him Tom, though they did when Burton wasn't nearby. Expecting the summons, he stood in the doorway, a swatch of thick fair hair angled towards his eyes, the third son, already up to his father's shoulders. He had left school before learning anything because Burton needed him now and again to help in the forge, intending to make a blacksmith out of him as well, though Ivy of the sharp tongue said Thomas was too slow to have qualified in the classroom anyway. From talking to his sisters in the yard, he now stood sullenly by.

Burton had never known them to do anything as willingly as he'd had to do. 'Feed the pigs. Edith, help him to get the mash from the outhouse. The stuff that was made today.'

The eldest daughter, she was a vivacious seventeen-year-old with golden-blonde hair. 'I was just going out for the evening.'

'Do as I say.' Seeing them start to obey, he closed the door, but as his back turned Edith gargoyled her face, then went to help Thomas.

Oliver came from the pantry with a yoke across the back of his neck, and a steel bucket in each hand. 'When you've done that,' Burton said, as if never to leave him alone, 'you can get some coal in.'

Softly whistling, Oliver was happy to be liberated from the pall of his father, and set off along the path between chicken coops and the house wall. Passing the front door, the long garden gave off its smell of dry soil, a scent of fresh flowers, and a tang of rotting potato tops that he would later gather up. Every week he and Thomas, under Burton's critical eye, lest they slacken on the distance or spill a drop, manoeuvred iron buckets reeking also of creosote from the outhouse to furrows indicated in the garden, and splashed it liberally about, nothing from the house being wasted. The garden gave shining red beetroot, potatoes, onions, carrots, marrows, cucumbers, lettuces and kidney beans, as well as sweet peas and mint, while raspberries, gooseberries and redcurrants made pies, puddings and jam.

The well up the slope was covered by a triangular wooden roof and, however many times Oliver had laboured to and from to get water he liked the sight of its fairy-tale shape, as depicted in books brought home as an infant from Sunday School. The vision of magical enactments at midnight, or even during daylight, summer or winter, when he wasn't there, set him cheerfully whistling *To be a Farmer's Boy*, letting the chain that Burton had made rattle the bucket from its roller and hit the water with a satisfying smack, before it sank and began to fill. Turning the handle, he brought up the first overflowing bucket.

All the others at work, Burton in the kitchen enjoyed his usual pinch of snuff after the evening meal, stood with back to the fire, as contented as could be after the day's work.

'Don't I get any money this week?' Mary Ann said.

'You always have.' He took cash from his pocket. 'Take this sovereign.'

'I was hoping for a bit more.'

'Have another five bob, then. Trade's been good.'

And that was all, though it was better than usual. She looked at the head of King George on one of the half-crowns, then put the coins into her pocket.

'I'm off to town for a couple of hours.' He stomped his way up the stairs to change.

Thomas was half bent over carrying a huge bucket of pig food from the wash house to the sty, Edith following with another, helped by fifteen-year-old Ivy, while Rebecca, Sabina and Emily looked on.

'I hate the old bastard.' Edith's words were smothered by the shrilling pigs, smelling their supper, already at the trough, as if to start on the bare wood. Thomas drove them away with a stick, then poured in the flood of mash, bran, slops and old seed potatoes, stepping aside to avoid the rush at his trousers.

'Don't hit them anymore,' Emily said. 'I like the piggies. They're my friends.'

'How can you be friends with pigs?' he jeered.

'Well, I am. I've got names for both of them.'

'And what are they, young madam?'

'That fat one's Lollipop, and the other's Kidney.'

'Percy the slaughterer's coming up from Woodhouse soon to cut their throats,' he said spitefully. 'And then we'll eat 'em.'

It was easy to make her cry. They sometimes called her Monkey Face, or Mrs Meagrim, or Dolly Dumpling, in spite of being told by Mary Ann to treat her kindly. 'I'll run away, then, and take them with me. We'll go and live together in Robin's Wood. I'll cook their dinners and wash their faces.'

'You like sausages and crackling and chitterlings and pork scratchings, don't you? I've seen you gobbling them up when Mam wasn't looking.' He turned to Edith. 'You'd better not let Burton hear you talking about him like that.'

'Well, I do hate the old bastard. I always have. Did you see Oliver's face? I've never seen such a bruise. He's always hitting people. I'm going to leave home the minute I can.'

Thomas stroked one of the guzzling pigs. 'And when will that be?'

Oliver came into the yard, two buckets on the yoke slopping water. He waved, and straightened his back before going into the house.

'I'll do it after I'm married,' Edith said. 'And he won't dare touch me then. Every time I go out he tells me not to be long. And when I don't go out he calls me in to do some work. And when I do go out I've always got to be back in bed by nine o'clock. I'm seventeen, and I've been working for four years.'

'You stopped out till eleven the other night.'

'Yes, and I'll blind you if you tell Burton.' The older girls, exploiting the inconvenience of a lavatory set apart from the house, sometimes made their way downstairs when Burton and Mary Ann were already in bed, as if to go there, then walked quietly through the gate and down the lane to see boyfriends in Woodhouse. They might not get back till midnight, but a piece of gravel at the window of their bedroom brought Sabina down to let them in. 'The only good thing about Burton,' Edith laughed, 'is that he sleeps so deep an earthquake wouldn't wake him, though if one should ever swallow him up it would be good riddance.'

'I'll run away from home,' Rebecca said, 'one of these days.'

Thomas smiled. 'You'd soon come back.'

'I bleddy wouldn't.'

'You might, if you got hungry,' Edith said, 'but once I go, that'll be that. He won't see me till after I'm married.'

'You're not twenty-one,' Thomas said, 'so he could fetch you back.'

Rebecca smoothed her long dark hair. 'He might be glad to get shut of us.'

'And where would you lay your head at night?' Thomas asked. 'Under Trent Bridge?'

'I would if I had to.'

'I'll always find a bed to sleep in,' Edith said, 'but I shan't say who with.'

'You'll get into trouble one of these days.' Thomas took the empty buckets back to the outhouse.

They were locked in notions of what they imagined freedom to be. 'I don't care.' Edith was adamant. 'It'll be better than staying here.'

Oliver placed the buckets under the large sink, came out of the pantry and picked up the long-handled woodsman's axe to tackle a heap of logs by the fence at the laneside. At the noisy opening of an upstairs window they saw Burton's face: 'Don't stand there. Get on with your work all of you.'

The house was small but adequate, one bedroom for the five girls, another for the three sons, and the largest for Burton and Mary Ann. There was a four-poster curtain-drawn bed, a wardrobe, and a chest of drawers with a swivel mirror above, which showed Burton putting on a laundered white shirt, a high collar, and square-ended bow tie.

Tucking the shirt into the trousers of his navy-blue suit, and fastening the thick leather belt into place, a sudden irritation took him again to the window. 'Thomas! Get your hands out of your pockets and come in to polish my boots. The black ones. They're in the parlour. And look sharp, or you'll get a stick across your back.'

A few minutes were needed to arrange the correct set of the tie, and finish turning him from a blacksmith at the forge into a smartly dressed man of consequence. He fixed the watch and chain across his waistcoat with its attached couple of sovereigns, and slipped the white folded handkerchief in his lapel pocket. Down in the parlour he held his boots against the window to make sure they had a sufficient shine, then drew both on and carefully laced them up.

He went to the back of the house, the evening warm and damp with plenty of gnats, and from the garden decapitated a chrysanthemum with a small pocket knife, to adorn his button hole, thus completing the presence he wished to show. Satisfied that everyone was at their allotted tasks in the yard, he strode onto the lane, leaving the gate open.

SIX

He pushed into the swing doors of the Crown Hotel, the smell of pipe smoke and ripe ale as familiar as if he had known it even since before birth. Walking to the bar he noted everyone with hardly a turn of the head, those known and unknown. Eli the barman had the same facial colour and white albino hair as his father had at the old White Hart. 'I'll have the usual.'

'Can't get enough, eh, Burton?' Morgan wiped froth from his long moustache. Burton had known him from a youth, but disliked such familiarity, at least so early in the evening.

Tom, who also worked with the ponies at Radford pit, hovered on the other side. 'He'll need a lot of ale to dowse the fire in him.'

Eli put the tankard down. 'That's a tanner you owe the till.'

He set a coin on the wood and, standing sufficiently apart in the crowded Saturday night taproom, said: 'Have you seen Florence?'

'She was serving in the jug-and-bottle. Then she went upstairs, but I expect she'll be down in a bit.'

Burton let the rest of his ale stand while lighting a cigarette. At work he rolled them, but for the weekend emptied a packet of twenty Virginias into a silver case. 'Is she all right?'

He was called to take another order. 'She will be, as soon as she sees you.'

'She's not for you, Burton,' Tom said.

Burton stared. 'Nobody's for anybody, unless you take them.'

'You'll need a horse to gallop away on if her husband sees you,' Morgan laughed.

'You think so?' Saturday night was a time for ease, but he was annoyed at them putting their noses into what could only be his business. 'I've never been on a horse in my life. I wouldn't trust one an inch. Nor would I trust a woman, unless I wanted her. Only a fool would risk his neck on a horse, or his life for a woman.'

He noticed her stance at the foot of the stairs, glad she saw only him, and even more so at her approach in response to his faint nod. A tall well-built woman of thirty, she wore a flowery blouse with a lace collar. Her thin lips and the expression, as if for the moment unaware of where she was, made her seem eternally threatened, and too serious for Burton's liking, until her smile changed to one of expectation, a lightening of the features he had noticed on first seeing her six months ago.

'I thought you'd be in last night,' she said. 'I don't like it when you don't come when you say you will. I think something's happened to you.'

'To me?'

'I know, but I can't help it.'

'I worked till ten.'

'I thought as much. But I waited.'

'You can't stop while there's work. Not in my trade.'

She fiddled with the string of jet beads at her bosom. 'It's nearly a week since we were together.'

Their heads close, people drew back to let them talk. 'Come for a walk tonight.'

'I'd like to, but I daren't risk it. I'm not sure when Herbert will be back.'

'I shouldn't let that bother you.'

'I've got to be careful, haven't I?'

She was called to serve another customer, so he turned back to Tom. 'Did you have anything on the races today?'

'A couple of bob on Vanity Fair, but I think the bogger must have been wearing hobnailed boots. I could have got to that winning post quicker myself.'

Burton watched Florence at work. 'If you ride on them they break your neck, and if you bet on them you might as well throw your hard-earned money in the dustbin.'

'You spend it on ale, though,' Morgan said, 'and that only gets swilled into the Trent.'

Burton's laugh was short and dry. 'But you enjoy it as it goes through your tripes.' He emptied his pint, and went closer to the bar, a ripple of agitation on his cheek. 'Florence!'

She gave change, then came at his call. 'You're short with me tonight.'

'Fill this up. What about tomorrow?'

'It might be all right.'

'Don't you know?'

'I'm not two people, am I?'

Her scent wafted against him as he leaned closer. 'I wish to God you were. I don't know which one I'd love more.'

She smiled at his rare compliment. 'I'll try,' then drew his beer and moved away.

Though the night was as black as Cherry Blossom boot polish Burton could have gone blindfold up the lane to Old Engine Cottages. Morgan and Tom, trying to follow his footsteps, swayed to either side between the hedges, and sang as if the noise would keep them free of potholes. 'Come in for a sup of ale,' Burton told them by the gate. 'I've got a bottle cooling in the pantry.'

'It's eleven, and I must be up early.'

'Me as well,' said Morgan.

'You'll get all the sleep you want when you're in hell. At least I shall.' He led them up the path and into the house. All three faces showed when he set the glass over the lamp wick. 'Close the door behind you quietly, then sit down. This is vintage Shipstone's.'

The smell of ale poured from the bottle brought heads closer to the glasses. 'How many have you got upstairs now, Burton?' Tom wanted to know.

'There were nine when I last counted. That was including Mary Ann.'

'I don't see them around much,' Morgan said.

'I set them to work, that's why. Five daughters are a handful at times, and you've got to keep an eye on them. One of the young 'uns is a pretty little thing, so I expect she'll be a bit of trouble when she grows up, if I don't tame her first.'

'We won't know if she's pretty unless you fetch her down,' Morgan said.

'You don't believe me?'

'I didn't say so.'

'You meant it, though. I'll go and get her.'

They heard his weight on the stairs, and a door opening. 'He's a hard bogger,' Tom said. 'I wouldn't like to be one of his nippers.'

Morgan drew out his pipe. 'He's got something on with that Florence, and she's married. Let's hope his missis never finds out.'

'Nor Florence's husband,' Tom laughed. 'But wedding bells never frightened Burton. He'd run his own son off if he got half the chance.'

Morgan detected a descending tread. 'Shut your rattle. Here he is.'

Ten-year-old Sabina was half-asleep in Burton's arms. She stood hazy-eyed in her nightgown, looking at them from the middle of the table. 'What did I tell you? Straight out of angel's sleep.'

'What a little beauty!'

'Come on, my duck,' Burton said. 'If you can't sing us a song, cock your leg up and do us a dance.'

She looked at the three men, a smile on pale lips, unable to think, hardly knowing where she was, but seeing her father in a mood unknown before, one she might never see again. Maybe he wasn't her father, but someone who had come out of the night from a forest where he lived, and if he wanted her to dance, then she had to.

One leg high, one leg low, she stepped around the table, lips apart and smiling in her aim to obey and please him who must be her father after all. Tom and Morgan threw pennies at her feet, which she picked up quickly. 'You should put her on the stage,' Morgan said, 'and make your fortune.'

'I'd break a stick across the back of any girl of mine who wanted to go there.' Burton, tired of the caper, heard Mary Ann coming down the stairs. He helped Sabina to the floor, and Mary Ann took her hand. Silence, except for the pendulum clock on the wall. 'This is a fine thing. In the middle of the night as well. You and your drunken friends from the alehouse.'

A smile twitched across Burton's downcurving lips. 'It was a bit of fun, that's all.'

'I suppose it was, if you say so.' She pushed Sabina before her. 'Let's get you back into bed where you belong.'

'I'd better be going,' Morgan said, 'or I'll get the rolling pin treatment as well.'

Burton pulled them close. 'I don't want another word from either of you about me and Florence, do you understand? Keep your mouths shut.'

Tom was amazed they had been overheard. 'We won't say a dickybird.'

'People talk,' Morgan said, on the porch.

'Let them.' Burton bolted the door, went into the parlour to take off his boots, and on getting upstairs found Mary Ann asleep.

After the move to Old Engine Cottages the children had played in the field between house and railway, and counted the wagons or carriages of trains steaming along the embankment from Radford station. Sitting on the fence, they argued over the numbers, then went hiding and seeking in the tall grass.

Sabina had always been fearful at the run of a startled rabbit – it might have been a dirty old man lying in wait – but as the wheat-cutter worked in from the hedges she saw how frightened the poor things were as they leapt for safety. She thought how important Farmer Taylor looked on the high seat of his dray, a large grey horse in the shafts fighting off flies.

'You'll have a good harvest this year,' Burton said.

Taylor's laugh was of a man never satisfied. 'I might think so if the price was right. You work every hour God sends, and get little enough for it. The market's bad for farmers, and this government doesn't like us. Who do you vote for?'

'The Liberal chap.' Burton didn't care who knew it.

Taylor snorted. 'They'll never do any good, whether they brought in the old-age pension or not.'

He can kiss my backside, if he's a mind to. 'You can't expect much from any of them, so it's no use complaining.'

Taylor stared at his gold half-hunter. 'Is Mary Ann cooking the men's dinner?'

The shilling or two earned went into her pocket, though sometimes the housekeeping. 'I expect it'll be ready directly.'

A bundle of brown fur hurled itself from a line of wheat, reaching a safe hedge in seconds. 'Another lucky one.'

'I'll get my gun,' Burton said.

Thomas in the garden was loading weeds into the wooden barrow whose iron supports Burton had beaten out in the forge. Oliver was up the slope winding a bucket from the well, and on wondering where Oswald was Burton saw him in the yard chopping the day's firewood.

Mary Ann and Ivy came into the field with a cauldron of boiled bacon and a tray of newly baked loaves, odours reminding him of hunger, after the slice of bread and fat bacon for breakfast at six. But rabbits were fleeing in all directions, and he wanted one for their supper, so went upstairs and pulled the shotgun and cartridges from their hiding-place under the bed. Pointing the barrel downwards he opened the window to let in a summer breeze.

The gun came from an auction and cost three guineas, a light breech-loading firearm worth twenty now. Mary Ann grumbled at having such a weapon in the house, but never turned down a rabbit or a couple of pigeons for the pot. Like most women she disliked the plucking and gutting, so got him to do it. It was easy work: draw off the skin, open it up, pull out the stomach (careful not to burst it because of the fearful stink), cut off the head, then give the carcase a good wash before the butchering.

Farmhands were eating by the hedge, and Burton positioned himself in the far corner of the field, took a stone from his trouser pocket picked up on his way through the garden, and hurled it over the limit of uncut wheat.

Waiting on one knee, he fired, and missed. Another pair took their chance, one pausing to cuff itself, too confident at clear land ahead. He squeezed the trigger on the one that ran – more sporting that way – and bowled it over.

A cartridge still in the breech, he laid the gun down gently and launched himself at the half-alive rabbit. The butcher or poultry shop would charge a shilling, and this one was free – well-fed on the choicest grass – bar the price of the cartridge.

The blade of a hand against its neck dropped it dead at his feet. 'This'll make us a good dinner,' he said in the house, the rabbit swinging from his hand. 'It's the third this year.'

Soft Emily ran to Mary Ann's skirt, tears pumping as she stroked the fur. 'Dad killed you, poor little thing. I'd like one of these for a cat!'

'Stop your blawting.' He rolled a cigarette, and descended into the cool pantry to tie the two back legs with a piece of twine, and put a pan under its head to catch blood. He took a slab of smoked bacon from its hook, and a large round loaf out of the panchion, and laid them on the kitchen table. 'Mary Ann, cut me something to eat.'

By afternoon the hay field was flat and sweet-smelling, men and horses gone, crows daggering their beaks among the stalks. He scythed around the edges not reached by the combine harvester. The girls would husk and boil it in the outhouse copper, to mix with whatever else there was for the pigs.

He advanced with a wide swing of the arms through each uneven path. Nothing escaped the gleaning blade sharpened with a stick of carborundum to as fine an edge as the razor he shaved with. From a gap in the hedge Emily watched the stern reaper she had always known him to be in her dreams, till she could bear the spectacle no longer and stood behind the nearest bush to hide.

Florence opened the gate and crossed a corner of the field. He worked rhythmically, as if never to stop, forward to the privet then back to sweep what had not been in his track, thoughtless endeavour fuelled by the slow advance of his feet till the job was done. He noted her parasol, light gloves, and anxious smile. 'What are you doing, so far out of your way?'

'I get fed up being in that pub all day. They let me out for a walk.'

He laid down the scythe. 'That was good of them.'

'One of the customers said Farmer Taylor was haymaking so I thought I might see you.'

'I'm glad you did.'

She smelled his sweat, and he took in the scent of fresh lavender when she came into his arms. 'Careful what you do,' he said. 'There might be somebody about.'

She stood away. 'I love you.'

There was no answer to that. His look would tell any fine woman that he wanted her, and if they fell in with it, as they sometimes did, they must know what they were doing. If they didn't, and as time went on there was something about it they didn't like, it was nothing to do with him. 'Go across the Cherry Orchard, and I'll see you by Robin's Wood. Take the back lane.'

'Don't be long, my love. I haven't got much time.'

You won't need it, he thought, the way I feel. Emily on the other side of the hedge picked at a cornflower as Burton strode to the house. 'There's some wheat to collect around the field,' he told Mary Ann. 'Get the girls to husk it. They know what to do.'

'I'll do it myself, as soon as I've cleaned these pans.'

'Don't leave it too long, in case there's rain. What did Taylor give you for cooking the men's dinner?'

'Half-a-crown.'

'He's a mean sort.'

'He paid for the bacon and bread.'

'So he should. I'm going back into the field for a bit.'

'Is Emily out there?'

'Not as I know.'

'That's where she said she'd be. Tell her to come in. I don't want her wandering near the railway line.'

'I'll see she don't.'

In the garden he pushed her towards the house. 'Your mother wants you.'

He followed the concealed way by the far edge of the cornfield, along a track overgrown with nettles and brambles, but in spring a bridle lane of Queen Anne's Lace. At the uneven expanse of the Cherry Orchard he wondered whether cherries had ever grown there, but didn't know, for it was now a large patch of scrubland, too open for what he had in mind, hoping not to be seen, taking care to cross only a corner. You were never alone, and he wished for the shotgun to frighten away the birds he felt were watching him.

Avoiding the worst humps and hollows, the features of Minnie Dyslin came to mind from so many years ago. How many, he didn't care to reckon, but he'd been twenty-one and in his heyday, yet at forty-eight he didn't feel much older than when Minnie told him she was having his child. He wondered what the boy was doing and what he looked like. At twenty-five he would be older than Oliver, and Minnie more than fifty. He didn't know why he should think of her after so many years.

Florence was just inside the wood, because she didn't want to be seen either. He pointed to the parasol. 'Fold that thing up.'

She followed. 'Perhaps there are children about.'

'There aren't. I'd have heard them. Or seen them. We'll be all right.' Through the glade a streamlet flowed. As a boy he had filled his belly with its clear water. He helped her across, preventing the branches of a bush from springing in her face. In a space of greensward he drew her close for a kiss. 'Here's a place.' When this way with his gun, out for plump wood pigeons or collared doves, he had imagined leading a woman to it. 'Only the birds will see us.'

She clasped him. 'I don't know why I keep on seeing you.'

'If you don't, I don't. Why should you know?'

'I love you,' she said. 'That's the trouble.'

'You have to know what you want, and if you get it, then there isn't any trouble.'

'I had to see you.'

'I'm glad you did. Let's lie here.'

'There's no one else in my life.'

A poor life, if she believed so. No one was in her life except her husband, and no one in his but Mary Ann. That's the way of the world. Why he was here he didn't know and didn't want to know, you just did what you could when you had the chance, and all he knew was that he wanted to, and had no option but to go into her, and hope she wouldn't make such a noise as the last time she spent, when they were behind the public house after closing time, and before that when they were upstairs in one of the rooms.

He closed the door carefully. Mary Ann, who had long since lit the lamp, sat by the fire, a sheet of clean sacking over her knees, clippings of various colours but of the same shape on the floor, to be fitted into any pattern that took her fancy. 'I've been waiting for you.'

He held a bunch of watercress. 'I found this in the wood. Wash it. It can go with my supper.'

'What were you doing in the wood?'

The black dog was a bit too comfortable before the fire, so he held it around the mouth with his strongest hand, till the animal struggled as if in a fit, its helpless whine filling the room.

'Leave the poor thing alone.'

He let it go, a hard slap at its ribs. 'Where is everybody?'

'In bed, except Oliver.'

He sat at the table. 'It's time he was in.'

'He will be presently.' She put the rug peg and clippings into a neat roll, got up to set out bread, cheese, and a bottle of ale. 'I'm off to bed.'

'And I shan't be long.'

She stood a moment. 'I hope you won't get on to Oliver when he comes in.'

'He's late.'

'I saw him walking down the lane with Alma Waterall.'

He wondered who else she might have seen. 'When was that?'

'Two hours since. She's a Sunday School teacher at Woodhouse.'

He grunted. 'That's a fine business.'

'Somebody's got to do it.'

He had sent their children to Sunday School, on the one afternoon of the week when he and Mary Ann could have a peaceful couple of hours in bed, because he was usually too exhausted after the normal day's work. The children came home every year with a prize for good conduct, books only looked at by Oliver. 'I thought you might have seen them in the wood.'

'There was nobody there but me.'

'Wasn't there?'

'What would a Sunday School teacher be doing in a place like that? Go to bed, then. I'll be there soon enough.'

He pushed the empty supper plate aside, no sitting still, every moment something to be done, anything, everything, but anything was better than nothing, than stillness. Stillness was inanition, idleness, death, putting yourself at the mercy of penury, the workhouse, or illness. If you weren't busy you didn't know who you were, so George said, but George was dead now, and he'd never known anything, either.

He took off his shirt, and in the pantry lifted a bucket of water fresh from the well, splashed a gallon into a tin bowl and then over him, soaping himself in reflected light from the living room lamp. Up the steps, towelling his neck, he saw Oliver. 'Where have you been? It's gone ten o'clock.'

'Walking, with a girl,' lips set as if to whistle a lively tune, happy, but standing some distance from his father. Out of the lane into sudden light, he blinked, like Burton in everything but with darker hair, and a mouth softened by resembling Mary Ann's. He would never grow a moustache to conceal the shape of his upper lip, in case he looked too much like Burton as a young man. 'I didn't know the time.'

'Get yourself a watch. Maybe that'll tell you when it's dark. I usually know, because I use my eyes.'

'I'd get a watch, if you paid me more.'

Burton's fist was clenched by his side. Such answering back called for a blow, but he knew that if *his* father had threatened such at that age he would have punched him to the ground. So he hesitated. A fully qualified blacksmith of twenty-three was beyond the stage of being knocked about, and in any case no one knew better than Burton that whatever you did to someone who had just been out tumbling a girl was unlikely to have any effect. Oliver didn't know how lucky he was to be young. 'Get up to bed.'

'Is there any supper?'

'You heard what I said.'

Not caring to argue, he went. The sweetness of Alma's caresses would be easy to live on till getting up for breakfast.

Burton walked across the yard to the closet, and wondered as he stood there whether it was true that thin people pissed more than fat people. Back in the kitchen he booted the dog out, and double-locked the door now that everyone was safe in bed.

He took off the apron and reached for his jacket. 'I'm going out for a while.'

The fire at full heat, Oliver noted a grunt of approval at the work he was doing. 'Where to?'

'Mind your own business. You're in charge.'

Wherever it was, Oliver was glad to see the back of him, and went to striking in the nail holes of the shoe he was making. Oswald came from seeing to a horse, dropped the money in a tin. 'There ain't much trade today. If it doesn't get better we'll be in Queer Street.'

'It goes up and down. It always did.' Oliver dipped the shoe, set it aside, and walked with his brother to the door. 'Which direction did he go in?'

'The pub way.'

'It's not like him, to go at midday, though when I saw him in the Crown last week he was very thick with that Florence. She was too busy talking to serve anybody else, and Burton didn't even greet me.'

'Not that he would.'

'No, but something's going on with them.'

'He met Mam when she was serving behind a bar,' Oswald said.

'Yes, and I think she's regretted it more than once.' Back in the forge he picked up the horsehoe, held it to the light, and considered it done. 'In those days barmaids were different. Mother was, anyway. But Florence is married, and if Mam finds out there'll be ructions. I hope she never does.'

He rolled two cigarettes from Burton's tobacco tin, and they went outside as if he might pick up the lingering fumes when he came back. 'He'll notice some's missing,' Oswald said. 'There'll be hell to pay.'

'If he went off in such a hurry as to forget his tobacco he can't be up to much good. Anyway, he treats me like a dog so I might as well behave like one.' A mouthful of delicious smoke drifted towards his brother. 'We'll enjoy it while we can.'

Emily and Sabina stood in the doorway with the men's dinners. Oliver set the cans on the bench. 'Did you see any lions and tigers on the way here?'

Sabina came forward. 'We saw two, our Oliver, when we crossed the wide road.'

'And did one of them have blood on its teeth?'

Emily glanced sideways at the ground, as if finding her brother too handsome to look at. 'It had lovely fur. It was ever so tame, and I stroked it.'

Alma Waterall, watching from across the lane, saw Oliver take a coin from his pocket and close a hand over it, then hold both hands towards Sabina. 'Which one is the penny in?'

She glanced, and pointed decisively. 'That one.'

He opened his fist. 'You little devil! Lucky first time. It's got His Majesty's head on it! Now it's cheeky Emily's turn. See if you win a prize as well.'

Her face a mockery of adult consideration, she tapped a knuckle and, on her lips going down to weep at the empty palm, Oliver put a hand to his left ear, rubbed at a simulated itch, and brought a penny away that had been hidden in the other hand. 'It was stuck in my tab-hole, but I pulled it out by the tail.'

She smiled like a daisy in spring. 'I've won! I've won! Now I can buy some toffees on my way to school,' and ran off hand-in-hand with Sabina.

Alma, a full-busted young woman with fair skin and a fringe of dark hair across her forehead, a retroussé nose but a well-shaped purposeful mouth, came from across the lane. 'I saw you, but couldn't believe it was true. You said you were a blacksmith, but didn't tell me this was where you worked. I happened to be passing.'

He led her into a place she hadn't been in before, and wiped the bench with a piece of rag for her to sit, though she preferred not to. He intended to kiss her, but she stood aside. 'I've seen your sisters at Sunday School. They're always well-behaved.'

'Unlike me, I suppose. But that's because I told them to be. We all went there because Mother and Father insisted on it.'

'We need whoever we can get. I wish every child would come.' Oswald called that a horse and cart was on its way. 'I'll be going, then,' she said.

'Don't you want to see us at our work?'

'I'd like to, but my Aunt Lydia's not well, and she lives on her own, so I call now and again. She's my father's sister, but they don't get on, and I try to make up for it.'

The carter pointed with his lit pipe to the horse. 'Can you put a shoe on this awkward bogger?'

'I'll have none of your swearing.' Oliver caught Burton's sharp tone behind his, but considered it justified. 'You can go somewhere else if there's to be any of that.'

The man laughed. 'I don't know if the horse would get that far, it's such a wayward nag. But I'm sorry I cursed, miss.' He turned to Oliver. 'He's gone fair lame.'

Alma coughed from the dust and fumes of the forge. 'Shall we meet soon?'

'What about Sunday? I'm not free till then.'

She nodded. 'I'd like that,' and went on her way, Oliver watching for a moment before turning to the carter. 'Now let's see what can be done for your old crock.'

SEVEN

Burton was glad to see so few in the Crown, not more than a couple of men who had left their wagons by the kerb. Florence was distracted. Well, she would be. She always was. There was only one thing that could bring her back into herself, but by the look of her he could tell she was wondering whether or not she'd had enough of him.

He was halfway through the pint he allowed himself at midday. 'Is it your husband you're frightened of?'

'It's not that so much. He might murder me, but apart from that I don't think he'd care one way or the other. The thing is, he's leaving his job, and we'll have to live in Chesterfield.'

'What does he want to go to a place like that for?'

She might be daft enough to think her husband didn't care, but he surmised otherwise. Yet you could never be sure of anything. She might be using the assumption that he did know what they were up to because she was fed up and wanted to pack the business in with him, though if her husband did know then maybe he wanted to get out of it because he couldn't stand and fight like a man for a woman worth fighting for. Let him try, though he wouldn't like Mary Ann to hear of it.

'His brother's in business at Chesterfield,' she went on.

'Get him to stay here.'

'I don't know as I can,' her tone implying she might not want to. 'He's set on it, anyway.'

He leaned closer, a hand on hers. 'I'm sure you can if you want to. He sounds the sort who will listen.'

The glitter of desire came into her brown eyes. 'Is that what you'd like?'

He was irritated by her emotional scheming. It wasn't up to

him to make up his mind. She must come to him, and if she didn't she wasn't worth having. 'It only matters if you want it to.'

She was looking beyond him, and he saw Mary Ann's reflection in the mirror, between liquor bottles on the shelf. Uneasy at the apparition he turned back to Florence, as if to go on talking would prove innocence. 'Don't let her bother you.'

'Who is she?'

'Some woman or other. I'd be sorry to lose you. I think a lot of you.'

'You ought to show it a bit more.'

'I don't often see you, in that way. But I always want to. Life is hard for everybody. We'll have to see what can be done.'

Mary Ann had witnessed all she needed. Pale, blood pulsing in every vein, she pulled at his arm. 'I was told you weren't at work, but I knew where to find you.'

He pushed her away, to finish his drink. Dignity was the dearest thing in the world, and he was shaken that she had come into the pub and dared to make a fuss. Florence realized who she was, and stood away with shame and sorrow at what she had become part of, and at what she felt to be her fault. Burton had courted her for weeks before she gave in, though she too had wanted him. And now this. She should have known it would happen.

The few drinkers looked on, as Mary Ann went for him. Nobody had tackled Burton in that way before, and it was extraordinary to witness. 'You've got eight kids to keep,' she said, 'and you're doing it on me with her.'

Words were wrenched out of him. 'We were talking.'

'I don't believe it. You think I'm a fool? I know what's going on.' She seemed about to strike him. 'Come back to your work. No wonder you give me hardly enough to keep the house going, carrying on with a trollop like that.' She took a piece of paper from her pocket, held it before his face so as to give him time to recognize their marriage lines, and threw it in two pieces on the bar. 'That's what I think of you!'

He flushed with shame and rage. 'Go home.'

'Only if you come with me.'

As a master blacksmith and man of the house, philanderer and favoured customer at the pub, something had to be done to counter this violation of his dignity, and in such a way that it would never happen again. Such an affront had never been dreamed of, and caused a ripple at the temples fit to burst his head. He gripped her arm and walked her to the door. 'Get off home,' and pushed her into the street.

In the silence he dared whoever looked on to deny that what he had done was anything but just. None could. They would have done the same. Or the worst of them would. He wasn't finished with Florence. 'Don't worry about that little set-to. We'll meet in the woods tomorrow evening.'

She handed him the two halves of the marriage certificate. 'You'd better have this, and see if you can put it together again.'

'That's cold.' But he took it.

'I shan't see you anymore.'

'Don't say that. Wait for me. I'll be back.' A few strides took him outside.

'His poor bloody wife's going to cop it now,' one of the carters laughed.

'Well, she could have hammered him in the house instead of showing him up in public.'

The closer to home the less was he able to think, and the faster he walked. No need to think at all, everything spoiled between him and Florence. Rage carried him through Woodhouse, under the railway bridge and up the lane, not caring to avoid puddles from yesterday's downpour. He passed his neighbour Harold Ollington, who wondered at not receiving the usual nod. Even God, had Burton recognized Him, would have got no greeting, pushed out of mind by the force of such catastrophic events. It wasn't so much that she had shown him up in a pub as that she'd had the gall to do something like that in the first place. As his wife she had lost all respect, flaunted intolerance of him as his own master when away from the house as well as in it. His boot hit the gate.

Mary Ann pegged out a line of clothes fresh from the copper. Work for the household must go on, but tears went down with drops from the sheets. What she had done to Burton served him right, though she'd be damned for her Irish temper. Emily had seen him in the field talking to that wicked woman, then he had stayed so late in the wood, and today she hadn't found him at work when he should have been, and had caught him in the public house talking to the barmaid in such a way it was plain what had been going on.

She felt only anger and wild resentment that he had betrayed her who had brought up their eight children on short money over so many years; nor did she suppose it was the first time he had done such a thing, which caused more tears to flow as she thrust wooden pegs onto cotton or cloth.

She heard nothing, then Burton pulled her around to face him. Dead grey eyes fixed her, then black and orange sparks exploded at a blow impossible to avoid. 'Don't ever interfere with anything I do, ever again. Never. Do you understand? Keep out of my business.' Ignoring her scream, he fixed her in readiness for another across the mouth.

A third blow was held back. One was enough, and he had given two. Never lose control. He immediately knew he had done wrong, shouldn't have given even the first, because she was his wife and not a child or animal to be kept in order. George would never have done the same to Sarah. She caught him out once, though hadn't dared tackle him in public. George had done nothing more than laugh in her face, because fair was fair, he told Ernest, who was now sorry he hadn't recalled the incident on his way up the lane. He pushed Mary Ann aside, and slammed the door into the house.

Annie Ollington looked over the fence at the commotion, and hurried around by the front gate. She sat Mary Ann on a log. 'Oh, what a terrible thing! Look what a mess he's made of your mouth. But you'll be all right in a bit, duck.' She wiped her cheeks with a handkerchief, shook it square, and saw smears of red. 'Does he do this often?'

'He's never hit me before. I wish I could die.'

'Don't talk like that. But if he does it again you ought to set your lads onto him. I never thought Burton would do a thing like this. And he thinks himself such a gentleman! If anybody treated me like this I'd take the carving knife to their guts.' She put an arm around her. 'I've never seen anything like it, though I know a lot of it goes on.'

Burton came with a bowl of water and a cloth. 'What do you want?'

'Can't you see? I'm trying to help. What did you hit her like that for?'

'It's none of your business. Clear off, and don't come here again.' A hand jerked, as if to throw the water should she move any closer. 'She'll be all right.'

'Not with a beast like you she won't.'

'Have less of your lip.'

In answering back she was more brave than she knew.

'You'd better go,' Mary Ann said.

She saw the glint in Burton's eyes, and went quickly down the path. He dabbed at Mary Ann's face. 'I was only talking to the barmaid, passing the time. I'd had a heavy morning at work, and thought I'd go to the Crown for a drink. There was no need to show me up in front of everybody.'

If that's all he had been doing why was he so enraged? He couldn't get out of it like that. 'Whatever you were up to God will pay you out for hitting me.'

'God? And where does *He* live? What job does *He* do? Does He get good money while He's at it? Hold still, and let me see to you.'

'There is a God, though, and He'll have it in for you.'

'Not if I know it.'

'You shouldn't have hit me.'

He helped her to stand. 'I wish I could undo it. Come into the house.'

Nowhere else to go, she had made no better home for him and all of them, and because he was her husband she let him guide her to a chair by the fire. The world had turned in a way she'd never imagined. To say she had loved him was unnecessary. He was the main factor of her life and she would never complain, had made her bed and must lie on it. She got up, hoping her face would pain less if she busied herself.

A huge horned gramophone stood on the round mahogany table in the parlour, as if to bellow condemnation at what he had done. He pushed it aside on sitting down. The room was Mary Ann's creation, and she cleaned it every week, though rarely had company to show it off. She sometimes enjoyed its comforting solitude, and did her sewing there.

On a smaller table lay a neatly boxed set of dominoes, while a series of whatnot shelves fixed to a corner of the room held pottery pieces from seaside or Matlock. The bookcase was filled with prizes brought from Sunday School, which he had sent the children to hoping they would get knowledge into their heads that had never entered his. They might also be taught to behave, so that Burton wouldn't have to do it – as he once heard sharp-tongued Ivy remark to her sisters, not knowing he was near.

Mary Ann cared for the books, liked the idea of several a year coming into the house, and noted with pleasure how the shelves slowly filled. Only Oliver took interest in them, but she supposed that was encouragement enough. She had been with Burton on Alfreton Road and saw the glass-fronted case in Jacky Pownall's junk yard, standing in the drizzle by a stack of bedsteads, the perfect piece of furniture for storing books, instead of them staying heaped on the table, so she robbed him of a week's drink to pay for it, and got him to push it the mile or so home on a rented handcart.

It stood for a week in the warm kitchen to dry, and he took several evenings with rag, scraper and turpentine to remove the sickly green paint, then cleaned and polished to reveal the splendour of original wood.

The picture on the wall over the fireplace, a wedding present from George, was of a youth handing a bunch of flowers to a young girl, the couplet underneath an avowal of love that Burton knew well but didn't care to repeat at the moment. He sat with a hand over his eyes, as if they were paining him, or would be if he thought more about what he had done, aware that what was done could never be undone.

In a cupboard facing the fireplace was his bottle of whisky, rarely broached, but he went to it and poured a small glass, noticing that the level had gone down from when he had last taken a nip, wondering whether any of the children had been helping themselves.

Things couldn't be worse. He was losing Florence, and had

been angry enough to hit Mary Ann, having always said he would never knock any woman about. But none had ever given him cause to, and when your blood boiled there was little to stop you doing it – though there ought to have been. It was no use saying he wouldn't do it again. It was already done. The only way to make amends, if they could ever be made, was to let time go by, but that wasn't good enough. Thoughts went in a circle, till the only way to get out of their grip – nothing at the moment could make up for what he had done – was to be certain that Florence no longer wanted him.

He poured a larger dram. If Florence wanted to go on with him nothing should stand in her way, and since he wanted to go on with her he couldn't imagine she wouldn't want to.

He put the glass of whisky before Mary Ann. 'Try some of this. It might help a bit.'

'Nothing will.' But she sipped, not averse to the taste. 'What would you do to me if you caught me doing the same thing?'

'Kill the man, and you as well – except I wasn't doing anything I shouldn't.'

She thought it better to stay quiet. He stood at the door. 'Where are you going?'

'To see how those two idlers are getting on at the forge.' She had never questioned him before. As for telling a lie, what could you do when you didn't want to tell the truth? You never lied because you wanted to, he would always rather not, but only when people drove you to it, and to save them from worry. She should have had more sense than to ask, and if she doesn't believe me that's her lookout. Never tell anybody what they don't need to know.

He pondered the matter, but on reaching the main road his thoughts were only of Florence. Few women meant what they said. Getting her to keep on with him was as important to his pride as the need to use her body.

Eli took his time serving other customers, before coming to ask what he wanted.

'Where's Florence?'

'Gone. Packed her job in. Walked out just after you did. And she won't be coming back, she said.'

Burton's head tilted with disappointment, and indignation. 'That was a foolish thing to do.'

'You lost us a good wench,' Eli said. 'There's some things a woman won't put up with.'

'It's nothing to do with you. I'll have a pint.' The first mouthful tasted as if pumped out of the Trent, but he drank nevertheless, deciding never to go into the place again.

Tears fell into the mist of lavender, whose smell reminded her of early days at home when her mother and grandmother scented clothes and underwear in the same way. She was blinded with regret at ever having delivered herself into the hands of Burton. Emma Lewin had told her more than once that she ought not to.

She wondered if Burton had at one time found the florin she was looking for, and spent it on ale, or used it to treat some fancywoman – that holy florin she had vowed to keep till death.

The underwear drawer was her domain, so he would never have done such a thing, though if the thought occurred to him in the future he wouldn't find it. In any case he didn't know she still had that keepsake coin passed over the bar at the White Hart for buying her pair of gloves. She had those as well, though neither tokens could any more mean what they had.

The coin was wrapped in the same scrap of newspaper given him to go and buy the gloves, held firmly as if it might come alive and try to escape. She went up the slope to the well from which all water came for the house, moved the wooden lid aside and saw the glint at the bottom. She would throw the florin in, and say goodbye to her love for Burton, chuck herself into oblivion after it, water soothing her wounded face while she died, a reward of that peace and rest she seemed never to have had since marrying, and which she now thought she deserved.

She sat so still on the parapet that a thrush alighted and looked at her. You're free, she said. You have a hard life, but at least you don't think, or suffer misery fit to shred your insides. Its tail shook as if in greeting, then it lifted and flew at the twitch of her fingers.

Opening her hand, the florin tilted on her palm. She held it awhile, in two minds whether to let it drop. She wouldn't unless, taking on a life of its own, the decision was made for her. She levelled her hand. A chill wind increased the ache on her face, and she wanted the warmth of the house.

On going through the door the florin was still in her hand, and she looked at the elderly head of Queen Victoria who for better or worse had lost her husband early. Then the superstitious worry came, as if the Queen was sending a message from the grave, that if she had dropped the florin in the well something dreadful would have happened to Burton. She didn't want that, so the only thing was to return the coin to its hiding-place among the sweetness of lavender.

He made his way over the hill and into town, in the hope that the effort of walking would still his regret at what had been done, though nothing ever would. In a jeweller's window at Chapel Bar he saw a display of Galway claddach rings, and remembered that Mary Ann had admired them for as long as he had known her, but had given up hope of getting one. The price of twenty shillings dug into the reserve he kept should anything happen to her or the children, and the cost of having her mouth mended would also take some money.

The ring in his pocket, he bought twopennorth of tram ride along Castle Boulevard to Lenton. He recalled that nearly a hundred years ago ten people were killed and as many injured when a barge moored off Canal Street carrying a ton of gunpowder exploded. It was being held for pits in Derbyshire, but on being carried from the boat to the warehouse left a trail along the towpath. A man who saw it thought he would have a lark – as the damned fool must have told himself – and threw a hot coal down. He never knew what happened, his troubles gone in a flash, though he took nine others with him and ruined half the quayside.

Some men are like that, nothing in their heads but mischief, though on the top deck of the clanking tram he wondered whether it was worth going home. A beneficial explosion would nicely settle him, yet he wouldn't want anyone's company on the ride into hell.

On the other hand he could call at the forge, collect sufficient tools, and go back to being a journeyman-blacksmith as in his younger days when he had worked for George in Wales, those carefree times of knowing Minnie Dyslin and the girls of Tredegar. If Minnie was still there he would call and see the son she'd had. Perhaps she was married again, and had as many by now as Mary Ann. He could think of no better thing for her, and hoped she was happy.

Easy to understand why George had taken himself off to earn his living in Wales for a year or two, and left Sarah with the children. Having a forge of your own brought the bother of keeping it going, not to mention a home with a wife and eight children around your neck. A journeyman's pay might not be as much as a settled blacksmith's, but at least you had no responsibilities.

He let the tram carry him, because the world wasn't yours to do as you pleased with, as he had always known. The world owned you, though you had a fight to stop it doing you in. Storm clouds were everywhere, now and again a patch of blue to give you a bit of fun – until you put your foot in it and made a mistake. Then you got to thinking it was time to be off, yet knew you couldn't go. He was married to Mary Ann, and that was that. It was a harder road than the prayer book said, a bond that anchored him to solid concrete. Though Mary Ann would be pleased at getting the ring, he hardly expected the gesture to make any difference.

He went to the forge for an hour's work before the day ended. 'The old man's quieter than usual,' Oliver said to Oswald as he was seeing to a horse. 'I wonder why?'

'When he's like that we should keep out of his way.'

Burton sent them home first, and closed the place himself.

The table hadn't been set for the evening meal, ash dim at the bars, gloom so thick you could cut it with a knife but, Oliver thought, you couldn't eat it, and they were hungry. They wanted food, but something had happened, as if news had come that someone had died. Neither son had ever seen Mary Ann sitting by the cooling fire as if turned to stone. The house could die for all she seemed aware of it. 'What's gone wrong?'

She turned her head. 'Ask Burton.'

Thomas stayed by the door, fearing to come close but calling: 'Where's our supper?'

Her voice wasn't right. 'I'll get it in a bit.'

'You're crying,' Oliver said.

Her mouth was bruised and twisted. 'Can't you see?'

Oswald cried out. 'How did you do that?'

'I caught Burton in the Crown talking to a woman. I lost my temper, and showed him up in front of everybody.'

'Temper be damned.' Oliver's anguish brought more tears. 'Look at her. You don't do that to a woman, not for anything.'

She went to and from the pantry with none of her usual quickness while Oliver, weary after the day's work and wanting a meal, poked ash from the grate and put sticks on embers that still had heat. Thomas used the bellows, set larger wood and then coal to bring the fire to a state for cooking.

'Don't say anything to Burton,' she said. 'It's best if the whole thing blows over.'

'Somebody's got to.' Oliver didn't relish the role, knowing how it would end. 'We can't let him behave like that.'

'Go upstairs,' she told Thomas, 'and get Edith and Rebecca to come down and help me with the dinner.'

'Did you put anything on your face?' Oswald asked.

'Annie came with some witch-hazel after Burton had gone.'

'You finished ours on me a few days ago,' Oliver said. 'It's like being in a war, living in this house.'

'It helped a bit. She came with some Collis Browne's as well but I told her I wasn't a baby who'd got colic. She said it might buck me up, and it did for a while. At least I've got a good neighbour.'

'I'll make sure he never lives this down,' Oliver said.

Edith took knives and forks from the drawer. 'You've seen what that old fucker's done?'

'Don't swear like that,' Mary Ann said, 'or I'll make you wash your mouth out with soap. I won't have that sort of talk in this house.'

'I can't help it. He wants blinding, except that it would be too good for him.'

'And don't talk like that about your father, or God will pay you out as well.'

'If He paid me out for saying anything against Burton there wouldn't be any God.'

'It won't change him,' Oliver said. 'I can't think what will. He won't even alter after he's dead and gone.'

Edith laughed. 'Somebody ought to kill him. That's what he deserves.'

'He's not worth hanging for,' Oswald said.

'Let's get on with supper,' Mary Ann told them, as if only eating would stop such talk. 'He'll be in directly, and if it's not ready there'll be hell to pay.'

'Make it as hot as you can,' Edith said, 'and chuck it in his face.'

'Now stop,' Mary Ann said angrily. 'You can give me some help. Crack the eggs for the pudding and beat them in the big yellow bowl.' Her face pained, and two of her teeth were loose, alarming because she had always feared for her looks, but such murderous words from the children inclined her to take Burton's side.

She didn't like the notion that he had sowed the wind and would reap the whirlwind, not from her children anyway. He behaved as he did because it was his nature, and he didn't know any better, not realizing that do as you would be done by was the only way to live. If there was one thing worse than what he had done it was to have the children set against him with so much hatred. No woman deserves what she'd had, but no man deserves that, either. She had, after all, enraged him by doing the worst possible thing, humiliating him before other men, when she ought to have tackled him at home. She regretted her loss of temper, but it was too late to say so. He had never hit her before, and never would again.

Oliver nodded to his brothers. 'Let's go in the yard and get this muck off our faces.'

The fully leaved beech tree on the mellow August evening gave shade and shelter to both sides of the fence. Oliver took two bowls from under the worn rickety table and filled them from a bucket. Drawing off their shirts, they lathered themselves with pleasant-smelling White Windsor soap and, after much swilling and towelling, fetched clean shirts and trousers from the house. Thomas, the last to dress, went along the yard to get wood for the fire and, from the gate, signalled that Burton was on his way.

It would be an evil deed to strike your own father, and the intention troubled and frightened Oliver. Knowing that something had to be done, he regretted being the chosen one to do it. 'I rely on you two to give me a hand.'

Burton came from under the bridge in his usual smith-alone way, on up the lane towards home, back straight and looking only in front, as if nothing was visible for a thousand miles, therefore too far off to be bothered by. Victim though master of his thoughts, he was weary at wondering whether there would be any advantage in going to Florence's house and calling her out to talk, because a job left undone was a bad one, and he wanted to see the matter through. Then he decided that he wouldn't chase her. It wasn't worth it, was beneath his dignity, whether or not there was any hope of carrying on with her again. Let her come to him if she wanted, but he knew she wouldn't, a strong-minded woman never going back on her word.

A young man coming down the lane made no move to step aside, and when they collided Burton sent him staggering against the bank.

'Watch what you're doing, can't you?' the youth cried.

Burton knew him as someone from Woodhouse, and considered giving him as good a hiding as he deserved. A tall robust lad, he had broken his parents' hearts, so he'd heard, because they hadn't had the sense to bring him up properly. Well-muscled and able to work, he spent what time he could at the boozer, though he was barely eighteen. At least none of the girls in the family, nor his sons for that matter, would have anything to do with an idler who went poaching and was often in trouble with the police.

Doddoe sensed what was coming, and moved deftly from Burton's way, walking quickly and calling: 'You think you own the fucking world!'

Too near the house to bother, Burton was only anxious in some small way to mollify Mary Ann with the gift in his pocket.

Oliver stepped from the washhouse door, and placed himself in Burton's way as if having something to say about work at the forge, though fear increased when his father stopped to listen: 'What is it?'

'Why did you hit our mother like that?'

Burton disliked being pulled out of his world, except in his own time and when he cared for it, so he was merely startled. 'Eh?'

Oliver, legs shaking, called to his brothers standing by the pigsty: 'Back me up, then.'

Burton took a quick pace away.

'I asked why you hit our mother?'

A blow sent Oliver to one side, and before he could recover his stance Burton had gone into the house. 'That's a fine thing.' Oliver turned to Oswald and Thomas. 'I thought you were going to help me.'

'It would only cause more ructions,' Oswald said, 'and upset Mam even more.'

'No it won't. He's got to pay for what he did. He just can't do a thing like that.'

Burton put a hand over Mary Ann's shoulders, and held the small white box open before her. 'That won't make up for it,' she said. 'Though it might be a start.' She placed it in her pocket, and hoped that her sons, having seen the gesture, wouldn't now make a fuss about what had been done.

They sat down to eat. Edith, knowing that things hadn't gone well in the yard, winked at Oliver, as a hint that he should say something to Burton again. Knowing he needed encouragement, she sent a further signal.

Though only halfway finished he laid the cutlery across his plate. 'Burton, I want an explanation as to why you hit our mother like that.'

Ivy trembled, and looked away, while Rebecca's features showed only loathing. Emily and Sabina grinned, as if not caring what the tension was about. Oswald and Thomas stayed silent and fearful.

'Stop it,' Mary Ann said, 'and finish your dinner. It was my fault as much as his. I shouldn't have shamed him in the pub like that.'

'I don't care what you did. I expect he asked for it. There must have been something behind whatever you said.'

Burton ate, everyone knowing he wouldn't for long. His exertion of more control than they had ever known reduced them to terror. The veins at his temples twitched at Mary Ann saying she had shamed him. He was incapable of shame, and had struck her because she had done what no woman should. She had forgotten her place.

'I'm waiting for an answer,' Oliver said.

'Just eat your meal.' Mary Ann had little hope that he would, at times just as stubborn a man as his father. 'It's got nothing to do with you.'

'I want to hear what he's got to say for himself.' He turned to Burton again. 'You're a bloody savage.'

Burton, who never swore, and didn't like to hear it from his children, went on cutting at what meat remained on his plate. You couldn't sit down to your food in this family and say a word without starting an argument. 'You know the answer you'll get if you don't close your lips?'

'It won't happen again,' Mary Ann said.

'I'll see that it doesn't.' Oliver thought he had said enough, that honour was satisfied, so looked again at his plate. He had told his brothers he would tax Burton, and he had, and felt happy about it, was even proud to have gone as far as to let Burton know that he couldn't hit their mother and not be told off about it. Beyond that, Burton was immovable, nothing more to be said or done.

Burton was nagged by the reflection that if there was one thing worse than a wife not knowing her place it was having a son with no firm understanding of his. Unable to tolerate any confusion in the matter, and not seeing why he should, after a day in which nothing had gone as he would have liked, he stood, and launched his fist across the table with such speed that it struck Oliver full on the chest, seemingly before he saw it coming, and sent him sprawling with chair and plate across the floor.

If there was one nightmare in Mary Ann's life worse than any other it was that of violence breaking out in the family. 'Why did you do that?' she cried at Burton, already on her way to help Oliver, but he was on his feet, gesturing her to one side.

Burton, a piece of meat back on his fork, wanted only to finish the meal, before soothing himself with work in the garden. He was therefore not so intent on avoiding a blow that, had it properly landed, would have been at least equal to the one he had given. Adept at dodging sparks of coal and steel from the crucible of the forge, there was no one more alert than a black-smith, but he had been slow, which realization enraged him even more.

Oliver, both hands up to defend himself, was terrified at what he had dared to do. He was mesmerized by Burton standing slowly up in so unusual a way that Oliver wondered whether he wasn't going to come forward and forgive him, as if the weird smile never seen before meant that Burton might only tell him to sit down and finish eating.

He ran to save his life, for in two strides Burton reached the pantry door and picked up the sharp-bladed woodsman's axe. Mary Ann saw Burton about to commit murder, as Oliver pulled at the latch to get out, in despair that the others sat like statues, who would not help to pull their father down.

Burton stood at the door like an executioner, but Oliver's equally long legs had taken him quickly down the yard and onto the lane, leaving the gate wide open in his hurry, not caring who would have to close it.

Burton would not demean himself by chasing his son onto a public bridleway, so came back to lean the axe in its usual place. He sat to finish his meal. 'That's the end of him. He never comes into this house again, or works for me anymore.'

'Don't say such a terrible thing,' Mary Ann cried out.

'Never again does he sleep in this house.' He turned to Oswald. 'Who are you staring at? Do you want to go as well?'

He didn't. No one did. Where would they go? The hardest thing to do was find a haven from tyranny, though Edith didn't doubt she would do so one day, as she lifted Oliver's jacket from the door. Burton's mouth was open to call her back, to threaten if she didn't obey, but he stayed quiet, as if something in him halfway approved of what she intended.

She ran along the lane, afraid Oliver would be lost·to them forever if she didn't catch up. He was liked by his sisters as well as loved by them, and she couldn't bear the thought of him having nowhere to sleep and nothing to eat, or going away without his jacket.

He walked disconsolately along the embowered track, a lost and lonely place she would never go to on her own. 'Oliver! Wait for me.' From behind he might have been mistaken for Burton, with the high proud walk she had often noticed. She caught up with him, and sat on the bank. 'Where shall you go?'

He was hungry still, full of grief and anger, and shame at having run away. 'I heard they needed a blacksmith to look after the horses at Brown's sawmills. I'm going there.'

'Where shall you sleep tonight?'

'In one of their sheds. I don't care. It'll be dry and warm. I shan't be near *him* at least.'

'Have you got any money?'

He picked a twig and shredded it. 'I'll earn some. If they set me on they'll lend me ten bob to get by. I can never go back home.'

'You'll break Mam's heart if you don't.'

'I can't help that. Burton will kill me if I poke my face in the house. Or I'll kill him. Either way, murder will be done, and it'll be his fault. He's never liked me.'

'Yes he has. You're his favourite, but he just doesn't know how to treat you. I know what he's like. It's the same with the rest of us.'

'I'd like to think so, but I can't.' She felt he was going to cry, but he went on: 'You lot will have to look after Mother, since I can't be there anymore. I thought Oswald and Thomas were going to help, but they didn't.'

'They're cowards.' She took a shilling from her pocket. 'Here, have this.'

'I can't take your money.'

'Go on, you can get a pint at the Rodney. And you can buy some bread and butter. It's not my last, honest.'

'I'll pay you back soon.'

'And don't worry about Mam.' She took his hand. 'She'll feel a lot better when I tell her I've seen you, though I shan't say anything to Burton, even if he starts to worry.'

His laugh was bitter. 'He won't do that. But thanks for bringing my coat.' He brushed the grass from his trousers. 'I must be off. Mr Brown will still be there, and I'm sure he'll have some work for me.'

'Give my love to Alma then, when you see her. She's lovely.'

'We're meeting tomorrow, and now I have a coat to put on.' He kissed her. 'At least I've got a good sister.'

She watched him turn a bend in the lane, then ran back to the house.

EIGHT

All metal in a blacksmith's house had to shine, and the females were told to make sure it did, so Ivy, Rebecca and Edith gathered on Sunday morning for the ritual of polishing. Heaps of cutlery, prize horseshoes, and brass ornaments from the parlour shelves lay by their hands, tins of Brasso and silver polish in the middle of the table.

'I bumped into Tommy Jackson on his way home from work the other day.' Edith picked a rag from the heap, and fell silent when Burton came into the room.

Ivy wouldn't be put off. 'Tommy's at the bike factory, isn't he?'

Burton looked on. In the early days, before having so many children, he sat at the table on Sunday morning cleaning horseshoes and ornaments himself, but with so many daughters, and so much to be polished, there were other things to do with his time. Mary Ann recalled how, in his shirtsleeves, he had never been happier, glistening the metal and rocking Oliver's cradle with a stockinged foot. Glamorous Emma Lewin, who had never trusted him to be good to Mary Ann, called one morning to see them, Burton so happy at her visit he promised a special horseshoe to hang in the pub, sent by a boy before the week was out. How much water had gone under the bridge since then! Too often the liquid flowing through had been muddy enough, but she could not stop loving him more than she feared him.

'Tommy Jackson dresses very smart,' Edith said. 'I saw him walking along the street yesterday, and he winked at me.'

Burton laced his boots by the fireplace, grunting in disapproval at such talk.

'He asked me to go a walk along the canal. "No fear," I told him, "you might chuck me in." "No," he said, straight back, just like that, the cheeky devil: "It's you as might chuck me in. You're as big as I am."'

Geraniums by the open window seemed to shake at their laughter. 'He's ever so nice,' Rebecca said. 'I once saw him with a flower in his buttonhole.'

Burton looked at the girls' work, pieked a spoon from the table, and turned it over, handing it to Edith. 'Do that one again.'

'Isn't it clean enough?'

'You heard. The rag's not black. You do it till there's black on the rag. Then you give it a final polish. How many times do I have to tell you? I want it to shine so's I can see myself to shave in it.' He examined a horseshoe closely. 'Whose is this? It's good, but it's not mine.'

'Oliver made it.'

He threw it onto the settle. 'Give it back to him if you see him. Me and your mother's going to the Admiral Rodney for an hour. When you've got everything clean and shining put them back in their right places. Make sure they're straight. And don't get polish on the table. It leaves a stain.'

'I'll try not to.'

'There's a spot there. Rub it off.'

Mary Ann wore her best jacket with gold embroidery along the wide lapels and around the pronounced cuffs at the wrists. Four buttons on the left kept the garment open to show a white highnecked blouse, fastened at the waist with two short ribbons. A long matching skirt went almost down to boots laced up with a buttonhook, such a rigout crowned with a flamboyant hat of golden feathers to make her seem taller and more stately.

Burton, who liked to be seen with her at such times, recalled how stylish she had been when he courted her twenty-five years ago. She pulled on her shining leather gloves, and picked up a small neatly rolled umbrella. 'You two cook the dinner,' she said to Ivy and Rebecca. 'You know where everything is.'

'We should, by now,' Ivy said.

'Don't answer your mother back,' he said, 'or you'll feel my fist.'

'I didn't mean to.' The answering back was aimed at him, which he well knew.

'Thomas can get the beans and potatoes out of the garden,' Mary Ann said, 'and Oswald is to keep the fire going.'

Burton turned to Ivy. 'What do you call that?'

A small pot of Colman's mustard lay before her. 'It's for your dinner.'

'I know it is. I'm not blind. But do you know what it looks like?'

'No, I don't.'

'It looks as if a canary's done its mess. Put a lot more in. I like it hot. You should know by now.' He turned to Mary Ann. 'I'll wait in the yard.'

When the door closed behind him, fearing Burton's renowned ability to hear through walls, she said in a low voice to Edith: 'When you take Oliver's dinner don't idle along the way, or it'll get cold.'

Only girls in the house, Edith held the pot of mustard at arm's length, to imitate the way Burton stood to drink his ale, and with a gargoyle face drew it to her mouth. She hawked up what phlegm was in her chest, regretting it should be so little, and unloaded it into the mustard. The others did the same, and Ivy stirred it vigorously in, to the laughter of them all.

Mary Ann walked the customary few paces behind him down the lane. Halfway to the railway tunnel he sensed she no longer followed. 'Are you coming, or aren't you?'

She poked the tip of her umbrella at a pothole. 'I want you to ask Oliver to come home.'

He looked askance, but had been expecting her request. 'I'll be damned if I will.'

'I shan't come to the pub then.'

If he did walk on she might not follow, a stubbornness about her that even he at times could make head nor tail of. It was understandable that she wanted Oliver back. So did he, half-smiling at the thought that if there was one thing worse than having an argumentative son in the house it was having him out of it so that he could no longer be got at. 'I'll think about it.' For the moment that had to be good enough, and he left her to come after him.

A few paces later she stopped again.

'What is it this time?'

'I don't like walking under that dark tunnel on my own.'

A full smile and, ever willing to be gallant before a woman's weakness, he held out his arm. 'When we get to the Rodney I'll buy you a glass of port.'

Edith walked between machinery and large sheds, and hogsbacks of pristine sawdust on which she and her sisters had romped as children. Seasoning trunks were laid on trestles by neat pyramids of cut planks. Oliver stopped whistling on seeing her. Collarless shirt open at the neck, he looked even more happy and relaxed at getting a basket of the best dinner he could imagine. Mary Ann, away from the eye of Burton, had also slipped in some groceries. Edith spread the cloth on the smooth flat of a tree stump, and laid out the meal as if for Burton himself.

'That's a good sister.'

'What do you do for your breakfast?'

He picked up the shining cutlery, cut into vegetables and potatoes. 'I've got a packet of tea in the hut, and fetch milk from Mrs Baker near Robin's Wood. She gave me a slice of smoked bacon and two eggs yesterday, and wouldn't take any money.'

He was popular and handsome, and she was glad to help as well. 'What about water to wash in?'

'There's a pump near the house.'

'And when you want to go to the lavatory?' she asked mischievously.

'I dig a hole among the bushes with a trowel. But how's Mother getting on? I hope she's all right.'

'She is, but she wants you to come home.'

'What does Burton say about that?'

'He hasn't said anything, but everybody sees how he misses getting on at you.'

He passed her a piece of pork on his fork. 'I'll bet he does. I like it very much here. I don't have to pay my board, so I'm all right for money, and living like Robinson Crusoe suits me a treat.'

It was a disappointment that he could be so adaptable, because if there was one thing she and the others missed at home it was not having a brother they could joke and laugh with. 'Where do you sleep?'

'In that long hut, on the planks at the far end. I'm as warm as toast. Mrs Brown gave me some old blankets.'

'You'll be cold in winter.'

'I'll get lodgings by then.'

'Can you afford to?'

'I'm saving up. I'm earning a pound a week, which is more than I ever got from Burton. I mend machines, and shoe the horses. I feel a new man not having him ordering me around with never a thank you for all I do. He isn't going to knock me about anymore.' He pulled the basket forward and searched under the cloth. 'Did you bring that book?'

She had forgotten. 'I couldn't find it.'

'You'd forget your head if it was loose. Don't you remember? It's called *Famous Engineers*. It's on the top shelf in the middle of the bookcase. You can read, can't you?'

'You know I can. I'll bring it tomorrow. I can't do it this afternoon.'

'I suppose you're too busy going after the lads. Who's your young man now?'

'Mind your own business,' she flushed.

'Let me guess.' He danced around her. 'Oh I know: it's Tommy Jackson. I used to be at school with him. He once threw an apple at Miss Soames, and got the strap for it. Hey, what's that paper bag in your hand?'

She held it close to her chest. 'It's pepper.'

'Pepper? You don't put pepper on blackberries, and you know I don't like it on my dinner. What's it for?'

'It's lonely walking along that lane,' she said, embarrassed to admit her fears. 'Nobody ever goes there, not even in daytime, and I get frightened. If a man jumps out from the hedge I can chuck pepper in his eyes and blind him. Then I'd run like hell!'

He laughed. 'Who put a daft idea like that into your head?'

'Mother said her grandma used to do it when they lived in Ireland.'

'Poor old Mam! She's frightened of her own shadow. I can't

think who'd jump out of the bushes on an ugly thing like you.
He'd run a mile as soon as he saw your face.'

'I'm going, if you talk like that.'

'No, don't. I want to rag you some more.'

'I can't stay. I've got to see that the others set the table
properly.'

'Well, don't forget to bring my book. I want something to
read after finishing work.'

'Aren't you coming back to live at home?'

He stood up tall and straight – like his father. 'Not even if
Burton came and pleaded with me on bended knees.'

'But you will if Mam asks you?'

'I might. But I'll never work for him again.'

She went through the bushes towards the canal with the basket
on her arm, and he laughed about the bag of pepper. A big
comely girl like Edith should be able to knock any man senseless who bothered her, but the trouble was that women didn't
often know the strength they had, and those who did were afraid
to use it as they should.

Few tables were taken in the yard of the Admiral Rodney at
Wollaton village. The day was too fresh, though perfect for
Burton, who liked a breeze after the stink of burning coals and
searing metal all week. He drank with more pleasure in such
weather.

A well-dressed man with a friendly smile paused at their table.
'Good morning, Burton.'

He gave a nod that only someone unfamiliar with his ways
would find offensive. 'Who was that?' Mary Ann wanted to know.

'Some damned fool.'

'I don't suppose there's anybody around here who doesn't
know you, but he seemed pleasant enough.'

'He brings his horses to be shod, and complains when I charge
two bob. They're all cripples, the way he uses them.'

'He won't bring them anymore if you treat him that way.'

'He can please himself. You'll be getting drunk,' he said, at
her modest sip, 'if you go on gobbling it up like that.'

'It's nice, but I could never take much.' The small glass was still almost full. 'I used to see people getting tipsy all the time when I was in service.'

'I wasn't one of them.'

'I know, but I like to keep a clear head when I'm thinking about Oliver.'

He snorted. 'He's got too much to say for himself.'

'All young men have. I expect you did when you was a youth.'

'Not to my own father. It was more than I dared do.'

'Oliver was concerned about me. You can't blame him for that.'

'I look after you,' he said, 'not him.'

She thought that even he might take such a statement with a pinch of salt – which accounted for the few moments of silence. 'I wish you'd let him come back home. He's sleeping on planks at the sawmill.'

'I've slept on worse.'

'I miss him, though.'

'I expect you do.'

Morgan came through the gate, and stood as if for a talk, spruce and affable in a bowler hat, a sovereign and some farrier regalia dangling from his waistcoat. Burton hadn't seen him since Sabina had danced on the table. 'Hey up, Burton! Things all right?'

'So you can see.'

'Can I get you and your missis a jar?'

'We've got them already.'

'I'll see you, then.'

Burton watched him stride to the pub back door. 'Another damned fool.'

'I ought to have been introduced to him properly,' Mary Ann complained.

'You don't want to know him. He talks too much for his own good.' He finished his drink. 'I suppose I am missing Oliver's cheek. You'd better knock that jollop back, or we'll be here all day.'

She needed no telling. He was relenting, and it was about time. The house was a miserable place without Oliver. Even Burton would agree, though never say so. 'If we walk back along the canal we pass the sawmill.'

'What are you in such a hurry for?' He drew her chair away. 'A button's loose from your glove. You'd better take it off or you'll lose it.'

They followed the wall-lined road bordering Wollaton Park, away from the village. Mary Ann walked her few paces behind, at times almost catching up, which he wouldn't like. Clouds flowing low from the west put the wind at their backs. She all but clipped his heels. 'I don't know why you're in such a hurry,' he said. 'The dinner won't get cold. You'll be running me down if you're not careful.'

'Do you think he'll come home?'

'He will if I tell him.'

Having a child away from the house was like a brick missing from the wall and letting the weather in, she'd heard her grandmother say. 'I'm sure he will, then,' and she smiled, happier than for many a day.

They turned up a lane through the wood, till sawmill sheds were visible, a deep lock of the canal at their backs. 'Oliver!' he shouted, then turned to Mary Ann. 'You go home, and leave this to me.' He looked at his watch. 'Make sure dinner's on the table in half an hour.'

The arrangement was good enough, and she would happily face the darkness of the railway tunnel now that Oliver was coming back. 'Don't be late, though, or the pudding will go flat.'

He would be on time whenever he arrived, late or not. He stopped on seeing Oliver talking to a young woman. 'Did you hear, when I called you?'

'Yes.'

'You can come home.'

Oliver let go of her hand. 'I'm not working for you.'

'Please yourself.' Mindful of his shining boots, he avoided the higher mounds of sawdust. 'Who's the young lady?'

In her early twenties, he guessed, perhaps a little older than Oliver. He noted the blue eyes, fair hair done into a bun, and the palest of skin, a straight line of jaw from ear to a well-rounded chin when she turned to him. Perfect teeth as she smiled at Oliver's reaction to the erect well-dressed man who could only be his father.

Her plain white shirt had a narrow collar, no brooch to adorn, and the sun throwing a haze over her face created such a vision that Burton wondered how it was he hadn't seen such an unusual girl in the district before, as if she was a throwback to a very good family, amused in thinking she was far too good for his son.

'This is Alma Waterall,' and to her Oliver said: 'Burton, my father.'

Burton nodded – he never shook hands – but the gesture teamed with an uncommon stare, used fully, knowing its effect on an uncommon woman. His grey eyes looked – though not for too long – as they always did in order to test, and to optimistically ensnare any woman who took his fancy. He recalled turning such a gaze on Minnie Dyslin, and Mary Ann, and Florence, and not a few in between, an appraisal without seeming to be in any way entranced, yet long enough to take in a woman as yet uncontaminated by a world she might come to know if she responded to him – which she would do, he thought, if there was anything special about her.

She imagined she knew more than she did, on giving a stern and knowing look, trying to take in what sort of a man he was, yet not quite able to. Hard to tell what was in her mind. Such curiosity would get her nowhere. She didn't even know what to look for, but if she did satisfy her enquiring mood the responsibility for what ensued would be entirely her own.

He smiled, a mere flick of the lips before turning to Oliver. 'You're wasting your time working at this place. Come back to me, and you'll soon be the best blacksmith in the trade.'

Oliver knew he was so already, and had no further need of his father's slave-driving tuition. Burton waited long enough for an answer to know that none would be forthcoming, aware that his eldest and favourite son was as proud as himself, which wasn't much for either to be pleased about. 'Your mother's got your dinner on the table.'

'I've eaten already.'

He knew they'd been feeding him behind his back. 'I'd have been glad to eat ten dinners at your age. Anyway, you heard what I said. Your mother wants you to come home.'

Watching him go back in the direction of the canal, Oliver knew that an invitation of equal welcome would never have come from Burton, so there had been no use expecting it. He drew Alma close for a kiss, and wondered why her embrace was more ardent than he'd so far had that day.

'So he was your father?'

They stood apart. 'Yes, more's the pity.'

'What's his Christian name?'

The bitter laugh widened her eyes with surprise. 'Christian? Him? His name's Ernest, but we never use it. We call him Burton. Even our mother does, except I suppose when they're on their own.'

'He doesn't say much.'

'His fists talk a lot.'

'He dresses smartly. I wish my father did. He drinks more alcohol than he should, which causes trouble at home. I tried to get him to sign the pledge and join a temperance society but he just laughed. When Mother shouts at him for not working hard enough he starts crying, and then hits her. I don't think he can be all there. And he looks even more awful when he's supposed to be dressed up.'

'Let's not talk about them. It's you I want, all of you.' He kissed her again. 'There's a warm place in one of the sheds. Nobody will see us.'

Impossible to know what thoughts curdled behind her blank stare. 'I can't.'

'Don't you want to?'

She turned from him, did and didn't, would and wouldn't, only not now, but felt enough heat in herself to give in, a confusion making her blush. 'Will you walk me home?'

'I would, except they're waiting for the return of the Prodigal Son. I'll take you as far as the road, then meet you at the school this afternoon. We can go for a walk, when you've finished drumming God into the poor little devils.'

He came back and rolled his belongings into a blanket, tied the ends, draped the bundle around his shoulder, and followed his father's footsteps through the bushes with the same high-headed walk.

*   *   *

Burton enjoyed seeing neat girls in their Sunday best, noted how lively they were at Oliver's return, and Oliver's happiness at being among them. Mary Ann served Yorkshire pudding to begin, crisp at the edge and light in the middle, succulent to lips and tongue, a trickle of rich gravy from the sauceboat. The plates were afterwards laden with broad beans, slices of marrow, small boiled onions and potatoes fresh from the garden. Burton's long knife flashed along the steel for carving the leg of pork from their home-reared pig. He laid out portions in his usual silence, Oliver receiving two instead of one. 'Who was that girl you were with?'

In spite of his previous meal, he ate with appetite. 'Someone from Woodhouse.'

'She looks a rum wench.'

He wondered why Burton must push his nose into everything. 'I like her.'

'I'm sure you do.'

'I met her three months ago.'

'She's lovely.' Edith, as always, took her favourite brother's part. 'I saw her when I took his dinner to the sawmill.' She put a hand to her lips not so much out of fear as to mock herself. Rebecca and Ivy laughed, while Burton thought that Mary Ann was too soft-hearted. 'Well,' Edith went on, 'he needs a hot dinner every day when he's courting.'

Emily sang out: 'I saw Dad courting.'

She dropped her fork at Burton's stare but, close to tears, turned too Mary Ann. 'Mam, what's courting?'

'It's what two people do before they get married.'

'What does her father do?' Burton wanted to know.

'He's a jobbing builder,' Oliver told him.

'That's a poor trade.'

'Before that he was a soldier.'

'That's the worst trade of the lot.' He looked around the table. 'Now be quiet, all of you, and get on with your dinners.'

NINE

Oliver felt more himself among the comforting odours of the house, a mixture of lamp oil, pumice stone, carbolic soap, of baking bread and cooking, and the lavender Mary Ann sprinkled between newly ironed clothes. Camping out had been a treat, but the civilized embrace of the family house was unbeatable, in spite of Burton.

The flagstoned scullery was cold to the feet when he took off his clothes for a sluice-and-soap all over from one of the buckets. Underwear went into the washing basket, and he put on fresh with a clean shirt. The tang of his brothers' sweat in the bedroom was more noticeable after nights among the wood planks and clean air coming through the slats of the shed.

He put on his brown suit, and polished his boots to a shine that might have been mistaken for Burton's, assuming the good habits of his father but, he hoped, none of the worst.

The silver watch bought from a man at the mill for five bob adorned his waistcoat, a pleasure to have when asked in the street what time it was. Such an object gave status, he thought, combing his hair at the downstairs mirror.

The sunken lane was bordered by pink willow herb, in hedgerows overlapped with plates of white elderflower. He pressed a berry between his fingers, the smell mixing with mellow high summer. Life indeed was better than yesterday.

Woodhouse was a settlement of three short cul-de-sacs ending at the railway embankment, and the first turning beyond the bridge brought a forlorn lifting and falling moan of song from the Sunday School that reminded him of childhood. Inside the door, arms folded, he didn't much believe in the religion but enjoyed the stories.

He knew many of the variously dressed children, from the respectable to those who lived in squalid poverty. The buttons of Albert Dawes' cardigan were done up unevenly, and he looked as if he had fallen into the canal and, battered about the head for the trouble he had given, been hung on the clothesline to dry. The Warrener lad of twelve in his lop-sided Eton collar (though he was well-shod) was kicking at Bessie Atkin's ankles, who wore a white pinafore and a blue ribbon in her long hair, till a look from Alma drew his boot away.

Aaron Beaseley's tongue showed beyond his lips, but his jacket and waistcoat were tidily fastened, though his ironed collar was askew. Alice Smith's mauve frock matched her face, as if she was still locked in a frightening dream from last night. The same mixture of children was found in every school, and Oliver felt pity whether they were well-dressed or not, at the mere fact of them being children. He recalled that he and his brothers and sisters had always been well enough dressed and shod, never knowing how Mary Ann had managed on the money Burton gave her.

Alma's head over the book, and the sound of her voice, told him that she at any rate believed, and demanded it from her listeners. 'Charlie, stop that fidgeting, and pay attention. "And He said, Take now thy son, thine only son, Isaac . . . and offer him there for a burnt offering upon one of the mountains which I shall tell thee of." Abraham was told to sacrifice his firstborn, as proof that he loved and feared God. Bertha Abbis, pay attention to what I'm reading. But when "Abraham stretched forth his hand, and took the knife to slay his son" – in other words, just as he was about to kill him (Oliver noticed the silence at this lift of the tale) the Angel of the Lord came and said (now she acted the words, and he was amused) "Lay not thine hand upon the lad."'

She expanded her arms till they became wings, assumed a more sombre tone, at which the floors shivered, and windows rattled fit to shatter, the skylight grew dim with a shadow of overflying smoke, and she waited for the trembling of the earth to settle, for the heavy goods train not many yards behind the room to pass, before going back to her recitation. '"Neither do thou any thing unto him: for now I know that thou fearest God, seeing thou hast not withheld thy son, thine only son from me. And Abraham lifted up his eyes, and looked, and behold behind him a ram caught in a thicket by his horns; and Abraham went and took the ram, and offered him up for a burnt offering in the stead of his son.'''

She paused for comment, which came soon enough from ragged Charlie, whose elder brother, Oliver knew, was named Isaac. 'Please miss, why did God want the father to kill his son Isaac?'

Oliver had often thought to ask why a man could contemplate, even to please God, the murder of his long-awaited and only son. He imagined the reply playing in her head like sparks, till she said: 'Because there is no greater proof of love than for someone to kill his firstborn son, the son he adores most in the world, a son who is most precious to him.' She smiled at Oliver in the hope that he approved of her response. 'Bertha, whatever are you crying about?'

The girl lowered her head, shuffled in her seat, words hardly audible. 'Why did Abraham have to kill the poor little ram, miss?'

Alma smiled. 'I'll talk about that next week. You can all go home, but don't make too much noise as you go up the street.' A few moments, and the room was cleared. 'I'm glad you could come. Is everything all right at home now?'

'For a while I expect it will be. You never know what might blow up with someone like Burton.'

She locked the door, put the key in her pocket. 'You'll have to do what he tells you, then, and be a good son.' He didn't think he had ever been anything else, that it was Burton who should be a better father.

She took his arm as they walked away from the hall. 'He seems a just and upright person to me.'

'I'd rather not go into his so-called virtues.' They walked by the limekilns bordering the canal and on towards the main road leading into town. 'Let's talk of something else.'

Hard to know what to talk about, coming from a family of few words, though he had never found any shortage with his sisters. With Alma also it was a matter of 'still waters run deep', except when before her catechism class. Maybe the waters ran too deep for him as well, but the more packed into your head to say the harder it was to get out words that made sense, or didn't make you sound a fool.

The rise of the road was too steep for speech, both being quick walkers – as she had to be to keep up with him – so you waited for the descent to chat on things that didn't matter. In the Market Square he suggested an excursion to Misk Hill.

'It's a long way,' she said.

'Not if we catch a threepenny tram to Bulwell, and walk from there.'

'It's too late in the day, but let's go next week. I'll get a replacement for the Bible class.'

Which was the best thing he'd heard all day. 'You must be tired. We'll go to the Oriental Café on Mansfield Road and have some tea.'

Burton carried two buckets of slop to the pigsty, and Oliver was by the door before being seen. 'Where have you been?'

'Out. With Alma.'

He let the mess into the trough, avoiding the usual pigs' rush at his trousers. 'I need some help in the garden.'

The last kiss from Alma, sweet on his lips, was undisturbed by the smell of bran and pig muck wafting from the sty. 'I want to read my book.'

'There's no time for that.' Burton sensed how little he wanted to help. 'Pigs can't tell when it's Sunday. Nor do the vegetables.'

'I don't suppose they can.' He was too dispirited to make trouble. Burton looked at his son, long since out of his grasp, not only a fine blacksmith but he'd also been sent to school, a combination to stifle any regard between them. 'Go and get changed, and put some proper clothes on your back.'

Sunday trains were few, the carriage crowded, but he found the one spare seat for Alma. Sweat and Woodbine smoke thickened the air, and she couldn't know that looking at her between various heads gave a more complete view than if he had been by her side. Even so, he couldn't tell what she was thinking behind such placid but determined features. A clue might now and again help to build assumptions, as when her eyelashes flickered to show her changing from one subject to another, but that wasn't good enough for his intense and loving curiosity.

He couldn't ask. She wouldn't thank him if he did. Nobody would. People had to be left alone, because their thoughts belonged only to them. They weren't to be disturbed, just as you wouldn't like it if someone tried to break into your mind with questions you didn't care to answer, even if you had one ready to give.

They threaded streets away from Hucknall station, leading into the country. 'How is it you know your way so well?'

'I've been twice before,' he said. 'I walked the whole way from home once. I knew it was near Hucknall, and then I asked the way. Ernie Warrener promised to come, but let me down at the last minute, so I did it on my own.' Across the lane from the reservoir was Beacon Hill. 'See that hut on top, with the pole outside?'

'What about it?'

'Two young chaps from Hucknall who knew all about wireless set it up. They heard the SOS from the *Titanic* a couple of years ago, and before that they got the signals of a German zeppelin going down in France.'

'Are you having me on?'

'I read about it in the newspaper. I'm interested in mechanical things.'

By a farm fence a ferocious Alsatian seemed about to leap over and assail them. He chose a good-sized stone, and gave such a commanding shout for it to keep its distance that she looked at him as much with surprise as relief, but glad he knew so readily what to do.

He realized such behaviour to be as crude as Burton's, except that he might well have walked by in silence and, had the dog come close, booted it out of the way with never a word. 'He's blind in one eye,' letting the stone fall, 'so he couldn't have harmed us.'

Over a stile near Misk Farm he led her onto a path almost arched by briars and wild roses, pushing them aside and holding an outstretched hand. 'We're five hundred and twenty feet above sea level,' he said on the open plateau.

'Where did you hear that startling fact?' – as if suggesting he had no right to know it.

'They showed us on a map at school. It's the highest point near Nottingham.' He took her by the shoulder. 'You can see Newstead Abbey over there,' and pointed – which Mary Ann had told him he must never do, though he couldn't think why. 'If you look you can see Linby pit, and Papplewick just beyond. It's a marvellous view,' as if wanting thanks for his tuition. 'To the right you can see Hucknall and Eastwood.'

They trod the purple vetch and white clover. 'I expect you can even see Trent Bridge,' she said, 'if you squint hard enough. It's not very clear.'

'I know, but you can tell where you are when you're so high up. Everything's good because it's far away. If I could fly I'd go over it, as far as other countries. I'd be like a Wandering Israelite. Burton's only ever been to Wales, and to hear him talk you'd think it was the other side of the moon. I could save the fare and go to Canada. A blacksmith can always get work. On the other hand maybe I'll only dream about it. Unless you come with me.'

'I might want to leave one day,' she said, 'but for the time being I'll stay where I am. I hope to become a proper full-time teacher.'

The idea fell like a blow, as if a blacksmith in that case couldn't win her. 'You never told me before.'

'I didn't know. I still don't. The Reverend Walker said he'd try to get me a place where I can train, but it could take a few years. Maybe it will never happen, because so many want to become teachers. But I liked school, and was good at my lessons.'

'I wasn't, particularly, so I suppose I'm a bit of a numbskull.'

She allowed a kiss, to let him know that he was far from it, though didn't like saying so, while he was surprised at her assumption that he had used the word seriously.

It was unthinkable that he might not like it here. 'Why do you want to go on your travels?'

'Wherever I went I'd always have this place with me. I want to see as many different countries as I can while I'm alive. Maybe the only way would be to go for a soldier.' He brought her close for a kiss. 'Except that it would break my mother's heart.'

'Those boys will see us.'

'Let them.' He sat to light a cigarette. 'I suppose they've seen their mothers and fathers do it before now.'

Neither spoke, till he thought it was up to him to do so. It was his day, but needed effort to keep it pleasant. 'There's a picture hanging in our parlour, of a youth and his sweetheart, and underneath it's written: "If you love me as I love you, nothing can ever part us two".'

'It sounds,' she said with a laugh which was no laugh to him, 'like a postcard from the seaside.' She joined him on the grass. 'Is it supposed to be your father and mother?'

'It could be you and me, though it might have been them at one time. When Mother was a barmaid she asked Burton to go and buy a pair of gloves, expecting him to wait till after his work, but he went straightaway, and she was so impressed that when he came back with them and asked her to marry him she said yes.'

'What a romantic story. He's very goodlooking, and smart as well. He stands out from everybody else.'

'It was the worst move she ever made. I can't help but despise him.'

'Does your mother, though?'

He was afraid to say how vilely Burton treated her in case she might think such traits would pass to him. 'I'm sure she doesn't. She's far too long-suffering.'

'It says in the Bible that you must honour your father and your mother.'

'I'd like to honour Burton, but it's not in me.'

'You look a lot like him at times.'

'It would be surprising if I didn't, but thank goodness I'm different in every way.' She seemed to get a more lively tone in her voice when they talked about Burton. He took another kiss, and held a hand for her to stand. 'We should start walking back. There's a place in Hucknall to stop for tea. Then we can go to Bulwell and catch the tram from there.'

'I hope so. I'm tired.'

Talk declined, there was a limit to his store of things to say. Tea should have refreshed them, but the walking had been too

much for her. She was pale and looked exhausted when they got
to Woodhouse.

'When shall I see you again?'

'I'll call for you next Saturday evening,' she said.

'I'd rather meet by your house.'

'I like the stroll up the lane to yours. I'll be there about half-
past seven.'

'I'll never love anybody else but you,' he said, for which she
let him kiss her, though neither readily nor tenderly. As he walked
away he found it hard to decide what in the day had gone right.

TEN

Thomas took a bar of iron from the heat to shape a horseshoe, Burton looking over his shoulder: 'What do you think you're doing?'

Working hard to make a fair job, but feeling his father's critical presence, he missed a beat of the hammer, expecting a blow he could do nothing to avoid. 'I'm bending it, like you said.'

The bony fist struck his shoulder. 'You don't do it that way. You're lifting the hammer too high. Your mind's not on what you're doing. You've got so much confidence you don't know how to take care. Not to think about what you're doing is idleness, so stop thinking about yourself and think of the job.' Thomas's tears angered him even more. 'I've told you a hundred times how to do it.'

'I was doing it like you said.'

'Don't answer back, or you'll get another.'

'I'm tired, because there's too much work.'

Burton couldn't dispute it, and knew he'd been too harsh. 'Don't complain, do you hear me? Never complain.'

Thomas had heard it said so often he was fed up with the words, knowing he'd always had plenty to complain about.

'Oliver would make ten of you. Put the shoe back and heat it up again. It's the colour you've got to watch. From now on do it the way I've taught you.'

'Will Oliver be coming to work with us?'

'Not if I know it.' Burton wanted Oliver to ask for his job back, but no number of hints could make him see sense. Trade was good again, and he could do with help, but he preferred his soft place at the sawmill. He would regret it one day, as you did everything you said no to. He called from the doorway: 'Oswald, when you've finished that horse come in and show this daft ha'porth how to go on.' If he never did anything else he would turn his sons into good blacksmiths.

A wad of wool in his ears might deaden the high whine and tearing screech of the bandsaws, though the torment of such inhuman noise lessened when he forgot about it in the attention given to his work. Being Saturday, he would be going home soon to his dinner and, after a wash and change, stand by the gate for a glimpse of Alma on her way up the lane. She would want to go to the village, but he preferred strolling across the Cherry Orchard and into the cover of the wood, to find a dry place and go all the way in making love. The prospect was never out of his mind, though who could hope for such intimacy with a Sunday School teacher?

He backed a horse into the shafts, wondering how many more had to be done. The animal reflected his own weariness but passed a few moments by releasing a column of amber piss into the sawdust. Thirteen-year-old Sidney Camb stood by, a bedraggled specimen who, Oliver thought, should have been in school. The boy looked uncared-for, more exhausted than himself or the horse. A cap sat on a bunch of fair curls, and his too-big waistcoat had half the buttons missing. 'Look sharp, Sidney, and fasten him in. Earn your five bob a week. We can get our wages and go home soon.'

He liked Oliver calling him Sidney, instead of plain Sid as all the other men did: 'My money won't do much good.'

'It must be a help to your mother.'

He spat, to seem grown-up. 'It would be, if my dad didn't drink it all away.'

His father was a carter, and so often rocked at the reins it was a wonder he didn't injure himself, or get thrown out of his job. 'As long as you don't take after him. Here's Mr Brown with our money.'

A corpulent bald-headed man, under his bowler hat, walked from the main shed clutching a leather wage bag. His hand dug deep for the last to be paid. 'Here you are, Oliver, a sovereign this week. Not bad for a young chap, but I must admit you've earned it. I expect you'll be getting married on it soon.'

'It's always possible.' If Alma didn't know her own mind he could put a baby into her and go into wedlock on a foreceput. All would be honey and spice once they were married. Or perhaps not, because the real struggle would begin, like the hard life his parents had always led. Better to take the way of a journeyman and get to Canada for five years, returning with more gold in his pocket than could be made by staying put. He would ask Alma, and find what his fate was to be.

Brown ticked his name off the pay sheet. 'Remember me to Burton when you see him. He must have been a good father, to teach you the trade so well.' He handed Sidney his two half-crowns for the week.

'Thank you, sir.'

'And don't spend it all at once.'

'No, sir, I shan't.' He turned, cleared his throat of wood dust and bile, and emptied it by his boot. 'I never do, sir.'

'Oh yes,' Brown said to Oliver. 'I almost forgot: you'll be staying on a bit longer tonight. We've got six horses back from late deliveries, and they'll all need seeing to.' Oliver's frown was plain. 'You'll be done by nine, so I expect she'll wait, whoever the lucky girl is.'

'Of all the evenings,' he said when Brown walked back towards the house, 'it would have to be this.'

'I'll go and see her for you.' Sidney barely avoided the fist that flew at his face. 'I'll take her for a walk up Colliers' Pad.'

He could use his feet, collect his belongings and tell Brown to put his job where a monkey shoved its nuts, as no doubt Burton would in a like situation. When he ran from the White Hart to get Mary Ann's gloves there must have been a queue of urgent work at the forge, his father cursing and wondering where he was. But Oliver knew that if he walked away he would lose his job, at a time when another might be hard to find. Then how could he ask Alma to marry him?

On the other hand if he did go Burton would happily set him on, but asking him would strike at the roots of his pride. And then, Brown had kindly taken him in after his quarrel with

Burton. The first two drays came at the crack of whips from between the sheds. He would have to see Alma another time.

Hens and cockerels scattered when Burton went into the poultry compound. Panic and clumsy flight at his marauding fingers around the hatches, he came out with four eggs. Halfway to the house he heard the gate latch click and saw a young man come up the path.

'What do you want?' It didn't take long to know where he had seen him, the same young bully who had given him some lip when they had accidentally collided on the lane. Doddoe Atkin, who a few days ago had passed the gate on his way to do some poaching. Whatever he got from selling rabbits was spent in the pub.

Doddoe halted a few steps away, Burton noting that he didn't take off his cap before speaking: 'I'm looking for work. Some chap in Woodhouse said you might want an extra hand in your forge.'

He must have heard that Oliver was working elsewhere. 'Not as I know it.'

'I acted as striker once at the pit.'

Burton thought he was impertinent in thinking himself capable of doing any work he might give. Even if hard up for help he would never employ someone like that. Though big and hefty, he was fit for nothing. 'I don't have anything for you.'

Lips lifted, a slight gap between otherwise perfect teeth, and he spoke as if his life depended on a better response. 'In that case, can you spare a copper or two? I'm on my uppers.'

'There's nothing for you here.'

Half into the house Burton heard a shout from the gate – which Doddoe closed as if to wrench the hinges off. 'You're a mean old fucker!' – convincing him that nothing but trouble would be any man's lot who took him on.

Mary Ann at the table sewed buttons on a shirt, and Emily played on the floor with empty cotton reels. 'Oh, big white chucky-eggs!'

Burton put them into her hands, to show Mary Ann: 'We'll have one each for breakfast. Fry the others for Oliver's tea when he comes in.'

He took his rubber-rollered machine and a pouch from the cupboard, made five neat cigarettes and laid them in a row beside Mary Ann's sewing box. 'Oliver's late,' she said.

'I expect he's dawdling with some girl or other.'

'I thought I heard him in the yard just now.'

'It was a young lout from Woodhouse wondering whether I could give him some work. I told him I couldn't, then he asked for money, the damned fool.'

'Poor young man.' She would never send a beggar from the door with nothing. 'I'd have given him a cup of tea.'

'I know you would. You're too soft. But that wasn't what he wanted. He wanted money for booze. Nobody should meddle with his sort. He's been up a time or two before the magistrates for poaching.'

'There's always somebody worse off than us,' she said. 'A lot of young men don't have work these days.'

'There's plenty, if you look hard enough. Where did that come from?' he asked, when she picked up a newspaper.

'Oswald brought it back.'

'They're a waste of money.' A knock at the door, and he wondered whether Doddoe had been mad enough to come back, but looked down on a little scruff in his working clothes. 'What do you want?'

'Your Oliver said to tell you he'd be staying late at the sawmill tonight,' Sidney called from a few feet away, cap in hand. 'A lot of horses want seeing to.'

Burton gave him a penny for his trouble, and closed the door. 'You heard that?'

'I hope they pay him extra.'

'That's cold. Brown's a mean one.'

'Oliver should leave the job, then.'

'He's too loyal, at least with other people, though I can't think why.'

She picked up the newspaper. 'They say there might be a war soon.'

'What for?'

'With Germany it looks like.'

His grunt was more contemptuous than usual. 'The world's

daft enough for anything.' He got up, unable to sit for long. 'I'm going down the lane to get some ale.'

He thumped around upstairs, changing into a neater jacket and trousers, then came down, went through the kitchen, and strode across the yard onto the lane.

Halfway to the railway bridge a young woman came towards him. 'Hello,' he said, 'where are you going?'

'I'm calling on Oliver.'

'Do you remember me?'

Alma smiled, having hoped for a glimpse of him, even if from a distance. 'Of course I do.'

He saw the freshness of youth in her eyes and skin, and in the shape under her blouse, such beauty he would like to get closer to. 'Now you've met me.'

'He said he'd be waiting.'

'A lad came from the sawmill and told us he was working late this evening.'

'Did he say when till?'

'He couldn't say. It might be as late as ten. That's what it sounded like.'

'I'd better go home, then. I expect he'll tell me the reason when I see him again.'

'I'm going your way. I'll see you safe under the bridge. I'm sure you won't mind walking with me.'

Despite the lack of rain the evening smelled cool and fresh between the thick green hedgerows. She laughed. 'How can you think I'm afraid?'

'Every young woman's frightened of something.'

'I'm not.'

'You get some rum characters around here.'

'They wouldn't dare bother me.'

'What about the big bad wolf?'

'That's just a fairy story.'

He wondered whether she would know a wolf if she saw one. 'It might not be, and if it isn't it won't get you, if you're with me.'

The company of a young woman brought back the lechery of youth, as he walked a few steps in front to test her seriousness about following him. She came level. 'Where is it you're going?'

'To get some beer. But we'll call at the pub, and I'll buy you a drink.'

'I don't go into such places. They ruin people.'

Such naivety was fetching. 'They do if they throw their money away by getting drunk. I've never done that. Here's the tunnel. Take my arm, if you like. My girls are frightened of going under it by themselves.'

'I don't see why they should be.'

'Nor do I. But people are funny that way.'

He was amazed that she put a hand on his arm in the half-dark, the lightest touch of warm soft fingers. At the middle he thought about a kiss, but it was too soon. Had it been muddy he was amused to think he could have offered to carry her through. Back in daylight he asked where she worked.

She took her hand away. 'At Hollins's mill.'

'I expect you get thirsty, in all that dust. I'll bet you could do with a drink of something.'

'Are you sure Oliver won't be back till ten?'

'I only know what I was told. It's happened before. And I wouldn't tell a lie.'

At the corner of the street Doddoe leaned against the wall of the beer-off, eyes beamed above an upended bottle. Burton looked, daring him to say something, but he turned and brought the bottle down – empty, in any case – happy not to be called to account for his swearing.

'It's a warm evening,' she said, 'so I could have a glass of lemonade.'

'You shall have whatever you like, if you take my arm like you did back there.' She hadn't, yet she must have if he said so, but she didn't know, couldn't remember, alarmed at having forgotten, if she had. They walked towards the main road. 'If you don't want to be seen inside a pub we'll find a seat in the yard. It's a nice enough evening.'

His day at the forge was far away, and now he had the energy to enjoy leisure. They passed the limekilns, and the keeper's cottage outlined in the pallor of dusk. Every leaf of its garden tree seemed to hold a bird, the noise intense and piercing. A hooter sounded from a barge approaching the lock.

Hard to keep up with his stride, didn't want to be left behind, tried to stay level, his assurance a comforting umbrella she was allowed to share. He was a more complete man than Oliver could be on his own, and she'd marry Oliver without hesitation if he had been his father, whom she so much liked being with, though without knowing why.

Burton indicated the table she was to wait at while he went in for drinks. She stood by uncertainly, wondering what she was doing here, though it was a cosy place, with the full-headed over-hanging tree shadowing the last of the sun. Talk and laughter came from inside, and she could hardly fault people for their relaxation after a day's work. They sounded content, and happy. Even so, she felt an urge to leave, but wasn't able to move, waited anxiously for him to come back, a state impossible to explain. Perhaps he'd met an acquaintance and forgotten her, a notion so intolerable she had to wait and see if it was true.

'I got you a shandy.' He set the glasses down. 'It won't buck you up all that much, but it'll taste better than plain lemonade.'

'You know I can't drink alcohol, so why did you buy it?'

'Because I like you.' He smiled as she took a sip. 'They only put a thimbleful of beer in, to give it colour. You can see that, but it doesn't taste. In fact I like you very much. How old are you?'

She swallowed again. 'Twenty-three.'

'And do you like me?'

Her smile, though suggesting the question was unnecessary, didn't make it easy for him to know which way her answer would go. 'How can I say?'

'You mean you might think so?'

'I suppose I could.'

He looked at any woman as if reading all her secret thoughts, and as if knowing she knew that he did. 'You've got to know your own mind, and get used to answering a question when somebody asks. If you're twenty-three you should be able to.'

He was telling her what to do, how to behave, and she couldn't dislike it. Oliver had not been truthful in saying his father never talked. 'I can't always explain myself.'

'Let me ask you this, then, do you ever go in Robin's Wood?'

His enquiry seemed innocent enough. 'I did when I was younger.'

'To pick bluebells, I suppose? It's famous for them.' He drank more ale, smoothed his moustache. With no hope of getting her he might as well come out with what was in his mind. 'People come from all over to get them when they're in bloom.'

'I used to love it there,' she said. 'In spring there was wood-sorrel, primroses and violets, all kinds of flowers. When I took some home and put them in water though, they died. My mother used to say they smelled then as if somebody had wet the bed.'

He didn't want to hear about her mother. 'I go there for a stroll on Sunday afternoon. If you come you might see me.'

'I'll be in Sunday School. I read Bible stories to a class of children.'

'So I heard. How did you get that job?'

'It's not a job. I don't get paid for it. One of the preachers heard me telling a story I thought the children hadn't understood. He asked me to do it in front of the class, and I did. Then he coached me till I could do it better. He gave me a Bible to read at home. I was sixteen. One day I hope to be a real teacher. I don't want to work at Hollins's mill all my life.'

He laughed, and reached for her hand. 'I'd like to hear you talking to the children, though I'd rather you came for a walk with me in Robin's Wood. Send word to the Sunday School that you've been run over and can't go in that day. They'll believe you.'

She drew back, while not wanting to. 'I don't think they would.'

'They'll believe anything. That's their trade. And if you can't come this week, come next.' Her cheeks flushed at the pressure on her wrist. 'I can show you something better than flowers.'

She drank more shandy, as if it would lessen the flame of her colour. 'Oliver told me you're one of the best blacksmiths in the county.'

He was sparing with his smiles, even talking to this handsome girl. 'Did he?' It wasn't the time to hear Oliver's opinion. 'I've been in competitions, if that means anything.' From her mood he thought she might after all be tempted to walk in the wood. A woman's uncertainty was always the beginning of getting what you wanted. She might not come tomorrow, but that would give a whole week for the notion to sink in, to worry her, to turn her bed thoughts lickerish, and tempt her into wanting to find out what he meant. The prospect was possible, and he was prepared to wait, though he was surprised to be thinking so already.

Being twice her age made no difference if he wanted her. All you had to do was want hard enough, and let her know you did, that you wanted it so hard she didn't have to make up her mind about whether or not she wanted you. You also had to let her know that as far as you were concerned she could take it or leave it, which made the chances even better that she would take it, though if she didn't nothing was lost. Often enough a woman did take it, and when you got what you had made it known in no uncertain terms you wanted she would have no cause to complain at giving in, not if the result made her halfway happy.

He enjoyed the sight of her pale skin and lustrous hair, fair bust and ready lips, wanted to spread her legs and go into her, sending his steady gaze across the table, which she had found so hard to meet at first but now looked at with curiosity, helplessness, admiration, and even hopelessness at being drawn into something from which he was making sure there would be no escape.

To question himself as to what he was doing was a weakness he wouldn't allow. If you wanted something, you did and said all that was necessary to get it. Consequences were for the future, had nothing to do with you, because the future was never with you, was always the present. Tell a woman you loved her as if you meant it, and she would believe you whether you did or not, though he always meant it at the time. On the other hand it could be a bit of a game which, should it turn out to have been no more, was pleasant enough, with nothing lost.

She closed her eyes, opened them quickly, and not to be on her guard, either. He had seen it before, the barriers coming down in a full-blooded woman who didn't know they were doing so. But they were. He took care that the movement of his lips would be taken for a smile. 'Have something a bit stronger now.'

*　　　*　　　*

The last shoe was hammered into place. 'Hold still, will you?'

Lights yellowed through the trees from the house, where Brown and his wife were sitting to a well-earned meal, always late on Saturday night. After a hard day the horse bridled, sent a blow at Oliver's thigh. He had seen it coming, so avoided the worst, but walked a circle knowing he would have a dark bruise for a week.

An elderly blacksmith once told him how, as a young man, a horse had trodden on his foot, and the pain stayed with him for life. His already subsiding, he went back to the horse, talking as he stroked its mane. 'You didn't mean to knock me for six, did you, you poor beast? I wish you hadn't tried, though, because I'm as much of a slave as you are.'

Level with its nostrils, he touched with one hand and sent up comforting breath, taking the horse's part, familiar with its hard-working day, its weariness and agitation. Burton had drilled into him that if you knew how to whisper to a horse you'd never come to harm, but he should have done so before putting on the shoes. Missing the date with Alma had clouded the mind. Burton said often enough – but Burton had said too bloody much – that nothing should be on your mind while shoeing a horse, otherwise you were asking for it. He'd hammered the nails flush into the shoe, so saw no reason for the trouble. 'You can't be half as fed-up as I am.'

Brown came from the house, a comforting cigar smoking between his lips. 'I'll take him off your hands, Oliver, and make sure he gets a good feed. You've done well. I shan't forget it.'

Nor shall I, he thought, walking between the blending shadows of the footpath, weary in bone and sinew.

Mary Ann got up from the fireside as soon as he came in. 'Aren't you going to wash?'

He hung his jacket and sat at the table. 'In a minute. Give me a bit of bread and something first.'

She cracked two eggs into a pan of fat.

'What are those?'

'Your father said I was to fry them for you. They're straight out of the hens. You can eat them before the supper.'

He cut away the whites to eat first, as she had so often seen Burton do. 'Has somebody called for me?'

'Only a young lad, who said you'd be working late. Were you expecting someone?' She took a pan of bacon and roast potatoes, a crock of peas and carrots from the oven, and set them on his plate. A speared potato went into his mouth but, being too hot, he let it fall into his palm and put it on the plate. 'A young woman promised to call.'

She came back from the pantry with a square loaf not long baked, glad to see such a spread for him on the table. 'You look half-dead. You'll feel better after you've eaten.'

'She said about half-past seven.'

'It's as well she changed her mind, because you wouldn't have been here.'

'It's strange. She's always been on time.'

'I expect you'll see her at Sunday School, if it's Miss Waterall you're talking about.'

Done with eating, and sufficient energy back, he refreshed himself in the scullery with soap and cold water. From the steps he asked: 'Where's Burton?'

'He was in the yard a while ago. Then he went to Woodhouse to get some ale.'

'I should have told her to meet me at the sawmill, but didn't want to be seen in my working clothes.'

'You look handsome in whatever you wear.' She put a suet pudding and a boat of treacle before him, held his hand as he picked up the spoon and, remembering him as a fair-haired boy running about the yard full of delight, kissed him on the cheek. 'When you see her tomorrow you can tell her what happened.'

A rattling of the doorlatch signified Burton on his way in. His eyes glistened as he pointed to the pudding. 'You can give me a bit of that.'

'Where were you?'

'I stopped for a jar.'

She wondered at his unusually ready answer, though a whiff of beer suggested the truth, and proved it on him taking a quart bottle from his pocket. He set it before Oliver. 'Drink this. I know you've worked hard enough.'

He made no move to pick it up. 'Don't *you* want it?'

'I'm giving it to you. It's not poison, so drink. You look thirsty.'

Mary Ann put a glass before him in case Burton should change his mind, or feel insulted if Oliver still refused to drink, and when Oliver squeezed off the rubber top to pour, her heart softened at seeing them like father and son at last.

ELEVEN

Burton walked silently around the house and behind the garden, till covered by the hedge. The track beyond the well, thick with vegetation, was pushed through and trodden down to reach the trees. He turned at the edge of Robin's Wood, to see anyone crossing the Cherry Orchard.

Uncertain that she would come, he knew there was a chance, otherwise why was he here? Where a woman was concerned it was every man for himself, and if Oliver couldn't make sure of her that was his lookout. He hadn't been acquainted with such a woman before, and in any case all women were different, equally young and fresh if you hadn't yet had them. A rise at the thought of her, he regretted that, having so much Sunday School business, she might not turn up.

An hour went by, and felt like it, but the breeze was cool, and bushes lush even at the beginning of August. Birds sang more sweetly here than in the town, reinforcing his love for fields and woods. Skylarks whistling in the heat would guide her to where he lurked. Though careful to stay hidden he would make sure she saw him.

A pigeon scrambled noisily out of a tree as he gazed at the way of her approach. The route from Woodhouse led by the house, but unless someone was looking over the fence she would get by without being seen, and who would realize she was on her way to meet him? She might in any case think herself only out for a walk, hardly knowing what she was doing. Such things happened that way.

Putting yourself in the mind of another person was only useful for passing the time. Others would do what they would do, and you could only hope for the best when you wanted them to do what you wanted them to do very much indeed. You had enough in your head thinking for yourself.

She was close before he saw her, from an unexpected direction, proving that she had a head on her shoulders, and knew what she was doing, telling him that the innocent could be as cunning as their elders, though perhaps not more than once. She had been hurrying, and her heart beat heavily. 'Did anyone see you?'

'I don't think so. I came the way you told me, but then I zig-zagged a bit.'

'I waited a long time.'

'I shouldn't be here.'

'Now you are.'

'It doesn't seem right.'

'It's right enough for me.'

'I came as if I had no say in it.'

'That's the only way.' He had clipped his moustache, and shaved with special care, smoothing his skin for the give and take of kisses. 'Come into the wood.'

She stepped backwards. 'I don't know that I should.'

'Should or shouldn't,' he said. 'I love you more than I ever loved anybody.' There was a time to bully and a time to coax, and he hardly knew which would be more effective. 'You came all this way, so we might as well stroll inside. It's a bit hot in the sun.'

Twenty-three, but she wasn't much more than a child in her understanding, and he drew her along to save arguing with herself, better for her not to be certain which way things were going. That she had deeper feelings than he thought was better in the end. Neither did he know whether he was doing good or ill, but whoever did, and what was the point in knowing whether you were or not if it stopped you getting what you wanted?

She noted the strong athletic boughs he walked among, and prepared herself either to stay out of range, or field them with open hands should they shoot towards her. None of it necessary, she so much in mind that he stopped the twigs and branches springing against her, careful also to tread down the virile nettles that would sting even through her skirt and stockings because they had matured under a damp canopy of trees.

A man only ever took a woman into a wood for one thing, and a woman only followed for the same purpose. He helped her over the narrow brook he had drunk from as a boy after escaping George's wrath. She thought his snort at the memory was because of her, and went into his arms for kisses of reassurance, so passionately received that she knew she had done right to meet him.

She followed close on his strides, and when he stopped without warning went into his back. 'What is it?'

'I can't,' he said.

She thought he meant walk on because of some obstacle. 'What do you mean?'

He turned, and though throbbing at the groin to take her, he could control it, as any man should be able to. He had never had to force any woman, but getting her here had been too easy. It was the sort of mad year in which young girls had become more lax in their ways, as he knew from his own. He could deceive Mary Ann as long as she didn't get to know, and trick another man by taking his wife (because that was never anybody's fault but the man's) but he didn't relish the notion of doing it on Oliver. 'We'll go back.'

The pleading on her features shocked him. 'No, please, it's too late now.'

The knot in his brain fused. He hadn't banked on her pushing the boat out, yet it was he who had cut the ropes. There was no more to be said as he led her to a glade where they wouldn't be seen. 'We'll lay down here.'

Overarching trees hid the sky. He hung his broad leather belt in the fork of a tree, and helped her into place, a picture among the green he could never have hoped to see, her soap and scent smell mixing with the sweat of hurry over the fields, a fragrance to set any man aflame, though he sensed uncertainty in her still, and knew he must not hurry.

She seemed uninterested in his kisses, pressed her arms around his neck with more force than he thought necessary. The rustle of her skirts was hidden by the noise of the birds, and he went smoothly past the garters to get at her drawers. When they were off she pulled him in.

Oliver went to the Mission Hall and was told that another mistress had taken Alma's duties. When he knocked at the door of the house where she lived, her father stood on the step in braces and collarless shirt, to tell him she wasn't in. Calling again, her worried mother in apron and sud-stained hands said the same thing. Alma was out, and she had no idea where.

He wanted to knock her father down, or kick the door in when her mother slammed it in his face, and force a way inside to find where Alma was hiding. He was tall enough and strong enough, but shame prevented him.

If he found her she might even lie as to where she had been, but he wouldn't care as long as they could talk, if only for a few minutes, because he was sure she would be back in his arms and never lie to him again. Imagining she would tell a lie was hardly fair, it was just that she didn't want to see him, though if not, why not? It was griping that he didn't know, longed to find out if it was true. He had thought of asking her to marry him when they met, and the ache of love was in him more than ever.

A long goods train rumbled along the embankment, and Edith coming from under the bridge wanted to know why he was standing so forlorn. 'I was wondering which way to go for a walk,' he said.

'What difference does it make? You've walked everywhere before. We all have. I'm fed up living in the same place, and traipsing the same dreary footpaths. I'm nearly eighteen, and I've worn every one out with my shoes. I just want to get away.'

'Is that why you're wearing your Sunday finery? I'll bet you're going to meet Tommy Jackson.'

'You are a sharpshit!' She laughed. 'He promised we'd walk into town and go rowing on the Trent. Or he might take me on an excursion boat to Colwick.'

'Don't fall in the water, will you? I worry about you. It's a warm day, but it's still cold among the fishes, and you'd get wet.' He came close, and looked into her unfearing eyes. 'If you see any orange peel on the road, pick it up for me.'

'Orange peel? What for?'

'I'm collecting it. When I get a sackful I can sell it. I've already got a lot at home.'

'I haven't seen it.'

'It's hidden under the bed, in a pillow slip.'

'Oh, you are daft, you and your jokes. You're always pulling our legs. Are you waiting to see Alma?'

'I would be if she was waiting to see me.'

The pain on his face was plain. 'She hasn't chucked you, has she?'

'I'm beginning to wonder.'

'She's no good if she has.'

'Don't say that.'

'There's plenty more pebbles on the beach.'

'You'd better go. Tommy won't wait long for any girl.'

'I'll blind him if he doesn't wait for me.'

'Remember me to him. We were at school together. But I'm serious about the orange peel. If you see any, bring it home to me.'

She held his hands. 'Are you all right, Oliver?'

He regained his normal voice. 'Tell Tommy how lucky he is to have you for a sweetheart.'

'I do that every time. I like him a lot.'

'But I do want some orange peel.'

'If I see any I'll put it in my pocket.'

'That's a good sister. Tell Tommy to get some for me as well.' Now why did I say all that? He watched her walk up the road, and only when she was well in front did he go in the same direction, and turn onto the canal for a stroll among the Sunday fishermen casting their lines from its banks. Some sat without thought, gazing at small points of exploding water, or watching waterbeetles making rings around the minnows, then going about their inexplicable business. They were as content for an hour or so as any men could be on this earth, which was how he would like to be, though the sight of them calmed him.

This is where they start to cry, but she didn't, either made of better stuff, or not knowing what she had done, or what she had let herself in for. Experience told him it was something of both, so she might need humouring. 'I don't suppose they ever saw you like this at that Bible class?'

She sat peacefully, drawers off and stockings down. The calmness puzzled him, and her look told him she knew it. Realizing her dishevelment, more from his gaze than her own feelings, she put things right, and tied the band of blue ribbon around her hair. 'I haven't done this before.'

'I could tell. But you've done it now. It's a good job I always have a red handkerchief about me.' As if uncertain of their haven's safety he pulled up his braces and reached for his belt. 'Was that why you wanted to?'

'Yes, but only with you.' She stood against the green background to straighten her skirt and be again the young woman who explained the Bible to children. He was bemused by the glint of accomplishment in her blue eyes, not to mention the smile of mischief on her lips when he looked more closely, telling himself he would give a guinea to know what was hurtling through her mind. He lit a cigarette in the certainty that he would never know. 'Were you good at school?'

She leaned against him. 'I didn't want to leave, but my father said I had to earn some money.'

'I suppose he would say that.'

'Not that I hold it against him. We were always short.'

'It's not easy, keeping your children.' An idea came to him. 'Have you ever been to Matlock?'

'The Sunday School went once, but I was ill with bronchitis, and couldn't go. The others talked about it for ages when they got back.'

'We'll go together, and put up for the night. Not under the bushes, either. We'll find a boarding house, and have a bed to ourselves.'

'What could I tell them at home?'

'Say you'll be staying the weekend with an aunt. You must have one.'

'I don't like telling lies.'

'Nobody does. But you'd better get used to it. I'll meet you at Radford station next Saturday morning, at eight o'clock.'

She looked around. 'I've lost an earring.'

'So you have.' He scraped among grasses and leaves, but it was hopeless. 'I'll buy you another pair.'

She held the odd one. 'No, don't. I'll keep this as a memento.'

He thought it just as well. 'You're a strange girl to me.'

'Am I?' As if wondering what advantage there was in it for him. He found her as vulnerable as a winged bird, though a wayward and beautiful one. When they embraced she whispered: 'I love you,' and as they turned to go out of the wood: 'I can't wait to do it again.'

'Nor me. You spent, didn't you? I know you did.' You've got to be sure the woman enjoys it or she might not want to see you anymore.

'Now I know what it means. I love you so much I don't feel like going home.'

'Nor do I, but we've got to.' There was pity in his tone, impossible to say for whom. Sending sweet words into a woman's ear was the same as when your warm breath whispered them up the nostrils of an intractable horse. 'You'll like Matlock. We can take more time over it. Then we'll go out, and walk by the river.'

Her bosom shivered against his ribs as she put her face up for another kiss, warm and protected by a man of such self-confidence. 'What about Sunday School?'

'Tell them you've got the mumps.' Beyond the kiss, eyes ever open, he saw Ivy and Emily coming hand-in-hand across the Cherry Orchard. They roamed everywhere, at any time, but maybe Mary Ann had sent them to find out where he was. He wouldn't put it past her, though to be so distrusted was more than a man should have to endure. He pulled her to denser cover. 'A couple of my youngsters are over there, and I shouldn't like them to see us.'

Her heart beat almost to sickness at the peril of meeting children from her class, and she allowed him to steer her to the other side of the wood. 'Go home,' he said, 'and take the long way. See me at the station on Saturday morning. And don't keep me waiting.'

When Burton passed them he looked, Ivy told herself, like thunder, and didn't say a word. Well, he wouldn't, would he?

TWELVE

Uniformed musicians in the bandstand embarked on a lively tune from *The Quaker Girl*, all threepenny chairs taken, people crowding the outer fringes. Burton, tall and upright in his best suit, a bowler hat flatly on and the usual flower at his lapel, beat out the rhythm on a chairback.

Alma's hat of sprouting feathers almost reached his height. The ring on her finger, fashioned from a piece of metal at the forge, was exactly the right size, though Burton had made no measurements. 'I wish it was real,' she said on taking it from him in the train.

'And so might I.' He watched her put it on, playing his wife for a couple of days.

When everyone stood for the National Anthem he drew her between the chairs. 'Let's get out of this' – heeding no one's stares.

'Why didn't you stand like the rest?'

They were crossing the river. 'I don't do that, not even for God Almighty.'

'People should, when they play *God Save the King*.'

He walked ahead, a slight squeak in his boots, but waiting to guide her over the road between brakes and wagonettes, a motor car now and again. 'Nobody forces anybody to do anything. They stand up like dummies for a piece of music because they want to. That's their business. I don't care what they do, but it's got nothing to do with me.'

It worried her that he stood so far apart from the sentiment of the crowd. You can hide yourself just as well by doing the same as everybody else, and yet if he had been like other people she wouldn't have wanted him so much, and he'd never have brought her here.

They weren't married, so he could allow her to take his arm, patient when she paused at windows showing sticks of peppermint rock, mineral specimens and fishing tackle. The smell of frying floated everywhere. 'We'd better find a boarding house. They get full later on.'

He seemed to know where to look, went along the road towards Matlock Town. After knocking twice the door was opened by a short grey-haired woman in a black apron. 'We want to be put up for the night.'

She led them upstairs to a room with a wardrobe, chest of drawers, chair and small table, and linoleum on the floor. 'This'll do,' he said.

'It's four shillings and sixpence a night each, bed and breakfast. And you're lucky, because it's the last one. Somebody cancelled. Doors close at ten, and breakfast is at eight sharp. What name is it?'

'Mr and Mrs Worthington,' his mother's before marriage.

'Where's your luggage?'

'At the station. Where's the bathroom?'

'That door across the way. You can pay me now. The hot water won't come on till morning, and that's an extra sixpence.'

He gave out the coins in silver, as if far more than she deserved. 'Cold is all I'll need for the bath.'

'Too much lip,' he said when she'd gone, opening the window to let in fresh air. 'Do you like it?'

She turned from looking at woods across road, river and railway. 'It's clean and pleasant.'

'If it hadn't been we'd have found somewhere else.' For their honeymoon Mary Ann had booked a more comely place by telegram. He put jacket and waistcoat on hangers into the wardrobe. She looked on at his orderliness, till held for a kiss. 'You get undressed as well.'

She took out the pin and set her hat carefully on the chair, undid the small pearl buttons of her blouse. 'I've never seen such a picture as you make,' he said.

'I find that hard to believe.'

'You wouldn't if you could see yourself. If I'd met you earlier in life things would have been different.' Love grew the more he saw her skin unworn by work, flesh unblemished from having children. Such beauty called for tenderness, but she would have had eight young ones by now, and I'd be the same as I've always been, so it's no use dreaming. 'Are you sorry I made you miss Sunday School?' he said with a subtly malevolent smile.

'You seem to like the idea.'

'No woman's missed Sunday School for me before, and that's a fact. I'll never forget it.' She was enough of a Nottingham girl to remind him of younger days, and the sight of her made him want to live forever. The fact that neither of them could brought a moment of sadness; though as far as he was concerned there was no such thing as yesterday, nor the future, either. He turned to take off his trousers, undo suspenders, lay socks aside. She uncovered her breasts and held out her arms.

It was a delight to see her so well-bosomed, and all for him. The bedroom was like no other, she as no other girl, and he a man of distinction to have her in the same room – though she couldn't fail to note how far he stayed inside the shell of himself when they lay down.

He passed her clothes. 'Get your shimmy on, and we'll go out.'

'Will you take me on the river?'

'I'll do whatever you want.' He watched her dress. 'You can put your hat on as well.'

The Derwent forced a bottle-green track between steep wooded banks, heading for Derby and the Trent. After a ten-minute wait he helped her into a fragile skiff. 'Look sharp, or you'll get your ankles wet.'

'Don't go too close to the weir, sir,' the boatmaster called. 'We've lost a few people that way over the years.'

'He must think me a damned fool.'

She settled herself as he moved them quickly midstream, her finger dipping into the water. 'Where exactly are you supposed to be today?'

'It's none of your business.'

'I just wondered.'

'It's best if you don't.' He noted a sulk at his reticence.

'There's no harm you knowing. I'm in Sheffield, looking over something for the forge.'

'But it's Sunday tomorrow.'

'Business is always business there.' He missed a boat by inches to reach less traffic. 'And where are you supposed to be?'

'With my Aunt Lydia. I told her a gentleman friend wanted me to visit his family.'

'What did she say to that?'

'She said good luck to me. She thinks women don't get much opportunity to enjoy themselves. She said times were changing, and she was glad they were, even though she might be too old to get the benefit.'

'Times don't change.'

She thought they did. 'But people do.'

'They do if they don't know themselves.'

'If things happen to them, they change.' She took her hand from the water. 'It's cold.'

'It always is.' But it hadn't rained for weeks. 'We could do with some of it out of the sky.'

She wasn't listening. 'I wish we could stay in Matlock for good.'

He pulled more strongly, cutting through the wake of another boat. 'You think I don't?'

'Why can't we stay here? I'd find a job, and you could work at your trade.'

He grunted. 'Yes, I know, you could sell sticks of rock in a shop, while I'd show people around the caverns and get their pennies at the end when I held out my cap like a beggar.' She waved the gnats away, so he paused in his rowing to light a cigarette. 'That's a daft idea.'

'Why should it be?'

'If we stayed here do you think they'd let you teach in Sunday School?'

'I don't suppose I'll be able to do that again wherever I am. But we could be happy together.'

'Could we?' He didn't care for such talk and, feeling the pull of the weir, headed towards the boathouse. 'We'll go up the Heights of Abraham tomorrow. You'll like it there.'

He was incapable of thinking about anything. He was empty inside and couldn't think at all. 'I love you.'

'I can't deny that's what I like to hear,' he said. 'But do you know what love is?'

'Of course I do.' She put a hand on her heart. 'I feel it here, for you.'

'You can't know. You will one day, but not yet. It's when you've got eight children, and you break your back working every hour God sends to keep them and yourself out of the workhouse. I can't leave that, much as my flesh and bones might want to.'

'It doesn't sound like love to me.'

'It's the only one I know, and I'm chained to it. Every day at the forge I want to walk out and never go back. But I know I shan't because there's something stronger than chains to hold me there. You have to go on working, and never complain. You might think I'm complaining now, but I'm not. I'm telling you how it is. You'll have a lot better life with the sort of man you can get than running off with me.'

Yards from the weir again, drawn to its line of toppling water, she thought the best thing would be if they went over together and drowned. Or, most of all, if she did, though her heart throbbed so fiercely she knew the body wouldn't allow such a convenient fate.

A few more pulls at the oars got them to safety, and her tone was regretful. 'How strong you are!'

He knew what she had been thinking. 'It's a good job I am. You don't die until you have to.'

She laughed. 'Can't you swim?'

'No more than Saint Clement. They tied an anchor to his leg and threw him in, or so I heard.'

'Who did?'

'That I don't know. I heard he was a blacksmith, but he still drowned.'

'I can't swim, either, but I shall learn one day.'

'We'd better go back. The hour's about finished. And I'm hungry for my dinner, so you must be.'

The stale cheese smell of fish bait came from a tackle shop, postcards dazzling in the sun by the door of a gift emporium, placards blazoned outside a stationer's front. A boy laden with newspapers shouted his way along the promenade: 'Special! Special! Telegram to Berlin!'

'What does that mean?'

'There'll be a war with Germany,' she said.

People stopped to buy papers. 'As if there isn't enough trouble in the world. Anybody must be daft in the head to want war.' They came to a restaurant. 'Let's go in and fill our bellies. We've earned it, one way or another.'

A clerkly man on his way to take the only vacant table was frustrated by Burton's long strides, who put his hat on one chair, and pulled the other out for Alma. Exhausted and hungry, she loved him for getting a place so soon.

'You can read that for me, as well.' He gave her the menu as she sat down. 'I worked almost as soon as I could stand, and had no time for schooling.' Smithing's my trade, he added to himself, and you don't need letters for that.

'What would you like?'

'Two hot dinners should settle us.'

'There's beef, and there's lamb.'

The waitress was a gawky tom-laddish woman whose apron looked none too clean. 'Bring me beef,' he told her, 'with plenty of fat on it.'

'I'll have the lamb,' Alma said.

Burton pointed to food left on plates at the next table. 'What do you do with all that?'

The waitress wrote their orders. 'Throw it away.'

He grunted at such waste. 'If you kept a couple of pigs on it they'd think it was Christmas every day.'

Her eyebrows lifted, as if he wasn't in his right mind. 'Tell it to the manageress.' She looked at Alma, wondering how she could put up with a man like that, and Alma was half-inclined to tell her, as if quite taken with her, while Burton speculated on what might be done in bed with such a woman. 'She's a bit of a rum 'un,' he said, on her zig-zagging away.

Alma smiled. 'She didn't know what you were talking about.'

'She might one day. People waste too much.' Her plainly troubled eyes could not meet his, her thoughts whirling in all directions, but he had no intention of guessing why. A woman's eyes always showed when her mind was on the boil, and he knew he was right on her saying: 'What are we going to do?'

'We're waiting to eat.'

She turned her knife in a circle. 'I love you. You're my whole life now.' Passion joined them, but he lived in too wilful a world to want the cargo of her troubles. She needed kind words, promises, even lies, but he couldn't help because he saw no future, only the present. 'We're enjoying outselves,' he told her. 'It's a holiday. What more do you want?'

She held his wrist. 'There's more to it than that, isn't there?'

Disliking to be touched in public, he drew his hand away. 'If there is, I don't know what it can be.'

The waitress set Alma's soup on the table. 'Enjoy it, duck!'

He reached a piece of bread. 'Get that down you,' and touched her hand, adding gently: 'It'll make you fit for when we're in bed tonight.' The big-eared waitress, who made an enquiring face at his words, could think what she liked. Alma smiled, as if for the moment his advice was what she wanted to hear.

Plates of meat and Yorkshire pudding, potatoes roast and boiled, peas and cabbage were set on the cloth, the waitress glaring at Burton as if to say he could lump it if he didn't like it. He looked at Alma over his uplifted fork, before bringing it to his mouth. 'You're famished, aren't you? You should be. I know I am.'

She leaned forward and said that she was. 'The sight of you makes me hungry, but the trouble is I can't come down from the stars so soon.'

Oliver, usually finding distraction in a book, couldn't now. Shirtsleeves rolled, he wore neither coat nor waistcoat. Burton would have been shocked, since he was always fully dressed when beyond the bounds of the house and garden, even in the hottest weather.

Emily moved loving fingers among flowers by the brook. She counted the daisies but, though knowing her numbers, got them in the wrong order. From his seat on a fallen tree he held back a laugh for fear of hurting her raw pride. Out of love the others often made her cry so that they could take her in their arms and cradle her back to happiness, always easy to do. Mary Ann, making sure she lacked for nothing to appear normal, had tied a ribbon in her hair, and put on a clean pinafore. She never let Burton bully her, and was glad the others looked after her, even though they often treated her as a pet.

Burton regarded her as dense enough to be quite a long way on the wrong side of normal, therefore so little receptive to his discipline that he hardly cared to look at her. She had neither the fair features nor the liveliness of the others, and could be left alone.

'What are you sitting there for, our Oliver? You're ever so quiet. Why don't you say something?'

'I'm trying to read.'

'Reading's daft.'

'You won't say that when you can do it' – though she never would.

'What's the book saying?'

'It's about famous engineers.' He flipped the pages to their frontispiece. 'Men who built trains and ships and bridges.'

'You won't do anything, if you only read.'

'Where did you get that idea?'

'I heard Dad say it.'

'He would. But I'm also waiting.'

'What for?'

'To die.'

Her features were wrenched into distress, so he pulled her close and stroked her face. 'I'm not really. Look, your ribbon's got tangled. Let me see to it.'

Her smile came back. 'Shall you go to heaven when you die?'

'Nobody knows till they get there.'

'I shall. They said so at Sunday School. But when I laughed and couldn't stop they made me stand in the street.' Every indignity was stored in her heart, never to be forgotten. 'Can you pick daisies in heaven?'

'I expect they'll find some for you.' He offered his hand. 'Let's go home, and get our tea.'

She was eight, and would never make her way in the world.

He feared for her future, but vowed to see she never came to harm. His tears almost broke as she hugged him. 'We'll have sliced cucumber and salmon, pineapple chunks and jam pasties,' she cried. 'I love Sunday tea.'

'Come on, then, you greedy little devil.' Burton would not be in the house to spoil her teatime. He had gone to Sheffield, or so he said, though not all of Ahab's horses would get the truth out of him.

Her merriment covered any anxiety about Alma, though when he looked across the blank stretch of the field his misery came swamping back. Emily lingered at the edge of the wood, loving greenery and flowers. 'Run!' he called. 'There'll be buttercups in heaven as well when you get there in a hundred years.'

The broad and shaded track went steeply through the woods, Alma breathless by the summit. Burton walked beyond the lookout tower to the shelter of a tree where they could be more alone. The neighing of a horse from a trippers' wagonette came on a warm breeze from the valley. He kissed her, and she sat on the dry bracken. 'I went on a motorbus to Skegness last year, with some girls from work.'

'Did you?'

'I couldn't stop looking at the waves coming up the sand. I was going to walk into them but the girls pulled me back.'

He enjoyed the taste of a cigarette. 'I've heard they're dangerous.'

'Because I can't swim, the waves looked so strong and beautiful, like a wall I wanted to walk through. I was sure if I went into them they'd be warm and soft.'

She was beginning to sound like daft Emily, not knowing there were things you could think but not say, though he smiled. 'I'm strong, and you're lovely, so we get all we want between us.'

'I still think there's something missing.'

He caught her regret. 'It was all right in bed.'

'Oh, I know.'

'You're a funny thing. You know I love you. You're a miracle to me.'

'You're a lot more than that to me.'

She wanted to stay but, hearing laughter on the path below he held out a hand for her to get up. 'You're as light as a feather. We'll go down now.' On the descent she kept a hand in his, praying he wouldn't take it away, as was his habit. He didn't, more aware now as to how she felt about him, though at people coming towards them he put the hand by his side. She kept up with his strides: 'I've never had a weekend like this.'

'Let's hope it's not the last.'

He was remote and unfeeling, except when storms within showed by a sign at his cheeks, which he couldn't always control. He was the opposite to all that her father was, but she hoped that wasn't the reason she loved him. They paused by a small stone shelter under the trees, built into a sort of grotto. 'I like being with you. Wouldn't it be wonderful if we could live in that little place?'

Anguish unsettled his features, though only for a moment. 'That's a rare notion.'

She would never break through. Even make-believe wasn't part of his nature. 'Oh, why is it? I could live anywhere with you.'

'And me with you, but not in this world. And there isn't any other. We might want to do all sorts of things, but we can't.'

'I don't believe it. Imagine how happy we would be. I could teach you to read and write,' thinking he would prize the capability.

'There are plenty of others to do that.' He put a comforting hand on her shoulder, feeling warm flesh under the blouse. 'There's no hope for us staying here, but don't you think I wish there was?'

She began to weep. A man and his girl stared on their way by. Burton steeled himself. 'Let's get down. There's a train to catch.' He'd had enough, wanted to be a thousand miles away. Yet she was right. The picture of a new life dazzled, perhaps brighter for him than for her, but nothing could be done about it.

Crossing the bridge, a train whistle warned everyone to get a move on, a melancholy signal for Alma, who knew they would never be here again. She wanted to tell him, but said: 'We shall miss it, unless we run.'

'I never run. There'll be another in an hour. And if we miss that, we can walk.'

'But it's twenty-five miles.'

'I know. I did it once.' He had been young, and ale inside helped on the way. He was pulled from mulling on that dull incessant walk by seeing Florence come out of the station. She gazed ahead, a stately vision in a high hat, carrying a folded parasol. She looked older, as if tragedy had struck, though he knew it hadn't. The man must have been her husband, middle-aged and neatly dressed, a bowler hat on and carrying an ivory-handled stick, so cock of the walk he could never have known about the behaviour of his wife. Burton ensured mutual recognition before she turned her head and walked on, her husband hurrying to catch up.

'Who was that?'

'Somebody I was acquainted with, once upon a time.'

It was obvious she believed something else, though he was glad no more was said. 'We can still catch the train if we hurry.'

'I thought you wanted to stay?' He shouldn't have said so, but on such a weekend how could you listen to every word in your mind before letting it from your lips? She wanted to get the day over, and so did he now that all enjoyment had gone, but it would end soon enough.

Torment burned her insides: 'We can't stay forever, I know, so what's the point in another hour? If we could stay forever I would.' She turned on him. 'You're not alive. You're not even awake. You don't know how to live.'

'I don't know anybody who does, but I didn't come here to do your bidding.' He pulled her along. 'The train's still in. We'll catch it.'

People got out of the way like minnows before a bigger fish as he walked through the crowd, saw above everyone's head, thrust her into a carriage, and found seats.

The train threaded the wooded vale towards Derby. Neither spoke, in the withdrawal from a pleasure they felt would have to be paid for. His features were set, when all she wanted to hear was how he expected her to pass the rest of her life, which could only be unreal compared to the one already lived. Two days in

Matlock had set her years apart from her previous existence, and she would never understand what madness had driven her into going away with him.

Whatever he could say – if he wanted to open his mouth, which he didn't – would help neither. They would be better hardened for whatever might happen if they didn't indulge in entangling speech.

The train slowed through flat land close to Nottingham, and he ignored her as if they weren't together, when the thought of what had been done to Oliver was so overwhelming that she cried as quietly as could be done in the crowded carriage. People looked as if wanting to speak words of comfort, till Burton said: 'Didn't you enjoy yourself? I know I did.'

'You don't realize what's hurting me. I want to die.'

Allow me to open the door so that you can jump out and have your will against me, he said to himself, though the train's going too slow at the moment to do much damage, which you must know, or you wouldn't have said it. Despair or disappointment was no excuse for weakness.

'I know what you mean,' he had to say, 'more than you think in that young head of yours, but we had a good time, so stop blawting about it. You ought to be happy, that's all I can say.' But he didn't know what had been done, nor wanted to know, nor could in any way know, in his assumption that all things would take care of themselves.

He'd had a good weekend, and spent something like two pounds, so she ought to be glad. But she wasn't, and he couldn't think why she expected a good time to go on forever, because they never could nor had, and though she was inexperienced enough to hope they would, it was unreasonable of her to think so. He liked her young body but not her immature thoughts, which served him right for taking up with such a woman, though he couldn't blame himself because who wouldn't have done his best to get her into bed, and miss Sunday School for him into the bargain?

The train shunted into Radford station. 'I don't want to see you again,' which he thought a bit soon to hear.

Usually, by the time such words were said, he was more than

halfway wanting to tell the woman himself, since everybody got fed up with each other sooner or later. 'That's a fine thing to say.'

She dried her cheeks. 'It's true.'

'That's that, then.' He drew her upright as the door opened, and helped her to the platform, hoping she would want to see him again, however she felt. 'Go out of the station first.'

She walked quickly up the steps to join the tread of men's boots across the wooden floor of the booking hall. The lamps were lit, though it was still daylight outside, a subtle odour of gas, their mantles glowing with fairy incandescence. Burton lit a cigarette, and let her get well in front, not wanting them to be seen so close to home.

Oliver, opposite the station entrance, was hoping to see someone he knew, for company on the way to Woodhouse, though doubting anyone would be able to keep up with him in his present mood. He had been in and out of town at such a rate as to erase all thoughts of Alma, and the sight of her turned him pale, an unbelievable apparition he hadn't hoped to see.

He recalled her kisses among the pungent sheds of the sawmill, their dalliance on Misk Hill, her homely entertainment of children at the Mission Hall, but since that short time ago her face had changed. As if not sure she was the same person he let her go a few yards, before running across the road and taking her arm. 'Where have you been? I couldn't find you anywhere.'

'I went to Matlock.'

'Who with?'

'On my own.'

He wanted to believe, but her features had no fear, and settled into a hardness he found strange. 'You must have been with someone. I'm not daft. I can tell.' He couldn't, particularly, but it was a way of attacking her as he knew she deserved. 'Nobody goes to Matlock on their own.'

'I did. And it's got nothing to do with you.'

Distress in her eyes told him that guilt was responsible for the unfamiliar tone, which she had no way of hiding. 'By heck, it's got a lot to do with me.' He calmed himself. 'Who were you with?'

'I was by myself.' The words were forced out. A fortnight ago her dull life had been so marvellously peaceful, but she had been drawn to Burton on seeing him at the sawmill, and had met him on the lane when her only thought had been to call on Oliver. If only he hadn't been still at work, though she despised herself for thinking that everything was his fault.

'I never thought you would lie to me,' he said calmly, looking back towards the station. She knew who he would see. 'So that's how it is?'

Burton, bowler hat at a non-caring angle, cigarette still burning, went downhill towards the river.

'I knew that was the case.' His throat closed as if to choke him. 'It was a nightmare I couldn't believe in.' He clamped a fist tight at his side, because a son of Burton knew better than to hit a woman. 'Why did you do that to me?'

The day had started in the bedroom at Matlock, when Burton's long body had leaned over her, and she was so happy when he came into her, but she should have known it would lead to this. Tears burning like vinegar, she wanted to run back to the station and fall under a train. 'I don't know. I wish I hadn't.'

She walked away, but he followed, stopping so suddenly he knocked into her. 'Is it him you love, or me?'

'Don't touch me.' When her hat fell lopsided she put it quickly back in place, steeling herself into dignity, holding down her sorrows and regrets. 'Leave me alone. How can I love anybody?'

He walked so that she would never catch up, supposing she wanted to, to soften her distress. She was a scourge, and he wasn't the man to relish pain. Any talk of what she and his father had been up to would be too sickening to hear.

THIRTEEN

Burton stood in the doorway hoping for an afternoon breeze to dry his sweat. Three idlers watched Oswald shoeing a placid grey carthorse.

'They're calling up the Territorials,' a man said from behind his newspaper.

'The queue at the drill hall stretched halfway down Derby Road this morning,' said the other man, who looked too old for soldiering. 'They won't get me. I've got a family to keep. But they say it'll be over by Christmas, anyway.'

Burton's sceptical grunt said: 'Which one?'

'Anything's better than staying around here and sweating your tod off for bogger-all,' a youth of eighteen said. 'At least in the army you get beer money and a suit on your back.' He looked at his feet. 'And a new pair of boots as well.'

You couldn't even waste compassion on such stupidity. 'If you still haven't gone in six months,' Burton said, 'come to me, and I'll give you a pair of boots.' But he knew he was on a winner, because the damned fool would go.

'A shilling a day,' the family man said, 'and they've got you body and soul. You wouldn't really sign up, would you, Ken?'

'Half the lads in our street have gone already,' the youth replied. 'Some of the married men as well.'

'How many do you think will come back?' Burton asked.

'I'll see France, won't I?'

'For all the good it will do you. Only fools enlist.'

Ken didn't like the opinion of a man over twice his age. 'Lots of people are waiting to jump into my job at the brewery, so I shan't be missed.'

Burton tapped Oswald on the shoulder. 'Finish what you're

154

doing, then we'll lock up and go home.' He went in to make sure all tools were in place for the morning.

The long dry summer made each day's walk more wearying, and evening brought no ease, the sunken lane holding in so much heat it was lousy with gnats. He lit a cigarette to smoke them off. Since Matlock he'd hoped Alma would call at the forge, or show herself on one of his strolls in Robin's Wood, couldn't think why she was sulking, or brooding. He never believed anyone who said they'd never do this, or never do that, because whenever anybody did say they'd never do something it was usually a way of letting the matter rest till they did exactly that again. On the other hand if she really did mean she had packed him in, being a more determined woman than he'd imagined, well then – he spat out a strand of tobacco – she can kiss my behind.

A long low booming sound crossed the almost clear sky, and though hard to tell where the storm was coming from he hoped it would bring rain, though he would only believe it when water splashed on his cap.

A flash of more immediate light, and a gunclap of noise, reverberated through the empty kitchen. The wide open door told him where to find Mary Ann. Since childhood she had been terrified of thunderbolts spinning down the chimney and exploding in the fireplace. Or they would flash through a window and create hell in the parlour, bouncing from wall to wall and scorching them black, perhaps setting fire to the house in their malevolent playfulness, killing or horribly injuring anyone in the room.

So she kept the doors open, to encourage any such fireball to leave after the minimum of damage. It was better to take precautions, and stay out of their way.

Burton knew every thought in Mary Ann's head, much disliking those put there by her grandmother. 'I wonder where she can be?' Oswald said, at another splintering of light and burst of thunder.

'I know where.' Burton hung up his jacket, then tapped the door to the cubby hole under the stairs. 'Mary Ann! I know you're in there.'

A small oil lamp at half-glow came before a pale hand and bare forearm. She stumbled into the kitchen, and almost turned back at another flash covering the window. Burton, while softened by her look of terror, couldn't understand why anybody should be afraid. 'I always know where to find you.'

She put her lamp on the table and turned it off. 'I get so frightened.'

'I've told you time and time again that lightning never strikes a blacksmith's house, but you won't be said.'

'It might. You can never tell. I'm going back under the stairs till it's over.'

'No you're not,' Burton said. 'Get my beer, and some snap. I've been at work all day, and I'm clambed.'

'I'll do it when the storm's finished.'

At such unreasonable fear he took a bunch of steel cutlery from the table drawer. 'I'll show you that lightning can't hurt us.'

Wondering what he had in mind, her fright multiplied when he opened the window and held out the bundle of knives and forks as far as his arm would go. She had never wished anybody dead. 'Ernest, don't!'

'He's enjoying himself,' Oswald said.

The veins at his temples twitched. 'Come on! Strike me!'

Mary Ann was transfixed.

'Here's your chance! Strike me dead!' he shouted at the sky. A sizzle of lightning sheeted the window, and Oswald thought how pleased Oliver and all of them might be if he was scorched to a cinder.

He rattled the cutlery to give whoever it was a second chance, but the flash was weaker, as if it couldn't be bothered with such as him. He turned. 'What did I tell you? It didn't strike me, did it?'

Oswald, who had never seen his mother so pale, inwardly cursed Burton.

'No,' she said.

'It never will, either.' He patted her on the shoulder, and it was as much as she could do not to shrink away, but he smiled at his prank. 'It won't harm you, either, and that's all I care about.'

'God will do it when He wants to,' she said, 'in His own good time.'

'If He didn't do it then, He never will. Anyway, He missed his chance.'

'I suppose that makes you happy?'

'He can take me or leave me.' Glass and bottle were put before him. The storm had gone, and left no rain, and to staunch their hunger she put out bread and a piece of bacon. 'Who was that young woman you were seen with at Matlock last weekend, when you should have been in Sheffield?'

'What woman was that? I know of no woman.'

'I've heard different.'

No option but to answer, he could never give himself cause to hit her again, would regret to his dying day that he had already done so. 'I did the business sooner than expected, and came back through Matlock. I wanted to see if it had altered since we were there.'

'And had it?'

'Not as I could tell.'

'People talk.' Batter went into a bowl for the pudding. 'They always have, and they always will.'

'And who the hell was it who did?'

Oswald stopped eating at his savage tone, wondering what could be done if Burton thought to knock her about. He didn't fancy going for him without Thomas and Oliver to back him up.

'Never mind who it was,' she said.

The names of those who might have blabbed were gone through almost as quickly as the lightning that had flashed so uselessly at his bundle of steel. Perhaps Florence had talked: he wouldn't put it past her, or Annie Ollington from next door had been in Matlock that day. She had it in for him, but there was no point speculating on who had panmouthed. 'I stopped to ask somebody if they knew the place to get a good dinner.'

'Couldn't you remember the one we went to after we married?'

'That was a long time ago. Places change.'

'It seems like yesterday to me.'

'Me as well, at times. But I didn't think.'

A likely story. She went into the pantry to calm herself, knowing that the only way to end an argument was to say no more. 'Here's something else till your dinner's ready,' she said, laying a pasty on Oswald's plate.

'Don't I get one?' Burton had eaten enough for the moment,

and any more would spoil his zest for dinner, but he had to ask.

'You'll get it when I'm good and ready. I only have one pair of hands.'

He was uncertain whether to show concern about Oliver, yet wanted to know where he was.

'I expect he's still at the sawmill,' Oswald said. 'They work all hours.'

'I don't know. I worry about him these days,' Mary Ann said. 'He came in half an hour ago, for something to eat. Then he changed and went out again, saying he wouldn't be long. When I asked what was the matter he just smiled.'

Burton sharpened his dinner knife with the steel. 'He's young. He'll get over what's bothering him.'

Restless as ever, after the meal he walked across the Cherry Orchard, boots crunching over stubble, grass parched to a dusty unhealthy brown. The storm had left no rain to make any difference. Nothing but a deluge would bring the colour back, though there'd be plenty in the autumn. Robin's Wood spread to either side, every tree clear, a place of memories, causing a momentary smile. A breeze against his face, he felt at peace, and went between the nearest parting of the trunks.

Rain or not, brambles and nettles had found enough sustenance to overgrow the path. He pushed his way through, and at a rustle in the undergrowth wondered if a rabbit was close. Oliver stood with the double-barrelled twelve-bore signposting his father's stomach.

'Put that thing down,' Burton said.

'If you move, I'll kill you, and put the other in myself.'

Burton noted his hands not too firm at the firearm, though steady enough to put the ice forever in his belly: 'It's loaded. And I can use it.'

'I know you can. I showed you when you were thirteen. I showed you everything you know.'

'You deserve to die.'

'You think I care? There's many a day I've wanted to. But if you kill me, Mary Ann loses both of us.'

The gun wavered, so much misery on Oliver's face. 'You ran me off with Alma. How could you have done such a thing?'

'I shan't touch her again.'

'I don't care. It's too late, anyway.'

'Nothing's too late. Where did you get that gun?' Not the man to waste talk, but knowing that only words would save them, to look as if not much caring whether he lived or died. 'I took you shooting over the fields, remember? I made you stand behind me when I fired so that you wouldn't come to harm.'

'I was in love with Alma.'

Burton scoffed. 'How was I to know? A young man has lots of girls. I know I did. Any woman is any man's meat – except your wife.'

Oliver thought that whoever spouted such a philosophy was little better than a brute. Burton was irredeemable.

'I didn't force her. If anyone had taken a girl from me in my young days I'd have thought good luck to him, and bided my time till I could do the same back, unless I was too busy with other girls by then. Anyway, I've told you, I shan't bother with her again.'

Oliver marvelled at hearing more words from his father than he ever had. Burton lunged forward and pushed the gun clear. 'You young fool. I'll have this.'

'I'll hate you till my dying day.'

'That's a long time to hate, if you think anybody's worth it. Get out of my way before I brain you.' The safety catch had been off, and two cartridges leapt from the breech when he opened it. It was that close. Unable to say anything, he put the shells in his pocket, and threw the gun back. 'Carry it home.'

Striding away, he regretted not having given him one between the eyes, even two, though glad at having saved him from murder. No man looked pretty swinging from a gibbet. The sun was going down over the wood behind, and he hoped for such a dowsing of rain as would cool the air and make everything grow. For weeks his sons and daughters had carried every drop, from washing either themselves or the pots, into the garden, and watered at least some of the vegetables. He supposed they hadn't done so when he wasn't there, because they'd do anything to get back at him, even though the garden provided food for them all. He'd also splashed a few buckets on the marrows and cucumbers, but water was getting low in the well and was barely good enough to drink.

Shadows covered the bushes, it would be dark in half an hour, and as he thought of hurrying to give the garden its last look of the day a shot clattered from the wood, a startling sound ripping through the still evening. If you wanted to kill your father and didn't have the guts or the firm enough wish the next thing you might think of, having the means to do it, was to kill yourself. He scoffed at such an idea, but his heart jerked, almost stopped, and though aching from the day's work he multiplied his rate of strides back to the wood. He's done it, the mad stupid youth, because I didn't think to search his pockets and find the shell he'd hidden from me. Careless, careless, I should have known he was ripe for anything.

He crashed between the trees. 'Oliver! Where are you?'

He stood before him, a dead pigeon dangling from his hand. 'I'm here, Father.'

Burton wanted to take him in his arms and hold him, never to let go. 'I heard the shot, and came back to see what it was.'

Oliver smiled. 'You thought I'd committed suicide.'

'I never supposed you'd do such a thing. I only wanted to know what you'd caught.'

'A plump wood pigeon for Mother's supper, though more by luck than judgement.'

'I'll pluck it for her when we get home,' Burton said.

'No, I'll do it.'

'We'll need a few buckets of water on the garden first. It'll be dark soon, so we'd better hurry.' He pointed to the gun. 'Are there any more in there?'

Oliver held up the dead bird. 'I used the last on this.' He smiled, serene and sure at having one final blow to deal his father, which he would not mention now, something unluckily that would upset the rest of the family as well, but things had gone too far to bother about that.

'Don't let your mother see the gun, or you'll frighten her half to death.' As he strode across the common, relying on his son to follow, he wished he had never set eyes on Alma, and regretted that Oliver didn't have another bullet to put in his back.

He could think of nothing more than to enlist in the South Nottinghamshire Hussars, and do his bit for the war like everybody else. No queue at the drill hall, a sergeant at the table inside told him the lists were full.

'We've got over five hundred men, and that's all the regiment needs for the time being.' He picked up a four-ounce tin of Craven 'A' Mixture, and sat back in his chair as if after a good day's work in enrolling so many, to light his pipe from a box of Swan Vestas. 'I'll tell you what, you look as if you'd make a good soldier, so why don't you put your name down for the Robin Hoods? It's a fine regiment.'

Oliver had seen the Hussars parading in the Market Place five years ago, and told himself that if ever he decided to become a soldier (though hardly intending to) he would join that body of men, or none. It was all the same whether he belonged or not, because how else could he get rid of the misery of Alma's betrayal? What better than to forget by going for a soldier? The Robin Hoods would be as good a regiment as any, and being with the infantry would get him killed sooner. He turned to leave.

'There's one trade we're short of,' the sergeant called, 'but the people in it seem a bit shy of coming forward.'

'What's that?'

'Blacksmiths. Shoeing smiths. Farriers. With so many horses we're dead short of 'em.'

'I'm a blacksmith, and I've got my articles.'

'You aren't codding me, just to get in?'

'It's as true as I'm standing here. I'll sign up, but I must go home and let my mother know.'

'Of course you must, my lad. But first I'll put your name down. You'll be on the roll as a shoeing smith. What name do you go by?'

'Oliver Burton. I'm twenty-three.'

'The colonel will be as pleased as Punch. Even he's waiting to get his charger shod.' He shuffled a few lists. 'You'll be in the Wollaton squadron, under Major Ley. They've been out all day bringing in horses. A lot came from Shipstone's brewery, which'll mean less ale for the drunkards in town tomorrow.' He smoothed his bushy grey moustache, and smiled widely, turned loquacious at getting a farrier, pleased to let his pipe go cold. 'The colonel's been up Eastwood way, and his party brought over twenty back, though I can't say how good they'll be. Anyway, the regiment's off to Norfolk in the morning. You'll join them in a week or two, after we've made a smart trooper out of you.'

The first day's pay of one-and-twopence in his pocket signified the prospect of adventure and put elation into his walk, as if the war had broken out for him alone. Anguish falling away, he was no longer his own master, but when had he been? The army wouldn't be so strange, because he would be dealing with horses, and any sergeant-major's bark couldn't be worse than Burton's had always been.

The forlorn yet familiar hooting of steam whistles from Radford station swamped him with the reality of what he had done, and he could hardly bear to face his mother without explaining Burton's perfidy to her, which he could not do. Lighting a cigarette, he decided to put off the encounter by calling at the sawmill to say he wouldn't be working there anymore.

'I knew you'd enlist, Oliver.' Brown asked him into the parlour. 'I told my wife only an hour ago we'd be losing you. "A fine upstanding chap like young Burton is bound to go now that his country needs him," I said, didn't I, Doris?'

She sat in an armchair, as if not at all agreeing with what her husband had said. 'We'll be sorry to see the back of you,' he went on. 'You're the best chap we've got. But it's always the best who go first.' He felt in his pocket. 'Here's a little something to help you on the road. And when you come back, as I know you will, you'll always find work here.'

Such a time was too far off to imagine, or to hope for. He'd heard Brown talking to the foreman about buying a couple of motor lorries to speed up deliveries, so when he came back there would be no horses left to need looking after. He took the sovereign, shook hands, and turned smartly to go.

*　　　*　　　*

He looked on from the hedge at how busy they were. Thomas plied his fork into a heap of sunburnt weeds at the end of the garden, loaded them on the barrow for burning. Oswald and Burton dug shallow trenches for autumn planting, a reel of string on a stick to get the alignments straight. Burton peered along the line, a twitch of the head. 'Left a bit. Now a shade to the right.' He lifted a hand towards Thomas. 'Weed the marrows when you've finished that. I said to the right a bit,' he shouted to Oswald. 'Get it straight, can't you? And Thomas, give them a bit more water from the well.' He saw Oliver. 'There's plenty to do if you'd like to get stuck in.'

'I've enlisted.'

Burton stood at full height. 'You've what?'

He plucked a gooseberry from the bush and ate it. 'I'm a trooper in the South Nottinghamshire Hussars. They've taken me on as a shoeing smith, and I've got to be back at the drill hall in half an hour.'

Oswald looked up. 'What did you want to do that for?'

'There wasn't much left to do. Burton might know.'

'You don't do that for anything,' Oswald said.

Burton recovered himself. 'You're a bigger fool than I took you for.'

'Perhaps. But I've done it.'

'Don't go. I'll buy you out.' He would get the money even if he had to sell up at the forge. A young man from Woodhouse had signed on a few years ago after quarrelling with his parents, the worse thing he could have done, the sort of disgrace they would never live down, and now it was Burton's turn to feel the same. But the young man's father had been able to get him out by paying five pounds.

'There's a war on,' Oliver said, 'and I'm over twenty-one.'

'That's got nothing to do with us. War never did anybody any good.' If only he'd killed me in the wood, Burton thought. No one on either side of the family had ever 'gone for a soldier'. Had they done so the service of the dead would have been said over them, no other way to outlive the shame.

Oliver was no longer sure he had done the right thing. 'I've taken the King's shilling.'

'Give it back. I'll pay a lot more to get you out.'

The girls were eating dinner, and Oliver stood in the doorway to tell them what he had done. Mary Ann turned white, all ten more silent than they had ever been in the same room together.

'If he'd come and told me he was thinking of joining up,' Burton said, an accurate spit at the bars of the fire, 'I'd have talked some sense into him.'

Oliver hoped to calm them. 'Everybody's enlisting.'

'That's even less reason to go. You never do what everybody else is doing.'

Mary Ann, hands to her face, fell half-fainting into the Windsor chair only Burton ever used. 'Oh, why did you do it?'

He no longer wondered, propelled by a force he could neither understand nor control. Everyone was going, all the young men and quite a few of the old, and he wouldn't be left behind, might well have gone even if he had never met Alma.

'Maybe it's not so bad.' Thomas held back tears at his mother's pain. 'He's a blacksmith, and they don't put them in the firing line.'

'I've got to be back at the drill hall soon,' was all he could say. 'So I should be off.'

Edith, Rebecca and Sabina began to cry because their favourite brother was not only leaving home but was setting off for war. 'Oliver's going to be a soldier,' Emily sobbed.

'Stop your blawting.' Burton too felt wrenched by the misery of Mary Ann, who in her moaning saw her firstborn as a young boy, now on his way to being dead forever. Burton knew that soldiers didn't come back for years, if ever they did, though he couldn't say so. 'He didn't think of any of us when he took that paltry shilling.'

Oliver's tears blended with the girls' on kissing them goodbye. 'Edith, you're the eldest now, so look after the others.' Mary Ann sat quiet and still at this unexpected and bitter disruption to their lives. 'Goodbye, Mother. I'll see you as soon as I can.'

She stood. 'And when will that be? I won't see you again. I know I won't,' unable to take in how someone as loving as Oliver could have made such a pitiless move.

His smile withered. 'Don't be daft, Mother. Of course you

164

will.' How many times had the young hero of a Henty novel said familiar farewells to father, uncaring or tyrannical uncle, or mother? The comparison buoyed him as he offered a hand to Burton. 'Goodbye, Father.'

Burton pushed it aside. 'There's no call for that.' He wanted to take the hand, yet couldn't. If he did he might not see his dearly loved son again. Then he thought how terrible it would be if Oliver never did come back, and he had to live for the rest of his life with the knowledge that he had spurned the goodbye hand. He took it, and pressed it with all the love he could decently show in front of the family, as near to tears as he had ever been. 'Come back to us soon.'

Oliver kissed his mother again, and went stricken out of the house. At the gate he looked over the yard in which he had played and worked, and waved to his sisters, brothers and mother who stood around the door to watch him go, Burton's austere face above their heads.

Walking down the lane, alone at last, relieved that the news had been given, his youthful spirit reasserted itself, and by the time he reached the railway tunnel, wishing he was on the train that rumbled overhead, he was singing aloud, and happy to be on his way.

FOURTEEN

'You're lucky,' the quartermaster said. 'A lot of men rushing to the colours have to wait weeks for their uniforms and equipment.' But the Hussars were the darling regiment of Nottingham, and had all they wanted, so he ought to be proud they had taken him. He put on the khaki and fitted a peaked cap. Winding puttees around his legs wasn't easy – he didn't see the sense of them – but patience taught the knack. A small metal horseshoe, prongs pointing downwards, was stitched onto the upper left sleeve of his tunic, the distinguishing sign of a shoeing smith which pleased him because most others had nothing to show for their status.

It took a fortnight to give him the semblance of a cavalryman, training which normally needed twelve weeks. Footdrill and disciplined equitation was almost a pleasure, and learning to care for horses in the military fashion easy. A course of musketry with the Short Lee Enfield was concurrent with how to handle (and kill with) the sword. Fascinated by maps since the teacher had shown one with the height of Misk Hill – that curséd place he had walked to with Alma – he went downhill into town and bought a pocket manual on how to read them.

The sergeant was surprised at his ability to estimate distances, soon regarding him as a smart enough soldier to join the regiment in Norfolk. 'You'll go up through the ranks like a knife through butter once you're abroad and we take casualties. You might even end up with a commission before this war's done. Don't believe all that nonsense about it being over by Christmas. None of us old sweats do.'

Some troopers were billeted at home, coming on parade every morning, but Oliver needed much of the day and night to care for the horses, and was found a bed at the barracks. Calling once more on the family, the farewell was not so harrowing. He took his civilian clothes for them to look after until he came back. 'At least I shall have something to remember you by,' Mary Ann said, seemingly less in despair at what he had done.

She asked him to have his photograph taken at a studio in town, which he found time to do, the first and only snapshot of his life. When Mary Ann sent Edith to the barracks with handkerchiefs and underwear in a bag he gave her the photograph to take home.

He didn't tell anyone he had signed on to serve overseas, as had the whole regiment. If he was killed, so be it. He didn't much care. That was in the future, and though he might hope for death he couldn't imagine it would happen, because what you wanted you never got. Someone who went to the Boer War to get himself killed because of a disappointment in love had survived the bloodiest battles, while another had gone to fight saying he would never be killed and died of fever in a Bulawayo hospital, proving there was something more than yourself with a say in what happened. All you could do was keep whistling, and go on with your work.

They had difficulty getting the horses into the wagons, until Oliver coaxed the most placid up the ramp, and the rest followed. As a blacksmith he was wanted urgently in Norfolk, so was on his way with other troopers and their remounts. He arranged each horse in the cattle truck, for them not to face passing trains head on, and when they seemed snug enough took off their bits and slackened the girths.

Four hundred and fifty-two officers and men had already gone, entrained with their horses from the Low Level station on 14 August. Several thousand people had gathered to see their heroes off, unlike *their* unobserved departure.

The corporal split the party into shifts of two hours, keeping a couple of men on hand to make sure the horses came to no harm. Army beasts were more fractious than those Oliver had dealt with so far, either due to hard treatment and the uncertainty of their lives, or from too many changes of master.

Wanting never to see Nottingham again, he was impatient at

the slow train huffing towards Grantham. A ration box between the seats made a table for their game of ha'penny brag. He could afford to lose a coin or two, change from Brown's sovereign still rattling in his pocket, and in the ups and downs of the game he won a shilling.

'Lucky at cards, unlucky with women.' Kirkby, a saddler who had worked at the same sawmill, had a long pale scar ending in a whiter circle of skin as big as a florin, where somebody had gone at him with an awl during an argument in one of the sheds. 'I don't know how you do it, Burton. Must be the aces up your sleeve.'

'I'd rather be lucky with women.' Time off from King and Country was taking him painlessly away, but he was riled at Kirkby calling him Burton. 'It just happens, like everything else.'

'As long as you're lucky at something,' Kirkby said. 'I know a few poor bleeders who don't have any in all their lives.'

Oliver looked at scenery little different to that at home. 'It says we're at Sleaford. They seem to be shunting us all over the place.'

'You'll get used to it.' The corporal opened a tin of corned beef, a tongue-wetting aroma when air hissed out. Hardtack biscuits and a tin between two filled their stomachs. 'My mother used to make a stew for the whole family out of one like this.' Beardmore the carter had done five years as a Territorial. 'Sparetime soldiering kept me on the straight and narrow,' he told them, his smile almost diagonal. 'And the perquisites were welcome. But one tin of bully for six had to be enough, though we loved it when Mam put carrots and onions in as well, and the fattier the better. These biscuits'll break my teeth, if I'm not careful.'

'You've got to crumble them with your fingers.' The corporal opened his clasp knife. A thatch of black hair came almost to his eyes, Oliver wondering how good he would be when using his brains. Tim the Ostler, if ever there was one, though he knew his trade in most respects. 'You put it in your fodder box, but don't swallow till the spit's melted it, or you'll get toothache terrible.'

'It's a good thing an old sweat like you's with us,' Kirkby said, 'to tell us how to go on.'

'He wasn't very clever at getting the horses on board,' Beardmore said. 'A good job Burton put us right.'

'Shut your fucking mouth,' the corporal said, 'or you'll be on a charge when we get to Diss.'

'Try any of that, and you'll go flying off the train, when it speeds up a bit,' Beardmore said. 'You shouldn't swear in front of enlisted men. It's against regulations.' The trucks jerked at the sound of a whistle. 'What else is there to eat? My guts are still rumbling.'

'We'll be boxed up in here for weeks,' Kirkby said.

'As long as we're on the train we aren't working,' Beardmore laughed. 'It suits me down to the ground.'

Kirkby looked at Oliver. 'How about another of them lovely fags?'

Whatever you had, you shared. His father might well have kept them to himself, but Mary Ann said you must give what you could when asked for something. Soldiers were your mates, not beggars, and he passed them out, though the corporal huffed and told him to keep it, Oliver thinking that some people were born unhappy.

'I'll make it right with you.' Kirkby held a match for them. To use only one, he waited till the flame was about to burn out, then spat on two fingers and held the charred piece, and while the flame consumed the rest of the wood he was able to light the last cigarette. 'When we get to where we're going I'll be put on saddling.' Smoke towards the window bounced back on him, a cloud he waved away. 'It'll suit me, because I've always done it. Do you know what it takes to make one? All you've got to remember is: eight stitches to the inch. That's what I was taught. I can hear my father now. In fact I'll never forget the old bastard till my dying day. He bawled it when he set me to work at thirteen, and I made a mess of things. "Eight stitches to the inch." Smack – right on the chops. "Did you hear me, you careless lump?" Smack, again. "Eight stitches to an inch, not one more and not one less." Thump. And if I didn't get it exactly right from then on it was a boot up the arse, after the biggest bang of all on the napper.'

'As for me,' Oliver said, 'it was seven nails to a horseshoe. The old man didn't care if I couldn't count up to ten, as long as I knew what seven meant. Not that you dared get it wrong, with him hanging over you like the Sword of Damocles.' He held out the rest of his Gold Flake, and by the time they were passing Ely the compartment was filled with comforting smoke. 'Have one now, Corporal?'

He let go of his sulk, and puffed amicably with the others. 'Parents?' he said. 'I've shit 'em. They're all the same, though they can't bother us anymore. That's one thing the army's good for. My father's in jail, and serve the bogger right. He tried to murder my mother. I ought to kill him when he gets out in five years, but I shan't want to know the swine. I don't fancy swinging, anyway. All I do know is that if they put him in the army he'd frighten the Germans to death.'

None had been up a whole night before, so those not looking out for the horses dozed, the corporal's head against the window, mouth open as if never to wake again. The air vibrated from an orchestra of rhythmic snoring, and Oliver as the only man with a watch was left to call the changes of shift, which gave him little rest. He stayed alert, till prodding them awake when they got to Diss.

Arms piled on the gravel of the siding, they unbolted the doors, easier than expected to get the horses off. Oliver found the trooper sent to meet them smoking his pipe in the station-master's office. He looked up: 'You've come, then?'

'Doesn't it look like it?'

'I've been waiting for you, and you're none too soon. So many horses have gone sick. I hope those you've brought don't start pining for Sherwood Forest like the others.' He stretched, and knocked the ash from his pipe, which Oliver thought was going to take all day. 'I'll give you a hand to get them off.'

'They're out already.'

The cavalcade trotted to Palgrave leaving a trail of dung they had been too nervous to let go on the train. 'There's a good breakfast waiting for you,' the trooper shouted into Oliver's ear. 'Coffee as well, piping hot, as long as it ain't all gone. The eggs are fresh and the bacon's good, and the bread ovens have been working full-time. But now let me tell you what you'll really have. Bully beef, hard tack that the navy threw out and, oh yes, if you're lucky, a bit of mousetrap cheese. But there's all the tea you can swill down, cauldrons and cauldrons of it – without sugar.'

'What bleddy concert party did they pick you out of?' Beardmore called.

Only the names were different to the area he had left but, having marched, entrained, and ridden to get here, he felt so carefree as never to doubt he would come back safe from the war. He wondered whether *The Golden Treasury* had been put together in the village they trotted through, so bright and homely in the early dawn that he regretted not having brought the Sunday School prize from home, though in the next letter he might ask his mother to post it.

He was happy at the jingle of harness, occasional neighing, shouts and handclaps from children at the doors and bedroom windows, urging them on as if they were the most important people in the world which, he smiled, they were, at the moment. Out of doors was the only place to be, however dozy he felt after all night in the close air of the carriage. The early breeze was a treat to freshen the senses, a trace of cloud to look down and wish them well.

Pennants fluttered from marquees among the lines of tents, a bugler sounding reveille in the central square of the Hussars' area. Men swilled themselves at the ablution troughs, queued for breakfast, or groomed their horses.

The trooper dismounted beside Oliver, who looked at a squadron of Lancers cantering by from the Diss direction. 'They've been on patrol, as far as the coast,' he was told, 'to see whether the Germans have landed. We're all part of the Mounted Division, and that's what we're here for. There's rumours every night that the Germans are coming, but it'll be the day of our lives if they do. Every man-jack's as keen as mustard.'

In line for breakfast, mess tin and irons in hand, he thought: I'm here to kill Germans if I get the chance, and if they don't kill me first – though they'd have a job should they try. Sweat under his cap from the sun's heat, and heavy khaki cloying his body, a slight soreness at the feet, he exulted in the way he felt because it was no longer up to him how much time would be spent where he was, nor to what part of England or even the world he would be going next. Everything was new, and to be on the move was all that mattered.

The roughest food tasted good when you were hungry, which he always was, commons of some sort turning up. Kirkby kept a seat for him at the trestle-table, sparrows darting for crumbs or alighting on horse manure to pick out undigested bits. The regiment owned him yet he felt more free than when under the basilisk eye of Burton where he had at times been no more than a slave. Here he was among friends and equals, and those above in the hierarchy could never be as harsh and villainous as his father.

The neat mechanical contraption of a mobile forge was little different in principle to what he had been used to, and simple enough on being shown its workings. Much to be done, the days passed. From five o'clock reveille and through till dusk he made shoes for horses which had lost them on patrol, or worn them so far down they needed replacing. The sergeant-artificer said the army had no use for horses that went lame, while all Oliver knew was that nobody had.

Handmade shoes were put together from new bars of iron or, more often, from worn-out shoes, because not enough could be carried on the wagons to make new ones. Of the different types of shoe the first four sizes were for cavalry and small horses, and others for heavier breeds of the artillery and engineers. Years under Burton's tuition made everything easy. Out of two worn shoes he produced a strong and sufficiently blended piece of metal from which a new shoe could be made, adept at wasting nothing because Burton, whenever trade was slack, always set him to making new shoes from heaps of cast-offs. With such skill he thought the army had him cheap, but he was satisfied with the arrangement because food and shelter were taken care of.

Farriers also learned to ride without saddles or stirrups, or became part of a line galloping for the kill across the fields. Before the war, eight months were needed to fit a man for the saddle but, as the sergeant bellowed, we have to train you in as many weeks, till you're second to none, and will go through any Hun cavalry screen as if it's made of brown paper.

Sword in hand brought out a wilder Burton, surprising Oliver, a primitive inner force never suspected, a space being filled almost against his will, but he was spurred on for the charge with a weapon that had its uses, no time for thought except what concerned the hill or wood in front.

Horses were made to lie down on their own and come to the trooper when called, and even if shots were fired they must remain standing. Scouts who knew map-reading rode cross-country by day, marched on compass bearings in the dark, got from place to place under as much cover as possible. On field exercises they were given the map reference of a supposed enemy position and told to get there, Oliver regretting that farrier work kept him from much of this.

Exhausted by close of day, he washed and changed into walking-out uniform, lucky to be let off once for work well done. It was still light and he walked into Palgrave for a pint. Officers went to the Crown Hotel in Diss, some in motor cars, others on their chargers, but he found a pub corner, smoked a cigarette, and supped a strange brew, though welcome to a farrier's throat. Alma came to mind, but he tore the vision away, to speculate on work to be done in the morning, or to wonder where in England the regiment would go next. Anywhere would do.

The beer went in a straight drain down his throat, his tankard empty on the ironlegged table. He watched a darts game, till a man in gaiters and deerstalker hat put another pint by his elbow: 'Can't see a hussar without a drink.'

'Thank you, sir.' He stood, to shake the offered hand, of a farmer perhaps, with his pink face and affectionate blue eyes. The man went abruptly back to his whisky at the bar, as if embarrassed by his action, and Oliver thought the spirit of the country good if this was how soldiers were treated.

In spite of money in his pocket he put on his cap and went back to camp. He folded his clothes carefully in the crowded tent, before going through the gate of oblivion into sleep.

*　　　*　　　*

They grumbled at the bullshit of a kit inspection, every item to be accounted for, smartened up, and laid out. The regiment paraded in full field service order, alignment perfect for the march to Diss. They filed into the first of four trains taking them to Colchester and through Chelmsford. Eight men to a compartment, talk was low, they seemed awed by the murky spread, the endless cuttings and buildings of London. The train jumped points every few hundred yards, buildings so close they might come together and stop them getting on.

The country beyond was flat and nondescript. They played cards, broke into their rations, and made a home out of every space as if, Oliver said, they were on an excursion to Skegness.

They detrained at Reading, cookwagons waiting to hand out a meal of stew and bread. Oliver found warmth for the night in a hut of the cattle market near the station, others bedding down in the sheep pens. As the sergeant said – and you could always rely on him to say something – this is the Savoy Hotel compared with what you'll put up with later. Right or wrong, Oliver didn't care, and set his pack down for a pillow. Talk and laughter went on into the night, blotted out by passing trains or the shunting of trucks. The scrape of a mouth organ fell silent at the sergeant's command.

Oliver saw in his little pocket diary that it was 1 September. The regiment mounted and formed up by the station. When the thousand-yard column clattered out of the cattle market and went through the silent streets Oliver felt like a king on his high horse riding to war, laughing at the thought that though never making a king he would surely be going to war.

The Thames flowed under the bridge, a boat steaming in the London direction, trees and bushes dawn-black along the banks, a cotton-wool drift of smoke between the houses. To be on the march was the only tonic for an enlisted man, cutting away tendrils of the past still clinging to his boots. Yet family and house were close, and he hoped letters would be given out when they reached Churn Camp.

Fresh air swept his brow. To take his cap off would be very heaven, but he enjoyed the jingle of harness and clip-clop of massed hooves jostling with birdsong. The sky was clear and he was hot in uniform, but so was everyone. Cool-looking woods patched the hills to either side, and he thought how pleasant it would be to sit in a glade and read.

They bivouacked at Woodcote, officers finding billets in cottages, the men to bed down in barns and stables. Oliver spread his groundsheet behind a headstone in the churchyard, sufficient protection from the night's chill.

A morning's march led them to the riverside village of South Stoke, where the usual bell tents were ready, twelve men to circle clockwise with their feet at the centre, such accommodations scattering the Berkshire uplands. Water for the horses was drawn in canvas buckets twice a day from the Thames.

On fine afternoons young men and women cycled from Oxford to see soldiers at work, march and gallop. Oliver smiled at Kirkby's Nottingham shouts, unfit for anyone's ears: 'Come down here, duck, and see what this throstle's made on!' Beardmore joined in: 'How about a bit of hearthrug pie? Can I take you courting on the Forest?' colouring the young men's cheeks more than those of the girls, who often blew kisses and waved back.

People on steamboats fluttered handkerchiefs, but the hussars soon couldn't be bothered, thinking it strange that buntinged vessels were still in service, however far away the battle line was. Two young women, all hats and ribbons, came close in a rowing boat: 'Remember us to Paris!'

'Berlin more like,' a soldier cried, but rumours every day that they'd be packing up for France were always false.

Filling buckets was mindless enough work to bring Oliver's mother and sisters vividly to mind. Burton's face was wilfully blanked away, though Mary Ann would no doubt tell him not to think evil of his father, even if she knew what he had done, because without Burton she wouldn't be able to go on living, in spite of the hard times he had given her. Everyone was redeemable, and Oliver knew he should endeavour to go by her laws rather than Burton's, who could hardly be said to have any.

When in charge of a detail for watering the horses it worried him to hear Burton's voice behind his own, a persona that had its uses though he tried not to feel ashamed, because it was always effective when the men began larking about.

Off duty, a cloud the shape of Baffin Land on the map followed a boat to London. He watched the placid smokey green stretch of water flowing by, and listened to birds fighting for space to manoeuvre overhead, or squabbling for food around the bushes, such intricate music mingling with shouts of command and the neighing of horses.

Soldiers in the gnat-filled twilight stood outside the tents to sing *O My Darling Clementine* and *Danny Boy*, popular but sombre tunes. Oliver preferred to listen, not knowing why, though he liked hearing the songs.

Letters were given out at the Divisional Post Office, items bundled alphabetically, meaning Oliver's name was called early. From the postmark and the writing a letter could only have come from Alma. The previous one, in his tunic pocket, had been sent on from the drill hall, and he'd thought of throwing it into the fire, because nothing she could tell would be what he wanted to know. Their lives were divided, so whatever was written could only intensify the pain, and he wasn't Christian enough to forgive.

He opened his mother's letter, a single sheet telling that all was right at home. A folded postal order for two shillings came: 'From me and your father, who sends his love.' He smiled at Burton being prevailed on to part with money, and as for his love, he knew what he could do with that.

Albert Beardmore, seeing Oliver with a pad writing hastily to his mother, said he wasn't much of a scholar, so had no way of staying in touch with his sweetheart. 'I never liked school. The teacher was always hitting me, so I ran away.'

'If your girl can read,' Oliver said, 'I'll drop her a line, but you must tell me what to say.'

'Her name's Dora,' Beardmore told him. 'I'll treat you to a pint if you do.'

'No need of that. I'll write to your mother as well, if you like. She can get a neighbour to read it.'

Oliver couldn't think what kind of girl Dora was, but was amused when Albert dictated that he couldn't wait to get back to Radford for another walk up the cut, to that bit of wood called The Roughs near Wollaton colliery, where he would get her drawers down and give her juicy purse a sweet taste of the mutton dagger.'

'Are you sure you want to say all that?'

'Oh yes. She'll like to be reminded. We had some lovely times. We didn't have a bed to jump into so we took all the chances we could get and fucked in the fresh air like rabbits in a thunderstorm. She was fifteen when we started, but we didn't care about that. I don't mind if I have to marry her one day.'

FIFTEEN

Burton's hammerblow brought forth Oliver's image, a smile from that sensitive yet determined mouth in the fire's dull glow. The bellows pumped up a man much like himself, hoping to spot something in the distance before whatever it was saw him.

Now that Oliver had gone the atmosphere in the house was ominous. Burton had never worried about his children as far as health and life were concerned. They worked, played, and were sometimes a torment to him, but they were fed, clothed and shod to the limit of what he earned and of Mary Ann's care. No reason to worry, yet Oliver's absence was painful, and not only because he could no longer get at him.

Mary Ann pined because he wasn't there to be looked after, and Burton sometimes thought he was too much influenced by her, who always lived as if the world was about to end. What comfort he gave didn't make a blind bit of difference.

Thomas and Oswald would tell her time and time again that shoeing smiths were too much thought of to be sent to where the danger was, but it was natural that she ached now that he wasn't at home. Nor could she be consoled that thousands of families suffered the same way. If he had gone off to get married it would have been different, a matter of joy that she could still see him, and make a friend of his wife.

Sons and husbands gleefully broke their bonds, having waited all their lives for the chance to spite their families and escape. They ran to feel the hot shilling in their palm, Burton went on, and he hoped they'd be happy, though knew they wouldn't for long. Every man was caught by the madness of wanting to get out of the country, even at the risk of his life, as if it was a Sunday

School excursion and they could come back the moment they found it wasn't.

The others were in bed, and he sat waiting for Edith. Ten o'clock had gone. A train hooted along the embankment across the field, the dog growled and dragged its chain around the kennel, and wind rattled the door so that, thinking it might be her, he looked to make sure the stick was in its place. It was, but he stared into the fireplace until eleven o'clock, enraged at his enforced idleness, or the sleep he was missing. Mary Ann came down in her nightdress: 'Where do you think she can be?'

'Go back to bed. It's no use two of us waiting.'

'I can't sleep while she isn't here.'

Neither could he. Everyone of the brood had to be under the roof before he could close his eyes. He set out mashcans and knapsack on the table Mary Ann had already laid for breakfast. 'She knows that if she comes in at this time she'll have a sore back for a week.'

'You shouldn't hit her.'

'But where is she? It's pitch-black outside, and she deserves what she'll get for not thinking about how upset you'll be. But she's gone, I'm sure she has. So go to bed.' He riddled the ash from the fireplace bars. 'She won't come back.'

'Something might have happened to her coming up the lane.'

'Not if I know her.' Of the Burton girls Edith was the one most able to care for herself. She had liveliness and good looks, but was also strong and with a mind to match. She could give as good as she got from anyone. 'We'll know soon enough where she is. Let's go upstairs, then.'

Little to do, he left Oswald in charge and walked to the Nottingham Arms. The army had commandeered so many horses that times were getting hard. Some forges had closed because even farriers were joining up. Harry the bartender came to serve. 'How's your Oliver?'

The first gulp tasted of soap. 'He was all right when we last heard.'

'Morgan's two lads have gone. They're with the Robin Hood Rifles, in Hertfordshire.'

Not worth talking about. He drank, and at the click of a door-latch saw Alma looking at him from a few feet away. 'What are you doing in a place like this?' he asked.

'Oswald said you'd be here.' She had much to say, features taut, eyes red, and hair he saw as untidy, which disappointed him. He would drum it into Oswald that he must never again tell anybody where he was. 'What is it you want?'

'I don't know. There isn't much I can want. And if there was I wouldn't get it from you.'

He called Harry. 'A whisky and water over here,' then turned back to her. 'If there's anything I can do for you just let me know.'

She sat by a table. 'I've sent Oliver two letters, and he hasn't written back.'

'Nobody can make him, though I expect you'll hear soon. He's a young soldier. A young fool as well, but no more than anybody else these days.' From his full height he reached her warm and pulsating wrist. 'I'd write to a nice young woman like you if I was in his place. Or I'd get someone else to do it for me.'

She sipped her drink, and smiled, as if pleased at so many words from him. 'My letters were long. He should let me know if he's received them at least.'

'Give him time. I expect he's busy. He'll come round.'

'I'd like to think so, but don't see how I can. Not after he found out about us.' The whisky gave neither strength nor pleasure, and her face twisted into weeping. 'I don't know who I am anymore. I only want to die.'

Not another one, he said to himself. Mary Ann, all of his daughters, and now her. Oliver can't know how lucky he is to have so many women blawting over him just because he went for a soldier. And if she didn't know herself, then she should. He expected everyone to know themselves, otherwise why were they alive? She would have to know herself one day, because if she didn't nobody would do it for her. 'You're too young to die,' he said kindly. 'And too good looking. Drink that, and have another. It'll buck you up.'

'I'll be sick.'

It looked as if she might. 'Not with all that water in it.'

She looked away. 'I was sick this morning, before I had anything to eat or drink. Perhaps I'm getting a cold.'

He gave a grunt of premonition, but hoped he was wrong. 'You must look after yourself. Oliver will be back one of these days. People say it'll be over by Christmas, and even fools have been known to be right. Are you sure you won't have another?'

She wiped her tears. 'I have to go.'

Oliver was a double fool for ignoring such a fine young woman, in spite of what had happened. He watched her to the door, disappointed that she hadn't taken another drink, because they might then have talked and become friendly again.

Thomas was sent home with the housekeeping money, and found Mary Ann sitting by the window with her glasses on glancing through Mrs Beeton's cookery book, which Burton had gone downtown to buy for her on hearing she would like to have one, not long after he had struck her, when even the claddach ring seemed too feeble an apology.

She recalled Emma Lewin engrossed in her Mrs Beeton, and to have one herself was a connection to the happiness of the past. On seeing her squint at the small type Burton had also taken her to be fitted with spectacles, a further good deed he was glad to do, but considered sufficient to be going on with.

She put the coins in her pinafore pocket, and took Oliver's latest letter from behind the clock. 'On the train to Norfolk we passed Ely, and I was sorry we couldn't get closer to St Neots, where you said you had grown up . . . The train was so slow at times going through London that I thought what a lark it would be if I jumped off and came back to see you all. What a surprise that would have been. But I was with my pals, and you don't do that in the regiment. I'd have relished the surprise on your faces though as I burst through the door. I've got stamps and an envelope, and will put this in a pillar box when we get to where we're going.' She always told Burton that Oliver sent his best wishes, which couldn't have been a lie, because even though it wasn't on paper it must have been in the lad's heart to say so.

With Oliver away she had no place in the world, didn't belong anywhere, had no anchor unless seeing his face at table or knowing he was busy about the yard or garden. She couldn't think how she lived much of the time, though she cleaned and cooked and served and kept the house running, almost as if she was two people where before she had been one.

She tried to imagine him on his horse, or shoeing one, or sitting on a stool outside a tent much like the illustration on the Camp Coffee bottle. Or he'd have a pad on his knee writing her a letter, or be eating from a tin plate, or standing in a pub with friends, a pint to his lips.

It was no use talking about him to people in Woodhouse while shopping because they had similar worries, other thoughts bothering them. Then again there was Edith to think about. They hadn't heard anything for weeks. Burton as well was nagged with anxiety on both counts – though less so about Edith – but what could they say to each other that hadn't already been said? Whatever he thought he kept inside, but she knew it could be no less troubling than what went on in her own mind. These days he listened with more patience when she mentioned her fears about Oliver, telling her to stop worrying, that the lad would be safe, that in a year or two he would come back. A comforting hand on her shoulder, he would say: 'There aren't any Germans in Norfolk. He's just in camp there.'

Happen so, but she was hearing all the time of young men killed or wounded in the fighting, photographs displayed day after day in the *Journal* and *Evening Post*. She wasn't worrying for nothing. In no time at all Oliver could be in France, and the weekly gap between his letters became ages of torment. Burton wondered how she would feel when he did go overseas.

A letter from Edith told them she had married Tommy Jackson by special licence. How she had managed it they didn't know, but Edith had always found ways of doing what she wanted. 'It's a terrible thing to do, not telling us,' Mary Ann said. 'We could have given them a proper wedding.'

Burton grunted his agreement, though Edith's headstrong act had no doubt saved them a bob or two. Tommy then joined up as a gunner in the Royal Artillery, after a few days honeymoon at his parents' house. 'Another fool in the army,' Burton said. 'I would have expected better from him.'

Mary Ann wrote that Edith could live at home until her husband came back from the war, hoping she would, but Edith replied that she never wanted to be in the same house as Burton again, to which Burton responded, on Mary Ann hinting as much: 'She can please herself.'

At least Mary Ann had no more cause to worry about her, and in spite of his daughter's opinion, never much of a secret, Burton said she could come home any time, though trying to talk sense to her had been like shouting at a brick wall with your back to it.

When Tommy went to France, Edith got a situation as cook in a hotel at Mablethorpe, intending to stay till her husband came home. Burton was disappointed but, with no liking for the fact, couldn't dispute that times were changing.

Mary Ann took up a basket and went down the lane to shop in Woodhouse, hoping the tent Oliver lived in didn't leak, that the weather was as warm there as it was here, that it would never be raining wherever he was sent, wanting only sunshine in his life, looking on him as a blacksmith rather than a soldier (she still couldn't think of him as one of those) and praying he would never have to kill anybody so that nobody would need to kill him, yet full of fear in knowing that those who lived by the sword inevitably died by the sword.

SIXTEEN

A small feed had been given to the horses, and now the start was delayed for them to drink, which they were often reluctant to do so early in the morning. Major Ley, the inspecting officer – eyes all too aware, large ears that missed no sound, and a broad nose above a well-marked dark moustache – walked the squadron lines to make sure the saddlery was correct, that the withers weren't pinched or pressed on, nor pressure put on the horse's spine, that the shoulder-blade bones had free movement, and that weight was on the ribs rather than the loins.

Oliver, erect in the saddle, knew that his mount was well groomed, accountrements wiped, greased, soaped, scrubbed, polished and, above all, shining. Up since four, everything was in place, and they were ready to go. His sword blade was keen enough to shave with, and his mother would have been frightened half to death to see him wield it.

Much work and little sleep convinced him there was no other life than that of a soldier for scraping away the past, a life even better when the regiment was on the move. Wherever they were at the end of the day it would be one stage closer to France. A rumour floating about spoke even of Egypt, and if so he would see the Nile where Baby Moses was found among the bulrushes by Pharaoh's fair daughter. Alma would envy him, but her letters stayed unopened in his tunic pocket.

The squadron moved through Moulsford, Oliver and other smiths at the rear should horses hang back and have to be looked after. Some NCOs also followed behind in case any men fell out, though none would today. The level stretch called Fair Mile seemed longer than that, for he wanted to get on and see new vistas.

They crossed the ground of ten days ago, where the division of two thousand men had been inspected by the King. Oliver noted his bearded figure and frozenly severe aspect, changing to benign kindness and concern on speaking to the next man. The King was nowhere as tall as himself, something else to tell his parents when he saw them. Even Burton by then might, after time overseas, have more respect for him.

An invigorating tang of caustic horse droppings sharpened the air, fodder that had worked through many an irritable stomach. Five hundred horses traversing the hills would leave soil for flowers and cabbages to thrive. Such fertilizer made the garden sprout at home, Burton often sending the girls to collect what had been left along the lane.

Churn Hill was a green hump in the sky behind, but a good soldier never looks back, the sergeant once bawled. After half an hour they halted on the open downs to check saddles, and for fifteen minutes of the hour, or every three miles at regulation pace, they dismounted and led their mounts on foot, keeping to trail or lane and maintaining a proper distance from the horse in front. A ten-minute break every two hours allowed for a quick smoke or swallow of water, or to loosen the horse's girth and turn its head to any breeze.

The springy turf was easy to ride on, and despite no laxness in dressage the sergeants barked them to attention on approaching a village. They needed little telling, as children clapped from garden walls, men and women waving from the fields.

They halted at East Ilsley among red roofs and bowering trees in a steep hollow of the hills, its pubs increasing every man's thirst. Through a cup-shaped hollow of bare chalk, over the hills to Peasmore, beyond Leckhamstead and on by Hangman's Stone, then down to Welford where Oliver imagined spending the rest of his life it was so embowered in trees, yet so taken with the ride over such fine country he was happier at going on, till flies tormented men and horses, and the trek seemed an endless up hill and down dale, each rider with his thoughts, the camp of morning far into the past, and the place they were going never to appear.

Faces dusty, beiged by sun and wind, they descended to the

Great West Road and crossed the cool Kennet, Oliver craving a swim among its reeds. Eighteen miles, and near to dusk, slow-walking the horses for them to breathe before going into camp, they passed through Kintbury to Hungerford Park, and into the squadron lines made ready.

'If they don't feed us soon I'll eat my bleeding horse.' Kirkby dismounted, and slapped its sweating flank. 'Won't I, Bunty? You'd give me a steak off your arse any time, wouldn't you, my old duck?'

No one got hungrier than a soldier, though Oliver recalled how famished he often was when knocking off from the forge, though hardly as much after such a day's ride over the downs. But animals had to be seen to first.

Beardmore came from the troughs, two buckets slopping water. He handed one to Oliver. 'We're going to be here for the winter, some chaps just said.'

'I hope not.'

Kirkby observed the neat rows of tents. 'I expect you'll get your wish before long.'

Horses unsaddled, rubbed down and tied in the lines, men were told off for guard and fatigue duties. No matter how little daylight was left, a soldier's day never ended. Yet it did. Shirtsleeves rolled after shoeing two horses, he leaned on a five-barred gate to let the breeze dry his face, and lit a cigarette to drive off gnats and flies, which fed on the horse muck. Fatigue parties gathered it up but there was always plenty. The line of hills darkened across the valley, smoke hovering above cottage chimneys as if it couldn't make up its mind which way to go for extinction. Hungerford Park seemed like home already, but so would any place after you'd been there a couple of hours.

From fixing his puttees in the morning to winding them into rolls at night and getting his head down for sleep, the welfare of horses was his concern: rope galls to be doctored, legs to be bandaged, the lame and halt to be attended to, shoes to be made and fitted. Recalling half-forgotten information from Burton made him as much a veterinary officer as a blacksmith.

Days and even weeks went quickly, the flitting hours barely

noticed, work continuous – though when hadn't it been? Only in sleep were you free, until parading in the morning for inspection, taking your place in line for breakfast, dinner and tea.

He was glad when the squadron formed up to collect its fortnightly pay, but an equally good time was the delivery of letters, except that he was stung at another from Alma, because what was there to ask that he could give, and what could he tell her that she would like to hear? He thought of throwing her missives in fragments to the birds, watch them chase as though they were scraps of food. He wanted to lie on the earth and howl at what the letters might contain, except that a soldier must stay strong within the stockade of skin and uniform and get on with his duties. Destroying the letters would be too close to the violence he had enlisted to take part in, so he buttoned the envelope into his tunic pocket with the others, and turned to Beardmore's, which came from Dora. She wrote in no uncertain terms, in spite of faulty spelling and punctuation, that the letter Oliver had written had been welcome and enjoyed. He handed it back. 'You should learn to read and write. I'll help you sometime.'

Sergeant Wilkinson stopped Oliver. 'Burton, you're to go to the sidings in Hungerford and collect a couple of remounts for the colonel. Sign for them, then bring them back to the Park.'

'Yes, Sergeant.'

'And get that scruff Beardmore to give you a hand.'

'Come on,' he said to Albert who still perused his magical letter, 'we've got some horses to pick up.'

Albert took his arm. 'Shall you read me Dora's letter again when we get back?'

'If there's time I will.'

'You're a pal. I'll look after you when we get to France,' at which Oliver grunted, and pushed his hand away.

'That one's a bugger.' The corporal opened the waggon door and pointed to a fierce-eyed grey stallion of more than fifteen hands stamping a hoof in its impatience to get free. 'He's given trouble all the way from Marlborough. I don't know where they get them. People sell anything to the army. Before the war we wouldn't have touched it.'

Oliver steadied the horse onto the station platform and, laying a hand on its mane, it sheered away. 'You won't be the worst horse I've had to deal with, so do as you're told.'

Deeply-arched neck, ribs full and finely bent, chin broad and straight, the rear round and full, legs fine and pasterns short, it was a handsome horse but a lot to handle. The colonel would have some fun taming it.

A few homely words calmed it for a while, then a loop under its upper lip and over the poll with a slipknot brought a slight jerk of renewed restiveness. 'You've had some bad usage, but you'll be all right with us.'

He kept the led horse to the nearside of the road. 'They knew what they was doing, sending you to collect him,' Albert called from his more tractable animal. 'If we go the long way back it'll be nice and quiet before the colonel gets him. Not that I don't think we deserve a pint. What about you?'

He couldn't consider it yet, as they passed the church along the High Street. Albert whistled a couple of girls who, he said at Oliver's chiding, expected no less. 'Maybe a bit of a canter will soothe your nag. Make the bogger pant for its living.'

Keeping the regulation distance from the nearside of the road, he held the reins in his left hand, shortening them by a foot, such an awkward cuss it hardly seemed to have a mind of its own, unless it had borrowed one from somewhere and hadn't yet got used to it.

He steadied the horse into the pub backyard, thinking any man deserved a drink after riding such a beast. Whoever gets him will need a few months to bring him to heel. 'I'd rather be in the trenches than manage this one.'

'I don't suppose you'll say that when you get there.' Albert tied his horse up. 'It's always better to stay where you are. I heard we'll be going back to Norfolk for a while, but let's get a drink. The colonel can wait an extra ten minutes.' He filled his pipe, as if it might be longer than that. 'He's too busy to know the difference, and if he isn't he ought to be. I'll go in and see what I can do.'

Oliver dismounted, and passed over a shilling. 'It's my turn. Pay out of this.' A bucket brimming under the pump provided drink for the horses, but he let the awkward one wait till the last, thinking it might mend its ways if feeling neglected. 'At least we got you off the train quick enough, didn't we, you mean-hearted so-and-so? I wouldn't like to be near you in a thunderstorm. Hold still, while I light up.'

Two men in the yard were arguing, hard to fathom what about for a while, two carters, or farm labourers, family men of about fifty, too old to heed the call from Kitchener's boss-eyes. Oliver presumed that one was from Inkpen, and the other from Combe. The Combe man said that the gibbet on the hill between the two villages belonged to Combe, because those who lived there spent money on maintaining it. The man from Inkpen swore that the gibbet throughout history had belonged to his village.

'Then why is it called Combe gibbet?' the man from Combe said.

'It ain't called Combe gibbet. It's called the Inkpen gibbet,' the Inkpen man retorted.

'That's the first I ever heard.'

'Well, you're hearing it now. My little girls run up there to play. It's all bracken by the woody bit called the Bull's Tail because of its shape. They go up everyday from Inkpen.'

'So I hear you say, but it's still the Combe gibbet.'

'No it ain't. It's Inkpen Hill, so it's the Inkpen gibbet.'

'It ain't on Inkpen Hill. That's half a mile away. It's on Gallows Down. You can see it from the Bath road, as plain as a pint pot at harvest time.'

'Perhaps you can, but it's still the Inkpen gibbet.'

The man laughed with throaty self-assurance. 'Then how is it Combe maintains it?'

'It don't maintain it. Inkpen does. I'll bet you a quart pot to a pickled onion.'

Their argument went on vociferously, as if they had tackled the matter many a time before, and Oliver might have been amused had the subject been less gloomy.

A barmaid followed Beardmore, carrying two pints, and two small whiskies on a tray: 'Compliments of the landlord,' she said. 'He took for the jars but sent you the whiskies buckshee.'

The men stopped their hammer-and-tongs about the gibbet

at such generosity, one calling: 'He's got a soft spot for hussars. His son's in the Royal Berkshires.'

The grey stallion, gleaming malignly, settled itself for a long piss, as if to lessen its weight for another bout of mischief. The rest of the horses took time to do the same business. Oliver lifted his pint, wondering why they had bothered to water the horses since, judging by low cloud and a sudden chill in the wind, they would get enough of it from the sky in a while. 'What's your name, love?'

With her creamy complexion and pile of fair hair he thought her about sixteen, and he smiled when she actually curtseyed. 'Jenny. What's yours?'

He laughed at her cheek in asking. 'Burton, since you want to know.'

'Why shouldn't I?'

'It's no use getting off with him,' Albert said. 'He'd fall over his own toes to get to France. But I'm in no hurry, and our camp's just up the road, so what are you doing tonight, duck?'

'I'm not a duck,' eyes glistening at Oliver as she placed the shorts on a weather-worn table under the window. 'I'll be serving in the bar for you, though.'

He stood erect, arm held out, and brought the jar in for a well-earned measure in the throat. It had been drummed into them that a hussar was ever on duty, so they must be on their way. 'We'd better not have the whisky, though it's bad manners to hand them back.' He drew out a letter to his mother. 'Will you post this for me?'

'I'd like to,' she said, 'but there's people in the pub waiting to be served.'

'It's to his sweetheart.' Beardmore lifted his ale. 'Every girl in Nottingham's hanging on his coat tails.'

'I'm not surprised,' she said. 'But there's a box just round the corner, by the gate. You can't miss it.'

'Look after the horses,' he told Albert. 'I'll be back in a minute.'

'Aren't you going to drink the whiskies?'

'We daren't,' Beardmore said. 'It's bad enough if the officers smell beer on your breath, but if it's neat stuff we'll be for the high jump.'

'Our boss will be ever so disappointed. What shall I tell him?'

'Just pour them on the ground where the horses have done their business. They've made such a flood already. Then you can take them back empty and tell your gaffer how much we appreciated it.'

As he turned to knock ash and dottle from his pipe she slopped the whiskies into the remaining half-bucket of water, then went indoors.

Oliver came back and picked up the same bucket to give the awkward horse a last drink before the final half-mile to camp, pleased to see it drink so avidly. Jenny returned for the tray, and he put an arm around her, a quick kiss on the cheek before she could break free. 'You're red like a beetroot.' He smiled at her excitement. 'It was only a kiss! But you look lovelier than any beetroot. I'll come and say hello when I can get half an hour off from my duties. Perhaps we'll go for a stroll.'

'I'm living in,' she said. 'I can't come out till a week next Sunday.'

Burton had courted a barmaid, but he wouldn't let that put him off. 'I'll see you, unless we're packed off to France. I'm not so sure I want to go now.' He steadied the spiralling horse, deciding to ride it instead of lead. 'Hold still, you damned Tishbite!' He apologized to Jenny for such language, saluted her, and rode out onto the lane.

'Looks like you got off with her,' Albert called from behind.

'A lot of good it'll do me. But she's a lovely girl.'

'I wouldn't mind getting her under a bush, either.'

'Don't be filthy.' The horse reared, and he saw only a troubled moiling of grey cloud. 'This mount's a swine to look after.' A touch of the spurs might bring it to order, but that was a mark of failure. Bad treatment could only make a horse worse, and in any case spurs were discouraged in the regiment, except at certain times.

'It wants a bat across the arse with an iron shovel,' Beardmore cried. 'We'll get it back as quick as we can, then it can torment the colonel.'

The crinkle of the letters on moving his arms called Alma to mind. Perhaps he should have burned them after all, to obliterate her memory. Love died bitterly, and you lived in limbo till another person came along who, in all freshness, you began to love more. He was twenty-four, and hoped to cut all ropes that held him to the past. He felt old, as if he had lived two lives already, yet everything was vividly reflected in the mirror of the past, constantly forcing him to look in and see faces he fought to forget. He wanted strange and open landscapes yet thought what heaven to walk up and down the High Street with Jenny or someone like her, whether or not it delayed his going to France.

Perhaps she flirted with every hussar who called for a drink, though he preferred not to think so. Her blue eyes, like cornflowers plucked from the edge of a wheatfield in August, held the promise of seeing her again. A few minutes' chat across the bar would obtain her full name, and permission to write while on active service. Letters would be a way of falling in love, and if he was alive and in one piece by the end of the war they could marry, and live till death did them part.

Fresh leaves fell on the mottled ones of last year, spots of rain clattering to help them down. 'We shall get drowned in this,' Albert said, 'but we'll be there soon, so it's no use unrolling our capes.'

At the first view of tents Oliver was pulled from his dreams by so forceful a lunge that he jumped before being thrown, disorientated but on his feet. The horse neighed and reared again, galloped through a gate into a field of stubble.

Albert leapt down. 'I'll hold the bogger.'

'You won't do much good. Leave him to me.' If a horse goes mad on you, Burton once said, in his rasping self-assured voice, the only thing is to shoot it. But if you care to risk your life, walk backwards till you're by its side, only don't touch. Talk gently to see if you can calm it. I did once, to see whether or not I could, but swore I'd never do so again. No horse is worth a man's life, or any injury, so get out of the way of a mad horse till you have a gun in your hand, then shoot the devil.

Oliver went forward, but the coal-burning eyes lifted before him, hooves uprising, a pair of neat shoes terrifyingly outlined. He ran, at its feet drumming down and circling the field.

Burton's advice might be good, but he didn't know every-thing. The horse was an awkward cuss, not much worse than others he had known. Albert watched as Oliver went close, using all caution, talking in as gentle a tone as a fast-beating heart would allow. 'Come on, then, Neddy, the world's not such a bad place. We'll get you to the lines and give you a good feed. You can roll about in a sandbath up there, though it's only for horses who behave themselves.'

The horse charged. The escarpment of its chest frightened them both. 'We'll have to tackle the brute, or we'll be late getting back,' Oliver said, running after it.

Such a horse gave no warning. The power of its curving chest came down, a hoof glancing his forearm. He saw no reason for it to be unsatisfied with its existence, but some malevolence against mankind, and him in particular, lodged in its brain. It couldn't have been well cared for, and whoever had sold the swine to the army must have been happy that day. Maybe it had been some gentleman's horse and, on being taken away, could not adapt to new surroundings.

Albert stood well aside and said fervently: 'Oliver, leave the fucker. It ain't worth it.'

His Burton will was up. He would not be beaten. He would pacify the beast, but with ever more caution, as he imagined his father would have shown, and relying on agility to avoid what-ever viciousness played in the horse's mind, he went forward. The earth spiralled to a few square yards of conflict, the horse a falling monument. He swivelled to avoid the hooves, power under his feet to jerk clear, saw nostrils widened with emotion, snot and rain running down, as if more in terror of the world than even he was, but such a dangerous animal he'd never been close to, the mouth open showing a flash of teeth not much worn, evil in the eyes – he was frightened and knew the time had come to get out of the way.

A building on legs, of sheer muscle and flesh coming down, he hoped the horse in its madness would fall over on trying to kick, but a hoof as big as an anvil splayed wide with lightning suddenness on an unforeseen trajectory, unthinking tons of angry flesh behind. He misjudged the speed, and with a cry fell to the ground. Blood spurted, covered a whole side of his face by the time Albert reached him. He left the three horses, and set off in a gallop to the camp.

SEVENTEEN

Verses read to children from the Bible came out of days when she had been happy and in control of her life.

'The vapour of fire wastes the blacksmith's flesh, and he fights with the heat of the furnace; the noise of the hammer and anvil is always in his ears, and his eyes still look on the pattern of the thing that he makes.'

No idlers around the entrance, one glance into the forge was enough to show Burton wiping sweat from a face more lined than when they had been in Matlock. Talking to a man who hammered and shaped at the anvil as if only that gave meaning to his life would be futile. Unseen, she stayed a moment, since no one would notice.

Burton, lucky to be out of the cold rain, was never one to let another's troubles concern him. The hiss of fiery metal in water by his side overcame the sound of rain striking slate tiles, and the slam of hammers followed her up the lane and by the church, head down as if not to be blinded by what she must face, tormented by no longer seeming to know who she was, yet so solid in mind and body that the anguish was unbearable.

A convoy of army wagons rattled on before she could cross the road. Letters to Oliver had gone to waste, a heartbreak written into each, but requests for forgiveness or understanding could not be expected from someone so stiffnecked. The son was like the father in refusing to soften her misery.

Yet she remembered his blameless features when he had taken her to Misk Hill, a memory now too spoiled to give comfort. To enjoy such a poignant vision was a romantic indulgence from days which could never come back. The madness with Burton could not be undone. People looked at rain mixing with her tears as they went by – just another woman crying. She wanted to be dead, but whatever you wanted wouldn't happen. The simple wisdoms of the world were hard to learn, and God alone made the rules.

Lydia was the only person to talk to, or so she hoped, standing by the step, rain washing off traces of soap and pumice. By custom she should have gone down the entry way to the back door but couldn't move, and after a while knocked again, with her fist. If her aunt wasn't in she would go to Trent Bridge, climb the parapet before anyone could pull her back, feel her flight through the air, and then an unbreakable envelope of cold water would welcome her in.

Two bolts were unshot, and her aunt stood in the doorframe, peering through steel-rimmed glasses. 'What a surprise! I thought you were at work.'

'I felt too ill to go in.'

She stepped aside. 'You're all soaked. Why didn't you bring an umbrella?'

She had known Lydia's parlour, even as a young child, to be unlike the smelly untidiness of the one at home. Everything was still in place, familiar and comforting, the round table covered by a lace cloth, an aspidistra plant of outcurving leaves in a laminated metal bowl set in the middle, a small Bible close by, brass clasps always shining, a book she used to open and try to read. A sewing machine in a black case stood on the dresser, and a corner what-not was crowded with seaside pottery figures and coats of arms from trips to the coast and countryside. Alma had played at putting them in ranks on the rug and, not yet able to read, speculated on where they came from.

A framed photograph of her father as a smart soldier in dress uniform, with a pillbox hat and swagger-stick, was far from the wreck of his appearance now. After seven years in the army he was without rectitude of any sort, never able to profit from his work and business, perhaps because he had no sergeant-major to bully him, so turned into an idler only happy after a few pints. Sitting in the pub, he would lament his bad luck, till the beer began to inspire, then tell stories about his service in India.

She followed her aunt into the kitchen-living room, with its piles of lace which Lydia, with other women in the district, fetched as outwork from the factory at the end of the street, collecting her load every few days in an old pram. Working all hours without complaint, she made a living, did so much every day, and if she was unwell and couldn't, laboured into the night to make up for it when she was better. Instead of a ten-hour shift in the mill she preferred working at home, even if it took far more of her time, unable to tolerate the heat and dust in the factory, and the foulmouthed women who tittle-tattled from going in to coming out about how they were up to no good.

Alma saw her busy every day with her mending at the table, time too valuable to waste, unlike her father who hadn't the backbone to go out and find work, and grumbled against whatever prevented him making a living. Yet she could no longer despise or condemn him, having fallen lower than was ever possible for a man.

In her trouble she had come to Lydia because there was no one else, Lydia who took care of herself because, she said, no one would do it for her, and she didn't want any man to do it either, having too often seen how young and happy women were turned into fearful mouse-like drudges soon after getting married.

Alma put a hand to her breast as if to stop the heart breaking through, and didn't see how anyone could help, though watching the care Lydia took at placing a kettle on the half-dead fire increased her hope.

'I'm economizing on coal, but it'll boil in a bit.' She was tall, sallow-faced and thin, arms sinewy below the elbows. Black hair was dappled with grey, and the stern line of her lips contrasted with signs of humour in her eyes. She took crockery from a glass-fronted cupboard. 'Get your coat off, and sit by the fire. You look half-dead, and it's not just the rain, either. Is it because your father's murdered your mother? Or have the bum-bailiffs been and chucked your furniture onto the pavement because my feckless brother hasn't paid the rent? Neither would surprise me.'

The kettle boiled, and she fetched a seedcake from the scullery. 'Have a slice of this. I made it myself. I've never seen you in such misery, so tell me what's the matter.'

Alma put a hand around the cup to warm her fingers, and to

stop it rattling against the saucer. 'On my way here I thought the best thing would be if I chucked myself off Trent Bridge.'

'Whatever do you mean?'

'I've been sick every morning this week. A woman at work said I must be having a baby.'

Lydia faced her from the rocking chair. 'That went through my mind when I saw you at the door.' She put her cup on the hearth. 'But I couldn't believe it.'

'I wish I couldn't.'

'Stand up, and let me have a look at you.' She pressed the stomach, and turned her. 'The woman at work must be right, though trust her to know. Who was it?'

She had dreaded the question. 'I can't say.'

'Eat your cake.' Anger flashed across her dark eyes. 'You'll be needing all you can get soon. So how many men were there?'

'It's not that.'

'I should hope not. He's married?'

'Yes.'

'Was it a teacher at that Sunday School?'

'No.'

She sat down, as if exhausted. 'I suppose I shall have to be satisfied with that for the moment. But whoever it was you can stop thinking about chucking yourself in the river. You'd go straight to hell if you did a thing like that, and I don't think someone like you would want to be in such a place. In any case it won't be necessary to kill yourself because your father will save you the trouble. I know Les. You can't have told him yet, or you wouldn't be here.'

'I thought you might want to kill me, as well.'

'I would if you hadn't always been my favourite. But how can you have been so daft as to get pregnant? It's a shock, I can tell you. But you looked after me when I had pleurisy. Nobody else did. But your father will have to know about it.'

'I'd better go and tell him.'

'Not on your own. Finish your tea, and we'll go together. You won't get drowned on the way because we'll take the big umbrella I use to cover the pram when it's raining and I don't want to get the lace wet.'

Lydia held her hand along the straight and narrow street, every door shut firm as if all inside were dead, water splashing from disordered drain pipes onto the pavement. 'We'll go by the Raleigh. It's quicker that way.'

Alma's footsteps slowed, wished herself far from trainsmoke coiling above the bridge. Low clouds were moving, and she wondered if one would pull her along if she put up a hand, taking her to anywhere but where she was. The rain stopped, and Lydia brought the umbrella down to fold. Lights glowed yellow at the factory windows, a heavy smell of oily disinfectant from rows of machines going full pelt inside. 'They're on war production,' Lydia said, 'though they still make a few bikes. A lot of women have been set on because of all the men joining up, but I'd never work there.'

Alma hoped only her mother would be home, but Les opened the door, the sleeves of his striped collarless shirt rolled to the elbows. The unlit pipe in his mouth was a bad sign. Once tall and slender on his soldier's rations, a stomach bulged under his belt. Having heard them coming, he stood on the step. 'I thought you were at work?'

'Aren't you going to ask us in?' Lydia said.

He moved aside. 'I suppose that's the least I can do for my only sister, who's always been too stuck-up to come and see me, and never even lent me a couple of bob when I was in need.' He grasped Alma's wrist. 'I asked why you weren't at work.'

Half a loaf and a dish of butter stood on the table, an aluminium teapot, cups and saucers, not a good day, they were always short of something, the money she gave them never going far. An empty firegrate smelled of cold soot, and a floorcloth hung over the lip of a half-filled bucket.

'I didn't go in.'

'I can see that. I'm not blind, am I? Why not? Do you want to lose your job?'

'I wasn't feeling well.'

He knew all about malingering. 'You look well enough. You're on your feet, aren't you?'

'She's going to have a baby,' Lydia said.

Hilda came in from the parlour, a small round-faced woman

whose eyes could never, or did not dare to, focus on her husband. She looked at her sister-in-law, having heard the revelation, and thought that for everyone's benefit it might have been spoken less directly.

Les made a fair job of bringing himself to full height, and called from the wreck of his parental authority. 'I could tell. It's obvious already. I had my suspicions a week or two ago, and said as much to Hilda, but that wet fish told me I must be wrong. She said I was a man and didn't know about such matters.' He turned to her: 'Well, you did say it, didn't you?'

'I know. But I feared the ructions if I said what I thought. I only hoped it wasn't true.'

Lydia leaned forward on her umbrella, tired at standing but too proud to request the use of a chair. She pitied Alma but was hardly less sorry for her brother, not nice for anyone to hear of his daughter's bad luck, or gormlessness. 'We thought you ought to know.'

To have it confirmed by his sister was doubly painful, since she had always treated him and his failings without an ounce of sympathy for what the world did to a man who tried his best to get work, and when he did, and slaved all the hours God sent to make a go of it, the client took a dislike and paid him off, which made him even harder done by, and now the present catastrophe stabbed him like a bayonet in the guts.

He stood before Alma and lifted her chin. 'Been whoring, have we, you dirty little bitch? Got your belly up, have we?' She shook her head clear, but the grip was brutal. 'Said you were at Sunday School when you were with some lad. Who was it?'

Hilda rubbed the lamp glass with a teacloth and set it gleaming on the table – anything for her hands to do. 'Don't say such things, Les. It won't help matters.'

'Won't it?' He turned to her. 'You can shut your mouth, for a start, and leave this to me. I always expected something like this.'

'It's not the end of the world,' Lydia said coolly, 'unless you want to make it so.'

'It's none of your business.' Half-fainting, Alma stood as if all life and hope had gone, but the hatred of her father kept her upright. His pot-coloured eyes glazed with rage. 'Who was it, then? We shall have to get you married, and I can only hope that whoever it was has a bob or two to pay for it. I'll wring his bloody neck if he tries to get out of it. Come on, who was it?'

'I can't say.'

'"Can't say"!' he mimicked. 'Oh yes you can.' He opened a tobacco tin in the hope of seeing a few shreds for his pipe, the inside so clear he saw his face and didn't like it, slinging pipe and tin onto the couch. 'Was it that young man who called on you in summer?'

'No, it wasn't.'

'Who was it, then? I want to know.'

His request was expected, and reasonable, but she had to say: 'I can't tell you.' If she did, and her father was mad enough to call on Burton, well, she was saving blood and tears by staying mute.

'You've always been stuck up and stubborn, but if you don't tell me I'll knock your teeth down your throat.'

Silence drove him to madness, and what she hoped would not happen came when the flat of his hand went against her head. She staggered into a mist of sparks, but stayed on her feet. 'I won't tell you,' she cried.

A heavier blow sent her onto the floor, curled in misery and waiting for a boot to strike. His short black moustache was wet with spit: 'Who was it?'

'Oh, Les, don't,' Hilda said. 'She'll tell me later. I know she will.'

He moved to give what his eyes promised, but Lydia stood between, and drew back her umbrella for the thrust. 'If you do that I'll stick this in your beer-belly. And don't think I won't.'

He recalled her temper as an elder sister when they were children, and stepped away. 'You got her into this. She told us she was stopping with you, when she was out whoring.'

Alma stood up, as if to strike back, but Lydia took her arm. 'Come on, you can't stay in this house.'

'You've disgraced me,' he shouted after them on the street. 'Never come back, you trollop.'

They walked silently for a while till Lydia said: 'I know he's my brother, but he's mental, and I can't think what made him like that. He had a lot to put up with as a child, but that's no excuse, because we all did.'

Alma covered the pain with her hands. 'I feel sorry for him. It's my fault, after all. I have to forgive him.'

'No you don't. There's too much forgiveness for what people do to each other, especially what men do to women. The things I hear when I go to collect the lace. Some women have had more black eyes than hot dinners.' Close to the main road she said: 'We'll do some shopping before getting home, and you can help me to carry it.'

Her flesh burned less on being hurried along at her aunt's pace, a blue and white landscape between the mountainous clouds, peaceful without houses or people, and she wanted to be walking on her own among them, the nearest relief from a death she wouldn't now think about.

'I've got some witch-hazel at home.' Lydia reached back for her hand. 'It's good for bruises. But if somebody asks what happened tell them you fell on your face when you weren't looking. They'll believe you. You do get that dreamy look sometimes. What a terrible waste,' she said, a column of soldiers passing on their way to Wollaton Park. 'All these idle men.'

They looked tired as ghosts going into some nether world where none could follow. 'Keep your eyes to the front,' the sergeant shouted. 'And step out.'

Lydia crossed when the first batch had gone. 'Won't you tell me who it was?'

A lamplighter was pulling the gas into flame with his pole, wet pavements shining in the half-dark as if covered with ice, so that Alma righted herself from slipping in a pool of light. The painful drumming in her bones told her she would one day get out of a place which was no part of her, and not by killing herself either. 'I can't tell you.'

'I shan't ask again.'

'Perhaps you'll know one day. But not now.' She was surprised at her strength in not even saying anything to Lydia, and hoped it was a promising sign for the future. 'I'll go on working at the mill as long as possible, so as to save all the money I can.'

'We're going to need it,' Lydia stopped at the grocer's window, 'but you'll be all right with me. One thing about the war is that wages are going up. Prices are as well, because everybody's got work. As for the men, I know I shouldn't say this, but let them kill each other if they want to.'

When she came out with her packets and bags Alma said: 'If I have a boy I'll call him Oliver.'

'So that's who it was.' She put some of the groceries into her arms. 'But Oliver who? It's got to have somebody's name.'

'It'll have mine,' she said.

EIGHTEEN

Four stretcher-bearers and Albert looked on as Surgeon-Captain Rowe spread his burberry so as not to get mud on his trousers when kneeling over Oliver, who lay pale and cold on the ground. The winded horse chewed clover by a hedge, too satisfied at what it had done to wonder about its fate. Albert stood erect, glad that rain concealed his tears, and hoped the bastard would be shot dead, the sooner the better.

Blood soaked the khaki serge to Oliver's shoulders. Rowe took off his cap for a clearer view, a small mirror at the wounded man's mouth showing the hardly-expected sheen of breath, the face narrowed with pain, lips ashy blue, pulse uncertain. A leg kicked out. 'He's a strong soldier.'

Albert felt himself the only man left on earth because he hadn't been able to help his friend, and struggled to straighten his features. 'He's very popular in the regiment, sir.'

'That's as maybe.'

Oliver's head was lowered, tunic opened at the neck. Second-Lieutenant Hanson said: 'How bad is he, sir? We can hardly afford to lose a farrier.'

'There isn't much to be done here in camp. It looks like a fracture at the base of the skull, and some lacerations of the brain I shouldn't be surprised. He must go to the Southern General Hospital.'

'That's about thirty miles away.'

'They'll be able to treat him properly there. The thing till then is to keep him comfortable and still. May God help the poor chap. The orderly will need plenty of morphine for when he comes to.'

Stretcher-bearers took him to the medical-aid tent, where

dressings were put around the wound. When a wagon was found a corporal and orderly were detailed to get him to Oxford. Rowe's signed authorization and particulars of the case were given to the corporal, who elected to drive. 'Go as fast as you safely can. A man's life depends on it. Once you're in Oxford ask for the hospital at St Peter's-in-the-East. Do you know the way?'

'It's through Wantage and Botley, sir.'

'At least you know your geography.'

'I've been there before, sir.'

'The Saturday traffic might be heavy. But take the light wagon. I noticed one free this morning.'

Hanson turned to Albert. 'The colonel will be sending for you, to find out how it happened. Meanwhile, get back to your work.'

Raincloud darkened as the corporal whipped the horse along the High Street. A barge sliding under the Kennet and Avon bridge looked so set apart from the world he wished himself asleep in the cabin, after a few pints from a wharfside pub, instead of driving the cart on a journey likely to be wasted.

The man was obviously near death, but hurry was the order because he was a lad of the regiment whose life depended on getting to Oxford as quick as the old nag would allow. You couldn't tell. Some people go like a straw in the wind, but others have come out of worse. If the poor chap dies he'll be the second since the regiment left Nottingham, because Sadler was crushed to death when a horse fell on him at Moulsford in September. Two dead, and the Germans hadn't fired a shot, though you had to expect casualties in the army, and there'll be plenty when we get abroad. It'll be interesting to see foreign places, but it'll be even more interesting to come back in one piece and tell the family what it had been like.

The orderly felt better off under cover, away from the rain on such a piss-ant day. Burton was so still it was hard to say whether he was here or in the next world already. He'd been told that if he came round and was in the sort of pain he looked like not being able to stand he must take a morphine tablet from the first-aid pack and put it under his tongue.

A rank odour of beerish nausea mingled with cold rain pelted the canvas. Drops came through in places, and it was funny how many different smells rain could have. If you were walking through a field in summer it might be sweet and warm, and you didn't mind such a pong. Along a canal bank there would be a touch of iron in it, he couldn't think why. Rain in town had a stink of horseshit and fag stumps, very unpleasant to the sniffer. The best rain was the sort that slapped against the window when you were in the kitchen, and smelled of nothing except toast and strong tea on its way to your gullet. The worst was that which reeked of soaking overcoat and leaky shoes on your way home dead beat from work on a dark night. But what was a few splashes of cold rain to a trooper?

Oliver's feet stirred, a troubled snore from nose and lips, both arms needed to stop him sliding off the stretcher at the bumps and bends. The corporal on his high seat tackled the hill to Hungerford New Town. A nice pub there, but they daren't stop, much as he would like to, speaking for himself, but the corporal from outside shouted that it was wrong even to think of it. A good enough stretch with little traffic took them over the hill to West Shefford, where a motor in the high street frightened the horse which had to be shouted at and called to order.

'It'll be ups and downs nearly to Oxford,' the corporal mused. 'Unless somebody flattened them out with a rolling pin since I was sent on one of the colonel's chargers to get a box of cakes from that posh pastry shop, though I hope nothing's been done with the more or less level bit beyond Wantage. After that there's only the big up until down into Botley, and we'll be nearly there.'

Oliver was trying to say something, all bubbles and blue spit, calling for his mother, the orderly didn't wonder, like they were supposed to, unless he was married and it's his wife he wants, though if he is married he ought not to be serving in the army but looking after her at home. Anyway, he's too young to look as if he is. What's that you say? Don't worry, you'll be as fit as a fiddle again, though I can't promise you'll shoe any more horses. Might as well make him think he's going to get over it, if he's hearing me at all. That's a nice-looking chain coming from his tunic pocket. I wonder if there's a watch on the end? Some blokes are born lucky to have one. Pity there's no fags. I could do with a smoke.

Clouds moiled and glowered, a dreary day for the job they'd been landed with. Why couldn't the horse have kicked him on a sunny day? Dour hedges lined the road, and a well-fed spaniel ran in front of the cart, from one field to another as if whistled by a bloke they couldn't see. A second dog followed, and he wondered how many more there were. Maybe the hunters were out. They didn't care about the weather. The hooves missed it by inches, and he squibbed his whip shouting: 'Watch out, you blind curs.'

Crows squawked from a great oak tree. On beer wafting its malt delights from a pub doorway the orderly poked his head from the tarpaulin to say again that he wouldn't mind a taste, but the corporal said they couldn't stop under any circumstances. They might, though, pick up a jar on the way back. It's a bloody long way to Tipperary, and I'm already fed-up slogging along this miserable road.

Sparks squealed from the brakes on a steep descent, a work-house two-thirds the way down, a place I might have been in if I hadn't joined the army, the corporal smiled, ready to tackle the obstacle of Wantage. 'Do you know what famous man was born here?'

The orderly moved the flap aside. 'Where?'

'In Wantage. Can't you see the houses?'

'Who was it born here, then?'

'You an Englishman, and you don't know?'

He stopped Oliver rolling, at a turn of the street. 'How the hell should I?'

'I don't know. Some mother's do have 'em. It was King Alfred, you bleddy dunce.'

'The chap who burnt the cakes?'

'Well, you do know that much. He started the navy, that's what he did.' It was a complicated place to find a way through, but an elderly constable whistled, shouted and waved to get them a space in the congestion. A file of cavalry halted to let their red-cross wagon go by, the lieutenant at its head lifting a hand in salute.

'He didn't start the bleddy army after he burnt the cakes, though, did he, that King Alfred?' the orderly shouted, smarting from his ignorance.

'Shut your rattle, while I drive out of this lot.' He turned left across the market place by the town hall, right into Grove Street, and down to the end of town. After the tramline came an awkward angle for a horse and wagon, then the way was clear into open country. The horse trotted across the railway and, a few miles on, over the Childrey Brook and the River Ock. The corporal took out a tuppenny packet of Woodbines, lit one, and even the horse seemed to clatter on more smartly at the smoke in his lungs.

Opening the flap the orderly called: 'You wouldn't have one of them fags for me, would you, Corporal?'

'No, I wouldn't.' The horse went slothful again, so he used the whip, thinking that a month or two before it must have been pulling slag and rammel around a builder's yard.

'They ought to have provided a motor van for what we've got on board,' the orderly shouted as the speed increased.

'Or they could have put him on a train,' the corporal said, when a scream came from Oliver on trying to move. 'He'd have got there quicker, the poor chap, and in a lot more comfort. Here, have a fag, then.'

'Thanks, Corporal. Swear like a trooper, smoke like a trooper, eh? They don't care. He's only an enlisted man.' Head and shoulders came in from the stinging rain. He put an ear to Oliver's lips, cigarette smoke over his face as if it might revive him. 'What's that? Your mother again? I wish she *was* here, instead of me. I expect she'd be a lot more use, though I don't suppose by all that much. Stop moving your legs like that. It'll make things worse if you manage it.'

Oliver struggled as if to get on his feet. The orderly opened his slack mouth, blood and spittle sliming his fingers, unravelled a twisted flattening tongue between the teeth, for a tablet to go in. 'That's the best thing. A bit of old knockout. The less you feel the better.'

Making him as comfortable as the jolt and rattle allowed, he slid fingers into the tunic pocket. 'You don't want to get it damaged, in all this rolling around. It would be a shame, such a lovely ticker.' Oliver's hand stopped him, an effort through dimming waves of sickness and pain, perhaps recalling the acronym of the Royal Army Medical Corps which the men always said meant: 'Rob All My Comrades'.

'Hang onto it, then, if you feel like that. I only wanted to look after it, to stop somebody else getting it off you. We're doing our best to get a move on, and I wouldn't mind if you did come round. Not that it looks like you're going to, but it'd make my job easier. We could talk, then. Or you could talk, and tell me what's best to do for you. When they've mended you in Oxford they'll send you back to your family. Let them fuss over you. I'll bet they will. You're out of the war, and no mistake, one way or the other, so perhaps some good will come of your accident, except it's taking us a long time to get to King Sawbones's Palace. Not that it's our fault. Your watch says it's over a couple of hours since we left, and we're doing the best lick we can, crossing most of Berkshire. Trouble is we'll come back over the hills in the dark, and that'll be a right dance. Lighting-up time's twenty-past seven, and we've only got one lamp for the dark road.'

Ending such a comforting speech he called: 'Do you want me to drive for a bit, Corporal?'

'You do your job, I'll do mine. You're best off where you are. But I hope they shot the horse that kicked him. If they do, I suppose there'll be meat pies for tea when we get back. It was a big horse. Corn in bleddy Egypt all next week.'

'They don't eat horses in the army, Corporal.'

'Not yet we don't.'

The orderly enjoyed talking to someone who could answer back. 'When I see leaves diving from the trees, Corporal, it makes me think we're in for a long war. I didn't think so when they was green and the sun was shining on 'em.'

'Shut your gravy-box, and look after your precious cargo. I've got this beast to manage.'

Oliver's fingers reached for the opposite pocket to that holding his watch. 'What's in there, mate? I'll get it out for you. It ain't good for you to struggle. We don't want your paybook getting covered in blood. Ah, it looks like letters. You don't need 'em, unless you want to make a poultice out of the paper. Maybe there's a ten-bob note inside. No, there ain't. What's this, though?' He opened a gap in the covering, let the wind take the letters away. 'I suppose it's good there's something on your mind, but don't upset yourself, I've put 'em back. What's this in the other pocket? A soldier carrying a folded handkerchief! There'll be plenty of clean hankies where you're going, and lots of nice nurses to mop you up.'

Oxford colleges and spires showed under a low sky from the top of the hill. An artillery column stalled them at the Witney road, men marching behind the shining barrels. 'They're so smart that the sergeants aren't swearing at them,' the corporal said in wonder, as the gunners stopped for nothing and went on.

Over the stream beyond Botley the road was taken up by carts and charabancs, motors and pony traps, wagons and omnibuses, neither space nor order in the eagerness to progress or disentangle. The corporal cracked his whip as they passed the station, a whiff of marmalade from Frank Cooper's factory. 'Makes your mouth water,' the orderly called.

The corporal tugged this way and that at the reins. 'I could walk faster than this. At least it's not raining so much anymore.' He talked to himself. 'Over the bridge and fork right, I think. It'll take me a fortnight to dry out. Then fork left.'

A military policeman at the Carfax crossroads, resplendent in red cap, was endeavouring to sort out the traffic. 'We've got a badly-injured soldier on board, Sergeant,' the corporal shouted. 'Can you tell us where the Southern General Hospital is?'

The whole six-foot-odd of him, coolly raising his swagger-stick, stopped all movement, and came over to talk. A deep fair moustache, blue eyes as hard as stone, well-filled cheeks, and Boer War medal ribbons above the left tunic pocket into which went a lanyard with no doubt a whistle on the end, made a vision of authority to be feared. 'How bad is he?'

'He'll be lucky to get there, Sergeant.'

He glared at the stalled traffic, as if daring a single wheel to turn, and in a blistering voice told a parson in a dog-cart to hold back and not shift till he was beckoned on. 'He will, if I can help it,' pointing the way onto the High Street. 'Keep going, past St Peter's-in-the-East, and over the bridge, then follow the Cowley road. Turn right when you come to a church. And good luck to him.' Waving his stick, he began to sort out the congestion.

'What a fucking bully he was,' the orderly said, halfway along the High Street. 'I thought he was going to incinerate us when he came over.'

'They're like that.' The corporal flicked his whip. 'That's their trade. But we wouldn't have got through without him. As soon as I said we had a soldier on board he was like a lamb to us.'

Soldiers and civilians strolled along the pavements by church and college fronts, those with urgent business using what roadway was free of traffic. Officer cadets were drilling or doing physical jerks inside the quadrangles. The corporal urged his horse on. 'It's like trying to drive through Goose Fair on Saturday night.' Two young women, arm-in-arm, thought him a tormenting brute, but he shook the whip at them, and they laughed on going into the Mitre Hotel.

Morphine no longer got through to the stars or landscapes of Oliver's mind. He clutched the bandages, to tear them away and see how much blood was there, mouth working as if in dialogue with his mother. He called in fear for Alma.

The orderly held his hands. 'Can you hear me when I talk to you? She must have been a nice sweetheart. But we're nearly there, and then your troubles will be over.'

'Father!'

'It's enough to break your heart,' the corporal said. 'This is the church the redcap mentioned. No more jerking around for him in this ramshackle contraption.' He began the turn.

'Perhaps they'll supply us with tea before we start our way back,' the orderly said. 'I'm knackered already, and we've only done thirty miles. Having this poor bloke on board's worn me out.'

'I'll bet it felt like three hundred miles to him.'

'He's very quiet suddenly.' The orderly leaned for another look. Nothing to be done. Only hope he stays in his coma. Leave well alone, is all I can think.

A couple of chaps in white overalls, chasing a tennis ball around the yard, took little notice of their cart entering the gate. Too common a sight for them to jump, but recalling the redcap's method the corporal raged that they had a dying man on board, and would they look sharp and give them a hand?

They unloaded the limp body onto a trolley, while others opened doors into reception. The nurse behind her glass office pressed a button, while the corporal showed his chits to a medical officer.

Oliver's face suggested little more wrong than had been sustained on rugger or football field – common soldiers could be so damned rough – but on turning the head the doctor called: 'Wheel him to the lift,' and to a nurse: 'He's to be made ready for the operating theatre.'

'That's our job done,' the corporal said.

'Now we can get our tea and buns.'

'Not before we've watered the horse. He's got to get us back to Hungerford. I don't suppose he's done sixty miles in one day before.'

After such duty by the stables the corporal talked to the nurse behind the desk about a meal. 'Matron will give you a chit,' she said, 'for the other-ranks' mess. I'll call her.'

The orderly looked at his watch before sitting at the trestle-table. 'We'd better hurry, or we won't get back till midnight, and it's church parade tomorrow.'

Cold potatoes, two slices of bully beef, a scoop of cabbage and a chunk of bread covered their plates.

'Where did you get that?'

The orderly took a long drink at his mug of tea. 'I've always had it. The old man gave it me as a present when I joined up.'

The corporal gripped his wrist. 'You lying thief. You've nicked a dying man's watch.'

He drew the hand away. 'You want to be careful what you're saying.'

'That's Burton's ticker. Hand it over. I'll see it gets back to his family – if he dies.'

'It's mine, I tell you.'

'It was for an hour. Say goodbye to it.'

'You'll only keep it for yourself.'

'If you don't give it me I'll knock you to the ground. And I'll make a report. Never in my born days have I known such a thing. And as well as that, I'll have that postal order you took.'

'Postal order?'

'You went through his pockets. Thought I was blind? Didn't know I had eyes in my arse, did you? A slip of paper it was, so it must have been a postal order. If you don't hand it to me *jildi-*like, I'm going to shake you up and down in front of the nurses till they see what tiny bollocks you've got.'

He gave up his loot. 'A right mate you are. Can't we go shares?'

'I'm not your mate. I'm an NCO in a crack cavalry regiment.' He folded the paper and put the watch in his pocket. 'Now that you've handed it over no more will be said, but just keep out of my way from now on. I don't think that sergeant-redcap at the crossroads would show much concern for your face if I told him what you'd done. I only hope the Germans put a bullet through your windpipe as soon as we get overseas. Now let's eat our grub. It'll be dark in an hour.'

NINETEEN

Morgan knocked raindrops from his billycock hat. 'There won't be many horses left soon, with so many taken by the army. I can't see a lot coming back. Soldiers don't know how to look after them.'

Oswald hammered a shoe on carefully because his father watched from the doorway. Burton hadn't felt well on getting out of bed, eyes less sharp and tongue coated, not from boozing but a touch of the ague – or age, he wondered – that a lot had now that the autumn rain was back. To be out of sorts was rare, never to be mentioned. He was tired and couldn't fathom why, nor cared to. A pain in the back, or a crick in the groin, or a tweak at the bend of an arm, or any sign of a headache, could only be a matter of wilful disobedience on the part of the body, regarded with the contempt it deserved, and if it didn't go away it would kill him in its own good time, but if it did go away there was nothing to worry about, and could be taken as a sign of his God-given right to go on living.

Oswald saw him in the forge uptilt a bottle of the jollop for seedy or sluggish horses and take a couple of swigs, so that by the time the cork was back and the bottle on its shelf, he seemed more his normal self. A grind of knuckle at the eyes diminished the spinal ache. 'Hit the nails a bit harder,' he called. 'They won't bite. You should know what you're doing after all this time.'

Oswald wasn't so afraid now that Oliver had gone. 'I'm doing it my way.'

'The only way is mine, so have less of your lip.' He wished Morgan would go, and let him get on with the work to be done. 'The army's got plenty of motors, though; there'll be so many on the roads we'll have a lot less trade.'

When Sabina came along the lane he felt anger at her being away from school, though it was strange that Mary Ann had put her in a white frock kept only for Sunday. 'What are you doing here at this time of the day?'

She stayed some yards off, her face a chaos of misery. 'Oliver's dead, our dad.'

He looked for a few seconds. 'What did you say?'

Oswald stopped work, and everyone around stood like images in a frieze. She called again: 'Oliver's dead. He's been killed. Mam got a telegram.'

Burton looked into the forge, the fire at half-glow, as if Oliver might be at his usual tasks. He came outside, pausing at the door to pick up tools from the ledge. 'What was that again?'

She wouldn't come closer in case he should smack her around the ears for bringing such news, and told him the third time, but this further demand had been a means of Burton keeping himself steady, and for him to remain still for a few seconds among the silent men waiting around, who seemed equally in shock, and then looking again at Sabina as if indeed wanting to boot her to Kingdom Come and back – to remark in an astonishingly sharp tone that made them realize even more how terrible the by now not unusual news must have been: 'I damned well knew it.'

'Mam says you've got to come home.' Sabina, crying into her frock, agony in each noisy sob, was to remember till her dying day the whiteness of Burton's face as he lit a cigarette. Oswald finished shoeing the horse, and Burton without thought manoeuvred it into the cartshafts. It didn't want to go, as if also feeling that someone's world had changed, and he got it in by force rather than persuasion, would have battered it to the ground had its resistance gone on too long.

'He was such a fine young man.' Morgan thought something must be said. 'He was the apple of your eye.'

Burton turned on him. 'Shut your mouth. We don't know if it's true yet.'

They did, but understood him wanting to doubt. Some mistake had been made. It couldn't be true. They'd got the wrong man. Burton was a common name, and there'd been a mix-up. He wasn't in France so how could he have been killed? They'd had a letter from him only the other day. 'Go home to your mother,' he told Oswald. 'Take Sabina.'

'She'll want all of us.'

'Do as I say. Some mistake's been made. Close the place up, Tom,' he said to Morgan.

'I'll be glad to.'

'Drop the keys in on your way home.'

With Oswald and Sabina gone away hand-in-hand, he put on jacket and cap, and walked in the opposite direction. The sky had fallen in. The slightest hint that Oliver had died was impossible to credit. Houses to either side went black, the church was black, the sky was black, the trams on the main road were black. Oliver wasn't anywhere near the war, so how could he have been killed? Trees along the boulevard were black. Sabina had called out that he was dead but how could it be true? Every word of the telegram was black. The idea of Oliver being dead created the blackest of fogs.

Let the sky fall, it could be no worse. If it was true, and the way he felt told him it was, he would find out how it happened. He would know who was responsible, though if it was the truth, then he would be dead too, and so do nothing. The world went on, and there were so many things you couldn't do or know.

The only building that wasn't black was the public house, massive outside, red-bricked, and rearing to the sky. He stood at the bar yet didn't call for a drink, features so abnormal Harry had to look twice. 'Are you all right, Burton?'

He struggled to open his lips. 'A glass of whisky. A double.' Was he dreaming? He hadn't been aware of dreams before, hard to know what he was doing if he wasn't in a dream, but if this was dreaming he wanted none, never having heard of dreams so heavy they would break your back, like when your son went off to the army and four months later was dead.

Harry took a bottle from under the bar. 'This is the best. Is anything wrong?'

'They say my eldest lad's been killed.'

'Your Oliver? I didn't know he was in France.'

The whisky went in one watery swallow. He turned to go home and see what could be done for Mary Ann.

He walked through Woodhouse, erect and high-headed. Everybody must know by now. On up the lane, he passed the house, unable to go there for the moment, as if a ten-foot thorn hedge held him back. A chalk mark would have been as effective. A traipse to the wood and back might stop the beating in his head, though he doubted anything would.

Mary Ann could not stop weeping. She couldn't be expected to, poor soul, didn't know what to do with herself, couldn't do anything in the scorching anguish that wouldn't leave her alone. It was unbearable to be near her with so much pain in himself. The day after the telegram he got up at five and went to work. Life had to go on. He dragged the lads out of bed to come with him, and earn enough so that everybody in the house could eat, though the hardest labour dulled nothing.

Children scattered as he crossed the Cherry Orchard, rooks creating a raucous palaver on the wet and misty day. The noise of redwings chattering overhead was buried by the rumble of a train. A wind told him that rain would soon be falling.

He took a cigarette from his tin but the match wouldn't light. The next one did, and he put the box in his pocket, at the spot where Oliver had pointed the shotgun. If only he had squeezed the trigger, and had injured me, and I had told everybody it was an accident, and then I had died, he would have been free of me, and might not have gone for a soldier. Keep your back straight, whatever you do, it hasn't even come into me yet what's happened, though I can feel it trying to kill me.

The words would never go away: 'I regret to inform you War Office reports Trooper O. Burton, South Nottinghamshire Hussars died 15 November Lord Kitchener expresses his sympathy' – neatly written on the telegraph form. A few days later a second message came: 'The King and Queen deeply regret the loss you and the army have sustained by the death of your son in the service of his country. Their majesties truly sympathize with you in your sorrow.' The news had been reported in the *Evening Post*: 'BURTON, shoeing smith, died from a kick while shoeing a horse, 15 November, 1914.'

The warbling of a wood pigeon mocked with its certainty of

life. Those doomed to lose their firstborn son hardly know them to be the apple of their eye until they are dead. Beecher's only lad was killed last week in France, and rows of photographs in the papers make it no better for the rest of us. As for Kitchener and their majesties, they've got more to gain from the war than people like us, so let them put their faces in the firing line.

Treading grass and live brambles in the wood, water soaked his trousers to the knees. The cooked smell of greenery came from the stream, where three children with their arses hanging out were putting potatoes, unearthed from Farmer Taylor's field, into a fire. One urchin on his belly was blowing his guts away to keep a small flame alive, and when a pair seemed about to scatter at his footsteps Burton went no closer: 'Don't let Farmer Taylor catch you digging up his spuds.'

One boy had a more knowing face, half-starved but merry. 'We can run faster than him!'

He envied their innocence. Perhaps one had lost a relative already. The world was hungry for young men, and King and Country was never a good excuse. The scum of the earth went into the army because they wanted a job and a nigger to wait on them – though Oliver had had no idea of that. If he joined up because of what I'd done more fool him, but I could blawt my eyes out, though it's too late for that, and tears are always wasted.

On a roundabout way home he stepped over a freshet of rain running to the bridge. In the yard he walked to the outhouse where pig food was stored, took up two buckets to fill with bran and seed potatoes. Ivy and Emily held hands and cried in their misery. 'Stop your blawting, or I'll give you something to blawt about.'

The look Ivy gave was as if she wanted to strike him dead, and if only she could, he thought, what a blessing that would be, though not for her after I'd gone. 'We can't help it, our dad,' Emily dared to say. 'Oliver's dead, and now he's in heaven.'

Grunting his disbelief that Oliver could be anywhere but at the undertaker's parlour, or on his way home by now to be buried, he scooped scraps and potato mash from the barrel. The world might come to an end but pigs must be fed. What had happened had nothing to do with them, whose fate would be decided when Percy came up to slaughter one next week. He worked to dull pain, though nothing could, dumped the stuff in to let the pigs sort it how they wanted.

He took the buckets back. 'Carry these to the well, and get them clean.' Work might ease the girl's minds, but such hope had no chance.

Thomas and Oswald were at the table with Sabina and Rebecca, no cloth spread, as if only alive to the white-faced pendulum clock on the wall, and the isolated heartbreak of a sob from one of the pale girls. 'Where's Mary Ann?'

'In the parlour.' Where you should be, Rebecca wanted to add but daren't, because with Burton you had to rehearse every word before letting it out, and then press your teeth into your tongue to hold it back, more often than not.

Curtains were drawn in mourning, though only a footpath passed the house. A small lamp was lit, and Burton faced her, the telegrams and a letter open between them. He nodded: 'That's all it takes, a few bits of paper.'

She said it again. She said it every day. She came out with it every time she saw him or anyone. 'He hadn't been away four months, and now he's gone forever.' She said it to herself with every breath, every few seconds, no use telling her how often she said it, because she would more than likely go on saying it every minute till the day she died. And so would he go on saying it, and though he would say it only to himself you had to say something aloud now and again in case it was thought you had no heart.

'He was killed by a horse, that's what I can't get over. The times I had to tell him to be careful. And he was careful, at least while I was looking. I know I did my duty in that respect. I drummed it into him from when he was a child. He knew as much about handling horses as I did. And then one had to kill him. It didn't take the army long to rob him of his life. That's what it must have been. The army killed him. If he hadn't joined up he'd have been here now.'

'It seems only yesterday that he was with us.'

'Blawting won't bring him back.'

'I know,' she wailed, 'oh, I know.'

'I could blawt as well, but it wouldn't help.' He spoke gently, afraid of too soft a tone in case he did weep.

'I still can't believe it,' she said.

'Nor can I. Read me the letter again, from his chaplain.'

Her fingers shook, voice barely audible, though he'd heard the words a few times already. '"Your son died while shoeing a horse."'

'That's wrong,' he said. 'He wasn't killed while shoeing a horse. That's a lie.'

'A parson wouldn't lie,' she said.

'Believe what you like. Go on.'

'"He received a blow at the head from which he never recovered. He was an excellent soldier, and his friends in the regiment will miss him sorely. I very much regret having to send you such sad news. You might like to know that the horse which killed him was shot."' She folded the letter carefully back into its envelope. 'A lot of good that did, to kill the horse. But it was kind of him to write and tell us what happened.'

'I only wish I'd been there to shoot the horse myself,' he said after a silence. 'If I had been it wouldn't have kicked him to death anyway. A few tricks up my sleeve would have settled its hash. It wouldn't have got on its legs again for a month, either. Or I'd have pulled Oliver away and told him to leave it alone.'

'You weren't there, though, were you?' She spoke as if he ought to have been, that it was his fault he hadn't been there, but he knew that whatever happened to one of your children had to be your fault for having got them into the world. So she was right in what she said, and all he could do was help her inch by inch through her grief, while enduring his own.

'I know a few more tricks than he did. I've had more experience. Our family's been blacksmiths for generations, and none of them was injured by a horse, beyond the odd nudge or two. But why did he try to shoe a mad horse in the first place? He should have run away. He could have done. Nobody's obliged to shoe a mad horse.'

'I pleaded with him not to enlist,' she said.

'So did I, but you couldn't tell him anything.'

'I can't believe it. I remember holding him up in my arms as a baby, and making him laugh. And how he used to laugh! I know what made him enlist. It had something to do with that girl.'

He had been waiting for that. 'No, it wasn't because of me. He didn't have to go. You can't blame anybody. Everybody was joining up. They still are. There was a queue at the barracks, and he got pulled in with the others.'

'It was about that girl,' she said. 'He didn't tell me, but I'm sure I'm right.'

There was no answer, and he could only let it rest, if ever it would, but if that was the case he's got me for life, and maybe longer. 'Blame it on me, if it'll help.'

'Nothing can help.'

Nor me, either, he was unable to say. His large working hands reached across, but she drew hers away. 'We've got to keep on living,' he said, 'that's all I know. The girls are in the kitchen waiting for something to eat. Oswald and Thomas have been at work all day, and they're hungry.' As I am, but he couldn't say that. 'It's time to get up and make the dinner. You look as if you could do with a bite.'

Remembering their courting when she had served his beer with such a smile at the White Hart, and the glistening of her eyes on his first night back from Wales, caused him to put out his hand again. She lifted it to her lips, and washed his fingers with her tears. He regretted that the house was so full of children, and when they stood to embrace he could tell that she did too.

There was nothing for it but to lead her into the kitchen so that she could start work on the meal everyone needed. Seeing the case of prize horseshoes on the wall he recalled how Oliver helped him put them in with the correct space between, an instinctively good eye for such arrangements, and enjoying that early confidence Burton placed in him.

Mary Ann came out of the parlour like a sleepwalker, but now, looking around the room, she seemed to wake up, and began telling the girls what to do.

*   *   *

An army wagon came from the railway station, a coffin on top with Oliver's body inside, a Union Jack draped over. People stood by their front doors as it passed through Woodhouse, and went under the bridge up the lane. Four soldiers laid it on trestles in the parlour. 'His sword's on the coffin,' the sergeant said, 'and we'll display it when we get to the church tomorrow.'

'It's a shame he wasn't wearing it at the time.' Burton took it from the scabbard. 'He sharpened it, didn't he?'

'Yes sir.'

'It looks a handy weapon. He ought to have rammed it into the horse.'

'They were only given out last month, and he wouldn't have had it at the time, being a shoeing smith.'

The lid was lifted, and Mary Ann began keening again, his death more believable now that she could see his body. 'They've done something to the face,' Burton said. 'He must have been knocked about a bit.' The texture was that of false fruit he had seen on peoples' tables, nothing like flesh, though he was glad it seemed normal enough to Mary Ann.

His face was not so much at rest as utterly dead, made of putty, like that in a photograph taken at the seaside, with the head poked through a hole surrounded by unusual scenery, a bad copy of the living man, eyes closed, and cheeks more filled. Either the army diet had improved him, or cotton wool had been stuffed into his mouth at the undertaker's parlour. The sword in its scabbard lay by his side, tunic buttons polished to shine like golden sovereigns.

Mary Ann kissed him as if tears, falling on cheeks and lips, would recolour his features and bring him back to life. Burton wished to God they would, he'd have spilt some of his own then, and blood as well, and been the happiest man on earth, but nothing could do that. The army had killed him, and what else could you expect? No army looked after its men when there were so many to draw on. His father and mother had died in the fullness of their lives, and so had Mary Ann's. Perhaps she was thinking of her parents but, whoever they had in mind, what was left of Oliver was here to receive the final kisses of Mary Ann and the rest of the family, a scene to break the heart if you did but let it.

He gave each soldier a glass of beer, and while they were drinking took the sergeant back into the parlour. 'Now you can tell me what really happened to my son.'

'How do you mean, sir?'

'He wasn't killed shoeing the horse when it kicked him.'

'That's what I was told.'

'That was what you were told to tell me, but you know that's not the truth.'

'I don't understand.'

'Well, I'll tell you. No blacksmith was ever kicked while shoeing a horse. If a horse tried to kick while being seen to in that way it would fall down. A horse can't kick on three legs. It's an impossibility.'

'I wouldn't like to say anything about that, sir.'

'I don't suppose you would.' He was lying, or he really didn't know, so Burton let him go. They would never tell the truth.

Emily, Sabina, Thomas, Oswald, Edith, Rebecca and Ivy: each face bore its misery as they stood at the coffin, resplendent happiness only on Emily's face: 'Oliver's gone to heaven. He always said he would.' Then her features distorted into tears.

'I've told you,' Burton said. 'There's to be no blawting in this family.'

'Why can't there be?' Edith wailed. 'He was worth a hundred of you.'

A tremor at his cheeks, but he said nothing. Let them cry, for all the good it would do. It wouldn't bring Oliver back. He was about to leave, unable to endure so much warranted grief, when the door rattled to let someone in.

They saw Alma standing there. A loosely buttoned coat hung about her as if it had been rained on for a week, or as if she had slept in it under a hedge. She looked older to Burton than she should have. 'What do you want?'

Anyone could come in who wanted to, so he needn't have spoken. One or two would call from Woodhouse or the sawmill, and the Ollington sons would show themselves on finishing work at Taylor's farm.

Alma pushed a way forward with bowed head to the coffin,

hands together as if in prayer. Crying stopped, not because Burton had cowed them by his impossible demand not to blawt, but at Alma's long intent look, eyes going from head to foot of the body as if to make sure all of it was there.

She's pregnant, Edith said to herself, like me, and then a weird scream of agonized distress shocked them, Alma's wail going on until everyone except Burton was pulled into an intensity of keening that seemed to vibrate the walls. The girls turned to each other as if for explanation as to why their control had gone, or to comfort each other as they stared down at Oliver, unable to believe he was dead, that he would never again make them laugh at his jokes and quips, wanting him to get up from his coffin and say he had only been pretending. They turned to Burton, who had always kept them in order, as if daring him to condemn their behaviour.

He looked at Alma, then over her shoulder to view Oliver, gazed about the room as if desperate to find refuge from the terrible unstoppable commotion on each mournful and individual face. After the long slow look his features suddenly shivered from their habitual iron composure, which none present had seen before and never would again. He drew out a large red handkerchief, and from the albeit noiseless movement behind the covering of his face, they knew that the soul was being torn out of him at last, Edith not alone in thinking that if it wasn't now it never would be.

Ivy and Rebecca helped Mary Ann to get the dinner ready, and Thomas went with Oswald to the well. Edith, having twigged what was wrong with Alma, walked arm-in-arm with her down the lane, since she had seemed too distressed to leave the house alone. 'I can see you're going to have a baby, duck. So am I. My husband's Tommy Jackson. He went off with the gunners to France, and I haven't heard from him for over a fortnight, so I'm beginning to wonder if he's all right, but then, I would, wouldn't I?'

'I knew him,' Alma said. 'He'd sometimes come to the Sunday School and collect his little sister.'

'That's him, all right!' Edith laughed. 'Though I shouldn't

think he ever went there himself, the way he carried on with me. "I've rented a hedgebottom for the weekend," he used to say. "It cost me the earth, but I know it's going to be worth it. Just come with me, and let me show you where it is. I've fixed it up with a double bed and a birdcage!" He's a real devil, but I've always loved him, and I know he loves me. What's a man for if he can't make you happy in that way? Oh, I'm sorry. You're crying again. I feel like that as well,' and they wept through the dim long tunnel, Edith stopping the moment they were in the open, unable to bear anyone seeing her upset. 'When I have my baby I'll call him Tommy, after his father, and I think I know what you'll call yours. Our Oliver was a bit of a lad. All the girls liked him, and it never took much to see why.'

She stammered. 'I'm not sure what I'll call him.'

'Well, you'd better decide, because if you don't have a name ready you might say the first one on the tip of your tongue, and afterwards it might not be the one you wanted. I must know what to call mine in case I blurt out my father's, which is Ernest, and I never want to do that, because he's been a bogger to me all my life, though he's better to me now I'm married.'

Alma felt close to Oliver's goodlooking confident sister. She liked her, and in her misery wanted to hold her. 'Mine might be a girl.'

'Well then,' Edith said, 'if mine is I'll call her Ivy, like my sister. My baby will always be Little Ivy, and my sister will be Big Ivy. That way there'd be a difference, and we'll always know who's who. I'll walk you to the top of the road, duck, but then I must go back to help my mother.' It was impossible not to weep. 'I can't believe our Oliver's dead. It don't seem true.'

'I can't believe it either. I never will.' They embraced in mutual misery and concern.

'I'll see you at the funeral tomorrow morning.' Edith kissed her wet cheek. 'It's at Lenton, at eleven. I don't suppose there'll be many there, but I'd like all Nottingham to come and say goodbye to Oliver.'

Mary Ann wept through the service, so many tears from the thirty or so in the church that you could rear a patch of prize marrows, Burton thought, who felt himself bleeding inside. Oliver deserved no less, but the vicar rattled on about what a good and upright Christian he had been, and what a pity God took him so young, as if the sanctimonious humbug had known him every day of his life. The army chaplain put in his sixpennyworth as well, and there were prayers and hymns, though the ceremony had to be drawn out if only for Mary Ann's sake. The few tears he had blawted in the house were enough for him, having the rest of his life to mourn a beloved son who would have made an even better blacksmith than himself. Whether there would have been much work, with so many motors coming on the road, was something else to think about.

The November sky over the cemetery increased the desolation as the people came out, mourners as if blind, hardly knowing where to stand, till vergers discreetly arranged the scene. Six troopers from Oliver's regiment carried the coffin to the graveside, marking his departure with full military honours.

The rain had waited specially, but what could you expect at a funeral? Fourteen riflemen formed up on either side of the grave, each file for the seven holes of a horseshoe, Burton surmised, a sergeant-major by the left hand row with three other NCOs. The vicar wore a cassock, and mortarboard with a tassel dropping behind, while the regimental chaplain in uniform stood close to Burton and Mary Ann. Eli and Tom and Harry and Morgan, all in their Sunday best, were further back by the wall, and others with nothing better to do had walked in from the street to see the show as if it was something on at the Theatre Royal. Away from everybody, and sharing a large umbrella with an older woman, Alma stood with a handkerchief to her mouth. Edith had told Burton of Alma's condition, and he didn't have to enquire whose baby it would be.

The vicar spouted as if he couldn't have enough of listening to his own voice:

> "'The sun shall be no more thy light by day,
> Neither for brightness shall the moon
> Give light unto thee;
> But the Lord shall be unto thee
> An everlasting light.'"

The sergeant-major barked: 'Present!'

All rifles pointed at the sky.

'Load!'

One blank cartridge went into each breech. 'Fire!'

Fourteen shots clattered into the dank air, and after the echoes had died away, and the lugubrious melody of *The Last Post* sounded, even traffic on the road seemed stopped by the slow notes of the bugle. The ceremonial scene was taken by the *Nottingham Post* photographer from his tripod a few yards behind the priests.

Soldiers lowered the coffin, and Mary Ann sent down the first handful of soil with tears never to be her last.

As Burton kept the gate open for her to come onto the road a man of the firing party said: 'Just a minute, sir.'

He held Mary Ann steady. 'What do you want?'

The corporal saluted, and took something from his pocket. 'This is your son's watch. I know he wanted me to give it to you.'

Burton looked at it, and put it into his pocket. 'Here's a shilling for some beer.'

'No, sir, that's all right. Oh, and there's something else.' He gave him a slip of paper. 'It's a postal order for two shillings.'

Mary Ann fainted, but Burton caught her before she could fall.

A bottle of White Horse and a few quarts of Shipstone's were laid out for those who came back to the house. Burton wanted to be at work, to lose himself in his own thoughts, but stood aside with a single whisky and let the others go to it, though few had much stomach for booze. The girls cut bread and butter, and brought in sandwiches on Mary Ann's best plates to the parlour table, which none outside the family had seen before.

Morgan stood by the fire. 'You've got a nice place here.'

He's keeping the heat from the rest of us. Burton nodded at the remark. Had they expected to come back to a slum?

'I suppose you'll be joining up next,' Morgan said to Harry the barman. 'You can't be a day over thirty.'

'They'll have to fetch me.' He upended his empty glass. 'I

must get back to work. There's still plenty of men clamouring for their pints, and some women as well, these days.'

A suitable guest, who drank and went. Burton nodded again, while Morgan turned to Tom. 'Shall you be joining up?'

'I will if you come with me. I've got children to look after. Kitchener's bleddy eyes don't frighten me. He wants to get in the trenches himself.'

'That sort never do,' Burton said, a hard look at Tom who was on his second glass of beer.

Ivy combed Rebecca's long hair, which Burton considered wrong behaviour at such a time, though didn't speak, which would have made it worse. At least they weren't crying. He gave Emily a hard look for biting her nails. The girls had always gnawed them to the quick, and he'd told them about it many a time, but they never took a blind bit of notice. Sabina the other day was going so greedily at her fingers you'd think she didn't get enough to eat. He clipped her ear, but knew she would do it again as soon as his back was turned. Such a detestable habit looked ugly on a young girl. Mary Ann said she used to do it, till her mother threatened to dip her hands in vinegar.

She sat unable to speak, a cup of tea and a ham sandwich undrunk and uneaten, as if a brick wall loomed an inch from her eyes. There would never be eight children again because she was too old to have any more, but at least she'd had them. Burton said that if she'd had another man instead of himself there might not have been such trouble between him and Oliver, who could therefore have been with them still, though he would probably have gone off to the army, with the daft notion of changing his life. When I said that God had taken my favourite he told me you shouldn't have any favourites among your children, they're all precious and equal. And so they are, I said, but any child of mine God took would be my favourite, whatever you say, and Oliver was always special, just like he was for you – which he didn't deny.

She cried again. Would she ever stop? Could she? If she couldn't it was easy to understand, because he was crying, the linings of lungs and stomach turning to salt. Last night he had woken up feeling torn and bloody from a dream of wrestling with Oliver, a bitter and inconclusive bout in the dark, but he couldn't say anything to others because you never told your dreams. You could only be on your own at such a time, knowing that a day would never come when you could be as easy again as before your son had died. He wasn't soft enough to hope for it. You go on, day by day, and if you live until tomorrow you'll have lived forever, though on going to sleep at night he hoped he wouldn't wake up again, and was sorry in the morning that he had, but you never revealed such things, nothing to be done about what was eating you with steel teeth.

Ivy opened the door of the parlour to show in Mr Brown from the sawmills. Bowler hat in hand, he held the other out to Burton, who pressed reluctantly, while Mary Ann folded it with both of hers. 'I'm sorry I couldn't get to the church,' he said. 'We're working full tilt making planks for trench supports. The army nags us morning noon and night for all we can give them.'

Mary Ann stood, to pour a whisky.

'Just a small one, Mrs Burton. We were so upset to hear about Oliver. He was such a fine man. My wife cried when she read it in the paper. She couldn't believe it.'

'Neither could we,' Burton said. 'But we had to.'

'He was the best man I ever had, but I was very proud when he enlisted so readily.'

'It was the worst move he ever made,' Burton said.

Brown sipped his drink. 'Young men have to go.'

The veins at Burton's temples twitched. 'They don't.'

'It's for King and Country. I don't know where we'd be if they didn't go.'

'Just where we are now.'

'Even young Sid Camb's gone. He went the other day to join the Robin Hoods. Told them he was eighteen, and he's only fifteen. But they took him. He couldn't wait to get in – a brave young lad.'

Oswald took a sandwich from the plate Sabina held before him. 'They were wrong to take him.'

'I can only pray for his mother,' Mary Ann said.

'Oliver wasn't shot by the Germans,' Burton said. 'He was killed by a horse, and it could have happened anywhere. But before this war's over,' choosing the first large number that came to mind, 'there'll be a million killed.'

Brown looked at his watch. 'I don't know what it's like to lose a son, Mr Burton, and I hope I never do. But my eldest went last week, into the Flying Corps, to be a pilot. He's just turned eighteen.' A sense of foreboding filled the cottage. 'As I said, I'm sorry. It's a terrible time. I must be going now.'

Rebecca showed him out. 'If he'd stayed much longer,' Burton said, finishing his whisky, 'I'd have knocked him down. Him and his "King and Country".'

'He means well,' Mary Ann said.

'No he doesn't. People like him know nothing. They were born grasping the wrong end of the stick, and they'll die that way.'

'I wanted to scratch his eyes out.' Edith handed her father a sandwich. 'I ain't heard from Tommy for a while, and I'm worried to death.'

Ivy put the slide into Rebecca's hair. 'Well, they can't kill everybody.'

'No, but they'll try,' Burton said. 'That's the trouble. But Tommy will be all right.' Edith had to take what comfort she could from that, yet he knew she looked for more, which he gave, knowing he might well be sorry if the worst happened: 'He's a good sort. He'll come back.'

Mary Ann couldn't stop her tears, and Edith went to her, and when she also wept Rebecca cut a piece of cake and passed it across, at which she wiped her face to eat. Burton put a hand on Mary Ann's shoulder, and looked towards Morgan and Tom, who, feeling the burn, said they had to be going, put their glasses down, and went out together.

The wake was over, as far as he was concerned. He was glad Alma hadn't drummed up the gall to come. Considering how easy it had been to get the brazen girl to bed at Matlock, she would certainly have called if she'd wanted to. He roused himself from thinking about scenes that weren't appropriate.

The best way to take everyone's mind off death was to set them working. 'Thomas! Oswald! Get changed. We're going to the forge. There's a lot to catch up on. We can put a few hours in before tonight. You girls can help your mother. She'll need it more than ever now.'

He was glad that people had come to wish Oliver goodbye, but on his way upstairs to get into working clothes he felt better now they had gone.

Part Three

1916 onwards

TWENTY

Mr Walker, superintendent of the local Sunday Schools, walked down the street, and she thought he might need to speak to her. 'Children, I want you to go in now, because it looks as if we're going to have some snow, so find your places quietly, and I'll be in in a minute. Emily, you're the eldest, so help to settle everybody down.'

Her brown hair, parted in the middle, was pulled back to show more pale forehead. Darkly dressed, a woollen coat covered a thinness Lydia complained about, as if losing weight was a crime. But it gave a look of endurance, and tiredness from working at the lace, fingers so much faster than her aunt's that they earned enough to keep their small family going.

With Baby Oliver nearly a year old and already weaned, she helped again at the Mission Hall. She had thought of applying for work at Chilwell Depot filling shells, with thousands of other women. 'You get twenty-five shillings a week, so I'd be a millionaire on that!'

'Chilwell's a terrible place,' Lydia said. 'You should see the women coming home at night. Most have such yellow faces from the gunpowder they look like canaries. I heard that one of them died of it.' The argument that decided her not to go was that she would see so little of Oliver, whereas by staying at home she could be with him all the time. 'You don't want him to grow up looking only at a crabby old witch like me, do you?'

Clouds turning the weather raw were grey in their fluidly mapped outlines, like cauliflowers fit only for pig food. Burton came to mind at times for no reason she could think of, and she was glad to hear Mr Walker say: 'We'll step inside the doorway, to be out of this wind.'

Seventy if a day, he wore no overcoat, and a small Bible bulged from a pocket of his Norfolk jacket. He wiped a dewdrop with a large white handkerchief. 'You've heard, I suppose, Miss Waterall, that Will Jones had been killed in action? And then that foolish young boy Sidney Camb was also killed.'

'I saw his mother yesterday,' she said, 'and she told me that one of Sidney's elder brothers has enlisted as well, and that if he got killed she would throw herself off Castle Rock. I tried to comfort her, but you can hardly expect to.'

'I'm sure you did your best. But Will Jones was a good teacher, and we're losing so many we can't be particular as to who we take on anymore. Didn't that girl Emily Burton lose her brother?'

She wanted to go inside, and quell the noise before beginning her lesson. 'He was a shoeing smith with the Hussars.'

He seemed to be saying a silent prayer, and perhaps he was, as many must these days, when the world had become so changed from two years ago. The war influenced everything, people only daring to live from day to day, and praying when they could for it to end.

'We fully realized what we were doing in taking you back instead of casting you out,' he said, 'and you've been such a good influence on the children of this area. It's rare for atten-dance to be so high, and in such capable hands.'

Well, she knew all that, and wondered what he was coming to, because his seriousness was never without a point.

'The thing in my mind, Miss Waterall,' he said, 'and it's been there for some time, is that we might eventually find you a post in some school, teaching full time. Everything is very unorthodox these days, as you know. You're not the only young woman who has been left in the lurch because of this dreadful war. I wonder whether there'll be any young men alive when it's finished. My wife and I pray every night for the safety of our soldiers, but God seems to move in more mysterious ways than we could ever have imagined. Of course, you'd have to go to Newark for your teaching practice, though I'm sure we could arrange a small stipend. But would you be able to manage, with your present responsibilities?'

She put up a hand to soften the beating of her heart, its rhythm hard to keep in bounds, at sensing a possible turning in her life. Working at heaps of lace with Lydia, and looking after Oliver, she set aside an hour each day to read books from the Free Library. 'I'd like to go. I'd manage somehow.'

'I'll put your name before the committee, and do all the persuading I can.' He took her warm hand, as if to bring life into his own freezing fingers, then drew a hand away to reset his glasses. 'I've already mentioned what an outstanding teacher you'd make.'

A warmth spread at her face as she followed two late children inside. He closed the door and stood at the back, pleased at how all became quiet when Alma went before them.

'This afternoon I'm going to tell you a story about the infant Moses, who was hidden among the bulrushes of the River Nile. The Pharaoh who ruled over Egypt gave orders that all Hebrew baby boys were to be killed, because he was frightened of their power and skill when they were grown up. I'll go on to read about how the Chosen People escaped from such wickedness, and safely crossed the Red Sea, while Pharaoh's soldiers pursuing them were drowned in the mighty waters.' She opened her Bible at the well-known place. 'And then we'll say a prayer and sing a hymn. And I shall want each of you to come out and read a few verses aloud.'

Audible grumbling at such a task, beyond the capability of some, made her smile and, looking over their heads, she saw that Mr Walker had gone, satisfied that she could finish the session, unable to know her anxiety while being watched, or how much she loved the children for being so attentive.

Coat drawn tight over a woollen shawl, she hurried to get home, the first snowflakes floating across her eyes. Men's laughter from a pub on the main road tempted her to go in for a warming drink, but Mr Walker's assumption that she would one day become a teacher gave more than enough heat to resist. Aware of every penny, she wouldn't go into such a place anyway. Such pothouse noises reminded her of Burton, whom she fought to forget, trying not to blame him for all that had happened to her, and more fatally to Oliver. Many other Hussars had died on service overseas since then, and no doubt still more would be lost. It was impossible to pick up a newspaper without seeing numerous photos of the dead.

She hurried home to be with Oliver. He would soon be walking but, as she told Lydia, he would never be a soldier. Lydia replied that he would only become one over her dead body, adding that she however would be dead before he was old enough to think about it.

They talked in the kitchen when at work. Time went faster and the labour was lighter with two to get it done. Oliver, a lively soul when he wasn't sleeping, looked on as if to make sure their fingers didn't slacken. They laid him well swaddled on bundles of lace, no more comfortable place for an angel to be.

Alma often trembled for him as he lay before her, as if the world he had come into was hostile to all human life. What would become of him if she and Lydia left him one day with a neighbour when they had to go out together and they were struck dead by lightning or fatally run over by a motor omnibus whose brakes had failed? A terrible life he would have, starved and abused in an orphanage, and growing up in utter misery.

The haunting picture didn't let her forget that children were in any case susceptible to measles, whooping cough, diphtheria, tonsillitis, the croup, and scores of other furtive sicknesses which if too virulent could bring on death. He was strong, healthy and big for his age, the only reason to be glad that a man like Burton was his father. Whatever she thought now, he had been conceived in love, and was more likely to survive because of it.

She hadn't seen Burton since the funeral, and hoped never to do so again. She supposed he would walk straight by her, as she would pass him without a word of recognition. To make sense out of her life you had to assume that both had got what they wanted, and as for Oliver growing up without a father, maybe it was better that way, because those who did have fathers invariably ended with more bad habits than if they only had a mother. When Lydia said she ought one day to think of getting married so as to give the child a father, Alma replied that she would never marry for such a reason. 'There'll be no men left to marry by the end of the war, anyway.'

'But you might not relish being an old maid when I'm dead and gone,' Lydia said.

She stepped into the small warm house, renewed by seeing Oliver clutching the bars of his crib and laughing at the face Lydia was making to amuse him. She took a plate from the oven, and cut two slices of bread. 'Come and eat this by the fire, and warm yourself up. The Baby Mikado will scream his little honeyguts out if you touch him. You'll turn him into an icicle.'

She was hungry for the potatoes and black pudding. 'It's all I could get,' Lydia said. 'The shops will be out of business soon. I heard they'd be selling horsemeat next, and I couldn't stomach that.'

'If we're starving we'll have to,' Alma said.

'I expect we would. A couple of years ago I couldn't afford bananas, and now we can there's none in the shops. I'd like to see Oliver's face when I can show him one. I mashed some potato with a drop of milk just before you came in and he gobbled the lot from a spoon.'

'You love to spoil him.'

'If we don't, who will? Maybe spoiled children grow up to be better people.'

She held Oliver, in paradise when so close, till he went to sleep. 'Mr Walker said he might get me taken on as a pupil-teacher in a few months.'

Lydia took up the scuttle, and filled it with coal from under the stairs. 'Is that what you want?'

The tone said so. 'More than anything. I've wanted to change my life ever since I was born.'

'Well, I've always supposed that. I never thought you'd live in a place like this forever.'

'It's not that. I can still be a teacher and live here. Unless you get fed up and chuck me out.'

'Oh, I shan't do that.' Oliver's blue eyes opened from milk-white dreams. 'I've got used to you, and to this little bundle as well.'

Ivy had started work at the tobacco factory, and Rebecca at Hollins's Mill in New Radford. Burton got them out of bed at five every morning in time to go down the lane at six with packets of sandwiches Mary Ann had made the evening before, holding hands because they were nervous at going under the long bridge in the dark. It was no use Burton telling them there was nothing to fear, and that the more frightened they were the worse it would get, because he secretly believed they enjoyed it that way.

As soon as she was thirteen Sabina would sign herself on at the same place as Rebecca, so that with eight shillings a week from each the house might seem more prosperous. As for daft Emily, she would never bring a farthing into the house. She'd been sent to school but, like Thomas, could neither read nor write. Perhaps being the last born had made her backward, Mary Ann as well by that time worn out.

With one girl married and two at work she had more to do in the house, not a bad thing if it diverted her mind from Oliver, though she knew that nothing ever would. The postcard-sized photograph taken after he had enlisted hung in the kitchen hugely enlarged and framed, so he was always looking down, willing them not to forget. He watched whatever was being done, a presence Mary Ann felt even when her back was turned. Burton noted his old familiar expression of not much caring to know what was going on, lips slightly pursed as if to begin whistling a tune, something he would occasionally do in life, a piercing melody to make more space around him in the crowded house. Burton sometimes thought he knew more about him than when he had been alive, but supposed that was because he was more on his mind now that he was dead.

He said to Mary Ann more than once: 'That khaki uniform makes him look like a tramp,' wanting to remember the well-dressed young man in suit and tie, boots well polished on Saturday night, walking down the lane. 'It's a shame we never thought of getting a proper photograph, before he put those khaki rags on; but who of us imagined he would end like that?'

Killed by a mad horse. It should have been roasted alive over a slow fire. Shooting was too good. I'd have made the animal know what it had done. I've handled worse horses. I was often alarmed when Oliver got on one and trotted down the lane from the forge, but I said nothing. Perhaps I should have dragged him off and banged his head, but he would only have hated me more. He thought he knew everything, like you do when you're young, while I would never trust any horse because all of them nurse a wild streak, more than anybody might realize. Getting on their backs was never for me, and shouldn't have been for him, either.

Mary Ann wrote to Oxford for the death certificate, hoping to learn more about how Oliver had died. She thought of him all the time, couldn't lay a meal without wondering whether or not he would be pleased should he come alive into the house. She wanted to know how he had spent every moment of his last day, and so did Burton, but the death certificate only said: 'Fracture at the base of the skull and lacerations of the brain following injuries received while following his calling.'

Which Burton thought wasn't saying much. There was more to it than that, and I'd like to get to the bottom of it. A horse can go mad and kill a man, but couldn't have done so to Oliver while he was shoeing one. The leg would have been between Oliver's thighs, him facing backwards from the horse's head, and if a horse tries to kick when the leg's up like that it falls over with such a bang it won't get back on its feet in a hurry, and would never try such a stunt again. It couldn't have happened while Oliver was following his calling.

It wasn't so much a matter of forgetting, nobody could do that, but of living with what you couldn't help but remember. Work was the only solace, and he went at it full tilt, as he had to in any case to pay Mary Ann enough for the household, a weekly sum to Thomas and Oswald, and have a few shillings left for himself. Old Nick and Tubal-Cain had shoed a hundred horses a day, or so he had heard tell, and if I did as many, he thought, I'd be a lot better off than I am now.

Mary Ann said the years went slowly after Oliver's death. You could count the minutes. Even when you were working they crawled around the clock. Yet according to the newspapers so much was happening in the world beyond, though Burton was scornful at their obvious lies when Mary Ann read to him. Battles called great victories never ended anything. Fighting and slaughter went on, Burton said, and we were always winning (whoever 'we' were) but things got worse and worse for the soldiers, who you had to feel sorry for, as well as for everyone else, most of all for those losing sons, husbands, brothers and fathers who had gone like fools when they shouldn't have let wild horses drag them away. If they were killed the family got a telegram and a photo in the paper, and as for the blind and the crippled, what would they do for a living when the war was over?

Lottie worked the white handle and pumped two quarts of ale through a funnel into Mary Ann's bottles, scooping away froth with the same piece of wood she had used for years. 'A pound of cheese, as well as four boxes of matches and a packet of Robins.'

The new slot machines by the beer-off wall fascinated Mary Ann, flashing emblems of various fruits, yellows and reds and greens, purples and blues, the incandescent colours of her youth long since discarded but regretted all the same, the favourite stockings, gloves, blouses and dresses resting in a separate drawer of the bedroom, rarely used but always a reminder of happier days. Burton smiled when she mused over them.

A penny from her change seemed to go into the small zinc slot by its own will. She pulled the handle with vigour, as if the harder she did the more chance of getting the kitty. 'We haven't had them long,' Lottie said. 'Mr Warrener makes them in a work-shop at the end of his garden.'

Oliver would put in the odd coppers from his wages if he was here, and come home to share a five-shilling win with his brothers and sisters, and even treat his father to a pint, so all she needed was to have three items of the same fruit come around the drums and stop in parallel. They didn't.

She ought to stop, but fate beckoned, and after a few pennies had gone she put half a crown from her purse on the counter and told Lottie to give more change, hoping not only to win back the first few pence but have the large amount visible through the glass window fall into her pinafore as well.

The coloured drums spun, her mindless heart praying that Oliver would come back safe, until she knew he couldn't. The hungry mouth was made of steel, a wicked little ravenous slot demanding what pennies she had. It took them all. Oliver was spinning a top in the yard, and she knew he was thinking: 'That top is me. Don't let it fall. Let the colours keep spinning, though if it does fall, well, I can set it going again.' Oh, the poor little boy won't do that anymore.

'Don't cry, duck,' Lottie said.

Having dug so deep into the housekeeping she must go on playing to get it back, wished she hadn't started, didn't know why she had, Burton would surely knock all her teeth out this time, and she would have no one to blame but herself, it would be her fault, and yet it wouldn't, something stronger controlled her arms, other eyes looking on, apart from hers, and laughing with malice when she lost, but the effort of using her arms to pull and pull and pull and hear the clink of machinery moving and see the gaudy colours spinning made her feel better.

Another woman who came into the shop was astonished at so much being lost, though she willed a cascade of coins to fall like an avalanche into Mary Ann's lap. 'Can't you stop her?'

'I've tried, but she takes no notice.'

Mary Ann gave her a florin for more change. One penny eaten, another slotted in. The machine was big, it demanded more. It wasn't so much the money she wanted – though she had to hope for it – but to open the prison of the machine and give freedom to all coins inside, as if that would put life back into her.

'She's losing all she's got,' the woman said.

'I don't know what to do. She hasn't been the same since her lad was killed.'

'It's terrible,' another customer said, 'this war. But I'll see if I can meet Burton. He passes about this time on his way from work. If he can't stop her, nobody can.'

Mary Ann requested more coppers, with such a glint that Lottie had to spread them along the counter and, arms folded over her chest, watch her pick them up quickly in case they grew legs and ran back to the till. Two more women came in, as if they had heard what was going on and wanted to watch the play.

No one else in the shop could hear the talking in her heart. 'I bore him and brought him up, the best lad that ever was. Dear God, bring him back to me. I want him in the house again.'

With the last of twelve pennies clattering into the steel pocket she knew herself close to getting the kitty. Three lemons showed, though diagonal to each other instead of in a winning row.

'Stop now, duck. You've spent enough.'

Lottie hoped no one would blame her should Mary Ann lose every last farthing. 'Somebody's gone to tell Burton. He's her husband.'

'Burton?' exclaimed one of the women. 'Oh bleddy hell! She'll get two black eyes for this,' and went off with her groceries as if not caring to see it.

'I don't know why you went.' As if Oliver was beside her, she worked through the last pile of coins. 'I'll never know,' and then, feeling a presence behind, knew who it must be. A hand gathered in the few coins. He gripped her by the shoulder. 'This is a fine way to carry on.'

She turned but, finding one last penny in her pocket, slotted it in before he could take it away, a desperate pulling of the handle, the same result as ever. 'I've always wanted to play on one of these.'

'Couldn't you have stopped her?' he said to Lottie.

'Not without chopping her hands off.'

'You could have rapped her over the knuckles.' He gave Mary Ann the sackcloth shopping bag with its bottles of beer and groceries. 'Come on, let's get you home.'

'It's no use blawting,' he said on their way up the lane. 'What's done is done, but I wish you hadn't done it. I've got a pound or two put by, and that should see us through till next week.'

Her heart beat faster on knowing she had thrown a whole week's living money away, and it was difficult to imagine that what she had so far heard from Burton, who walked ahead, would be the last of it.

He opened the gate for her to go into the yard, and she held her head high on passing, the tinkle of bottles playing a tune, as if she had gone through fire and nothing could harm her now. Even the scuffles and grunts of the pigs seemed to welcome her home.

Burton, telling the others about it round the table, turned the matter into a joke: 'I don't know what Oliver would have said if he got to know – if he was still alive. But if he's where you think he is it'll give him something to laugh about.'

TWENTY-ONE

A message from the farm manager at Wollaton Hall asked Burton if he would come and ring a couple of young bulls, and he had sent Thomas back to say he would. He slid out of bed at five o'clock without disturbing Mary Ann, who needed all the rest she could get, being more than ordinarily tired since Oliver's death, as if she lived the life he would have gone on living, as well as her own.

He called Ivy from the girls' bedroom, to come downstairs and make his breakfast sandwich. She asked where he was going, so he told her, and why. 'It's a cruel trade,' she said. 'I feel sorry for the poor young bulls.'

'So it is,' his tone was sharp, 'but bulls have to be ringed so that they can be easily led, and don't do any damage to men. They'll pay me ten shillings for doing each one. Another thing is, if I want your opinion I'll ask for it, so shut your rattle, and get on with what you're doing.'

He didn't see her glare of loathing but knew it was there. Not with all the tools in the forge would he be able to cut a way through the wall of her dislike, supposing he cared to, which in some way he did. She had hated him well before he had given her cause to, though all he'd ever done was to make her show sufficient respect to himself and her mother.

Thomas and Oswald were to open the forge, and handle what trade might turn up. No matter how many horses the army took there were still enough to keep them busy. Carts and drays always needed animals to haul them.

At six he went out of the house, a picture in mind of Ivy putting two fingers to her nose at his departure. High clouds suggested a fine day, birds coming noisily to life, new flowers sprouting in the hedges as he descended the lane to Woodhouse. The driver of the baker's van called out a greeting while feeding a crust to his horse, then walked across the pavement with fresh loaves for the shop. Burton disapproved of those who bought bread instead of making it themselves, as Mary Ann still did.

People walked up the road to work, but he turned for the canal, crossing by a lock gate to the towpath. A bargee lighting his morning pipe had a greeting returned, and smells of bacon from the hatchway where his wife was clearing up after breakfast made Burton momentarily hungry. As a magpie out for no good lifted grudgingly from the path to let him by he realized it was 2nd May and that he was fifty today. He wouldn't mention the fact at home, and didn't expect them to do so either, though Mary Ann would remind him, and have them take a tot of whisky together.

A few fishermen were throwing lines from the bank, though what they hoped to catch he couldn't imagine. A few stickle-backs for the cat, if they were lucky, but they looked as if they were retired, so it was a fair excuse to be idle. What was a birthday, anyway? You were a year older, but that was nobody else's business. Some people were given presents, and what was the good of that if you were one step nearer to getting old? Presents would only mean something if at every birthday you got younger.

He slithered down the bank and walked his rapid pace through the sawmill, no place without memories of Oliver which was, he supposed, why Mary Ann left the house as little as possible. He had taken her for a walk to the Rodney a fortnight ago, which she might have enjoyed if an unthinking fool hadn't blurted out what a shame about Oliver being killed. Not that it was his fault. A year of mourning was the least you needed, so it was said, though for Mary Ann, and himself as well, it would last a lifetime.

Coal wagons passed on the main road, huge grey Clydesdales hauling the loads. He smiled at a couple of ragged lads following in the hope of picking up dropped cobbles. At the park gates he called his surname to the man in the lodge, and went in the direction of the stables, crossing the large stretch of grass as if steering by compass, the breeze pleasant after yesterday's mowing of the lawns.

The great mansion on the hill – worth a glance – was built in olden times from the profits of coal. Nothing wrong with that. If he had owned the land he would have enjoyed it as well, except he'd heard that the man who'd had the Hall built had died bankrupt and miserable in London. Served him right, you could say, because extravagance never forgave.

He should have gone the back way so that no one would see him from the terrace, but if they did, and didn't like the sight of him, they could ring the bulls themselves, and see how far they got. Lord Middleton owned the cottage he lived in, but Burton knew he could always find another place. Mary Ann had wondered whether they ought to move, the house having so many memories of Oliver; but if they did she would have to leave them behind, so she decided to stay. In any case Oliver's framed photograph on the wall couldn't be moved, because when in the same room alone Mary Ann talked to him, Oliver liking to hear bits of gossip about the family, so it was clear he would always want to stay in the house he was brought up in.

Walking across the open ground he hoped he'd get a glimpse of some of the maids, even of Lady Middleton, not to mention her daughters, if she had any, he wasn't particular. A bit of young flesh would be pleasing, and there were plenty of bushes by the lake.

He'd first come with his father and George at fourteen, to ring five such awkward bulls as kept them busy from dawn until dusk. At midday a maid brought a tray of mugs and a pitcher up to the brim with beer. Her arms could barely hold it, another young wench following with chunks of bread and cheese. A wet April day, they sat on bales of hay in the stable, Father smoking his pipe while he and George eyed the girls tripping oh so daintily back and forth on their duties. The three of them were so exhausted by evening that the old man, in one of his happy moods, treated them to a pint of good ale at the public house. He had drunk most of the pitcher at midday while, it seemed to George and Ernest, they had done all the work.

He veered to the right of the Hall fair and square on its hill, and under the arch into the stable yard. He told a man besoming dung and straw from between the cobblestones to find Mr Parker and say he was wanted.

'Who shall I say wants him?'

'Burton. He'll know.' The smell of cows was healthy, or so he'd heard. A man was brushing a horse in one of the stalls, the broad arse of a placid animal visible over the half-door. If that one went mad a bar of iron at the back of a leg would drop it in no time, and it wouldn't get up again, which would be its lookout. Oliver should never have been killed like that.

Parker, a portly bull-tup in gaiters, moleskin waistcoat and bowler hat, strutted as if he and not Lord Middleton was gaffer of the Hall, though you couldn't fault him for that. His eyes were bloodshot, from putting back too much of his lordship's brandy, he supposed.

'Morning, Burton.'

Burton nodded.

'I'll show you where they are. They're a right lot of trouble. His lordship wonders whether you'll be able to do anything with them, because none of us can.'

Burton wasted little breath in his response. 'That's why I'm here.' He walked to another wing of the stables and looked over the gate, his victims standing at the back where the light was dim. One sensed his presence, and turned. Burton sent a stare back, at the well-muscled young bull, the deep purple of its orbs steadily gazing as if gauging the prowess of the man. The prouder the soul the poorer the beast, because it was going to be subdued, and he trained his eyes on it, to get the measure of the contest, any satisfaction from the coming struggle more appreciated at this stage than later, when pure force blotted out all thought.

The two bulls were young and calm, as if the world belonged to them, stocky, well-fed, and powerful, fresh enough to be confident that no one could bring them to docility. But you'll be eating out of peoples' hands next week, such an appraisal the most important part of Burton's task, the weighing-up, the beginning of confidence for him and defeat for them, a long look in the hope of making them realize that there could only be one end to the contest.

They didn't know what was coming, yet the second animal

turned, stamped, nudged the first out of the way, and took a step forward. The look wasn't aimed at Burton, who then knew, from the arrangement of its muscled rear and legs, that this was the one he would have most trouble with, because it had already tested itself against the other and won. To tackle it after the first one, which had succumbed to the steel of its gaze, had been beaten, would take some of its heart away. It would sense its impending fall from the alarms of defeat, so Burton would warm himself up with the first, and be in more fettle to crush the disheartened second.

They were similar in everything, except for their eyes, until those of the second, on suddenly taking the decision to weigh *him* up, became less expressionless, perhaps noting some extra detail of Burton and the surroundings outside. Its way of looking at things was more inquisitive than that of the other, not by too much, but added strength might make it more formidable.

He stood to one side, out of their sight, took the breakfast of a bacon sandwich from his pocket, and ate it in a few large bites, not much in bulk, but you didn't want to clutter the stomach with such a job on hand. Parker came back. 'What do you think?'

'There's no hurry.' He pointed over the gate. 'I'll begin with the one nearest the wall. In a few minutes you can sling a rope and haul him out.'

A couple of stable boys, and an aproned man who looked like a gardener, stood along the facing wall. There would be an audience. There usually was, always somebody to gawp. If he ringed bulls on stage at the Empire he would make a fortune, except that if one got loose in such a place all the toffs and idlers would have to run for their lives. His smile, barely recognized as such by those waiting for the show to begin, showed him to be in no hurry. Impatience, otherwise fear, had killed many a man, and he wasn't going to be one of them. The sandwich gone, he smoked a cigarette, then hung his jacket on a hook inside an empty stable. 'I'm ready when you are.'

Parker called two men with ropes. Another couple carried a smoking brazier, and a selection of thin sharp pokers.

'Not that one, you fool.' The thick rope had spiralled the wrong bull. He waited by the door. 'Get it right this time.' He supposed the increase of onlookers along the wall would applaud if he flexed his muscles like a boxer. The day was bright and dry, so no chance of slipping on his backside and getting ripped up out of carelessness. That's something they wouldn't see, however much they might like it as part of the show. He kept his sight on the door, and indicated that Parker move the audience to a safer place.

The bull walked out, as if on its own sweet way to the greenest of pastures. Taking time, it seemed invincible, nothing in the world to do it harm. At Burton's approach the bull went towards the arch, as he knew it had to because there was no other option. Two men pulled it to a halt by the length of rope. A head of fresh dandelion grew from the wall nearest Burton, which he calmly took out with his fingers, removing the blemish on an otherwise clean surface. Hooves clattered on the cobbles, and he waited till the bull turned.

To approach such a beast head-on was asking for trouble and so, repeating to himself the eternal rule that he must take his time, he walked towards it obliquely, and stared into eyes that unusual happenings had robbed of opaqueness. They were flat ovals, losing colour as well, their intensity not certain anymore, nor their idea as to what was happening. You had to watch them even more carefully. The bull moved away, then came straight at him. His fingertips touched a horn as it clobbered by. It wouldn't be easy, because none ever were.

Ropes held it against the wall, though the position wasn't too secure. 'Let it go again,' he said quietly, not wanting to give much time for it to make up its mind. A shake of the rope, and Burton moved to where he sensed it would go, pleased to hear the second bull banging itself around the stable as if riled at missing the excitement. 'Another jerk of the rope.'

They complied, and the animal ran to Burton, as if he wasn't there, or as if he were a stone post. He struck the back of the neck with the full force of his hand, and during the time in which it couldn't know whether it was coming or going, grasped both horns and fought it to a stop.

They watched in silence. Holding the horns took all his strength. The young bull resisted. Nothing like this had happened to it before, a fresh experience, totally unsettling, but it had to struggle, and Burton knew that if he didn't win at this stage the bull would begin to fight. Then there'd be hell to pay, or worse.

I've got your measure, or he hoped he had. Droplets of sweat fell onto his shirt. The eyes of the bull, visible from side-on, spun in all directions. He forced one way, then the other, subtle but strong alterations of will, all the pressure he had. He was wrestling for Oliver, whose face came to him, not from the photograph on the wall but from full reality as he had known him in life, the man who had been done to death by a mindless animal, and now his father, he who was not mindless, was pressing down, down, down, down, trying to save him as he would have had he been in that field or on that lane near Hungerford. Down, down, down with all his force. He hadn't been there, and couldn't help him now, but he would beat this one, and its mate as well, if it broke his back and took half his life – or all of it – he didn't care because he wouldn't need to.

Minutes of stalemate seemed to go by, seconds really, though he wasn't counting, couldn't afford to, then in a split second which left all time behind, he aimed a boot at one of its legs, a painful blow, a bolt coming from nowhere, and threw it down.

Fore and aft legs were tied with leather thongs, but he stayed alert, noting the ripple of muscles and volcanic snorting as it fought to rise. The brazier was brought side-on. 'Not too close, or you'll scorch my backside.' While a youth worked the bellows an iron stool was put under the animal's head.

Burton looked from full height, not caring much for what must now be done. He never did, but he had to do it. Serves you right for being born a bull, though Ivy was right, it was a cruel trade. She had no doubt got the phrase from Mary Ann, but animals were made to serve man, and if anybody doesn't think so let them go without meat. Ivy's got too much to say for herself. It's what bulls get done to them – and he stared into the animal's half-defeated eyes – but it'll soon be over, and when you try to look back on it you'll have a job to remember. Such words must have been in his father's mind as well, or probably not. They were a lot harder in those days, though everybody thinks that, the older they get, so maybe they were only as hard as I am now.

The thin poker, handed to him from the coals, was examined to make sure the colour was right, a shade down from white. He noted two black-uniformed maids among the gawpers, white ribbons flowing from their caps, and while in no way distracted from his work – dangerous if you were daft enough to let that happen – he appreciated their comeliness. They looked at him as if, should he take the liberty of asking (he would certainly do that) they might agree to go out walking.

They fled as he forced the burning rod through the bull's nose, but he hoped one would be back before long with his platter of whatever the kitchen could provide, thinking he'd be lucky to get a piece of bread and cheese at this place.

The shriek of the animal, as if cast into the fires of hell, alerted the second bull to what might be in store. Hammering at the half-gate with its hooves, no one knew or cared whether it was desperate to come out and help its brother, or wanted to make a run for it to avoid the same fate.

The smell of smoke and flesh made him hungry for his dinner. When the wound had healed in a few weeks a ring would be threaded through, so that it could be led docilely anywhere. He stepped aside, and looked at his watch. 'Let the other go in ten minutes.' A ringmaster at the game, his word was not to be disputed. 'When it comes out, it can run about a bit.'

The first animal was let up, two legs released, but hauled with difficulty, fighting against the dread of its torment going on, into a separate stable. It was no work of Burton's to help. He was only here to ring bulls. 'Make sure the top and bottom gates are locked.'

Try as they might, they couldn't get the other out. Half an hour went by before they could, which seemed a good sign to Burton. Resistance and indecision now would make it easier to quell. Half a dozen pulled and sweated at the ropes, Burton wary as they forced it into daylight like a deadweight. It came back to life, yet didn't run around and waste energy, used its animal intelligence more knowingly than the first. Burton worked long before he considered it to be under his control, yet thought it an easier job than the other, when he had it on the ground.

He felt as if he had already done a day's work, but took the trouble to keep any sign from his face. Not that tiredness could be allowed to bother him, because he still had to be at the forge for the rest of the day, even if only to make sure those two dozy idiots were getting on with what they'd been told to do. Meanwhile, where was that hot-bottomed maid with something to eat?

He was given the pound note by Parker. 'His lordship sent you this. He was looking from the window with his opera glasses, and said you'd done a very good job.'

'And what did her ladyship say?'

'She wasn't there.'

'Too tender-hearted, I expect.'

'She's in the greenhouse, cutting the day's flowers.'

'Best place for her.' Payment was a slip of green paper instead of the solid sovereign of a few years back, the government having called in the gold. Paper was much inferior, because it didn't jingle like good metal in the pocket, and could turn to pulp if soaked by the rain.

The bulls were bellowing as if the end of the world might be coming up, wanting to batter the doors off their hinges and leap out for vengeance, not knowing that their troubles were over. The maid was back in the stable yard, Burton glad his jacket was on and already buttoned. Taking the glass of whisky, he drank it straight down, wondering what abundance of hair was hiding under her cap. 'What's your name?'

'Millie.' Her blue eyes sparkled as she looked up at him. 'But her ladyship calls me Jane.'

'That's a cheek.'

She looked over her shoulder. 'Aren't them bulls making a noise?'

He smiled. 'So would you, if you'd just had a hot iron through your jaw.'

'It's wicked.'

'Lots of things are.'

She shuddered. 'Anyway, I don't mind working at this place. I get eighteen quid a year. And it's a situation. I get well looked after.'

'I'll bet you do. But if I was you I'd take a job in the gun factory, and earn two pounds a week.'

'Well, I won't. I'm better off here. It's all found, and I don't have to worry about anything. As long as I do what I'm told.'

'Don't you want people to call you by your proper name?'

'Why should I care? I know I'm me, don't I?'

'I'd care,' he said. 'At the gun factory they'd call you what you were christened, and if you worked there I could meet you in the Market Square now and again. I'd take you to the Trip to Jerusalem, or the Royal Children, or the Eight Bells, or the Rose of England or' – he was enjoying himself after such exertion – 'to the Peach Tree. I'm sure you've heard of all those places.'

'So that's your game? I might have known. I don't know what you're talking about.'

'When is your day off?' He stroked his moustache. 'I only ask because you're a very beautiful young woman. I mean it.' Try to say something nobody's had the gall to say to her before. 'I fell in love as soon as I saw you looking at me while I was working. "I hope she's the one who brings me my snap," I said to myself. "I'll go home and hang myself if it's somebody else, because I don't think I'll be able to live without another sight of her." Come into town on Saturday night, and we'll have a tripe supper at Pepper's, and go to the Empire afterwards.'

She listened with flushed cheeks, mouth slightly open (a good sign) a hand at her bosom as if to hold every word captive, or maybe to prevent her heart flying away. 'You know I can't.'

'You can do anything, if you want to.'

Freckles on cheeks and forehead looked like sparks of hell that had bedded there and only half gone out. 'Now you're tormenting me.'

'That's the last thing I'd do to a girl like you. I'll walk you around the corner, to say goodbye. Then you can go into the Hall and get on with your skivvying.' Taking her hand, he was surprised that the fingers curled so warmly into his.

Parker, having made sure the stable doors were locked, said to the man next to him: 'Just look at that, Burton going off with one of the maids. I hope nobody cops her. I've never seen anything like it.'

'What do you expect from a blacksmith who rings bulls? They're a law unto themselves.'

'Yes, but it's a bit much. What if his lordship sees them?'

'I expect he'd laugh his head off.'

Burton had thought of bringing Thomas, to show him the technique of the job, in case he was ever called on to do it, but was glad he hadn't, drawing Millie into a coign of the wall for a kiss, her bosom firm behind the rustle of her clothes.

'It's not when you look at me brazen,' she said, 'but it's you looking at me so sly that gives me a frizz.'

Sly be damned, he'd never imagined such a bonus on setting out that morning. If he had hoped for it, and wasted much thought in imagining it, as sure as hell it wouldn't have turned up so nicely. Only a Nottingham girl appreciated a man who ringed bulls, though when his smile was buried in her warm neck he wondered whether his birthday had anything to do with it. 'I do love you, you know.' Since Oliver's death there were times when Mary Ann couldn't bear to be touched in such a way, and he was never one to bother a woman who didn't want him.

'And I love you,' she said. 'You're so strong. The way you did those bulls gave me a frizz as well. But do be quick.'

Leaning on the wall presented a good view of the greensward falling away behind the Hall, so he would see anyone who came into the open, not wanting to get such a pleasant and obliging girl into trouble. As for whoever saw him and made objection, they could take his presence or leave it, and ring their own bulls, knowing they wouldn't get anyone else from the area to do it so well or so cheaply. He opened his trousers, and lifted her skirts deftly, then drew her onto him as if she was a toy come to life, and worked them together till she cried out and all that was in him poured into her.

A jerk of the head at her crucial moment threw her cap off, a mass of fair ringlets falling about her cheeks, the sun shining through as, barely finished with her pleasure, she coiled it rapidly back into place and fixed the cap on. She straightened her skirts. 'Oh, that was good. What a dirty devil you are! I loved it.'

'If you meet me again you can have some more.'

'I don't think I'll be able to. The trouble is, they watch us like hawks.'

'They didn't that time.' He stroked her face. 'Never mind though, my pretty love. It's my birthday today, and you couldn't have given me a better present.'

'Many happy returns, then.' She blushed, as he had often noticed them do, after being seen to rather than before, when he was too busy to realize and they were so eager to get it.

During the discreet buttoning-up he watched her go into a small side entrance, at which he turned back for the stables, to eat the food she had brought him.

TWENTY-TWO

A workman touched his cap to Lydia and stood so that she could take the seat and put three-year-old Oliver on her knees. She kept the shopping bag with its flask of tea, bottle of Dandelion and Burdock, and sandwiches safe from the rattling sway of the tram. As good as stifled by sour breath and tobacco smoke, Oliver looked with wide-open eyes at men and women going on afternoon shift at the gun factory, Lydia thinking that if he was happy so was she.

The tram almost emptied at the factory stop, and went on to its terminus by the river. 'We're going over a big bridge, and since you've been a good lad I'll let you look at the water. It's deep and wide, and flows as fast as a motor car.'

She walked at his dawdling gait, gave a ha'penny for her toll, the keeper seeing a child who could go free. A cart went by, and at hoofbeats Oliver stared at the horse, till she urged him further onto the bridge, a grip at his vibrant body as he was lifted to watch a boat rowed by two soldiers slide from under the arch. He looked into the sky with steady and knowing interest: 'Crowds.'

'Not "crowds",' she said. 'Say "clouds".'

'Clouds.'

She took him down. 'Now walk.'

'Where's Mam?'

'She'll come later. She won't be long. Look at the big river again. It's the biggest in the world, and flows right down to the sea, where I expect you'll go one day.' She traipsed him through Wilford village. Alma was being talked to by a board of inspectors about her teaching post, which Oliver wouldn't understand, so she turned his attention back to the grey velvet sweep of the Trent.

Through a gate, and over Fairham Brook by a footbridge, was

a space of dry land between the two watercourses. Cattle dotted meadows on the far side. 'You can play on the grass,' she said. 'Only don't go near the water.'

'Isn't water good?'

'If you drink it, but not if you drown in it. You must learn to swim first.' She called him close for half a cup of Dandelion and Burdock, which he couldn't finish so she drank the satisfying fizz herself.

A stalk of grass between his lips, he imitated a man on the tram with a cigarette, talked indecipherable words in the rhythm of counting lace bundles before wheeling them back to the factory. She laughed. 'You are a funny lad. I'd like to know who your father is, though don't suppose I ever shall. But he can't have been all that bad.'

The more words the more he would feel cared for. No baby talk allowed. He was intelligent, but words would make him more so, Alma said. Words were what mattered, they agreed. Speech was paramount. What was in the mind must come to your lips. People might look at you gone-out in talking plainly to a child, but let them.

She and Alma went at it like a couple of sparrows in spring, chattering on every topic as they worked. Oliver put in his contribution, asked questions that were always answered, which only increased his curiosity. She wondered whether his father had talked all the time at that age.

'Come away from the water. It likes to suck little boys under and eat them for its dinner. You can only go close when you're grown up.'

She had no patience with people who didn't talk, or couldn't talk, or who wouldn't. You never knew what they would do next, so they weren't to be trusted. The less they talked the more miserable they looked, and the more threatening they could be. Often they only talked when they wanted something, and if that something they wanted was yours they would have it off you before you knew what was happening. If you had a bit more than them they broke the Commandment. And if they didn't covet they complained, which was worse.

Oliver looked at her, smiled as if knowing he owned not only her but the whole world and the air everyone breathed. 'Don't get your leggings dirty.'

He measured his paces one-two-three, footstepped them back again, and flattened himself on the earth to see how much his body covered. He ran to a hillock, and when he got to the top jumped up and down as if to make it lower.

'Have this slice of cake, my pretty little duck. You must be hungry after so much travelling around.' She offered a corner as if to a prize budgerigar, but he took the slice and went back to chuff-chuffing around the slope like a train. When he fell with a bump she waited for the howling indicated by his face, but the features straightened before reaching her. He drank too much for his throat. 'My nose is fizzy.'

'I might not know who your father is, but you're the spitten image of your mother.' Children took in everything, even at his age, so she must stop saying such things in case he later asked questions his mother wouldn't want to answer.

The gate clicked, and she saw Alma coming along the path.

'Coo-ee, Oliver!' She picked him up, though he was beginning to weigh a ton. Lydia knew from the glow in her eyes that she had passed her test.

'I said everything right, would you believe it? I got a teaching post. Mr Walker congratulated me on the impression I made.' She wheeled Oliver around in a half-dance until out of breath. 'Oh, I'm so glad.'

'If you are, then I am. But you must have some tea and a sandwich.'

Having run from the house too nervous to eat, saying there wasn't time, she had been half an hour early for the appointment. She steadied herself to sit, as if all strength had been used up in a life that might now be passing. 'The only thing is I must work in Newark for a year, and I won't like being separated from my little bundle of shame!'

Lydia frowned. 'Newark's only twenty miles away, and Oliver will be as right as rain with me. Won't you, Little Nollie? He'll soon be a big Nollie, then I can set him on at the lace. You'd like that, wouldn't you?' She held him so that Alma could eat, then he ran back to his hillock.

'It's going to be a struggle.'

'When wasn't it?'

'But I shall miss him.'

'I know you will, but take it in your stride, and when you look back on it it won't have seemed too long. You'll see him every weekend, and he'll be safe with me, won't you,' she called, 'while your mother knocks some knowledge into all those ragamuffins?'

Sensing a cloud over the otherwise clear landscape, a tear ran down his cheek, which he caught on his tongue, and smiled at the taste of salt. Alma fastened the top on the flask. 'I could turn it down.'

'And disappoint Mr Walker? I wouldn't let you. Not now you've come this far.'

'I thought about it on my way here.'

Lydia stretched. 'My old bones get worse and worse. When you see what most women have to put up with we should consider ourselves lucky. We'd better go, though. It gets cold at dusk.'

They must work at the lace until midnight, to make up for the day's absence, and Alma thought, holding the gate for them to pass through, that compared to such drudgery her time in Newark couldn't come too soon.

'What's all this about?' Burton had to ask, at Edith in her mother's arms. He might have guessed, but didn't want to. Her bitter and desperate keening filled the kitchen, while two-year-old Douglas boxed the dog on the rug, an innocent with no notion of the disaster.

'It's Tommy,' Mary Ann said. 'She got the telegram, and came straight here to tell me.'

'The bloody bastards!' Edith didn't need to explain who they were. Nobody could at such a time. 'They've gone and killed him.' She picked up Douglas who, at the bang of her heart and the hard grip, began to howl.

Burton had noted more houses with blinds drawn on his way from work, meaning that someone in the family had been killed in action. Mary Ann read in the newspaper that the government disliked the custom of drawing blinds. It wasn't good for the national spirit. People saw how many there were. They talked, and grumbled. They might no longer believe in what the country was supposed to be fighting for. Drawn blinds indicated a plague of misery, and he wondered that people put up with it. Thousands of young men were now called up whether they wanted to go or not, and there soon wouldn't be enough wood to make crutches for the cripples to go around begging their bread. Wars kept the rich rich, and nobody but the poor ever paid for them.

He took off his cap, and smoothed the peak before hanging it up. He had even told Edith that he liked Tommy, which made her a little fonder of him, though not by much. He had respected him because he was a smartly dressed hardworking warehouseman at the bike factory, nothing wrong with him as the man for Edith, so he felt pity and anger at his death. She put Douglas close to the dog, and went into the parlour, banging the door behind her.

'I'll go and keep her company,' Mary Ann said.

Burton knew how terrible it was for his daughter, who'd expected to pass a lifetime with the man she loved, and now he was dead, a gunner blown to pieces, as like as not, and for no reason he could fathom, no home burial for him, to see his face and say goodbye. 'Leave her.' He sat at the table. 'The poor girl needs to be by herself a bit.'

Everyone hungry, they wanted food. Mary Ann, hair grey yet eyes as blue and bright as ever, couldn't face another's suffering. Her heart broke every day at the slightest upset, such tender feelings did she have. 'Sit down and eat with me,' he said.

She couldn't recall when he had last allowed that, perhaps at Matlock when there had been someone else to serve. Did he intend her to think of that happy time? 'Leave Edith alone,' he said. 'Take her dinner in later. She'll eat it then, I know. She's one of us. She's got to go on living, to take care of her lad.'

He lifted Douglas to his knee, the blank pale face wary, and at his squirming Burton put him down to go on tormenting the dog. 'Edith will mend,' he said. 'It'll take a while, but she will. She's young, and she'll get married again.'

He laid a choice slice of meat on Mary Ann's plate, took up the boat of mint sauce, spooned out potatoes, forked a boiled onion and some cauliflower. 'It's all from the garden,' she remarked.

'I know,' he said. 'I grow it for you,' glad at her beginning to eat. A tender nugget sent down on his fork to Douglas was clutched as if by right, but while making burbling noises at his good fortune the dog swallowed the meat, and would have dozed by the fire to digest it had not Burton shifted it away with his boot.

Only women can comfort women, were better at it than he could be. Mary Ann finished her food and went into the parlour, while he sat making a box of spills out of an old newspaper – all they were fit for – a mindless job, but Edith's fate didn't give him the peace to enjoy it. He would willingly put her grief on his shoulders, but grief wasn't transferable from the one who was stricken. To tolerate its pangs and let no one know his torment was the least he could do for his tall and one-time rebellious daughter, now bowed down in the certainty that she would never see Tommy Jackson again.

Mary Ann came back, and he asked how she was.

'She's crying her heart out,' as was she. 'The poor girl's broken by it. But she's eating her dinner.'

'I knew she would.' A blacksmith's daughter would get over it. His heart was breaking with hers, but a broken heart would always mend, if you lived long enough in hope. And if you didn't live long enough you took your broken heart to the grave and had it mended there. He well knew there was no other way.

Sabina had never been so late. He didn't like her being out after ten o'clock. She wasn't old enough to look after herself, if any young woman ever had been. Soldiers crowded the pubs before going to France, got drunk and hardly knew what they were doing when they came onto the street. Or perhaps they did. It didn't bear thinking about. Women made guns and shells in the factories for men to kill each other, earning more money than men ever had. They could even afford to get drunk, a cheerful lot, except those who'd had people close to them killed, and they were either glad of alcohol, or so mixed up with the others you didn't notice them.

Thinking of Alma, he wondered whether the child was boy or girl, what she was doing and where she lived. He wanted to see her but wouldn't enquire at the Sunday School in case Mary Ann heard of it, not caring to jeopardize himself in her eyes anymore. Alma must have left the district, otherwise he would have seen her, though if he did she would ignore him, and who could blame her?

Mary Ann seemed reconciled to the war going on forever. Victories reported in the newspapers were all of them disasters. He'd heard a drunken soldier on leave from the trenches say they were no more than bloodbaths, and to no purpose.

There were fewer at table these days, with Oliver dead and Edith gone, and now Rebecca had married a miner who lived in Yorkshire, a man who didn't have to go in the army because the government needed the coal. On the other hand he was a loud-mouth who spent every night in the boozer getting kay-lied, as if being well paid entitled him to it.

The gate rattled, the dog barked from its kennel, and Sabina came in, looking too pretty for her own good.

'Where have you been till this time of night?'

'I went down town, with two other girls.' She trembled, yet happy that time had been forgotten.

'Did you see the town hall clock?'

'It was foggy.'

He had seen stars glistening, on his way across the yard. 'Don't chelp me.'

She was defiant for the first time, not knowing or caring where it came from. 'I'm fifteen, and I'm earning my own living,' she said through her tears, 'so I've got a right to stay out a bit later.'

His smack across the head couldn't be avoided. 'Don't come in so late again. Now get to bed.'

'You aren't going to hit me anymore.'

Another flat-hander was once too often. She worked fifty hours a week, so he had no right to knock her about just for being in town with a couple of workmates. They'd had a tripe supper, and walked around the market square. She had kissed one of the youths, but what harm was there in that?

Much of the night she was trying to get the blankets from

Emily who, in the sort of sleep a zeppelin couldn't disturb, worked her hands like a machine to drag them back. Finally snug among her sisters, she knew she had to go. She folded a few clothes into a bag and went from the house before Burton got up.

The terror of the dark assailed her at the railway bridge, and tears, rage, exhaustion and hunger drove her from one wall to another, arms held out so as not to scrape herself against the cold stones, but she got through, and walked confidently up the lane.

'You shouldn't have hit her,' Mary Ann said, 'no matter what she'd done.'

'She said she'd been with two girls, but how was I to know if it was true?' He had never put it beyond his high-spirited daughters to tell lies, knowing where such a trait had come from. 'It wasn't that so much' – he pulled on his boots and sat down for breakfast – 'but she had to cheek me back.'

'I expect she was frightened.'

'So she should have been. She's got too much lip. I don't want her getting into trouble. I know what girls are like.'

'I'm sure you do.'

The bait wasn't taken. 'I've seen them walking around with soldiers. Some were painted up to the eyebrows. They couldn't have been older than fourteen.'

'Our girls are sensible enough not to get into trouble.'

The expected grunt of disbelief was not long in coming, as if he doubted that any young woman had ever been able to take care of herself in that way. He drank the strong tea she poured. 'The only girl I knew who never got into trouble was you.'

'And look where it got me,' the smile suggesting that in spite of everything, and whatever his faults, she would never stop loving him.

He sent a half-smile in return. 'That was because Mrs Lewin kept such a tight rein on you.'

'What a fine thing to say. You don't give me credit for anything.'

He put on his jacket and took up his lunch tin. 'I give you credit for everything, just as you deserve.' He looked pleased with himself for saying so. 'I can't think of anybody else I'd need to give it to.'

'It's nice to hear it from your lips now and again. But I'm worried to death about Sabina.'

He turned from the open door. 'You think I'm not? But worry won't help.'

'She's silly enough to sleep under a hedge.'

'The weather's still warm.'

'But it's cold at night. I can't think where she'll go.'

'She'll be back before long. The silly little devil will soon realize home's the best place. I'll call at the mill on my way to work, and ask what she thinks she's up to.'

'Don't hit her when you see her.'

He would lose an hour's work, the mill a fair detour from his route to the forge. 'I shan't, though she deserves it, a girl of her age running off without telling anyone.'

He hurried, not pleased at getting so much trouble from his feckless daughter, crossed to the Board School at Radford Bridge, where he had sent his children, then on by the station. Beyond the Jolly Higglers he noted that the pork butcher's window didn't display its customary abundance of food.

The tall brick façade of the mill, with its square tower, was on war work like every place, hundreds of women and girls turning out uniforms when the machines, he thought, would be better used putting proper clothes on people's backs.

Beyond the gate, at a wide doorway half-blocked by enormous square baskets on wheels, a man who wanted to know Burton's business was ignored. He went two at a time up the stone steps, avoiding a man coming down with a bale of khaki cloth, and found Luke the foreman looking through order sheets in his cubby hole of an office.

'I think I know why you're here.' Luke, acquainted with Burton from when he had come to see about Rebecca and Edith starting work, was a deformed man in his fifties, lame since birth, and with the firm all his life. Burton looked at the neat and tidy girls tending their machines in the long lit-up room, preferring those who were handsome to the merely pretty ones. 'Where is she?'

'Look for yourself,' Luke said. 'She came in first thing this morning and collected what money was owed. Then she left with a girl called Leah Allsop. They went off arm-in-arm, laughing at what they'd done.'

At least she wasn't on her own, though that needn't bode well, either. 'Where to?'

'I've no way of knowing. It was none of my business.'

'It was your business. They were young girls. You should have asked them.' He gave a last look at the rows of women, nodded to Luke, and went out onto the road. Mary Ann would have to be satisfied with that, and so would he. He had done all he could. Looking north, east, south and west, he had no idea of telling which way the daft girl had gone.

TWENTY-THREE

The Clydesdale shivered, nervousness in its eyes, warning Burton to be careful. Shoes had to be put on, and he wouldn't let Thomas or Oswald do it. The July day was no help, an empty milky sky with a sun that had burned for weeks. Nor was a bump in the air, telling that something like a bomb had gone off in the direction of Beeston, an ominous rumble and shake of the earth that sent the horse rearing.

Letting the foot go he jumped to one side and snatched at the reins. Hooves struck the ground with such a scrape he thought the horse might fall. Then it would take some getting back on its feet, and serve it right. Strength was needed to stop it going on hind legs, and he held firm as it kicked from behind. If it didn't stop he knew the exact spot in the ribcage where a solid punch would knock it to the ground. Even the strongest had their weaknesses, and a horse was no exception. 'You're all right now, so don't give me any more trouble. It was an explosion by the sound of it, but Old Nick's not coming for you yet, nor for me, either. Just hold still while I get these shoes on.'

'It was a big one,' Oswald said from the door. 'I felt the ground move. You did a good job with the horse though.'

He was glad neither of his sons had tried to help. 'Yes, but next time don't even stand at the door. Another face might upset it more, especially a long one like yours!'

On the way home they waited to cross Derby Road. Carts and wagons, and sometimes a motor lorry, carried wounded and bleeding victims into the city, many to die before reaching the hospital. A man told Burton that the shell-filling factory at Chilwell had gone up, hundreds killed and injured. A slaughterhouse. It didn't bear thinking about. As bad as in France.

Groans and screams came from the wagons, and Thomas went pale at blood painting its way onto the road. Nor was Oswald willing to look, Burton thinking them too much like their mother, which would do them no good. Smoke from the explosion floating up the hill scraped his throat. 'It's all part of this damned war,' he said.

Thomas stopped his whistling. 'None of our family works there, anyway.'

Burton wondered where Sabina was, and hoped none of his acquaintances or their family had been at Chilwell that day, glad when a gap in the traffic allowed them to cross. 'You work where you can, when you want bread for your children,' he said.

Thomas, ever hungry, bought a sausage pasty from a shop in Woodhouse, but after a bite slung it to a mongrel nosing along the gutter. 'It tastes as if they filled it with shit.'

'I expect they did.' Oswald saw him throw it down. 'But that's what you get, buying something like that from a shop.'

'Can't you wait for your dinner?' Burton said. 'It'll be on the table, unless it starts to thunder and Mary Ann's hiding under the stairs.' Rain spat at the end of the railway tunnel, as if the exploding tons of TNT had drawn in clouds to make a storm.

Bread, slices of bacon, and a dish of kidney beans were laid before them. 'I thought I heard thunder not long since,' Mary Ann said.

Thomas told her about the disaster.

'All those poor souls dead or maimed,' she said.

Burton also regretted their injuries. Unable to say so, he resented not being thought capable of such feeling. You couldn't object to that, either, because it was worse for them than for him if they didn't understand. 'Eat your dinners,' though it was hardly necessary to tell them.

Mary Ann sat with them for the main dish, at Burton's request. 'It's Sabina I worry about,' she said. 'I can't get her out of my mind. We haven't heard a word in months.'

He cut into the scrag-end of mutton she'd been able to get from the butcher's. A penny stamp cost nothing, and he was angry that Sabina hadn't written. What had he made her go to school for if she couldn't write a letter now and again? It was to annoy him, he knew, but she should realize it was Mary Ann who would suffer. 'She'll be back one day, but I won't have her in the house, after the way she's behaved.'

Mary Ann got up from the table, thinking it no privilege to sit with him if that was how he saw the matter. 'I'd never turn one of my own children away from the door.'

She was too soft-hearted, but she was his wife, and he had to take note of what she said now and again. He knew she knew that he did, and she knew also that he knew that he did. You couldn't be closer to someone than that, except when in bed at night or on Sunday afternoon, and even then it wasn't the same as knowing each other's mind. That was how they lived, no gainsaying it, though it didn't hurt to remind yourself that you must be careful what you said to questions you didn't want to answer. Life was difficult without having to give yourself away in talk, though keeping your trap shut wasn't hard, because he'd been used to it since birth. The youngest of ten, he'd had to let others do the talking before he dared open his mouth, and even then he might get a blow for his trouble, so after a while he had taken care not to. But whatever Mary Ann said about Sabina, he would never have her back in the house.

Frost was white on the ground, and on the bare twigs of the hedges, the garden derelict except for a few forlorn sprouts among the milky furrows. Sunday afternoon, he gazed over the fence onto the lane. Emily was in the parlour staring at the cat, Mary Ann was dozing by the fire, and Ivy had gone walking with Ernie Guyler, her latest boyfriend, while Oswald and Thomas were in Nottingham chasing the girls.

Everybody swore that times were changing, though if it was true he would do all he could to slow them down as the best way of caring for his family. They were changing because of a war he would have nothing to do with. Let people do their worst if they were mad enough. King and Country was a curse too many were afflicted with because they were too soft to know who they were unless they had such a thing to believe in.

Blistered ice covered the puddles, the lane empty, hedges so bare you could see across the fields as far as the bridge. Even a train along the embankment seemed slower because of the cold. He shivered in his jacket, a bitter start to the year. Changing times would make no difference to him. Old men were happy for their sons to go for soldiers, while women in factories made uniforms and guns to put into their hands. They would fight till the last man was dead, or so exhausted as to be useless. It didn't bear thinking about.

The government's taken my pigs, but even if they hadn't there'd be little enough to put in their bellies. Food's rationed, and Mary Ann queued for an hour to get a pound of sugar, but just as she reached the door the shopkeeper said there was no more left, and slammed the door in her face. I wish I had been there. They're even selling horsemeat, but I'd rather eat vegetables and bread than the flesh of beasts I've worked with all my life. He had ringed another bull last month, and Lord Middleton had sent him back with a leg of beef, which fed them for a while. Middleton might have thought it useful to keep him strong in case more such work was needed, but it was good of him all the same.

Someone came from under the bridge and walked slowly up the lane, avoiding ice and puddles, no coat on by the look of it, only a frock to keep out the cold, a jersey to the waist that didn't match. He supposed her a girl from Woodhouse taking the short cut to Aspley. Parents sent their children unprovided into any weather. You saw them every day, battered shoes keeping out neither rain nor snow. Wages from the factories were spent in pubs, with no thought for their children. Those who'd had barely a living wage before the war had been attentive to their families, but a lot now lived as if tomorrow never came, and if that was the change they had in mind he couldn't think it was for the better.

She stayed to the nearside of the lane, a sly little cat, walking slowly as if not wanting to be seen. Wondering who she was made him forget the cold. When she stopped by the leaning fence he could see only the top of her head.

'Dad, I'm badly. I think I've got tonsillitis. Can I come home?'

His limbs momentarily shook, though not from the cold. I won't have her in the house. I'll talk to her, then she can go back to where she came from. 'Stand across the lane, where I can see you.'

Sabina came close, bare arms folded, bluish features raddled with unhappiness. Snatched to the very middle, her shoes weren't fit for the feet of a tramp, though a slip of blue ribbon hung limp from her hair. The day wasn't even good for a dog to be out in.

She was flushed with illness, but through it all looked at him unafraid, eyes similar to his own, wanting to rush away from his brutal unfeeling look, should have thrown herself at a train or died of cold under a hedge. He would never take her in. If only he had been in the garden and Mary Ann at the door.

He read her easily because she was his own flesh. Neither she nor the others know me – observed her a few moments longer. 'Come into the house, and get yourself something to eat. You look as though you could do with it.'

She followed by the silent pigsty and into the large kitchen smelling of cinnamon and baked bread, thyme and curry, cleanliness and comfort, and the strong tea Emily had made, a medley of odours that must have been there even before she was born.

He closed the door and told her to sit by the fire. 'Not too close, or you'll get chilblains,' stood away from the table for a better look. He spat at the bars, its familiar sizzle part of the welcome she hadn't dared expect. 'Where did you go?'

'To Skegness. I worked in a hotel, but they treated me worse than a slave. I stuck it as long as I could, then ran away.' Tears smeared her cheeks, pride scorched at having pleaded to be taken in, but weeping with relief at not being turned away as she had dreaded. 'I was going to get a job filling shells at Chilwell, and go into lodgings, but Leah didn't want to.'

'She had some sense.' He spat at the bars again, always embarrassed by tears. 'You aren't having a baby, are you?'

'Oh, nothing like that.'

'Mary Ann will be in soon, to give you a meal.'

Emily took her cold hands and brought them back to warmth.

'It's lovely to see you, duck. You'll be all right now you've come home.'

'We'll have to get you some proper clothes.' He came back from the pantry with two buckets and the yoke. More water was necessary if Sabina was to have the bath she needed. And he might as well do something as stand idle, carry in tomorrow's coal, chop up a log or two of wood, make sure the house was comfortable now that a bird had flown back to the nest. 'Your mother will put you in the bath later, and scrub some of that muck off you.'

When the door closed on him Emily poured her a cup of tea, lifted a fresh loaf from the panchion, took the sharpest knife, and drew it through the bread towards her chest, a thick slice falling onto the table. She spread it copiously with margarine, spooned almost half a pot of homemade damson jam onto it, and looked with such pleasure at Sabina eating that she might have been her only daughter instead of a sister.

The war had to end sometime, and now it had. As with everything all you had to do was wait, but it had been like watching the hour hand of the clock go round, never seeming to move. The Armistice was signed, and you could buy meat, butter and sugar again, but the feeling was as if you had climbed out of a darkened room through a window onto a street hardly recognized.

The postman had delivered a small packet containing a large bronze medallion. The name OLIVER BURTON was engraved above a lion's head watched over by Britannia with a wreath in her hand. The accompanying paper, from Buckingham Palace said: 'I join with my grateful people in sending you this memorial of a brave life given for others in the Great War' – signed in facsimile by the King.

'As far as I'm concerned,' a rare occasion when Burton didn't curb his language before Mary Ann, 'the King can kiss my arse, and should have kept his trinket.' He wanted to throw it into the heat, but Mary Ann set it like a holy medal on the parlour shelf, giving it pride and sorrow of place among horse brasses and other ornaments. Burton would rather it had been nearer the fire, and used as a target to spit at.

Boots firmly on the pedals of Oswald's tall pushbike, he pumped his well-balanced upright way towards Woodhouse, speed as easily come by as fire in the forge on pressing the bellows as a child. The ratio of energy to distance made it much better than walking.

Every car, lorry and motorbike seemed to have come back from France. Enough buses had taken the place of horsedrawn brakes and charabancs to have an effect on the farrier's trade. Only a fool wouldn't see the way things were going.

Oswald had bought the bike for six pounds on the instalment plan, and paid most of it off, so Burton wondered about getting one himself, and was trying it out. The Co-op van went by, on its way to take the weekly order up the lane to Mary Ann, and by the time he reached the bridge it passed him on the way back.

A single morning glory in all its freshness guarded the wall of the house, a five-petal hand against the bricks. He leaned the bike by the old deal table under the tree and took off his clips, saw a clutch of dockweed sprouting, his ever-active fingers putting the leaves together, and yanking them clear by the single root, annoyed that neither of his sons had remedied the excrescence. He hurled the leaves in a bunch over the fence of the pigsty, smiling at two young porkers rousting themselves as if it was birthday time.

As always on greeting Mary Ann he took off his cap. Now in his fifties, his white head was almost shaved after yesterday's visit to the barber's. Emily on the floor violently stirred Yorkshire pudding batter around a large yellow bowl, the only thing she was good at. He bent down, and said in a lugubrious tone close to her ear: 'Not so much elbow grease, or it'll all go to froth.'

In her fright the spoon went handle-first into the yellowish mess. 'Now see what you've done,' he said.

'You made me do it, our dad.'

Mary Ann took the spoon out and gave her a clean one. 'Don't tease her.'

He set his lunch tin on the dresser. 'That's all she's good for.'

'No it isn't. She's a good help to me.'. When his jacket was on the back of the door and he sat at the table Mary Ann laid out his bottle and glass, with a piece of bacon and bread. She frowned at him shaking such a quantity of salt over his plate from a large pewter pot. 'You look tired.'

'It's not that,' he said. 'But trade's getting bad.'

She ignored that for the moment. 'I've made a blackberry and rhubarb pie.' Thomas put his lunch tin on the table before washing his hands. 'Take that thing off,' Burton said.

'It isn't harming anybody.'

'It's too close to my arm.'

He put it on the sideboard.

Mary Ann pushed a couple of sticks between the bars, giving the fire new life. 'Why is it bad?'

He wiped beer froth from his small white moustache. 'There's so many motors that nobody needs horseshoes. Or they soon won't want enough to keep three of us in work. They even make them by machine at a shilling each. I won't compete with that.'

She knew him well enough to think for him, to feel whatever disturbance tormented him, guess the anguish that wouldn't come from his lips. It was conduct never to be judged. 'What shall you do, then?'

Thomas drank from a large cup of tea, and Burton nodded in his direction. 'He'll have to get a job elsewhere, for a start.'

He had longed for the day when he would no longer be under his father's gaze. 'It won't bother me.'

'I don't suppose it will.' None of his sons had valued the good trade he had given them. Blacksmiths who took on different work were given the best of jobs.

'I'll go to the Raleigh,' Thomas said. 'They're turning out all the bikes they can. Motorbikes as well.'

Those, too, had robbed him of trade. Oswald joined them at table. 'Where have you been?' Burton asked, though he knew well enough. 'You shouldn't keep your mother waiting.'

'I was talking to Helen.'

Burton had seen them walking by the canal, Oswald introducing him to a dark-haired girl with a face too troubled by what she saw of the world, and by much that was uncertain in herself. He hoped Oswald would be able to take care of her, not sure whether he'd be lucky with her in the long run. 'She's a Roman

Catholic,' Oswald said, which none of the family saw as an issue between such a handsome man and so goodlooking a girl.

'You'll have to get a job, as well,' Burton told him, 'when we close up.'

'I've been expecting it. I heard they'll want a man to look after the canal locks between here and Trowell. There's a house to go with it, so I might apply. As a blacksmith I've got a good chance, and if I get it I'll ask Helen to marry me.'

Thomas pushed his cup aside to be refilled. 'Do you think she'll say yes?'

He smiled. 'I have high hopes.'

His smile reminded Mary Ann of Oliver's. 'She's a lovely girl.'

Burton emitted a rare grunt of approval: someone whose children would carry on his name. He stooped to unlace his boots. 'I'll close the place early next year, and see what I can get for it. Morgan said the other day they need blacksmiths at Wollaton pit for shoeing ponies and other work, and the pay he mentioned seemed about right. Then there's extra jobs I can do at the farms between here and Ilkeston, so we'll be all right for money. I'll keep what tools I need.' It was a step down, to be a journeyman again, yet the thought gave some pleasure because it would be like his younger days.

Ivy, home from the cigarette factory, came out of the scullery with a tray of washed crockery. 'I shall be going to put flowers on Oliver's grave tomorrow morning.' They were laid there every week, and would be while the forlorn portrait looked down from the wall.

'Take the clippers,' Burton said, 'and cut the grass. It needed doing last time I was there. I want to see it neat and tidy.'

They sat, seven when Sabina came in and took off her coat, a different girl, Burton thought, to the wounded sparrow pleading to be let into the house a couple of years ago. She was late, but he made no remark, knowing that she too would no doubt be getting married soon.

'Why don't you come with me and Emily tomorrow?' Ivy said to her father.

He cut into his meat. 'I only go on my own. You should know that by now.'

TWENTY-FOUR

He answered the knock, and a tall man in his thirties, spare, upright, unflinching eyes – something of the soldier about him – announced: 'My name is Albert Beardmore, late South Nottinghamshire Hussars. I was with your son Oliver when he had the accident.'

Burton stepped aside: 'Mary Ann!' – and invited the ex-soldier to sit at the parlour table. 'Your Oliver wasn't killed "while following his calling", as was written in the newspapers,' Beardmore said.

Burton put a hand on Mary Ann's shoulder, hoping she would stop crying and listen. 'I never believed it.'

'We got the horse off a train at Hungerford, and it was as wild a devil as I ever saw. We called for a drink at a pub, and Jenny the barmaid, as was found, put whisky in the horse's water. She did it without thinking, but the horse was already mad. The man who brought it from Marlborough said as much, so Jenny just got a ticking-off. I know all about it from her side. When I went back after the Armistice we got married, because we'd been writing to each other all during the war. We still talk about what a fine lad Oliver was. He was going to teach me to read and write, but another pal did it afterwards. I'm sure Jenny would have married Oliver like a shot though, if he hadn't been killed. But we've got three kids now, and live near Oxford. I'm in charge of some stables. This is the first time I've found the opportunity to look you up. I knew you'd want to know what really happened. The regiment lost sixty men killed altogether, as well as a lot wounded. I count myself lucky to have come through without a scratch.'

Burton refilled his glass. 'And all this was known about his death at the time?'

'They didn't want to tell you the truth, I can't think why. But I got into trouble as well. We shouldn't have stopped at the pub, but you know what soldiers are. Not that I think it would have made much difference with a horse like that, though I'll regret to my dying day what happened.'

Burton wore his navy-blue suit, a button-sized chrysanthemum in his lapel, the tip of a white handkerchief pointing from the opposite top pocket, a polished watch chain across his waistcoat, and a large flat cap in his hand. People at the cemetery were in twos and threes, but he stood alone, looked at the rectangular tombstone, a marble scroll at the head. The two prongs of an embossed horseshoe pointed down, and though unable to read, he knew the words well enough:

'IN MEMORY OF OLIVER THE BELOVED SON OF MARY ANN AND ERNEST BURTON WHO WAS ACCIDENTALLY KILLED WHILE DOING HIS DUTY NOVEMBER 15TH 1914. LATE FARRIER SOUTH NOTTINGHAMSHIRE HUSSARS.'

He stood by the grave, and at times Oliver was so fleshly vivid that he reached out to touch, and say a few words – before the agonizing truth came that his son was dead.

He threw the wilting flowers against the church wall, and carried the water-filled vase back to put the daffodils in, and stood upright, no words to his sorrow, as still as a dummy inadvertently left there, to stay until rotted into the soil by rain and be even closer to whoever was so intensely mourned.

Unwilling to go directly home, he replaced his cap and walked to the White Hart, to stand by the bar he had chatted over to Mary Ann thirty years ago. Emma Lewin, whom he had so much fancied, and who had been so good to them, was long since gone, and the landlord who gaffered in her place had ex-sergeant-major written all over his face, upright behind the pumps, pot-bellied and moustached, hair parted down his skull. A couple of chaps were listening to the story of his life, Burton getting little more than the end: 'I was in the Ordnance Corps, all through the war, and swore every day that when I got out I would have a pub of my own.'

He should run it, instead of jawing, Burton not stopping to discover how he had found the money to set himself up. Energy to wear down after his pint, he walked over the Leen and the canal, leaving houses behind, up and over the railway bridge. Far left across the meadows was the line he had travelled on to get the gloves for Mary Ann, and again for the coveted claddach ring in his attempt to mollify her after doing what no man ever should. Packed trees on the heights of Clifton were painted darkly under a clouded sky too high to threaten rain, though a shower would be welcome for a richer sniff of the grass.

Sense told him that you couldn't be on your own for long, but after being so close to Oliver it seemed an intrusion to hear a woman shouting: 'Come down, you little monkey, or you'll get your suit dirty.' She held a bunch of flowers, and turned to the two younger women. 'He'll never listen,' but laughing at her unnecessary concern.

Alma's dark and slender companion stylishly smoked a cigarette: 'I don't see why you go to that cemetery every month.'

Burton looked across the nondescript fields, lighting a cigarette before facing an encounter impossible to avoid, recalling their stay at Matlock as if it had been last weekend. Her face was more full – plainer – not as it had come back to him since last seeing her.

'I knew him,' she retorted. 'You don't have to worry. He's been dead a long time.'

'I didn't mean that,' the smarmy woman said.

'I shall go whenever I want to,' Alma said, 'whatever your dislikes, dear Rachel.'

Rachel let the spent cigarette fall from its holder. 'I shan't say any more.'

Lydia hoped not, but was used to quarrels boiling up out of nothing, couldn't understand why they shared a house when much of the time they seemed to like each other so little. In the beginning Alma had asked her to live with them, but Lydia knew that such a scheme would end in pain and turmoil, wanted in any case to stay where she was, small and dingy though her own place sometimes felt, bothering nobody and not being upset by them. The Old Age Pension was hardly enough, but she earned a few shillings dressmaking, and by looking after peoples' children. 'Oliver! Don't fall into that ditch.'

'I can see tadpoles.' He kneed himself up a low tree in his neat short-trousered suit, and waved from the top: 'I like it here. I'm the King of the Castle!'

Burton stood by the gate, and she noted his unmistakable stance, the same long jaw and firmly-angled chin, and though he looked at least the decade older he was still placed as if he owned the earth and was the only man on it. She couldn't think why she had given herself to him – so long ago – except there was always Oliver to remind her. I fell in love, and the villain took advantage of me, unless in a fit of juvenile madness I was the one who did that.

His look demanded recognition, everything they had done burning in his possessive stare, irony and some humour on his lips as a hand went to the rim of his cap, and glanced the smartly clipped moustache on coming down.

The last time she was reminded of him was on seeing a man in the Duke of Portland's retinue at an agricultural show that Rachel had wanted to attend, who wore a large flat cap in exactly the same way. She smiled, and went forward.

He was glad the two other women walked in different ways across the field. 'I hardly expected to see you around here,' he said.

'I call at Oliver's grave now and again, though I don't often come this way, unless to let my son run about.'

He wondered how much better she would have felt if the grave had been his. 'It's a wonder we didn't meet before, or that you saw some of my family there.'

'I came across Edith once.'

'Who's the lad up the tree?'

Whatever he'd done he'd given her something to make life worthwhile, and the worst of the struggle was behind her. 'Can't you tell?' she smiled.

A twitch at the left cheek told her he could. 'Why didn't you let me know?'

'Didn't Edith say I was pregnant?'

'She might have done.'

'I didn't want to let you know, with any of your family around.

You wouldn't have wanted that. In any case I thought it best not to bother you.'

Pleased more than not at such consideration, he nodded towards Oliver. 'So he's mine?'

'He can't be anyone else's.'

Rachel came back, stood aside with lips sourly closed, thinking it curious that Alma could have any connection to a man who looked like an old soldier from the war before the one before. Lydia had waited a long time, till this casual meeting with such a tall impressive man showed the last piece of her puzzle coming into place. You could see from the face, and the shape of his head, that he was Oliver's father.

'Fetch him over,' Burton said.

'Oliver, come here,' she called in her schoolteacher's voice as if he was miles away. 'Come here at once.'

He ran. 'What do you want?'

Burton noted the blue eyes and a fair curl over his forehead, while the shape of the nose, and the lips as if about to start whistling, reminded him of Oliver, though the lad was his right enough. He put a hand towards him: 'Shake this.'

'Why should I?'

Burton laughed. He must be mine. 'Do as I say.'

The tone gave no option, and Burton took the warm hand for a moment, then turned to Alma. 'You aren't married?'

'No,' she said, 'and I never shall be. I've been a teacher for five years. And this is my friend, Rachel.'

A jaunty, intriguing woman, she wore a dark costume with a scrap of lace at the throat, picked a fleck of tobacco from small white teeth with a painted nail. He sensed the sort of woman who would never do for him, and there weren't many he could say that about. Her reluctant hand came forward, so he offended her by a mere touch.

'We share a house in Carlton,' Alma said.

'That's why I didn't see you.'

'And this is my Aunt Lydia,' to whom he gave the full hand, realizing that she was the one who had covered for her in Matlock, and afterwards cared for her. 'We're going on holiday to France next month,' Alma told him.

'I expect you'd rather go to Skegness,' he said to Oliver.

'I've not been there yet, so I don't know what it's like, do I?' He had given up trying to understand the meaning behind all that was being said. 'But I've been to Rachel's cottage at Staithes.'

'Rachel and I will be going on our own,' Alma said, 'and he's to stay with Lydia.'

'We'll go into Belgium, to see my brother Charles's grave,' Rachel said. 'He was killed.'

'I'm sorry to hear it.'

Oliver grasped his hand. 'Who are you, Mister Man?'

The boy sensed more about Burton than his name, but what a bust-up it would cause if I told him, Alma thought.

'Everybody calls me Burton, so you can as well.'

'He seems to know you,' she said, not altogether liking the idea, though supposed that blood would always tell.

'A year ago I could have shown him the forge.'

'I don't think he'll ever be a blacksmith.'

'The trade's finished,' Burton said, seeing Rachel's eyebrows go up. 'There was none better. Both my sons have found good jobs because of it. I'll take the little chap off your hands, while you go to the grave.'

More an order than a request, though Rachel's lips curled in disapproval. He's mine, Alma thought, not yours, anyway, let him be with a man for once. 'Would you like to walk with Burton for half an hour?'

Oliver gripped his long legs. 'Oh yes! That's thirty whole minutes. Can it be thirty minutes and fifteen seconds?'

'Bring him back to Lydia's house on Park Street.' She told the number. 'We'll be having tea there.'

'I know where it is,' Burton said.

Rachel watched them striding the lane hand-in-hand. 'Why did you let him go off with that chap?'

She wanted to manage everything and everyone, and Alma wasn't sure how much longer she'd care to put up with it. 'I did it because I did.'

Burton bent his knees, to touch Oliver's head. 'The Trent's not far away.'

'Oh, not that same old dreary river.' He looked at the shapes and veins of leaves, and threw them down. 'I'd rather go to the Amazon.'

'And where might that be?'

'It's a mighty river in Brazil, with fish that eat your fingers to the bone. Not like the piddling Trent, full of minnows. Lydia often takes me there because she thinks I like it.'

'Don't you?'

'Of course not. But I tell her I do.'

'You're a real little sharpshit.'

'Rachel doesn't like swearing.'

'I'll bet she doesn't. Shall you tell her?' – rather hoping he would.

'I don't think so. She'd get on at me. My mother doesn't like it, either, but we sometimes swear at school, in the playground.'

'Do you learn a lot there?'

'I suppose so. But I'm good at reading and writing, and geography.'

The river was shot with cooling light, cloud lower above the ripples. He stopped by the dredger, and held out an arm, saying, 'Pull this finger.'

'What for?'

'It's giving me gyp. You'll make it better.'

Amused yet distrustful – Burton had seen the expression on the other Oliver. The blood had done some funny twists and turns. The boy got a grip on the long bony finger. 'You mean like this?'

He dampened a smile. 'You'll have to do better than that.'

Oliver pulled, angled against the ground, face reddening at the effort. 'I'm doing my best.'

Burton let out a long splintering fart. George had tried the same game with him as an infant, to the amusement of all the others, while he could still be treated as a pet, and before he grew old enough to work.

'Oh, you farted!'

He took the boy's hand. 'You'll be a rum lad when you grow up.' Spits of rain fell onto Oliver's hair, so Burton used it as a reason to end the outing. 'We'll go back now, or your mother will miss spoiling you.'

'She doesn't spoil me. But she'll miss me, I bet. She always worries about me.'

'That's no good.'

'That's what I say. And then Rachel gets on to me.'

He hurried the pace, to see if Oliver would keep up. 'It sounds like you have two mothers, and that's no good, either.'

His face twisted with dislike at the idea, a more delicate boy than he looked, which was even less good. 'You're a fine young lad,' he said sternly, 'but you must never let anything like that bother you. In fact you should never let anything bother you at all.'

'I shan't. But I'm tired, Burton.'

'You've walked a long way.' Back among the streets he arched his back down from full height. 'Climb up me as if I'm a lamp-post.' He had played it with Oliver and the others in their early years, recollection more than effort giving an ache at the heart. 'You can get on my shoulders, and you'll see as far as Brazil from there.'

He set him squarely on, and crossed the main road towards Park Street, where he knew of a pub called the Black's Head, good for a pint after he'd handed him back, knowing he would never see him again.

TWENTY-FIVE

Ivy pulled her coat collar up and fastened the scarf against a cold rain-laden wind, the smell of the air clean and good. Too dark to go along the canal and through the sawmill, it was even so lonely enough on the main road after leaving the building sites and the last glow of the nightwatchman's fire. She carried a tin of food to give Burton at Wollaton pit two miles away, because he had sent word with a collier on his way home that he would be working till midnight, and Mary Ann was not to wait up.

Tall and strong like all the Burton daughters, she still didn't fancy being alone in the dark, so carried the usual bag of pepper to sling in the face of anyone who might jump on her from a hedge, knowing that Mary Ann's arcane method of defence was more to reduce anxiety than have much effect.

A pony and trap went by, a light back and front, the crack of a whip in the dull air, creating such a clatter on its way towards Nottingham you'd think the devil himself had come out of hell for a drive to frighten people. She had been to the coalmine in daytime, but when it was dark Sabina or Emily would come with her, laughter certain to keep them safe. Tonight they had been allowed to go to the Ilkeston Road Picture Palace.

Mary Ann told her someone had called that evening to see Burton, a tall impressive man, well-dressed and quietly polite. 'Let your father know about it,' she said, and Ivy repeated the message aloud every few minutes so as not to forget, and to gain courage while walking. Startled by an owl's hoot from the marshes around Martin's Pond, she hurried by the park walls dimly seen across the road. Perhaps the man who had called for Burton was a lost relative come back from Australia, and the family would one day come into a fortune, and he might fall in love and want to marry her, which couldn't be, because Ernie Guyler was her sweetheart, and they would never chuck each other.

The lit-up Admiral Rodney was noisy with boozers, horses and carts and motor cars lined up outside. She felt safer, with only another half-mile to go. She and Ernie Guyler had walked in Shepherd's Wood last Sunday, and even though he had consumption, or maybe because of it, and knowing he might not have long to live, he was able to make her happy. And she could play her part as well in that way. People at work said you might get left on the shelf at twenty-five if you didn't look sharp, but she didn't worry about that, as long as she had a good time.

Yellow and orange lights at the pit were close, and the man on the gate told her she'd find Burton in the engineering shop. 'You can give the snap straight to him, duck.'

She made her way between sheds and buildings, so much machinery it was surprising anyone could hear what was being said. Coal, fire and sulphur gave a smell of the inferno and, behind Burton in the wide doorway, were enough jangling noises to go with it. He glared at her, as if not wanting to be seen in a place he didn't own, but he was only wondering whether she had brought bad news from home. 'What do you want?'

She put the tin forward. 'Mam sent you some supper.'

He wore a large leather apron, tools in hand, features even thinner in the half-light. In a sour mood, because nobody liked working till midnight, he also thought she had been put to unnecessary trouble in having to walk so far, when he could have managed without eating till the end of his work. He took the tin as if grudgingly. 'You needn't have bothered.'

She walked the whole way back with his unappreciative words so rankling that she felt no fear, thinking she ought to have opened the paper bag and thrown the pepper in his face at getting not even a thank you and having given up her evening for the errand. Only when putting her hand to the gate latch at home did she recall the message Mary Ann had insisted that she recite, about the strange man who had come to the house. Ivy regretted her lapse because maybe Burton would have told her who he was. Then she was glad at having forgotten, laughing at the thought that it served the old devil right.

Mary Ann waited up for him nevertheless. 'He was a very smart young man.' They were undressing by the curtain-drawn four-poster bed. 'He wouldn't say what he wanted, and I didn't like to seem nosy and ask, but you could tell by his voice he came from Wales.'

'Did he say he'd call again?'

'He mentioned tomorrow evening. I had a funny turn, because he looked a bit like your brother Edward when he was young.' He had resembled Burton more, having black hair instead of fair, but she wouldn't say so. 'Haven't you any idea who it might be?'

'It's a mystery to me.' One of his longest yawns ever signalled the end of the matter. 'I expect it'll be solved.' He got into bed and was soon on his way into sleep, taking speculation to be shared with no one.

A cup of Camp coffee in hand, he sat by the fire after his meal, while Mary Ann went to answer a firm knock at the door. 'It's that gentleman who came for you yesterday.'

'Tell him I'll be out directly.' He stood before the Sandeman mirror to straighten his shirt collar, draw a hand through bristly hair, and put on a jacket and cap, to appear as neat as anyone could just back from work.

Mary Ann was right regarding the man's likeness to the family, for he was tall and thin-faced, hair not quite as dark as she had said, more mousy, eyes grey and lips under a similar small moustache as if about to smile. He wore a pepper-and-salt suit, with a tie and well-ironed white collar, a good quality mackintosh over his arm, brogues highly polished. The feather of his smile was momentarily curbed when Burton, weighing him up in a second, asked: 'What is it you want?'

'Strangely enough,' he glanced towards the lane as if someone might appear to stop him talking just as he had found the person he'd been looking for. 'I'm in Nottingham for a few days, so thought it would be interesting to talk to you. My name's David

Ernest Dyslin. I was born near Pontllanfraith. I believe you know where that place is?'

A satisfactory speed of mind was necessary when faced with surprise or embarrassment but, all the same, he should have known what was coming. He grasped the man's arm. 'Walk to the end of the yard with me,' glad none of the family were near to crowd in and listen. To delay matters, whatever they might turn out to be – though he had a good idea – he asked: 'What line of trade might you be in?'

Dyslin smiled at such a question, the same faint curl of the lip as came onto Burton's when amused at giving information from an unassailable vantage point. 'I'm a solicitor, here on some will and property business for a client in Cardiff. I'll be going back tomorrow, so I'm more than happy to find you.'

'People don't make such a point of it for nothing.' He accepted the offered cigar from his leather case, as yet too astonished to think of him as his son, but refused a match and struck one of his own, holding the flame a few moments over the end of the cigar, then pressing the fire out with two fingers, and rubbing the burnt part of the match to a point. Making sure it was sharp enough, he stuck it in the end that would go into his mouth, firstly so that it could be held more securely between the teeth, and secondly that the juice would go into the wood instead of his mouth, and thirdly that the end of the cigar wouldn't get soggy. Smoke flew out over the lane. 'Now you've found me.'

'Do you recall anything about the name Dyslin?'

Burton puffed on the cigar – a good one – and looked into his eyes. 'I knew a woman in Wales who had it.'

'I'm her only child.'

Every day, no matter how far back, was only yesterday as far as he was concerned but, judging by the age of the man before him, he could acknowledge that thirty-six years had passed all too quickly. 'How is she?'

Dyslin, fascinated by Burton's procedure in lighting the cigar, thought he might follow it himself sometime. 'She died, two years ago.' He tapped ash on top of the fence while waiting for a phrase of regret – which didn't come. 'Before she died . . .'

Burton wondered if there'd be any blawting, which would be disgraceful in a grown man. It was two years ago, after all.

'She told me how I came into the world.'

'We met on a train.' Burton wished for such an adventure today, but knew it was unlikely to come more than once in a lifetime. 'She told me her husband had just died. He was an engineer at some pit in Staffordshire.'

'Your memory is good.'

'It's hard not to remember things like that.' When did you forget anything, especially when silly damned people reminded you so unexpectedly? 'You must have had a job finding me.'

'Not at all. She told me your name and your calling, and where you came from. I'm used to tracing people.'

There were many Burtons in Nottingham, but it could hardly be denied he'd found the right one. 'How did you become a solicitor?' Being told to mind his own business might provide sufficient reason for walking away, but Dyslin had the sense and politeness to tell him.

'My uncle, the Methodist minister who took in my mother, was a good man, and I did so well at school he paid the two-hundred-pound premium for me to be an articled clerk for five years. After I qualified I enlisted and went to the war, like everyone else, and didn't get into practice till I came out.' In spite of the silence Burton knew he had more to say. 'I got the notion of coming to see you as soon as the opportunity arose. I know my mother wanted it.'

They observed each other with an intensity that couldn't deny their connection, stance exactly alike, even something in the shape of their hands and the casual smoking of cigars. Dyslin was talkative, but Burton supposed he would be in such a situation. He could hardly have inherited the tongue-wag from his mother, who'd never said much. 'She didn't want to marry again?'

'She told me that the only person she ever loved was you.'

'I did think a lot of her, and it's good of you to let me know.'

'She said it, not me.' He showed less of a smile. 'But it's been on my mind the last year or so to talk to you. I'd assumed my father to be the mining engineer, and you can imagine my surprise, for a while anyway, when she told me just before her death that it could only have been you, a journeyman blacksmith.'

Burton gave a short dry laugh. 'Strange things happen in the world.'

'Anyway, you might like to know I'm getting on well in life.' His smile turned from one of amusement to irony: 'Though there were times during the war in France when I wished no one had ever met my mother.'

'I don't suppose you were the only one.'

'At least I stayed alive, and came out a captain in the South Wales Borderers. Now I have three children, all on their way to being grown up.'

So I'm a grandfather again, which makes seven, the last time I counted. 'I'm glad to hear it.'

He held something wrapped in tissue paper. 'My mother wanted me to give you this. She said you wiped her tears with it at the worst time of her life.'

Burton looked at the folded handkerchief. 'So I did.'

'I have a lot to thank you for.'

He put the handkerchief in his pocket, something precious to remind him of Minnie. The regret that he hadn't persisted in trying to marry her was caught by the tail as it sped through his mind. 'She was a very fine woman. Knowing her was one of the best times of my life.'

They stood in silence, till Dyslin said, 'I understand you not inviting me into your house, while your wife is there.'

'What happened between me and your mother was long before I got married.'

'I imagine so. The war altered many attitudes, otherwise my mother might not have told me about you.'

'Come and see me whenever you like.'

Dyslin's cigar went sparking into the lane. 'I might not have another chance. If you want to reach me, here's my address. My uncle was a father to me nearly all my life, but I don't mind thinking a little of you in that way, though I shan't bother you.'

He's just as obliging as his mother. Burton thought himself lucky that it ran in the family. The white piece of calling card fitted into his waistcoat pocket, well hidden for going into the house.

The handshake was so firm that Dyslin hoped no bones would need resetting before going back to the office, though whether the pressure made up for his putative father's off-handedness was still hard to decide.

Burton watched him striding down the lane, glad that at least one of his sons had made something of himself. He stood a few minutes, unable to move. Oliver had died, but he had gained another that had been growing up in Wales all the time Oliver was alive. The shock usually came long enough after the event to poleaxe him – for a moment or two. Life was long with so many happenings that you didn't know about and therefore couldn't control. He felt weirdly blinded as if, for reasons he couldn't fathom, he didn't belong in the world of smithery but in a more expansive, a richer and better style to which he was entitled yet had never been able to enter because he was doomed to be who he was.

A shake of the head, he knew it wouldn't do, and with the shadiness of dusk coming on went into the house to receive the expected questions from Mary Ann.

'Who was he?'

'The son of a friend I knew in Wales. He came to tell me his father died recently, and thought I'd like to know. They've done well for themselves. The chap was a solicitor up here on business. He didn't go much out of his way.'

'He looked a lot like you.'

'Some must. I can't help that.'

'Ivy thought so as well.'

'She would.'

There was no way of getting anything out of him if he didn't want to explain. 'We can't both be wrong. You don't tell anybody what they want to know.'

Why should I? It always pays to keep your trap shut. 'Is there any whisky left in that bottle?'

'It's only half-gone.'

'Make a pot of tea then, and we'll put a splash in.'

Pouring some into a glass, he complained it was tasteless. 'Oswald and Thomas have been guzzling from the bottle, and levelled it up with water.'

Such remarks weren't as serious as might be assumed, she knew, or his words didn't come out the way he wanted because he had held them back too long. Maybe he only spoke so as to hear the sound of his own voice, and when he did the children answered back and made him angry.

But she was sure Oliver would never have drunk his father's whisky on the sly, and the little I take, she thought, can't make much difference. God help anyone if he caught them. Luckily it's his nature to suspect everybody, then he can't settle onto who in particular it was.

Thomas and Oswald might well have glued their lips to it, Burton thought, and I wouldn't put it past Ivy to sip a drop, or even Emily, whose eyes glistened unnaturally from time to time when she acted a bit dafter than usual. Maybe the whole family was at it, queued up to take their turn for a good swig when he wasn't there, and if so they'd all end up a bit sillier than they already were, or with their livers eaten away, which would serve them right.

'I suppose that's what you used to do with your father's whisky when he wasn't looking,' Mary Ann said. 'But if you think it's the others you'd better lock it up.'

'I'll be damned if I'll do such a thing in my own house. If you can't rely on your children to keep their hands off what doesn't belong to them who can you rely on?'

He didn't wonder at her laugh, but she had her notions, and he had his. She was welcome to hers, and could say what she liked, but he would keep his to himself. In most ways he lived in the time of when they had fallen in love, she thought, and would never change, which didn't make her unhappy. Holding more or less the same views was good for both, no matter how old they were beginning to look. All the same, she realized somewhat more than him how times were changing.

He wanted to tell her about David Ernest Dyslin, being pleased more than not at the meeting, but nipped his tongue as she poured the tea, and he put a good measure of whisky in both cups. 'We might as well drink it before the others sup it away.'

If he wouldn't tell her who the man Dyslin was she wouldn't admit it was she who liked a tot from his bottle now and again.

'That's a devilish thing to say about your own children. They'd never dream of stealing your whisky. It's just that the older you get the stronger it has to be.'

He touched her hand. 'I've got them weighed up.'

'It takes one to know one.' She liked talking, as a drop of the fiery stuff took effect. 'That young man was your son, wasn't he? It had something to do with when you were in Wales.'

He gave a grunt, then smiled. 'It happened long before we put the banns up.'

'That's nice to know.'

'It's none of your business.'

'You ought to have brought him into the house.'

'Well, I didn't.'

'He'll go away thinking we're a pack of heathens, keeping him outside like that.'

'He had no business around here.'

'If he comes again I shall invite him in,' though he was unlikely to return with the welcome he'd had.

'He had to see what I looked like.'

'I hope he wasn't disappointed.'

'He can please himself. Have some more whisky. It won't harm you. It's mostly water, only next time you have a nip when I'm not here don't put too much in.'

It pained Mary Ann that the children had always hated and feared their father. With Ivy it was more hate than fear, whereas the others feared more than they hated. Edith both hated and feared, but regarded him with contempt as well, and defied him as much as she could get away with, which was why she had been the first to escape by marrying Tommy Jackson. There had always been more of Burton in her than Burton could put up with, and she had more waywardness than he was able to tolerate.

Pushing Douglas in his cot by Woodhouse on her way to see Mary Ann and her sisters, she stopped at the railway bridge because the way through was deep in mud, no dry place on either side to save her sinking in.

She'd been trained by Mary Ann to be a good cook and housekeeper, so after Jackson's death she had found work living in at a large house near Radcliffe. Douglas was looked after by Tommy's parents, and she only saw him for a couple of hours on Sunday, which was pain enough for her full heart.

She wondered how to avoid getting cold and wet to the ankles. The family was expecting her, and would worry if she didn't appear.

The tall bullish young man who came out of the beer-off wore a Norfolk jacket under his army greatcoat, and a white scarf hanging to his waist. 'What's wrong then, duck? Can't you get through?'

'It's not that.' She drew herself upright. 'It's just that I'm waiting for a nice big boat with a velvet seat to take me. One usually comes if I stand here long enough.'

'That's me, then,' he laughed. 'I'm not the Titanic, but I'll get you through all right.' Before she could think of anything really sarcastic he picked up the cot with Douglas in it and carried it into the tunnel. 'I'll come back for you in a bit.'

He splashed his way along, and lodged the cot safely in a dry part of the track. 'Just wait there, you little crumb,' he said to the child. 'And don't cry, or I'll stop your windpipe. Your mam'll be here soon.' Douglas opened his eyes and looked over the barrier with stolid curiosity, then smiled as if his father had come back undead from the war.

Well-built and strong, he cradled Edith in his arms, and before she could say what the hell do you think you're up to? he went splashing through the mud. 'This is like milk chocolate. It's nothing, a paddling pool. I was a gunner in the Royal Artillery at Wipers. Now that was what you could call mud. There was lakes of it. I was a sergeant, and they promoted me because everybody else was either dead, drowned in the mud, or in hospital.'

She could well believe it. His brutal authority had a certain attraction, but only for as long as he would use it to protect a woman from the world, and not turn it against her – a young man to be wary of.

'I hate mud more than death. I'd run from anything that looks like it. But this ain't mud as I've known it. It's more like cocoa, and fit to drink while I'm carrying somebody as nice and warm as you.' He set her down, and the gap between his otherwise white and even teeth gave him a mischievous and untrustworthy look. 'Don't I deserve a kiss now?'

'You deserve a couple, I suppose, but you aren't going to get one. Thanks, all the same.'

'I can wait,' he said. 'I'm going up the lane to the Cherry Orchard, so at least I can walk a little way with you. You can't deny me that. Here, I'll push your cot.' She let him. 'My name's Doddoe. That's what everybody calls me. Surname, Atkin. You can have my army number if you like. I'll never forget that. But I didn't hear what your name was. Must have been the guns that did my ears in.'

She wondered how to get rid of him. 'It's Edith. And this is Douglas.'

'Are you going very far, Edith? I'm going after rabbits in Robin's Wood.' He stopped the cot and stood closer than she liked, opened his coat to show nets spilling out. A ferret's sharp little eyes from another pocket frightened her. Such a big girl, he thought, as if it might run up her legs and bite her quim. If it did I'd skin the little devil alive. 'It's only Percy.' He laughed, and showed her a cosh. 'It don't even earn its keep, though it's a hungry little bleeder.' He resumed his pushing. 'I'll knock it on the napper one of these days and throw it to the cat. Or I'll sell him and buy myself a pint.'

His talk sickened her, glad to stop by the gate. 'I'm going in here, so you can let me have the cot now.'

He was startled. 'That's Burton's place.'

'I know it is. He's my father.'

He put a hand to his cap, pushed it further back over his tight fair curls. 'Bleddy hell! I don't want anything to do with him. He's a hard bogger. I once asked him for a job, and thought the swine was going to kill me.'

'Don't you talk about my father like that.'

'Well, that's how he is. But he's got an eye for the women, I do know that much.'

'You can piss off.' She pushed him from the cot handle, and he seemed willing enough to walk up the lane alone, muttering about Burton, she was sure, words she had at one time used herself but didn't care to hear from a poaching braggart like Doddoe Atkin. Burton was her father, after all.

She watched the one-man poaching machine turn into the Cherry Orchard, thinking she would never marry someone like that, helpful though he had been, repeating the words with more determination on leaving the cot in the shed across the yard so that it wouldn't get wet in the rain.

She pulled Douglas into the house. Burton sat in his Windsor chair by the fire. 'Emily, clear out of the way so that your married sister can sit down.'

Emily sat on the rug to play with Douglas, her talk confirming for Burton that she was just the right age for him. 'I thought I wouldn't get here,' Edith said. 'I've never seen such deep mud under the bridge. But a chap called Doddoe Atkin carried the cot, with Douglas inside, all through it. He was very considerate.'

She had heard many grunts from Burton but was long to recall the one he gave now. 'He's a bad sort, the worst of the lot. I know about him and his ways. The rest of his family's rotten, as well. He was in the pub the other night with some of his pals, and I think he must have got thrown out of the army for swearing.'

Edith thought nobody could be as bad as Burton said. To him everybody was bad, so whoever he said was bad could never be bad to her. 'He helped me a lot just now.'

Pleasant, comely, and fair to all men as she was, you couldn't tell her anything. People went to hell in their own way, and little could be done to stop them, but he didn't want her to fall under the pall of Doddoe Atkin, since she had already suffered enough. Because Burton had brought the girls up strictly Mary Ann also hoped they'd never marry men who would treat them worse than they thought Burton had.

Emily was spoiling Douglas with a jam pasty, and not doing much good to her own face either, while Edith sat with a cup of tea and a slice of caraway seed cake, talking about the place she worked at. 'The doctor's wife is so mean it's a wonder I'm not skin and bone. At teatime on Saturday she puts a big cake on the table, after the bread and butter, and her five kids sit too frightened to ask for some. Well, I stand there feeling sorry for the poor little things, because I know that when she locks it back in the cupboard I'm going to help myself. I know where she keeps the key, so I don't starve. I shouldn't stay there if I did. She must think a ghost gets in to gobble it down.'

'That's not honest,' Mary Ann commented. 'But you should tell her to feed you properly.'

At the bridge on her way back, when Edith thought there'd be no option but to push the cot through and spoil her shoes, a voice from the bushes said: 'Don't worry, duck. I'm still here. I came back early to help you.'

He was hard to make out in the half-dark. 'Doddoe?'

'You weren't waiting for somebody else, was you? I wondered if your husband might come to meet you. That's why I hid myself.'

'I haven't got one.'

'Some rotten swine left you in the lurch, did he?'

'He was killed in the war. He was in the Gunners, as well.'

'A terrible lot of 'em caught it.' He took hold of the cot. 'I nearly went west more than once. I had a charmed life, though. Just a few scratches, and not many could say that who was in it from start to finish. Wait here, duck. I'll get the lad through first.' He bent down and kissed him on the cheek. 'Won't I, Douglas? What a lovely lad you've got, Edith. You'll have to get him out of the cot and make him walk a bit more. Then he can come poaching with me.'

'He bleddy won't.'

'Go on! He'll love it.' He came back to say she would have to ride piggy-back. 'It's easier that way, because I'm tired, and you'll be more comfortable.'

'I think you're trying it on.'

'I am, duck. I've got to confess.' Even the darkness couldn't hide the dazzle of his smile, the faint gap between his teeth accentuating what charm he had. Her warm arms went around his neck, and she recalled Burton's harsh words, which he would have used against any man she mentioned, only wanting to spoil her life. Doddoe had even remembered Douglas's name. 'Where do you work?'

'I'm a bricklayer, and I'm earning good money. They're building a lot of houses fit for heroes.'

'Why do you go poaching?'

'For a bit of sport.'

'It's not very honest.'

The word shocked him. 'Honest? Well, it might not be, but everybody does it around here.'

'My father doesn't.'

'Burton wouldn't, would he?' Setting her down, he offered a Park Drive, but she didn't smoke. He lit one for himself. 'Even Shakespeare's mother got done for poaching.'

'Who's Shakespeare?' She recalled Oliver mentioning the name, so she was testing him.

'How the hell do I know? I heard somebody say it in the Jolly Higglers the other night. He might have been a teacher from across the road, showing off. "Shakespeare's mother was caught poaching," he said in his posh voice. I heard it as clear as a bell.'

'A likely story.'

'Anyway, duck, I've got three rabbits in my pocket, so I'm going to give you one. It'll make a nice stew for you and young Douglas. Won't it, you lardy titch?'

She wanted to say no, but thought what a blessing it would be for the Jacksons, who had little money and could do with some help. Now and again she gave them a pat of butter, some scrag-ends of meat and a few bones, or a cigar for old Jackson which she hoped wouldn't be missed from the doctor's leather case.

The smell of rain on the rabbit's fur almost made her stomach heave, its body as limp as that of a dead cat. The lane joined the main road. 'You can leave me now. I'll be all right from now on.'

'Do I get a kiss, or don't I?'

'No you don't, you fawce bogger.'

He laughed. 'Well, I've enjoyed talking to you. I'll see you at the bridge next week, in case the tunnel's still muddy. You never know. I might even be there if it's as dry as snuff.'

Burton at dinnertime berated Thomas for having stayed out late the previous night. 'Two o'clock in the morning's not good enough.'

'I'm over twenty-one, so I should have the key to the door.' He dared to answer back, as if surprised at his father's unworldliness. Earning his own wages from the factory led him to believe he could do as he liked.

Burton lifted his fist for a solid smack at his son's head, to let him know his place, as everyone must who was still in the house, but for once he wasn't quick enough. Thomas, eyes wide open at what he took as an unjustified telling-off, was caught out by an eruption of cock-o'-the-walk confidence born from being hard done by for so long, and at the idea that a man of his age, who worked hard, should not be able to come and go as he pleased as long as he paid his board and no one but himself was harmed by it. He got one in first, and a good one, such a blow at Burton's chest that at the unexpected ferocity he almost fell to the floor.

Thomas was more terrified at what he had done than his father was surprised that such a thing could happen. On his feet in a second, and even more enraged at Ivy so openly amused at what she saw as his downfall, Burton picked up the woodsman's axe and went for his son as if intending to kill him.

Thomas fled, and Mary Ann – she would, wouldn't she? – wondered where he had gone, but Burton said that someone like Thomas would always find a bed, probably with a woman, until her husband came back, or she got fed up with him, which in either case couldn't be for long. 'So stop worrying.'

Thomas's re-entry into the house was negotiated by Mary Ann, and in agreeing to it Burton may have wanted Thomas back so that, Ivy said to Oswald, he could take a stern revenge. Unashamed at his reverse, knowing that hard lessons were often the best, Burton was confident that in any future set-to he would get his blow in first. At the same time he was amused at having a son courageous enough to tackle him, but if he stopped chafing at his lateness it may have been in the hope that one night he wouldn't come back at all.

Oliver would never have behaved in such a way, and as for Oswald, he's married and taking care of Helen who is so weak and delicate you'd think she didn't have long for this world, though newly-born Howard would no doubt help to keep her in it. Oswald hadn't stayed on as a blacksmith, won't work at the colliery as I have to, though nobody can blame him because it's harder graft than walking along the canal tapping the lock gates now and again to make sure they're not leaking. Times might be changing, as Mary Ann always claims, but there are fewer and fewer men to do the hardest work.

When Edith decided to marry Doddoe, Burton said: 'Don't do it,' but she did, because when did they ever not do what you told them not to? You said don't, and they always did. Even if you'd said do it, hoping they would do the opposite to spite you, they'd have done it anyway, since they had no sense and couldn't avoid throwing themselves at men with no trade, no dignity, and no brains.

If his girls blamed him for the rough beds they had to lie on after getting married they were wrong, because only the wicked and the weak held their parents responsible for what happened to them. Even if the parents had done what their children complained about, whoever blamed them would become parents themselves one day, and do even worse to their children, or at least no better.

He spat in the fire. As for your own kids, it was best never to open your mouth, then you wouldn't get answers you didn't like, or they wouldn't do something to regret. But he was sorry for Edith, helpless under the reign of a brute and a bully such as Doddoe Atkin had always been, boozing what wages he got and never a thought for her or their children. Rebecca's coalminer in Yorkshire at least provided for his family, though that man Seaton, whom Sabina married last month, was a numbskull as well, an upholsterer only fit to work for his father.

He pushed the dog from the fire. He wanted his girls to marry men like himself, but there was only one of him, and there were too many of the other sort walking around. In choosing men different to himself the girls found that times hadn't altered as much as they had hoped. He remembered scorning his father for saying: 'Men are lightweights these days,' yet the old man had been right, because men who now worked as little as they could get away with didn't treat their families well.

'It's always been like that,' Mary Ann said, thinking he went on too long about it. 'At the White Hart I noticed how many used to spend money they should have given to their wives and children. It was sickening. If times don't change, as you say, it's only because they've always been the same.'

She went up to bed, so tired that earlier nights were needed. He poked the bars, the top layer of coal falling lower in the grate, then put a bundle of sticks in the oven to be tinder-dry for Mary Ann starting a fire in the morning.

Soft and idle Thomas, who wasn't yet in, was only interested in going after women. Well-built and over six feet tall, with short thick wavy hair, he had farseeing blue eyes which even so, Burton was convinced, showed nothing but what was immediately in front, and he came in most nights with lipstick on his collar (which Mary Ann had to wash off) whistling some senseless tune like a love-sick canary.

Pushed out of the door, the dog sloped off to its kennel across the yard. He came back and drew the rug away from the fire, because dead ash might throw a spark and send the house up in flames while they slept in their beds. You couldn't be too careful. He turned the lamp out, and felt his way upstairs.

TWENTY-SIX

A large red handkerchief covered his left eye, keeping the blood all but invisible. Pain drummed as if the hammers of six smiths beat against the anvil of his head, the rest of his face whitening as he rode his bicycle against the cold east wind. The way seemed endless, and he was tempted to call at Oswald's house at the top of Radford Bridge Road, for whisky to dull the agony, but he didn't want Helen to make a fuss at the sight of his wound. She was always so fluttery and nervous, unless too busy burbling over baby Howard, so he pedalled on through Woodhouse, unable to care who looked at him.

Mary Ann cried out when he stood at the mirror to untie the handkerchief. 'Ernest!' – a rare word for the living part of the house.

He noted it, but excused her, since he felt half-dead from pain and mortification.

'What have you done to yourself?'

He sat by the fire, deadened flesh and bones coming slowly to life. 'A piece of steel flew in my eye. Some fool of a striker got the angle wrong, and hit a bit too hard.' He lowered the handkerchief, to show torn flesh, the eye a circle of blue, dull yellow and red, as if the hammer and not a mere spark had flown at his face.

'Oh, God, you've been blinded.'

'Only in one eye.' He looked around, as if to see all that was visible from the other. 'It's lucky I was born with two. I shan't be eating tonight, but how much whisky's left? I'd like a pull or two, unless the others have gluttoned it.'

She fetched the bottle from the parlour. 'I'll heat some water, and bathe the wound.'

'If you think it'll do some good.'

'It looks terrible.'

'I don't want to be seen by anybody in this state. Hand me the whisky before you get started. It's giving me gyp.'

He didn't complain about the strength, or look for the mark he had mentally put there, but held the bottle to his mouth, which he had never done before. After her gentle dabbing with a swab of clean linen he went upstairs and got into his nightshirt, lay in the dark, sparks bombarding his head as if trying to break through skin and tissue to his brain.

He set off at five o'clock to do his day's stint at the pit. Mary Ann asked him not to, but he knew what he was doing: you only stopped when you stopped for good. He felt justified when within a week the swelling around the eye began to diminish, though he saw nothing from it, and didn't need telling that he never would again. He asked Mary Ann to make two eyepatches. 'I don't care to have anybody looking at the mess.'

'What do you need two for?'

'I'll tell you, only don't ask again. I want a brown one for everyday, and to go to work in – a piece of strong cloth will do. Then I want the smartest one you can make, from black velvet, for when I get dressed up and go out.'

The pain was so intense at times that he was unable to be among the family. He took the bottle of whisky into the parlour, drew the curtains, and sat in silence. Mary Ann told the others not to disturb him, or make any noise. On going to see how he was, the only person allowed to, he'd be sitting upright in a chair, glass and bottle before him on the table, the world not so sealed off that he didn't hear everything said in the living room.

The throbbing would have given even more gyp had he but let it. Pain burned a cavern in his head, a space which, by an effort, he imagined as four compartments. As if by some trick he prevented his senses from entering more than one, where he would corral the pain and endure it until, like a miracle, it went away sufficiently for him to go back among the family, whom he would astonish or dismay with his knowledge of all they had said in his absence.

Ivy said, though not in front of Mary Ann, that God had got

back at Burton twice in his life: once when He had taken his son, and again when He had put out his eye. What she couldn't know was that Burton saw just as well with the other, and that with only one eye his hearing became twice as sharp, for he overheard her saying it to Thomas, who told her to keep her thoughts to herself. Burton couldn't forgive such a depth of malice, which neither he nor anyone else in the family could reach. Had Emily made the statement she would not be responsible, though she wasn't hard-hearted enough to come up with anything like that. Ivy should have known better because, for all her bitter dislike, she had to go on living with him in the same house.

Nor was he unaware that she sometimes referred to him as 'Old Nelson-one-eye'. He heard her, from the bedroom window, say it to Edith while walking in the garden, a remark he found so disrespectful to level at someone who was not only her father but a man who suffered so much that he was unable to go down and give her the smack across the mouth she deserved, or even ever to say anything, for to accept that one of his own flesh and kin could be so uncaring was more than pride would take. Whoever could be so slighting about another's misfortune would one day suffer for it, and though he might not be alive as a witness, that didn't lessen his satisfaction at the prospect. He couldn't kick her out of the house as was deserved because she was, after all, part of the family, who probably thought that, hating him as she did, she had to stay at home for Mary Ann's sake, while he often assumed that she didn't clear out because she wanted to go on tormenting him.

The unease Ivy always felt in his presence was so thick, Burton said to Mary Ann, that you'd need a knife to cut into it. He wondered why no one ever asked her to marry him. She was well liked at work – so it seemed – knew plenty of men, and went out often enough, yet no one would take her on. He didn't have to think far for the reason. Her tongue was more bitter than a bumboy's arse, and he couldn't imagine what had made her that way. He may have brought the girls up too strictly, but Ivy had been treated no worse than the others.

Mary Ann said he ought to see a doctor, but he wouldn't, and went on suffering. In any industrial trouble he walked out with the others, which as a journeyman he wasn't obliged to do, so was respected at the pit. The union representative said he could get compensation from the colliery owners of a hundred and twenty-five pounds, but the eye would have to be removed by surgery first, and apart from not wanting any part of his flesh interfered with Burton suspected he would be left with an uglier hole than before.

'In any case, it was my fault,' he said to Mary Ann. 'I knew that striker was no good, but they were in a hurry for the piece. It was within my rights to say I didn't want him, but I didn't. For once in my life I was careless. I kicked him so hard afterwards I'll bet he didn't sit down for a week. One eye in my head or not, I got him right where I should have done. And since it was my fault there's one thing I do know: you have to pay for your mistakes.'

'All the same,' she said, 'you ought to put in a claim.'

'I don't beg for anything.'

'It isn't begging.'

'I don't ask, either.'

And that was that. He had never been to a hospital, and wouldn't go now. 'You always come out worse than before you went in,' he said and, being the man he was, his words were final.

Ivy was so in love with Ernie Guyler that Burton thought the time of getting shut of her couldn't be far off. He took more than usual care not to find fault with him when he called. He was distant, but polite and, though not asking him into the house, shook his hand gently, Guyler being so thin he seemed in danger of being blown away by the softest breeze, especially if it had perfume on it.

He halfway liked Guyler because he was tall and well-dressed: a brown suit with sharply creased trousers, a tie carefully knotted and fixed in place with a pin, a fashionable Fair Isle pullover, a raglan overcoat, brilliantly shining shoes, and a handkerchief in his lapel pocket ironed and folded into shape by a loving mother. His dark hair was brilliantined neatly back, the only fault being that he wore neither hat nor cap, but his gaunt though well-featured face was always pleasant, a half-smile due to sensing perhaps his more than usual impermanence in the world.

Ivy saw Burton's leniency towards her courtship as a hope that she would marry as soon as possible, but it wasn't so easy to get rid of her – and she knew this to be in Burton's mind. Having fallen in love with a man who had consumption from working two decades in the tobacco factory, he was sure to die soon after they were married, in which case she would certainly come home again.

Another thing was that if she married Ernie before he died she would lose her place at the factory, because no married woman was allowed to work there. Then if – or more likely when – Ernie died soon after the marriage, she would be a widow and out of a job as well, or at least not get such a good one again.

Burton indeed saw these pennies moving behind the reasonably clear glass of her mind, as he rested from chopping logs by the fence and watched them go hand-in-hand towards the Cherry Orchard on Sunday afternoon to get what they could while it was possible, for it was plain that Guyler would be dead before any wedding could take place, since the salty cough he eternally carried seemed to be shredding his lungs. Ivy certainly knew how to choose them.

They reached the huge elm whose inside had been burned out by lightning, in which two or more people could shelter from the rain. Ernie drew her close. 'Your father never says much.'

'He didn't to any of us at home, either.'

'I often wonder whether people like him have got something to hide.'

'No,' she said, 'he's as plain as a pikestaff, to me anyway.'

He wiped his mouth after a bout of coughing that rattled every bone in his body. 'Why don't you like him? He's your father, after all.'

'Because he's always been a swine to me, and to the others as well. He interferes in everything, and though he never uses bad language he can be so sarcastic that you want God to strike him dead. Still,' and he saw her smile in the dim light, 'God got back at him twice in his life – so far – when he took his firstborn son, and then when he knocked out his eye.'

He pressed her hand, though couldn't say whether he altogether liked her, but did when she leaned closer and offered her lips for a kiss.

She thought Ernie a bit slow on the uptake when talking about other people. 'Don't let's worry about that old so-and-so. We've got better things to do.'

He could only agree. They left their hiding-place, whose smell of burnt ash irritated his chest, and set out for Robin's Wood, hoping it wouldn't rain again before they did what they longed to do.

Brian was six when Sabina his mother first took him to Old Engine Cottages. The country footpath led through a land of wonders after the streets smelling of horse turds and melting gas tar. She held him on the parapet of the railway bridge to see a train go by, and watch the twirling spokes of the colliery headstocks that circled so merrily he felt sick and had to be pulled down.

She stopped at the gate to rub lipstick away. 'Your grandad wouldn't want to see me wearing this. Another thing is he likes to see little boys with a clean face, so be sure to have a good wash whenever you come on your own.'

The house was an oasis of calm and plenty compared to his dole-stricken home, because Burton worked at the pit, and Thomas and Ivy paid their board. At the weekend Ernie Guyler opened a twenty packet of Player's and gave him the cigarette card, as well as a ha'penny from the shilling packet if it came out of a machine.

Mary Ann saw a shadow of Oliver in Brian, for his curiosity about books, and the cast of his lips on breaking into a question, or his smile on asking for something to eat.

He sometimes stayed overnight in the same bed as his Uncle Thomas, which was no hardship because he shared one with two sisters and a brother at home. Sent upstairs at nine o'clock, he was still awake when Thomas came in at midnight whistling a tune from pub or dance hall, and having been with some woman or other (he was a great man for the ladies, Ivy said) and Brian would get a whiff of his scent, and hear the clash of silver and coppers emptying into a dish on the dressing table. Thomas smoothed the ironed handkerchief for further use, folded his trousers carefully on a clothes hanger behind the door, and Brian would feel the bed sag as his tall and handsome uncle fell in to sleep.

After a breakfast of sausage, bacon and fried potatoes, Thomas wheeled his bike from the wash house, checked every moving part, and inflated the tyres to as hard as concrete. He rode every Sunday along the canal bank as far as Trowell selling fishing tickets for the navigation company at twopence apiece to anglers, keeping a farthing to himself for each one. The day's takings on a warm weekend added a useful few shillings to his spending money. 'You can come with me, if you're a good lad.' Brian didn't think he had ever been anything else, as Thomas set him on the crossbar. 'But keep your legs away from the pedals.'

Ivy had told Brian that Thomas could neither read nor write, but he noticed that no mistakes were ever made in dealing with the clutch of blue tickets, or how much was to be deducted for each one sold. At the counting of pennies and threepenny bits back at the house Brian hoped there would be a coin for himself but, as Ivy also said – who did give him a penny now and again – Thomas was so mean (except perhaps with the women he kept on a string) that he wouldn't give you the skin off his nose.

Brian was always glad at not having stuck his feet in the spokes and brought them crashing onto the towpath, which possibility worried him every second, since it was difficult to keep his legs in the right position. When he got cramp he was shamed into asking his uncle to stop. He was also fearful on seeing from his high point the cliff-like brick sides of the deep locks, and wondered how he would climb out if his whistling and carefree uncle's feet slipped on the pedals and they both went in. But the bicycle and its burdens were like feathers under Thomas, a strong man in his thirties, charging along to claim money from the next fisherman, who glowered over the water as if to become invisible and not have to part with his tuppence.

In the garden Brian picked potatoes from their furrows and, collecting the tops, pulled them in the laden barrow to a corner where his grandfather lit a fire and left them to smoulder, a vegetable smell Brian took with him into sleep. Rotten potatoes were dumped into a compost heap within squared-off planks next to the field, a mulch taking the place of horse manure which was no longer common due to fewer horses on the road, Burton telling him that in any case thousands hadn't come back from the war.

When Brian scraped up shit and feathers, to leave the pigeon coop as clean as a living room, Burton, tall and straight, a finger in his waistcoat pocket, observed an eight-year-old who took care to do things well and was willing to work, probably to please him but also because he was happy to do it. He liked to see a child so absorbed, Brian not knowing that he had found a way to his grandfather's heart.

Whenever Burton thought to give him the reward of a penny he sorted the coin for size and feel before pulling it from his pocket, and held it under his nose. 'Take this, Nimrod!' Feigning a happy surprise, Brian thanked him, and ran down the lane to buy sweets.

Burton disliked Edith's children, those satanic offspring of Doddoe's, because they had turned into predators like their father. On once letting three into the yard he saw how they took pleasure in tormenting the pigs, and ran about the garden not caring where they trampled. From then on if he saw them coming up the lane he waved a stick to keep them off, and watched till they had gone to do their mischief in Robin's Wood.

Brian would sometimes go to Old Engine Cottages along the main road, passing Oswald's square redbricked cottage a few steps down from the pavement. He heard his cousin Howard practising the piano, random but pleasing notes tinkling in the air, sounds unconnected to any tune he knew but following him by Woodhouse and under the railway bridge, only leaving him when he got to the Burtons' door.

Howard was a strange grandson for Burton, and whenever off to the pub, or into Nottingham, and sometimes on his way from work, he called at the house to see Oswald, still the same dignified and handsome man, whereas Helen, with more uncertainties in her features than he had seen on any woman, seemed to live on an island whose landscape no one could know about but herself, and he marvelled that Oswald was able to look after her as well as he did.

Her sensitive nature had passed to Howard, and Burton was puzzled that such a delicate boy could be connected to a robust family such as his. He had shown a love for music at school, so Helen insisted they buy a piano on hire purchase, and arrange piano lessons. It had almost cost her life to give birth, and because there could be no other children he was more cherished than most. Burton hoped that as the first grandchild to bear his name he might one day do as well if not better in the world than his chance offspring in Wales.

Brian once noted the peculiar glint in Howard's eyes on passing him by the gate, so had no wish to become friendly, too proud to talk to him, because too sensible to be rebuffed. Howard would never be able to skim across the narrow lock gates and explore the intricate wooded paths around Brown's Sawmills, or climb trees, or jump ditches, or explore the deeper parts of Robin's Wood, or go with the Doddoe kids to scrump orchards and break into allotment gardens. All such activities were too rough and perilous for Howard to share, much as he might have wanted to, and probably did, for who wouldn't? He could only watch from the parlour window as they went down the lane in a gang, Brian scruffy and uncared-for, waving a stick and seeming without the bother of having to play the piano or do such a thing as homework after school. There had to be times when Howard longed to come out and ask what he was up to, but he never did, and his enigmatic yet forlorn face at the window made Brian feel perversely glad at not offering to let him take part in whatever exciting mischief he was heading for.

He didn't want Howard to come, because suppose one day he avoided his mother's vigilance and did, and joined an expedition to the woods, and in emulation of others he climbed a tree, and was so full of rapture at his achievement that on starting to come down, always the most dangerous stage (and how he would boast of it afterwards at home, to the horror of Helen, and perhaps the pride of his father) he missed his footing and crashed onto the turf twenty feet or more below? If he broke an arm or a leg, or bruised his angelic face, it would be put down as Brian's fault, and the trouble he'd get into didn't bear thinking about.

Neither could he imagine Howard working in the garden with Burton and getting his shoes muddy, or passing hours at the well dropping the bucket in the water and winding it up with handle and chain to see how many he could get onto the parapet before his arms felt they were dropping off. In the garden Howard might fall and cut his knee on a stone and get blood poisoning – Brian's heart nearly stopped at the prospect – or at the well he might lean too far over, looking at his face in the coin of water far below, and fall.

Howard only went to the Burtons' with his father, Helen not otherwise letting him out of sight for fear something should happen, despite Oswald's disapproval. To send him alone down the lane and under the bridge was also unthinkable, because he might get into the company of rough kids running up and down the dead-ends of Woodhouse. School was only a few hundred yards along the main Wollaton road, so that was all right, but she was anxious when he left in the morning, and kissed him with relief when he came back.

Burton saw it as a pity that he wasn't allowed to run free, but Oswald seemed too frightened of Helen to tackle her on the matter, or he wanted a quiet life. Instead of insisting that she let him loose he treated her objections as if she might hang herself, or run away if he spoke too plainly. Burton wasn't to know that Oswald didn't like Howard to be so sheltered from the world either, and argued with Helen, though in as mild a way as possible, trying not to contradict her too directly, since she was so easily upset.

When she took Howard to mass at St Barnabas Cathedral he always came back saying how he had liked the service, and had enjoyed talking to the priest. As far as Burton was concerned Helen's religion was her own affair, though Mary Ann was glad to have such an unusual woman in the family, being not irreligious herself, thinking that growing up in such a pious atmosphere went well with Howard's appearance.

No one was to know that in the playground, or toing and froing the short distance from school, Howard, at eight years of age, entertained and enthralled his friends with stories containing the most scandalous information, which his listeners lapped up like nobody's business, as one of his friends later related to Brian, who told nobody else in the family. He stood there, with his bright little face, coming out with things they'd hardly imagined.

He culled such details from his parents' quarrels, because, though Oswald had always loved Helen, he was, after all, a son of Burton, and was known to go after other women. Helen was a devout Catholic, and forgiving of a sinner, but was distressed to hear of his behaviour, nothing being secret for long in such a district.

Tears and anguish would bring Oswald to a state of repentance, compelling him to confess infidelities in detail so that she could forgive him more thoroughly. They imagined young Howard in the kind of deep slumber that angels were thought to enjoy, but his ear was warming the wall or bedroom door, and whatever half-strangled phrase came through was used next day in a narrative for the delectation of his schoolmates.

When Mary Ann's relations came to stay in the summer Howard was shown off as a unique being, while Brian was told to stay at home for a few days because of the full house.

Bill Goss, Mary Ann's cousin, drove his wife and ageing Aunt Bec from St Neots in a Rolls-Royce. Erect at the wheel in cap and leather gloves, he took care not to scrape the car while tackling the bridge and narrow lane. The stately vehicle going by Woodhouse set tongues flapping at the thought that Burton – amused at such a daft notion – might be connected to a millionaire who would one day die and see him right.

Thomas bedded down in the wash house, his room given, suitably aired, to Bill and his wife, while Aunt Bec slept on a sofa in the parlour. Tea and dinner services came out of glass-fronted cupboards for them to feed and drink from, Ivy and Emily washing every piece in hot water before they were used, since Mary Ann insisted on nothing but the best for her Huntingdonshire family.

When Burton in the parlour passed the soda syphon to Bill he didn't take whisky from the cupboard but opened a bottle of

Johnny Walker that could not have been interfered with. 'So business is good?'

'When was it not?' Bill said. 'You work hard, and have a bit of luck now and again.' Old Charles had started as a saddler, then taken to repairing bicycles, he reminded Burton. 'At your wedding the old man asked you to come and work for him at St Neots.'

'I saw no reason to,' Burton responded. 'And I still don't.'

Burton was set in his ways, and always would be, too attached to his district even as a young man to start somewhere else. 'You'd have been a bit more prosperous.'

Burton grunted. 'I might, but money isn't everything.'

From bicycles the Goss's had moved to dealing in motor cars, and bought a small filling station, earning enough for Bill to own his Rolls-Royce. 'You're quite right. The only time I relax is when I come up here to see you and Mary Ann.'

'You're welcome. Any time you like.' Burton meant it, as Mary Ann would want him to. 'In the morning we'll go and see Oswald and Helen, and perhaps Howard will give us a tune on the piano.'

'If he does we'll take him for a spin around Nottingham. Show him the Trent.'

He poured more drink for them both. 'When we come back here I'll show you the garden. I've put a lot of good things in this year, so you'll have plenty to take home.'

Curtains open, pots of geraniums nodding on the window ledge, summer light mellow outside, eight sat at table for the feast of welcome. Thomas and Ivy had wanted to go out, for a bit of courting it was supposed, but Burton said they must be in for the first dinner out of respect and politeness, for what Mary Ann, both girls, Aunt Bec and Bill's wife had been working hard in the kitchen to prepare.

On the train to St Neots' Burton recalled his carefree journey to South Wales, when he hadn't been encumbered with baskets of vegetables, and a cloth sack of loaves and cakes Mary Ann had baked the day before, gallantry insisting that he carry them on changing at Grantham.

Bill waited at Peterborough, and drove them to the Great

Northern Hotel for dinner, the best in that part of the country, he said, Burton replying that it needed to be, at six shillings a head.

Accommodation was more spacious in the Goss house, nobody being put out for Burton and Mary Ann, who noted how much easier he was on such a holiday. The Goss's were glad to see him, though amused on going out to see how he made what they regarded as the antediluvian request to Mary Ann that she walk a few paces behind.

He agreed one afternoon to have his photograph taken, but only out of politeness, for it was a disturbance to his privacy. He was seventy, and looked it, after a lifetime of work. Though high summer in the garden, he wore a dark suit and the usual highly polished boots for the occasion. His waistcoat was fastened left over right, a vertical line of six buttons on either side, thumbs stuck into the two lower pockets joined by the watch chain, the long fingers of his gnarled hands half-bent inwards from bony wrists. The tip of a handkerchief showing from the lapel pocket of the jacket was close to the buttonhole of a small white chrysanthemum. His 'dicky' collar was old-fashioned even for those days, but the bow tie was perfectly arranged.

He stood erect, confident yet unwilling to look too relaxed, the face overshadowed by his large flat cap, though sufficient features showed the sort of man he was, and had been all his life. The chin was firm and well-shaped, a small white moustache carefully clipped, lips infinitesimally apart as if to emit withering sarcasm should anyone dispute his right to any detail of the pose.

Nose and ears were prominent enough to emphasize his acuteness in both senses, and he stared as if daring the camera to take away the dignity which formed his soul (of which he had no fear) rather than do its job and record his merely physical presence, while obviously having some regard for the camera since he was so formally dressed to face it.

Emily stood to his left, head tilted slightly as if, should she get too close he might, as a reminder that she must know her place, jab her with his elbow – for not allowing him to make the picture all his own. A few paces to the other side was a handsome man of about thirty, the son of Mary Ann's sister, six feet tall yet overlooked by Burton.

Burton's gaze went beyond the range of any camera, as if into a land and a past – a way of life – that no one around could know about. His stand as if to defy both God and Man indicated that if ever it happened that he was the last person on earth, the continuation and endurance of another human race would grow out of all he knew, and flourish from his blacksmith's strength.

When Bill motored him to Cambridge he was amused at so many young men prancing around in gowns and mortarboards, though his observation of the architecture told him it was something to remember. High tea at the Blue Boar was acceptable, but he was as usual appalled at the waste of food around him.

His eye for goodlooking women was undiminished. 'You only need one for the purpose,' he said lightly to Bill, one of whose unmarried daughters was so fascinated by him, as he was with her, that she was invited to take his arm when the family went walking. And she did, making pressures which delighted him on the one hand but riled him on the other because there was no chance of doing anything about it. Mary Ann walking behind – not far enough for him – knew that every eye was on him and his admirer, so he could not get up to any hanky-panky.

'Or, indeed,' he laughed on the train to Nottingham when she complained about him and the young woman, 'any argy-bargy, either.'

TWENTY-SEVEN

Howard looked one way and then the other along the wide road, as had been drilled into him, saw it free enough of traffic and, wanting to get home for his piano lesson, never knew where the doubledecker bus came from. The front left wheel dragged him a hundred yards before the driver could stop. An ambulance took him to the General Hospital, his leg crushed, and a teacher from the school went to tell Helen.

Unable to believe, though fearing her heart would burst, she fainted at her worst nightmare. When Oswald came from the nearby canal she was brought around with a measure of whisky, and went with him to see how Howard was.

His ruined leg was cut away, and three weeks later he lay on the parlour sofa, crutches leaning behind. Everyone in the family was appalled that such an accident had happened to Helen's unusual and promising child. Burton wondered at so many hearts in the world to break, and called whenever he passed the house, stood by the sofa and said a few words to his grandson who, asked how he was, replied like a Burton after all that he was fine, thank you very much.

Burton detected a sheen of suffering about the skin, and a frightened vacancy at the eyes which the poor lad could not hide. Helen's tears were always running, which Howard saw, and though Burton couldn't deny it was a case for weeping, it was also a time to hide them.

Brian, told he was to give whatever silver paper he came across to Howard, who collected it for the hospital, tore apart every cigarette packet for the usual film of paper smelling pleasantly of tobacco, so that Howard could be patted on the head when he was wheeled to the hospital and handed in a bigger bundle than

315

anybody else. Brian always hoped to find a cigarette that the smoker had overlooked, and when that was the case he would have a few sick-inducing puffs behind a hedge, though if feeling charitable he would take it to his father in the hope of making him less miserable.

With enough silver paper for a worthwhile visit he noticed Helen's suffering face, her vacant, terrified eyes, and dark ringlets now touched with grey falling over thin shoulders as she showed him into the parlour. 'Howard, here's a friend come to see you.'

He lay tremulous and pale, thanked him for the scruffy ball laid on the shelf, and beckoned him close: 'I'm tired of everybody coming to ask how I am.' Eyes wide, he stared at the door, a hint Brian took to go.

On hearing the tinkling of the piano a few days later he assumed that Howard had hopped the few steps to play, as if music might bring him back to normal life. He was now even more the favourite grandchild of Burton and Mary Ann, which Brian hoped would improve his spirit at having only one leg.

Ivy and Thomas being out on Sunday afternoon, and Burton in bed with Mary Ann, Emily sat looking mindlessly at the fire until, knowing she would soon hear her father treading downstairs in stockinged feet, put the kettle on. She took the tea caddy from the cupboard and threw as many spoons into the pot, Brian noted, as would have lasted a whole day at home.

He called at the Burtons' as often as he thought they would put up with him, liked to be in a kitchen smelling of baking bread – roasting meat on Sunday morning – a medley of hunger-inducing odours depending on the day of the week. The window opening on the back garden path was as clean as if it had no glass, and splashes of blood-red geraniums on the ledge seemed to warn everyone passing not to look inside.

Fascinated by Emily's quiet though unpredictable ways, he wondered where the mischievous and brilliant light in her eyes came from. Thin lips were always working, as if she had an irreducible grain of hard sago between her teeth, and was talking in silence to an invisible listener. Sometimes she would take a ha'penny from her pinafore pocket, eyes a-glitter on holding it before him. 'Do you love me, duck?' and Brian always said yes, for she would then laugh, and drop the coin into his hand.

The first scalding sip of Emily's black tea tasted so strong to Burton that the inside of his head seemed to empty in alarm. He liked a fair brew, but she put too much tea in the pot, though he didn't chide her in case she became upset, for it was the one thing she was proud of being able to do.

She gazed at him drinking, impossible to say whether her eyes glowed with beady satisfaction at having him imbibe her heart-coating liquid, or whether she was waiting to be patted on the head at producing an effect that threatened to send him clawing up the wall and travelling halfway across the ceiling. Burton wanted to boot the knowing pest out of the house, but Mary Ann would hear of no such thing, which Emily well realized.

At thirty years of age she had never been able to keep a job, being too uncertain in her behaviour. She had a temper, and little patience in unfamiliar situations. When set to work by a local shopkeeper, a charitable Methodist preacher, all went well for a few days, until she decided she was being 'put upon'. They were asking her to do too much. They were mixing her up deliberately. They were laughing behind her back. They accused her of making mistakes when she hadn't, because she had only been doing what she had been told to do, and they were telling her, now that she was doing it, that they had told her to do something different. It wasn't right. They wanted to see her cry. Then they could laugh at her.

She began to drop things, change items around on the shelves, or put them in places where they shouldn't be, whether she had been told to or not. It wasn't right for them to mix her up. She was doing her best so didn't deserve it. She'd heard right the first time. She knew what they had said. She remembered everything. She wasn't daft. She'd only been doing what they had told her to do. She wasn't having it. She'd show them, she would and all, she'd show them if it was the last thing she did.

The assistants in the serving part of the shop wondered why it was so quiet in the store room, till she had been there long enough for the shopkeeper to go and see what she was doing. His brain was properly knocked about at witnessing such chaos never before experienced, though in one sense the rearrangement was imaginative, the aspect colourful, and the ingenuity unbelievable.

'Have you lost your tongue?' He hoped to find out why she had done what she had certainly done, but all he got was an imitation glower of Burton in a bad mood – which Burton would have been in because of something she had said or done to him – followed by a demented grin, until sensing in the half-lit attic of her mind that she might not have done right after all. Instinct triumphed, and she reached for her coat.

His move to evict her took more strength in his arms than had ever been called on for shifting boxes of groceries, but he got her through the door and onto the busy street, confirming for Emily that he'd spitefully had such intentions boiling in him from the beginning, and she little cared that it would take days for her reassortment of goods in the shop to be unravelled. She wasn't known in the family as 'Batchy Em' for nothing.

After talking to the manager of the Flying Horse hotel in the middle of town, Mary Ann got her taken on as a chambermaid, work which pleased Emily, at first, for if there was one thing she could do, and didn't dislike doing, it was making beds, which she'd been taught from an early age.

As far as the family understood, because accounts varied on both sides, some double-dyed wicked commercially travelling villain had tried to get her into bed and rape her. She wasn't the biggest of the Burton girls, but her upbringing had been as hard as the rest, so the man was shocked at her ferocity. She gave him a drubbing he would never forget, and had to be pulled away by four other chambermaids drawn to the room by his screams.

Emily was no beauty, but she was young and personable enough in the half-dark, and to someone probably drunk, who couldn't know the significance of the grim expression she put on even when not being interfered with. She must have seemed just another of those willing Nottingham girls the man had heard about, especially if he had just come up from Leicester.

He denied trying to molest her, swore she had attacked first on being asked to smooth one of his pillows. The manager knew he would never get the truth, so gave Emily five pounds, with the advice not to come back. From then on Mary Ann thought it best to keep her at home.

When gangrene attacked the remains of Howard's mutilated stump he was taken in an ambulance to the hospital, unconscious from morphine. Oswald stood by the door to watch him go, gritting on his anguish at the possibility of his son not seeing home again.

Helen stayed by Howard's bed for as long as was allowed, then went to church and lit candles for his recovery. On the way home she bought a bottle from each beer-off passed, and threw the empties into any convenient hedge, ashamed of drinking but desperate for oblivion. Oswald went to the hospital whenever work made it possible, but she wouldn't come home on the bus with him because one of those things had started it. 'Is my angel going to be all right?' she asked again and again on the way home. 'He's suffering like the Lord Jesus. Is God going to spare him? Please tell me he is.'

Oswald promised Howard's life, though aware that God was unable or unwilling to spare anybody. He walked with her so that she wouldn't drink, and stayed with her at home because if he didn't she would go to the Crown Hotel and get drunk. His son's pain and Helen's racking agony held his own in control.

Howard died, and the light went from Helen's life. Oswald had lost his only son, and Burton didn't wonder that the shades went down on Oswald's life as well. Helen could have no more children, and the blow was as close to mortal as any could be.

Careful not to slip on the mildewed steps, Brian went down from the lane and knocked on the door of his uncle's house. Sabina, with many of Mary Ann's good traits in thinking of others' misfortunes, had asked him to call, in the hope that the sight of a young face might give them encouragement to carry on living.

Oswald's handsome features reminded Brian of a Viking pictured in a book at school. And what better job could an uncle have than that of lockkeeper on a nearby canal? As for Aunt Helen, if he knew nothing else he saw her as beautiful, and interestingly unlike any of the Burton women, with dark and curly hair around her tenderly enquiring face when she talked to him. Her hair now grey, this strange and distant woman was the last person in the world who should have had to suffer such grief.

Oswald led him into the curtain-drawn living room, Helen unable to let in sunlight though Howard had been dead six months. 'Mam sends her regards,' he said to the tall raddled figure in the half-dark. 'To Aunt Helen as well.'

Oswald seemed hardly to know who he was, and pointed to his leftovers from breakfast, a couple of long bacon rinds with the fat still on, a few scraps of egg-white around the plate. 'Do you want to finish that up? I'll cut you some bread, if you like.'

He was hungry, hadn't yet had his own breakfast, and Helen might have offered something better, but she was in bed and not to be disturbed. Through the half-ajar parlour door was Howard's still-open piano, uneven ranks of crotchets and minims on the sheet of music crowding across the page like black ants on the march, to remind Howard in the grave, or maybe even in heaven, how his fingers had at one time turned them into sounds. The sorrowful gloom of mourning was too much and, having given the message, he wanted to resume his walk. 'No thanks. I'm not hungry.'

Helen hurried to church for solace every morning, and drank her way home when there was a shilling to spare. Her vice was no more a secret to Oswald than his going with other women had been to her. He was to recall how, after the first years of marriage, unable to be all the time under her pervading fits and miseries and imagined misfortunes long before Howard's accident, as well as the seeming impossibility of their ever achieving some kind of compatibility, he succumbed to the congenital Burton need to know more than one woman. But after Howard's death, loving Helen as he did and always had, he devoted himself to keeping her alive.

He nevertheless wondered about the person he might have married had he not been so in thrall to her, chosen a less complicated and demanding woman closer to what he thought of as his easygoing self. But he had fallen in love with Helen Drury who was more beautiful than any seen in his roamings as a young man, and it had been the same for her when he talked to her at the tram stop after she had come out of church. The sparks of attraction were more fiery and sure between those whose temperaments were so unmatched. They should have stayed entranced, and happy in the mutual quest of getting to know each other for the rest of their lives, but Howard's death drove Helen almost mad. Oswald endured with the stoicism Burton showed at the death of Oliver, in that having Helen to pity made it more feasible for him to carry on. Where, in that case, would he have been without her, and if he gave in to the same agony of grief, which he felt just as much, who would look after her? Each became a crutch to hold a single body upright.

He sometimes thought that only the secret drinking kept her going, yet tried to get her to dress in the colourful way she once had, even to take more interest in church affairs, but neither colour, sobriety or piety meant anything. When it seemed she might perish from lack of nourishment he cooked her a meal – the first time for any male Burton – but she stared as if the food was poison, and went back into her world of grief, with its visions of angelic Howard, leaving Oswald racked with guilt at not being able to hide his exasperation.

She prayed continually for Howard's soul in the cathedral, comforted by the priest telling her that the boy wasn't in any place but heaven, where he would one day greet her and say how happy he was that she had lived so long after him, but had come to join him at last.

Brian was embarrassed at her trembling hands and at the smell of stout on her breath when she greeted him in the street: 'Tell me, Brian, where is Howard now?'

'He's in heaven, Aunt Helen.'

'So he is. You're a good boy.' With the light in her eyes renewed she leaned over a little less on her way towards home.

Everyone in the family agreed – at least those who no longer lived in the same house – that Burton became more amiable as he went further into his sixties and seventies, though he was no less scornful of anyone regarded as a fool. When Brian sat reading on the rug Burton looked down on someone he thought privileged, in spite of his poor clothes, so absorbed by a world he couldn't get into. At least one child did not have to put up with what he'd had to at that age. Perhaps times had changed, and though he would never say whether or not it was for the better, he told Mary Ann that Brian was a lucky boy in being able to read and write.

Having fallen into Howard's place, Brian was all eyes and ears at the Burtons', taking everything in without giving any sign of doing so. His enjoyment was intense because the distractions were varied and the comforts assured, impressions staying more than he could know. Quiet under the living room lamp of a winter's evening he seemed engrossed only in his book, and whether or not they thought he had any gift of understanding didn't concern him, in the flesh of his own fortress, his mind belonging to himself alone, not to be disturbed by any outside influence.

Burton did not see such stolidity as slowness or inanition, while Brian didn't regard his grandfather as harsh or threatening. He only felt that when Burton watched him he seemed to know more about him than he knew of himself, though little was said between them, as if it did not need to be. He felt wanted because of Burton's obvious interest, while Mary Ann liked to see him take books from the glass-fronted bookcase in the parlour because it reminded her of Oliver. 'I don't know what he'll do when he grows up,' she said.

Burton grunted. 'I expect it'll be interesting, whatever it is.'

TWENTY-EIGHT

Ernie Guyler coughed himself to death, and Ivy wore black for the funeral. 'I'll have his grave to visit now, as well as Oliver's.'

Emily followed her out of the house. She loved a funeral. People cried as if they were bursting, but after the misery in church and wailing at the graveside there'd be food and drink, just like a party. She wanted to be there so that she could have a good cry with the rest of them. She loved a good cry, whoever it was had died. And at the feasting afterwards there might be an argument to watch. Somebody was bound to say something somebody didn't like, and give him a smack in the chops. Even two women might have a go, and while they did she would help herself to more of the drink, and get tipsy, which made her feel as she would like to feel all the time when she was sober. Having a guzzle of Burton's whisky now and again wasn't the same – well, it wasn't enough anyway – because she was sure he put water in it, while keeping his own special bottle locked up where nobody could get at it.

Ivy was her sister, so she couldn't let her go to Ernie Guyler's funeral on her own. In any case she wanted to see what his family was like, because she had never met them. Maybe there'd be a man there who would want to take her out. He might ask her to the pictures or the theatre, and if he tried to do anything to her afterwards she could biff him so hard he'd run away.

Ivy knew her sister's thoughts and didn't much like them, but was glad of her company because she felt there was nothing else to do on the way there except throw herself off a railway bridge when an express train was on its way. She said so as they walked down the lane, but Emily said what would become of Mary Ann if you did anything like that?

'Well, I don't mean it, do I?' Burton would be glad, so that was one reason not to do it. She would be dead, so that was another. 'It's only what I feel like. Ernie was the man I loved, and now he's gone. I know I'd been expecting it, and so had he, poor soul, but when it comes it's still like the end of the world. My heart used to bump when I saw him walking up to the house to call for me.' She began to weep again. 'I shall never get over it.'

Emily took her arm. 'Don't cry, duck, or I shall as well, and my frock will get wet.'

The death of a sweetheart was worse than the death of yourself. No more shilling teas in the Mikado, or walking hand-in-hand to the wood. No more worrying whether your period would start, though he'd always taken good care.

Back at work, Florence on the next machine commiserated. Ernie Guyler had lived in the same street. A good man, she said, one of the best. He laughed a lot, even in his illness, but you can't go on being faithful to a memory all your life. You've got to go on living.

'Any damned fool knows that.' Ivy denied that she could forget him. 'He won't be out of my mind till the day I die.'

'He will. I know there was no better chap,' Florence went on, 'but he's got to fade.' Ivy realized how good it was to have such a friend at work, and that life would be unimaginable if there was no factory for her to go to every morning.

Those employed by Player's received a tin of fifty cigarettes every month, and because Ivy smoked only a few she handed the rest to her brothers. Burton thought that he could do with one or two as well, but Ivy considered he had been so harsh to her all her life that he didn't even deserve the skin off her nose, and when she once reminded him of this Burton said: 'Then why don't you leave, if you don't like it here?'

She had thought of it more times than he could know, but if she did leave where would she go? How could she set herself up on her own with what she earned at Player's? She would have to find a house – and a mean little one it would be – and buy furniture to put in it.

Burton noted that she was never short of money to go on

trips with friends from work, so knew she wouldn't leave home where living was cheap. Besides, who but Mary Ann would have such good meals on the table the moment she came in the door? He had her weighed up right enough. She was more than well off, and would stay 'on the shelf' like a packet of Mazawattee tea, even if only to spite him.

If she gave Burton some cheek now and again it was, Ivy told herself, because nobody deserved it more. Years could go by when they hardly spoke to each other, and though she knew her hatred of him troubled the tender heart of Mary Ann, it was his fault because he ought to have known it would be bad for her mother if he gave her anything to hate him for.

Words from her lips couldn't say anything good of him, no more than words from his would say anything good about her. They found nothing to say to each other, lived within different worlds in the same house. Ivy's silent anger became more bitter on Burton not even realizing he was the cause of it, and he never would because he was too set in the ways of long ago. She had her life and wasn't going to be made miserable by a bully like him. He only wanted to see her having the same hard time as Rebecca and Edith and Sabina. If there was such a place as hell for a woman it was where she was tormented by a tyrannical husband who wouldn't support either her or the children properly. She would never get into a situation like that merely to amuse Burton.

Her one chance of happiness was gone because Ernie Guyler – poor soul – had died. She couldn't marry anyone else, so stayed at home in spite of Burton, and if ever she did leave it would only be when she was good and ready.

Miss Middleton, a schoolmistress, was shown around the factory by one of the subordinate directors. A party of girls could see how cigarettes were manufactured, and perhaps they would want to work there one day. Ivy was in charge of a dozen women packing the boxes, and when asked how many were completed every day Miss Middleton, looking intently for her answer, smiled before walking on. 'You can tell what sort she is,' Florence said to one of the girls, but Ivy didn't care what sort she was, only knowing that she had been smiled at in a way she never had before, by this self-confident schoolteacher woman.

Jane Middleton waited for her to come out of work, and took her to a restaurant in town. A case of mutual curiosity, Ivy turned girlish at the notion that a schoolmistress could find her interesting. During the meal Jane told her of a bus holiday through Germany the year before. 'We were all women, so a very pleasant time was had by all. Frankly, I don't like men. They're hopeless. All the best were killed in the war.' Ivy agreed, thinking of Oliver, but also because she had never had much luck with men either, unless you could count Ernie Guyler, who had died a year ago.

Jane, also in her middle thirties, a tall red-haired woman, had views which Ivy thought at times a little too close to Burton's, yet agreed with them because they didn't sound the same coming from someone to whom she was in thrall. They met every weekend, and went to Jane's flat in Mapperley. The following year she took Ivy on holiday to Normandy. Burton watched them walking arm-in-arm down the lane, and knew with chagrin that Ivy was as far from getting married as ever.

Ivy went on her own to see Rebecca and her husband who lived near Lydd in Kent. She was put up on a settee in the parlour of their cottage, and spent most of the time with her sister maligning Burton. She came back and told Brian how marvellous Kent was, promising to take him one day. 'We'll go through London, and look at Buckingham Palace, and then see the pretty countryside where hops grow in fields on long poles.'

She was too busy with Miss Middleton, and would never take him, but the secret dream belonged to him alone, though one dream which became real was staying all weekend at the Burtons', helping his grandfather in the garden, and running across the Cherry Orchard to make a bow and arrow in Robin's Wood. When it got cold and dark a warm house was waiting, with something to eat inside. Mary Ann baked cakes, and gave him the large yellow bowl to scrape clean of the batter with a wooden spoon, leaving a few currants to find.

Burton came in from the garden for breakfast, and Mary Ann put a slice of fat bacon and a fried egg on his plate, the orange yolk neatly centred in a zone of white. Brian had collected eggs from the coop but never seen one cooked. Burton, thinking him hungry, trimmed off the broad white border with his clasp knife, and halved the bread. 'Eat this.'

'Isn't it yours, Grandad?'

Spraying vinegar over the yolk, he sensed a possible hurt to Brian's pride at being given it so off-handedly. 'I don't like the white. I never did, Nimrod. Eat it for me.'

Hungry or not, he did as he was told, watching Burton tackle the heart of the egg, and thinking that one day he would get as many yolks as he could eat.

A prince at the Burton house, he could be alone yet feel himself one of them. In the darkened kitchen, rain thrashing against the window, Mary Ann told him you never turn a beggar away from the door. If you didn't have a penny to give there was always a cup of tea. This was the goodness of the Irish coming out in her, his mother Sabina said when he mentioned it. Nor should you ever be unkind to animals, Mary Ann went on, seeing him tormenting the cat unduly. She instilled into him that he must always care, and never – ever – tell lies.

Burton told him little, but he took in by example and from what others said about his grandfather. He learned to believe in himself, to doubt everything, to work, to stand up straight, never to have hands in his pockets, not to care what anyone said about him, to look on the world with a cold eye, to speak only when spoken to, and when words were fully formed and well-rehearsed, above all to distrust praise or flattery, and stand indifferent in face of denigration. He seemed not to take in any of this, but it went in all the same, the difficulty of merging both sets of precepts apparent only later.

Thomas expressed himself mainly by the melodious whistling of tunes he heard in pubs and dance halls, or from somebody else's wireless, which instrument Burton wouldn't allow in the house, regarding it as an intrusion of unwanted sound, a box of lies that might one day have the cheek to answer him back. Brian wondered how in that case a gramophone had found its way into the parlour. He had heard it played once, when his grandmother put on a Negro spiritual.

Standing on the table in its immovable wooden casing, a large horn expanding above like the mouth of a giant lily, and a steel handle almost as big as that for winding up a motor car, perhaps it was tolerated because at least it couldn't talk, and needed work to set it going.

Thomas could whistle as loud as he cared to in the noisy workshop of the Raleigh, where machinery swamped all human sound. In that place he was little bothered at not having an audience, and produced a concert mainly to entertain himself. Ivy wondered whether he whistled music in his courting, on pushing his handsome and neatly dressed presence onto some tractable woman. He always had one or two going mad about him, she said, but God help any who was daft enough to marry him, because he was as mean as a kidney bean. On the other hand he was more than willing to spend money on women in the hope of getting what he wanted.

As if unaware of where he was, Thomas set up a piercing whistle in the living room before sitting at table for his dinner. A glance from Burton's single and therefore more menacing eye broke through to Thomas's deepest core and immediately squashed his sibilant display. 'I'm surprised you've so much money in your pocket these days,' Burton said. 'You haven't won the pools and not told us, have you?'

Thomas filled in the Littlewoods coupons every week in the hope of winning a fortune, and then what women he would have! He knew all the teams but couldn't read, so Ivy had to point out the relevant names. 'I don't know why I help him,' she said, 'because if he wins he'll never give me anything.'

'Why is that?' Thomas asked his father.

Burton ran a long thin knife up and down the steel for carving the meat. 'You must swallow at least half a ton of bird seed every week to keep that noise up, and even I know the stuff doesn't come cheap.'

Brian considered the remark a fair example of that withering sarcasm Ivy complained about, yet thought his grandfather right in putting a stop to such whistling because, however pleasant the tune, it killed stone-dead what was going on in the mind.

Thomas ignored the setback to his performance – it was impossible to damage his self-esteem – and during the meal asked Burton if he would like to have his prize horseshoes taken to the

Raleigh and dipped in chrome, which would help in their preservation and give them a more handsome appearance.

Burton was wary. They looked good as they were. He had made them that way. The iron would last forever, as far as he knew. But he thought about it and, sipping his usual coffee after the pudding, took Thomas away from his football coupons and said that he could dip one of the shoes and see how it turned out.

'If you like it,' Thomas said, 'I'll do the others, two at a time though, otherwise I'd get the sack if I was caught dipping them all at once.'

Burton stood. 'It sounds a bit like cheating to me.'

'Oh no, we're allowed to do the odd thing now and again.'

Brian stayed for Christmas, and money was collected to buy him a trainset. He sat in front of the fire and lifted piece after piece from its box, wondering what it had cost as he slotted the lines together, and laid engine and trucks on the circuit.

Burton looked from his great height. 'You'll be so busy I don't suppose I'll have you working in the garden today.'

'There's nothing to do there, Grandad. Look at all that frost at the window. It's the middle of winter.'

'You're winding the engine up wrong.'

'I'm not.'

'Give it me.'

'You'll break it.'

'Not like you, if you don't do it right.' He turned the key gently clockwise – Ivy and Emily hoping for something to snap – and passed the toy back.

Thomas at the mirror had half a dozen goes at getting his tie straight, inflated features holding in the aria of a whistle he wouldn't dare let rip before reaching the lane.

'All you've got to do now,' Burton said, 'is take the brake off. I don't suppose you'll have your nose in a book today, either.'

Thomas brought back the first horseshoe from the Raleigh, chromed to a fine shade of silver. Burton saw how good it looked in a beam of January sun. 'It is beautiful,' Mary Ann said.

She was right. 'Do the others,' which was more praise from Burton than Thomas could remember.

Burton handed it to Brian, who took the perfectly shaped horseshoe made by the hands of his grandfather at the forge, turned it around, examined it from all angles, felt the solid weight, held the coolness to his cheek, and counted the nail holes. 'Why are there seven, Grandad?'

'How many days are there in a week?'

'Seven.'

'That's why. Four shoes on a horse's feet, and how many holes does that make?'

'Twenty-eight.'

'That's for a month, a moon of days.'

He passed it back. 'That's clever.'

'There's a lot of things you don't know, Nimrod. Some horse-shoes have eight holes, but a horse goes better on seven.'

'Why is that?'

'Seven hold just as well as eight, and they don't weigh as much. It's easier on the feet, and it won't go lame so quick.' He put the shoe in its case on the wall, took down another, and held it before Brian's eyes. 'You see this one?'

He felt the prongs with both hands. It was wide, heavy and flat. 'What's special about it?'

'It's for a carthorse. I made it in Wales.'

'Wales is a long way off.'

'I know it is.' He took it back. 'It's where I worked as a young man.'

'Why did you go there?'

'It was the only place I could get work.'

The rows of chromed horseshoes hung impressively in their place, and Brian wondered whether all or any would ever be fitted to a horse. 'No,' Burton told him. 'They're prize ones, and have to stay there. Now pick up that newspaper. I want to hear about Spain, where another damned lot is fighting a war for no good reason as I can see.'

On Saturday night Mary Ann stood in her slip to wash at a large bowl of water on the living room table, then dressed in a navy-blue skirt and white blouse. Brian stood at the fence to watch the handsome and stately couple walk down the lane, Mary Ann a few paces behind. When they were out of sight he went into his aunts' bedroom, attracted by unfamiliar smells of feminine indulgence, of powders and creams and unguents, of bedclothes giving off odours of lavender and clean wind that had swept over the sheets when on the line by the garden of fecund soil and growing vegetables. Such smells came straight out of heaven, if there was such a place, though he hoped there was, yet condemned all his life not to believe it.

TWENTY-NINE

Surveyors spread triangulation, marked out roads and gardens. Enormous black sewage pipes you could crawl through were lowered into trenches straight as a die. The foundations of identical houses covered the green acres walked on so many times. Walls and windows were installed, roofs put on. Nottingham was spreading west.

Mary Ann filled the workmen's billy-cans with tea at sixpence a time, Brian fetching the empties and taking them back full. Sometimes he forgot who the cans belonged to as he walked among heaps of gravel and stacks of tiles, smells in the air of resin and fresh sawdust.

He jinked between trucks and concrete mixers, changed the hot cans several times to stop burns, men hurrying up scaffolding with hods of bricks or slates, till someone claimed one of the mashcans, recognition swift to a man with a parched throat. Mary Ann did good business because her tea was sweet and strong, and Brian was glad of a few pennies at the end of the day.

Old Engine Cottages made space for new dwellings. Burton didn't want to quit, because the house had mellowed during a century and, in good condition still, could have lasted well into the next. Electricity had been in for a year, and running water laid on, but Farmer Taylor got a good price, and orders came that they had to go.

Burton was over seventy, as was Mary Ann, who was not sorry to move to a street in Woodhouse, though Burton regretted bulldozers smashing down a place they had lived in so long.

'They should have moved forty years ago,' Sabina said, 'then I wouldn't have had to walk under that dark and muddy bridge when I was a girl.' Ivy thought Burton would like living in

Woodhouse because it was near the beer-off and closer to the pub, but Mary Ann said sharply that he had never been averse to walking a mile or two to get to those places. 'And he's never drunk much.'

Burton disliked so many people crowding close. In the back yard you heard the noise of neighbours shouting and clattering about. Women screamed at kids, and kept the wireless on. Trains shunted along the railway night and day.

A year later, after the war had started, they moved to Radford Boulevard, further into the city. The nearest pub was the Gregory Hotel a hundred yards away, though Burton had little to spend from the old age pension. It helped that Thomas and Ivy paid their board, and Emily made up the rations to five. Burton being a sparse eater unlike – he remarked – that glutton Thomas, meant that sufficient was usually on the table, though not as much as in the days of autumn pig-killing when legs of pork, flitches of salted bacon, and strings of sausages swung in the pantry.

Burton and Mary Ann lived in a comfortable though at times spartan way. If Emily or Ivy or Thomas said or did something annoying, Burton might now hold back his response for fear of upsetting Mary Ann. Ivy was encouraged by Jane Middleton to buy a wireless on hire purchase, so Burton enjoyed music now and again, and listened to the nine o'clock news, but it was sparingly used, and never too loud.

Mary Ann had the *Evening Post* delivered, and sometimes stood on the front step looking for the paperboy. Brian's brother Arthur put it into her hands for a fortnight, when standing in for a pal on holiday. In cold weather Burton took it in to Mary Ann by the fire, so that she could read aloud what might inform him about the war. They also learned in this way of the prison sentences on Edith's sons, who had deserted from the army and taken to robbing shops and offices. He pitied Edith for having had such lawless children by Doddoe Atkin, though Tommy Jackson's son Douglas was also in jail. 'Idleness is the greatest cause of misery in the world,' he said.

Standing on the front step, chin up, staring right and left at people and traffic, he saw Brian walking along the boulevard, a girl holding his arm. He beckoned. 'How are you getting on, Nimrod?'

The name embarrassed him, having been at work for two years, and no longer a kid. But he had to lead Pauline forward for his grandfather's inspection.

Burton noted her brown hair, fringed at the front and long behind, took in a good figure through the open coat, and with knowing eyes reached for her hand. He smiled. 'How are you, then?'

Brian expected her to curtsey, so smarmily did she speak. 'I'm very well, thank you.'

She could have sworn Burton winked. He was well aware that Brian, from his expression, and from hers also, was getting all that a young man wanted. 'Is he a good lad to you?'

'He's got to be, hasn't he?' Brian noted that she seemed about to bite off her tongue at having to add: 'Well, he's all right, most of the time.'

'Tell him to bring you to the Gregory Hotel one evening so that I can buy you a drink. You'd like that, wouldn't you, my girl?'

'I'd love it.'

You bloody would, Brian said to himself.

Burton took her hand again, as if he couldn't feel it often enough, wanting her to know she could come for a stroll and take a chance with him any time she liked. 'But don't let me stop you going where you want to go.'

'Your grandad's nice,' she said, on their way to the cinema. 'And handsome.'

'I suppose he is. I can see him running me off if I'm not careful. He's a dirty old man.'

'I'll bet he was a dirty young one, as well,' she said. 'He must have been a smasher. He's got such warm hands.'

'Aren't mine warm?'

'Not like his are.'

He pulled her along. 'Come on, or we won't get there before the picture starts.'

'Of course we shall,' she said in a tone that riled him. He was aware that if he turned Burton would still be looking at her.

Tall, white-haired, and seventy-five, a black velvet patch over his dead eye giving a raffish and predatory look, Burton seemed charged with energy as he walked towards the Gregory Hotel. Still unable to sit in the house for long, he walked a mile to the Crown, and to call on Oswald and Helen. Or he strode uphill through Canning Circus and down into the city.

When he took Mary Ann out she noticed his eye wandering towards any personable woman in the pub or on the street, unnoticed by whoever he was observing, though she also could pick out a well-dressed woman, knowing that Burton would never fail to do likewise till the day he died.

He could be taken, by his marching stride, for an old soldier, by those who didn't know him, a comparison he would have scorned. In the coldest weather he carried a coat over his right arm for smartness rather than utility. Many old men younger than himself ought to stand straight and put another inch or two on their height to give more dignity. As for a walking stick, it was only all right to carry one if you didn't need to. They should at least close their mouths and hide the rotten teeth. Looking so dead on their feet would make the young dread what they might one day come to, instead of showing a person to respect. If a lifetime's work had broken them they should try not to appear so gormless. It cost nothing to be smart.

No one was more surprised than Burton when Thomas said he had fallen in love with the woman of his life. 'It's about time,' he said to Mary Ann.

Thomas must have realized that at forty it was now or never, and decided it had to be now. He sang *Drink To Me Only* in a fine tenor voice at the church hall reception, his wife Grace looking on as if she had found the perfect husband.

Poor woman, Burton thought, listening to a song whose message of sincerity his son would never live up to. Grace was a tall thin woman far too good for him, which Thomas was never to realize, not having cared about anyone from the day he was born. Grace expected much, after the courting of such an insincere cavalier. Thomas had pursued her because she seemed unattainable, and now that he had her she would need a lot of looking after. She should have had more sense than to deliver herself into his hands, Burton said to Mary Ann. 'He could charm himself into the bedroom of the Queen of Sheba.'

'Which was much like you and me when I put myself into your hands,' Mary Ann responded.

He didn't indicate whether or not this had occurred to him, and went on to say that Oswald had made a better job of married life than Thomas ever would, because Oswald was closer to being a son of his as any man could get. Thus Burton, who had never bothered about knowing himself – who needed to, if you *were* yourself? – speculated about Thomas, who had lived in the same house for so long, and yet was right.

Thomas rented a house across the boulevard, as if he couldn't bear to be far from a father he feared so much, though Mary Ann hoped to have a grandchild close now that Brian was working in a factory and too busy going after the girls to come and see them.

Thomas walked into the house at least once a day, till Burton wondered whether he thought he still lived there, and that Grace was his kept woman across the road. He looked smarter in his Home Guard uniform than most spare-time soldiers, no doubt in order to get off more easily with the women, whether married or not. 'I suppose you fancy yourself in that khaki suit?'

Thomas's smile showed white and perfect teeth as he reached for the tea Mary Ann poured from her best pewter pot. 'I like being in the Home Guard. It's interesting, and fills my spare time. I'm doing something for my country.' The tea went like a scalding sword into his throat, as if someone might take it away if he didn't hide it quickly enough. 'Anyway, when I'm in uniform I'm not wearing out my own clothes.'

He ignored Burton's contemptuous grunt at such a notion of economy. 'You earn enough to buy your own.'

Thomas could only smile, even now wary of 'answering back'. 'Our company CO likes us to look smart when we're on parade. His name's Captain Dyslin, a man of about fifty, though he doesn't look anywhere near it. He was in the South Wales Borderers in the last war.'

From the cul-de-sac of his thoughts Burton recalled a name

already heard, and wanted more information but couldn't ask directly. 'That's a rare name for a Nottingham man.'

'He's Welsh.' Thomas pushed his cup forward for his mother to fill again. She did. 'A tall smart man, wears a little moustache. He saw me in a pub the other day and treated me to a pint.'

Burton by the fire folded sheets of newspaper into spills for lighting cigarettes, wondering how Dyslin, if it was him, came to be in Nottingham, and why he'd had the effrontery to hobnob with his half-brother. Perhaps it's somebody else, because there must be more than one Dyslin in the world.

Thomas adjusted a cap Burton thought only fit to carry a penny-worth of chips in. 'I must be going. Captain Dyslin shouts at us if we're late on parade. He likes to keep us in line. He can be a real tyrant. Shoulders back, stomach in, chest out! But I sometimes think he's laughing inside when he goes on a bit too long like that.'

The sirens howled their warning message but Burton did not vary his walk, and ignored a warden shouting from the factory gate that he should get into an air-raid shelter. He considered himself too old to die young, though not too old to go on living.

He wouldn't have bothered to hide at any time in his life. If you were to die there was nothing to be done, though better of course to stay alive, the bonus of a year or two extra not to be turned down. There had been times when he hadn't cared to go on living, while knowing there was no cure for life this side of the grave, and that the grave was no cure at all. His snort on turning towards home was meant for all those in the world who had allowed the war to come about.

Anti-aircraft guns unloaded their crackerbarrels at German bombers, shrapnel falling like hard peas on roofs and along empty streets, sounds regarded as merely another manifestation of Old Nick trying to reap him in. A blackout curtain was drawn over the district, except for stars between moving cloud, but he used the kerb and lamp-posts as markers, instinct and local knowledge showing the way to his doorstep.

Mary Ann stood waiting, shaking with fear, had visions of him being killed or injured. 'I'd have sent Thomas to look for you, but he's gone on Home Guard duty.'

He gave a dry laugh on following her inside. 'You don't think a fool like him would have found me?'

'You might have got lost. You can't see a hand before you in this blackout,' she said in the kitchen. 'I told you not to leave the house.'

A warm hand touched her cheek. 'Don't make a fuss. You know I'll be all right.'

'But the sirens go nearly every night, and give me a pain in the stomach.' The finned shoulders of a bomb crumped into earth not far away. 'It's worse than the last war with the zeppelins,' she said, a gap in the clatter of gunfire. 'I never thought we'd have to put up with this again in our lives.'

He took off his jacket. 'Neither did I.'

'Don't you think we'd be better off in the cellar?'

'You can go down if you like. Where are the others?'

'Emily's in bed.'

'Leave her there. She sleeps like a stone.'

'And Ivy's staying at Miss Middleton's.'

'She should be safe enough there. They only bomb poor areas like this. Put the kettle on, and take a hot water bottle when you go down. A blanket as well, or you'll start shivering.'

'Won't you come with me?'

If a bomb hit the house it wouldn't matter whether they were in the cellar or not, and if they got buried together what more could they want? 'I'll look in later.'

Every gun-sound came like a clap of the direst thunderbolt, then a barrage from the naval guns behind Robin's Wood opened up, dozens of shells one after the other, then many all at once, an unbearable noise for a poor soul like Mary Ann, who trembled at every rattle of distant thunder, which he didn't expect she would mind now, though as far as he knew she was in the safest place of the house.

The cellar was swept and cleaned, and a few of Mary Ann's selfmade rugs spread on the floor. He had whitewashed the walls to make it much like another room, and hammered up a wooden bench for whoever wanted to sit down, glad he'd kept sufficient tools from his work at the pit to do that and other jobs about the house. The trouble was that at night the cellar could be as cold as an igloo, and staying there long brought pains around the lower part of his back. Mary Ann called it lumbago, and he let her rub the aches with lotion now and again.

When Jane Middleton, asked into the house one evening by Mary Ann, heard the mention of lumbago, she looked up through her fancy rimless glasses and, ignoring a signal from Ivy, piped up: 'Lumbago is a painful complaint in the muscles of the lower part of the back, or so I understand, and has something to do with rheumatism.'

As if he didn't know, but there was nothing he could say in reply, even supposing he cared to, which he didn't, only thinking Miss Hoity-Toity should have been left out on the pavement to wait for Ivy. There was no woman he wouldn't be polite to, and try to get something out of (even now, if they'd have him) but if Jane Middleton had any liking for a person such as Ivy she wasn't the sort he wanted to know.

He supposed his lumbago to have started on the first night of air-raid warnings, when Mary Ann asked him in a way he couldn't refuse to come with her to the cellar because she was afraid to be on her own. Sitting erect in the same position for an hour, the best way he knew of keeping the mind empty so that time would go more quickly, a stabbing cut across the small of his lumbar parts, and from then on it came back if he sat too long. Nothing had ever been wrong with his body, and though such a complaint wouldn't kill him, Mary Ann said he should go to the doctor, a suggestion – all it dared be – receiving such a sceptical grunt it wasn't mentioned again.

A couple of bombs from the direction of Old Engine Cottages shook the house. Had he been in the cellar with Mary Ann they wouldn't have heard themselves speak. Pot dogs rattled on the shelf as if wanting to leap off and hide under the table. Oliver's photograph looked down, seeming to wonder about noises he had briefly heard in his days as a soldier.

He put on his jacket and walked through the scullery, out the back door. At the end of the small garden was the lavatory, and even though it was the flushing sort he put the usual two-gallon tin of creosote by the pan. He never pulled the chain after a piss because it was a waste of water. The toilet roll on the wall was only for Mary Ann – though he was sure Ivy used it – while he and Emily used newspaper cut into squares. Though it meant black arses it was good enough for them.

Vibrations underfoot and an orange glow over the yards meant more bombs. The noise of guns itched his ears, and he sniffed smoke. A terrified moggie leapt over the wall into the next garden, hoping for safety. Shrapnel pinked, one piece missing his boots by inches. The sky was lighter towards town, as if the whole lot was going up. Aeroplanes flew low again and again, engines droning unevenly between the gunfire.

He thought of Edith and her family in the Meadows, where a lot of the bombs must be falling, hoping they'd be neither killed nor maimed. Rebecca had moved to Kent, and there'd been a danger last year that the Germans might land, though she would have given them what-for if they had. Luckily they were frightened of a drop of water.

In many years he hadn't thought about Alma, or the child she'd had the cheek to call Oliver. He went to the grave every week but without seeing her, nor anywhere on the street either, and he wondered whether she was curious about him. Perhaps she lived in a different part of town, but if she wanted to find him she knew where to look, and if she didn't then she didn't want to find him. He only hoped she was safe.

The windows rattled. Another bomb, and close this time. He went inside at more peppering of shrapnel, careful not to let the bulb glow, though it seemed the Germans had all the light they wanted. He put a half-filled kettle on the few embers, thrifty as ever with the gas. When it boiled he spooned tea into the pot and filled it. Mary Ann would like a cup, and he could do with one as well. Such flame and smoke outside parched the gorge. He opened the parlour cabinet to get the best cups, supposing that if the house were to go up they might as well drink in style.

Sugar was short, but a full spoon went in for Mary Ann's sweet tooth. He had stopped using it when rationing began, able to take it or leave it, not mattering to him, and so all the more for the others. Even Ivy didn't refuse his share. He opened the cellar door with his boot, and went carefully down the darkened narrow steps carrying the first tea he had mashed in his life.

He thought Mary Ann was asleep, leaning against the wall, hands by her side, till realizing nobody could be with such noise, except Emily upstairs who must have imagined in her weird dreams that it was Bonfire Night.

Her lips were slightly open, as if expecting something to be put between them, though he couldn't think what that might be. The pale forehead was luminous with a fear tightly locked in. She waited for the bombing to stop and the war to be over, like everybody else, he supposed, yet feared that every second would be her last. Poor woman! In the dim light were the features of the girl he had married, enough beauty still there for him to touch her lips with his.

She opened her eyes. 'You kissed me, Ernest!' – something only done in bed.

Better to grow old like Darby and Joan than Punch and Judy. In such light she hadn't seen the smile. 'With this lot going on you never know when it's time to say goodbye. Here, I made a pot of tea.'

She sipped, and with the other hand reached for his. An explosion made the house shudder as if it would crumble, smashing them and all their tranklements to smithereens, but she was less frightened now.

His tea went down scalding hot as he sat by her, head bent from the low ceiling of the cellar. She felt his warm face: 'Oliver would have been fifty if he'd lived.'

'I know. I reckon it up every year.' He spoke close because of the noise. 'Lean against me, if you like.'

His lumbago might come back, but it wouldn't kill him, and whatever did could hardly matter. With more than three score and ten under his belt, and Mary Ann the same beneath her pinafore, he could put a finger to his nose, and hope that those dropping the bombs would be killed, the sooner the better.

Mary Ann's grip at the cleanly piercing whistle was tighter than he'd ever known. She called out, but he kept his hand relaxed, because if she sensed his worry her terrified heart might give.

The whistle went on, as if to last forever, and though only for a few seconds he thought if this is it, so be it, a throb of rage because they were causing Mary Ann such distress. To calm himself he imagined it wasn't so much the German bombers as Beelzebub about to blind him in the other eye. She couldn't stop shaking against him. The whistle ended, as everything had to, and a shudder of explosions almost threw them off the bench.

He knocked his cap against the wall to get the dust off. 'I thought it was Thomas on his way in, with a whistle like that.'

He thanked God when she laughed and said: 'Thomas's whistle was never like that.' But she couldn't stop trembling, and went on without opening her eyes: 'God will pay the Germans out.' For the first time in his life he held back the grunt she expected.

Burton admitted, on his way to the Gregory Hotel, that he liked to keep a watch over his children, whether they were married or not. Ivy said it was because he wanted to interfere in their lives, but it wasn't. He was only interested in knowing what they were up to. When Thomas had been married two years he saw him in town arm-in-arm with a woman, out on her dinner break from a factory, he supposed, noting her overalls and the cigarette at her mouth.

Thomas said: 'Hello, Dad!' not saying who she was. Burton didn't want to know, but thought it brazen to be going behind Grace's back so soon.

When he saw him talking to the same woman in a pub it was obvious what was going on. Grace complained at him having to do Home Guard duty every night, but Burton told Mary Ann he knew very well whose home it was he was guarding, while her husband was in Egypt or some such place. It was hard to understand why his sons had married women too good for them, while three daughters had landed themselves with numbskulls or bullies. Thomas had married an unusual woman, and found her hard to live with, but what wife had ever been easy?

Walking to the bar he noticed a tall army chap with a swagger-stick under his arm, flat cap, moustache, and a row of medal ribbons, who said to him: 'Do you remember me?'

The Welsh accent brought a picture of Owen the Bible reader who had penned Mary Ann's postcards at Pontllanfraith, and he got rid of it by a rub at the eye. He knew very well who the man was. 'I didn't hear your name.'

'Dyslin – David Ernest. Captain in the Home Guard for the duration.'

Burton nodded, then finished his drink. 'Pleased to meet you again.'

'Thought I'd take another look.'

'Now you have,' not wanting to be too abrupt with a man who was, after all, his son. Sensing his wish to shake hands, he kept one firmly by his side, and the other on his empty jar. 'What are you doing here this time?'

'I ask that question myself now and then. But I got tired of South Wales – as I believe you did once – and tried my luck in London.'

Another journeyman: it must run in the blood. 'How did you get on there?'

'Not too badly. But my wife left me.'

He was astonished that a woman could do such a thing to a Burton. 'How did that happen?'

'And then the children grew up.'

'They all do.' Burton looked at his impressive son, a sight that, though he was in khaki, brought a pleasure he saw no reason not to enjoy.

Dyslin smiled. 'Just before the war I thought I'd try things in Nottingham, since I had some connection with it, you might say. And it's as good a place as any, perhaps better. I get on fine with the people.'

'You're doing well?'

'I'm in a partnership. The war's hit us, but we're holding on all right.'

'I'm glad to hear it.'

'I got a couple of chaps sent down a year or two ago who'd been robbing all over the place. There's a great deal more crime here than before the war.'

At least one of his sons had made a way in the world, so he accepted a pint, wondering what life would have been like to have had the chap growing up at Old Engine Cottages, the mood momentarily blighted on reflecting that with such a background he might not have done so well for himself – except that Mary Ann could have encouraged him enough to get to where he was now. Perhaps I would have been less harsh to him than the others.

Dyslin took a gentlemanly sip of his whisky. 'A son of yours is in my company, my half-brother of course, though I shan't let him know. Chance throws up some rare coincidences.'

Burton had to agree.

'As soon as his name came out at roll call I could tell the instant I looked at him. He has the makings of a good soldier, you might like to know. He learns quickly, and does what he's told.'

Burton drank half his pint. 'He's had a lot of practice.'

'I imagine he has.' He looked at himself in the mirror behind the bar for a while. 'But I'd been wanting to have another meeting with you. Who knows when it will be possible again, in this war?'

'How long do you think it'll go on?'

'Another three or four years. But the Russians are in with us now, so I expect they'll win a lot of it.'

'I don't think anybody ever won a war.'

'I always told myself the same, but we've got to fight this one.'

'So I believe.' The Germans had tried to kill him and Mary Ann. He took money from his pocket. 'I'll buy you a drink.'

Dyslin couldn't refuse the generosity of an old age pensioner, who was also his father, for whom he felt more affection than he thought became any man, as he placed his glass forward. 'That's very kind.'

Burton looked askance at Dyslin's facetious remark. 'No it isn't.' He may be my son, but he has to keep his place, in spite of the ribbons on his chest. 'It's my wish. I'm glad we met again.'

THIRTY

Mary Ann booked seats on the train so that she and Burton could stay a week in Kent with Rebecca, who lived so far away that Mary Ann hadn't seen as much of her children as she would have liked. 'We don't know how much longer we're going to live, and I want to see more of them before I die, even though they're all grown up.'

She worried about the trip, her glasses on while looking at timetables, and trying to make sense of the London Underground diagram the travel agent had given her, of how to get from St Pancras to Charing Cross. Burton said not to let the matter upset her, but he would say that, wouldn't he? He expected her to do the figuring merely because he had given the three pounds for the tickets out of money he'd put by. Up at five, he woke Mary Ann at six.

'You might have left me a bit longer,' she said.

'I'm getting hungry. I've got the fire going.'

At half-past eight they stood in their best clothes by the silent Gregory Hotel, and took a trolleybus to Old Market Square, changing there for the LMS station. He wasn't bored, with so much to see from the train, shading his eye when the sun worked through cloud. Near Bedford, Mary Ann looked in the St Neots direction, as if for a glimpse of her relations. When the train puffed up to the platform of St Pancras station Burton was first out to handle the cases.

'We must get on the blue line to cross London,' she said, 'but there's no hurry. After we change at Leicester Square there's only one more stop. Our train for Lydd doesn't leave until a quarter-past three.'

The Underground train seemed to pull up every few seconds,

his head so full of the wonder. 'If there's time I could do with a drink. And I expect you'll be wanting your pint of shandy.'

At Charing Cross she put their cases into the left luggage and, with two hours to spare before the Lydd train, she led him into Trafalgar Square, where they ate their sandwiches. 'This is what I've always wanted to see. That must be Lord Nelson up there.'

Twenty years ago an old sailor-looking villain had stomped on his wooden leg up the path at Old Engine Cottages, and sold her a piece of wood for half a crown, saying it was part of the ship Lord Nelson died on. She was proud to have it, until learning that the *Victory* was in Portsmouth and had never been broken up.

Rebecca and Fred met them at Lydd station, made all the fuss possible during their stay. Rebecca told Mary Ann when they were alone that Fred had used her all their married life as a rag to wipe the sweat of his forehead with. 'I wish I'd never set eyes on him, but then, what man would have been good enough for me to set eyes on? Bringing up six kids has been my penance, and there was no getting out of it.'

Burton regretted having come, counting every hour to going home. He was nagged to get back, though couldn't say why, said nothing about it, never would have, went to the pub with Fred, who was a happy but thoughtless man, solid in body and contemptuous of everyone, without having the presence to back up his opinions, Burton knowing that Fred, in maligning someone, only showed his own littleness. Most of all, he talked too much.

But Burton enjoyed being with Rebecca's grown sons and daughters, who were fascinated by him. One grandson walked him to the Pilot Inn at Dungeness, and eighty-year-old Burton walked so quickly he at one point left him behind.

Whatever was calling him home he wouldn't like when he discovered what it was. He only knew he wasn't where he wanted to be, as if neglecting an issue of crucial importance. The sooner he went back the better, a feeling so firm he was tempted to talk about it with Mary Ann. The only sign of his uncertainty to her was that he ate so little it was a wonder he could go on living, but when she mentioned it he said he had never been a big eater anyway.

Standing with his grandson by a field at harvest time he watched the machine reducing the area of wheat. He was sorry at not having a shotgun to get one of the rabbits running for safety, but on one coming close enough he snatched it up, and killed it by a cut at the neck. At the same instant a youth slung a piece of slate which caught Burton's hand, and made a gash that fetched blood.

Kids were only doing what they had always done, so he laid no blame, but strode down the lane to where his daughter Rebecca would bind the wound, blood dripping through his fingers, the dead rabbit swinging from the other hand.

Burton, the large flat cap under his arm, stood so as to give full advantage to his height, looked at the rectangular grave and marble scroll at its head. Under the embossed horseshoe were words he knew backwards and forwards, upside-down and right side up, the only writing he could recognize, every letter blazoned into his head.

He laid down the swatch of red roses and threw the bunch of daffodils laid there by Ivy and Emily onto a heap of decaying blooms by the church wall. He carried the vase of tap water to the grave and set his flowers in it, prime roses from a shop, not trash out of Thomas's allotment.

He wiped his large veined hands with a red and white spotted handkerchief. Wounds never healed. Knots didn't unravel. You couldn't expect them to, had no say in the matter. You were grieved unto death and maybe afterwards, though his doubts on that were such as not to worry. Life had been long, and at least he had lived it.

The sepulchral grunt was as if his heart could hold no more. The older he got the worse Oliver's death tormented him. He wondered how much longer he'd need to shoulder its weight. Your head seems as full as a bucket but, turn it upside-down, nothing comes out, glued in by memories you could well do without. Life was long enough to enjoy, but too short for torment. He turned abruptly and went onto the street, walking in so straight a line that an onlooker assumed he was following the marks of the paving stones.

Back from his usual pint, he said to Mary Ann that he was going up to bed. Sparks of pain moved across his chest, hot as toast yet as blunt as all get out, toing and froing in a sloweddown insistent way, hardly worth bothering about, but suddenly they clubbed together and gave a gyp he'd never known. She asked again what ailed him, but he wasn't the man for answers.

Ivy and Emily sat by the diminishing fire. It was even harder to get coal and coke than it had been during the war. Emily queued patiently at depots all around the town, and sometimes brought half a hundredweight back on her shoulders. 'It's time you two were in bed.' He went upstairs before knowing whether or not they obeyed.

There was nothing to do with such pain except get some kip and hope it would go. If it didn't, it was him who would, to some place he had never known, and there was damn-all to be done about it. He put his boots in their usual place by the door, to know where they'd be if needed again, and draped his suit on a hanger beside the brown one in the wardrobe. He unclipped his suspenders and sat on the bed to draw off his socks, dropped them in the hamper for Mary Ann to wash.

The pain seemed to settle, and he hoped he wasn't pampering himself, though it would get back into action if he didn't lie down. Shedding his long underwear, nakedness minus feet and face showed in the wardrobe mirror. The woollen nightshirt shook to his feet, and the last thing done before getting into bed was to take off his black velvet eyepatch, make sure it was smooth, and put it on the small table so that he would know where to find it. The wounded eye was less painful for some reason, though dazzled with colours never seen before.

Mary Ann stood in her nightdress. He hadn't heard her come in, unusual for a man who always noticed everything. She laid the fallen blankets over him, the bedroom icily cold. His face was the colour of chalk. 'You're not well, Ernest,' she said. 'What is it?'

He couldn't stare the pain into quiescence, lay with knees bent in a bed that had never been long enough. Maybe he would get one to fit, where he was going. He turned to her. 'Bricks in my chest are banging together. Don't ask any more.'

It was an illness that couldn't be palliated by Epsom salts mixed with hot tea in a large white saucer; or cured by friar's balsam, or held at bay by that mysterious concoction for horses given him by a gypsy in Wales, gurgled into his gullet from an upended position, fitness and colour coming into his face as the sombre liquid diminished in the bottle.

His back was to Mary Ann, who lay by his side. Drawing his knees up eased him. 'Are Emily and Ivy in bed?' Whatever I've got seems more than a cold, unless it's a bad case of the flu, though if it is I can't think where I caught it. Walking among people who are hawking and spitting, it jumps into your throat, then goes everywhere else in your body. I've never seen a doctor in my life, but might if this hasn't gone by morning. Drunken youths shouted along the boulevard. 'They are,' Mary Ann told him.

He wondered about his children. Edith had at last rid herself of Doddoe – after he'd been in prison a few times for poaching. He recalled how some years ago Doddoe had pawned Edith's sheets and finest underclothes to get money for beer. On his way to the pub he met Sabina's husband Harold, and the pair drank away every penny, while their children were hungry at home. Edith now lived with a man who looked after her as she deserved, though her jailbird lads called him blind and tormented him almost to madness.

Sabina lived down the road, and Rebecca was all right in Kent. Oswald did his best for Helen at home, and Thomas across the road was more likely chasing some woman instead of being in bed with Grace. You couldn't berate a man too much for that. In any case nobody ever altered.

He thought of his children but didn't want them close, for who would be gawped at when the devil was getting his claws into you? He took my favourite son, and now it's my time to go, when I was hoping for another ten years before the lights went out. 'You tossed and turned all night,' Mary Ann said. 'Drink this cup of tea, and then I'll get your breakfast.'

She covered him, put a hand to his fevered head. The pain had thinned him since yesterday. 'Thomas has gone for the doctor. He'll be here directly.'

'I don't want breakfast. A doctor won't do any good, either.' No use talking, I don't care to frighten her, though by her look and the tears on her cheeks she thinks I'm about to go. His voice was weak. 'None of your blawting. Not for me.'

The doctor was a short heavy man not long out of the navy. 'What's all this, Mr Burton?'

Less answer was necessary than there ever had been to any question, and he felt like swearing at being addressed in so familiar a manner. As with the wounded on the burning deck, he was shot full of diamorphine to make the pain more distant.

'I'll call later,' the doctor said to Mary Ann downstairs, 'and give him more of the same. The poor chap needs it.'

THIRTY-ONE

Burton was dying. Ivy knew that if he didn't now he never would though no one lives forever, and who would want *him* to? Certainly none of his family, so she believed. Immortality is not given to anyone born of the flesh, as she had heard long ago in Sunday School, and whoever came into the world other than that way, and told us all about it, would be shouted down as a barefaced liar.

Burton would go to hell when he went, because where else was there for a man like him? She had heard that everybody who did go to that place, no matter how old, were made into their prime of thirty-three. Those who went to heaven, on the other hand, stayed the same age as when they had died, because inno-cence was much cherished in that place.

She found it unpleasant to think of Burton back in his prime. He had been tall and domineering all his life, though a roisterer when young, and a womanizer since. When we did anything he didn't like or thought was wrong, and he was forced to speak to us about it, the fact of having to open his mouth at all, as if he had no energy to spare after a day's work at the forge, made him so angry he nearly always ended by hitting us. Above all, we must never *answer back*, because the response would be certain and devastating. He'd had more power over his family than a Persian satrap over a province.

Sometimes they sensed the moment coming, and slipped away before he could strike, thinking that when back within range he would have forgotten his anger. Hope stayed during their escape, but he never did forget what they had done or said before running away, so they always got whatever battering the lapse of time had convinced him even more they deserved. He'd never crushed them, though, oh no, but they did grow more bitter as they got older. Or at least she had.

She pictured Burton arriving at the gates of hell, where he was made into his prime of thirty-three. He would be at Old Nick's throat in no time. There'd be some argument or other, such as when Burton, a lifetime blacksmith, wanted to get closer to the fire, while others did what was expected by running from the flames. At the first sign of authority from Old Nick, who as the gaffer demanded fear and respect from everybody, Burton would send a wicked knucklebone crack at his chin, because at thirty-three Burton had been a smith of long standing, with five of his eight kids already born, and took no chelp from anybody. Old Nick, having more than his work cut out to hold Burton in check, would get the pasting of his life. All hell would break loose, you might say. The defence of Burton's behaviour could only be that he had only been himself, at a time when to be anybody else would have brought him and his family to destitution.

On hearing the din, and being told what it was about, God Almighty would send word for the culprit to come up and explain himself. Out of curiosity Burton would go, to see if there really was a God, and if so what He looked like, because hadn't he all his life heard from his chastised children, and even from Mary Ann, that God would one day *pay him out* for his wicked temper? All that could be said in his favour was that at least he had heard of God.

'Nobody in hell has ever made such a fuss.' God would shake a finger, though not too harshly, reluctant to upset anyone unnecessarily. 'So tell me what it was about.'

'He asked for it,' Burton would reply, if his mood was mischievous, which it rarely had been, certainly not at thirty-three. Though aware of being talked to by no less than God Himself, he wasn't the sort of man to answer a question from anyone.

'What do you mean by that?' God would ask more sternly, committing the ultimate sin, as far as Burton was concerned, of answering back, and before any of the angels realized what was happening God would be knocked from his golden throne and crawling around the floor looking for his glasses, as well as for the scythe that only a blacksmith like Burton could have made.

Burton would go back to where he knew he belonged, to live in as much peace as could be expected after the life he had led.

Ivy made a pot of tea for Mary Ann, who had only left Burton's side because, unable to fight off sleep, she had come down to doze in her rocking chair by the fire. Burton was beyond needing a cup, but Ivy wouldn't take him one, unless he asked her politely, which he was incapable of doing.

Standing on the doorstep a week ago she had seen him coming back from the pub with one of the last pints he would drink settled inside him. Under the sodium lights of the boulevard he held himself straight-backed, fully erect, striding along in his best suit, as if knowing that everyone would step aside for him. Halfway to the house he touched his cap to a young woman going by.

Ivy had been too close to know why women had always found him so attractive, but they had. She remembered standing in the jug-and-bottle to get some Guinness for Mary Ann, and when the door into the saloon bar opened for a few moments there was Burton talking to a woman young enough to be his granddaughter. She was all dolled up, smiling and nodding and looking ready to eat him, and happy that he laughed and touched her arm, as if he would like to eat her. God alone knew what he was telling her. It wasn't the first time she'd seen him trying to get off, unable to imagine why a young girl could be so taken by such an old man.

The last to know about a man were his own children, and all of them were between forty and fifty now. They had never acknowledged how hard he worked to keep them fed, shod and housed, but on the other hand his lifelong struggle had stopped him getting close to them, and had not allowed them to get close to him. Perhaps the only way of keeping himself going was to fight against any kind of bother.

Providing for a wife and eight children hadn't been easy on the money a blacksmith earned, and she admitted that he had never complained, or blamed anyone for whatever unpleasantness he'd had to face, even though such endurance had cut him off from getting love or consolation from his children. He had never wanted to know himself, thinking, if he had thought at all: 'I'm me, therefore I am.' It had always given her satisfaction to recall that God had got back at him twice in his life.

Those who had lived under his reign might dispute that they were the last people to know him. They could say it was easy to know all there was to know, because the expressive fist and vitriolic mask had been only too plain to understand, and that if *they* didn't know what was behind it, on running away with aching ribs or a sore back, then who could?

At the groan from upstairs she told herself that whatever pain he was in served him right. It was as well for God to pay him out as much as possible before he died, because who in fact could be certain there was a hell for him to go to afterwards?

The only thing was that he was about to kick the bucket, for which she had waited till the age of forty-five, more years than she'd ever wanted, but when you were born into a situation from which you couldn't escape there was nothing to do but put up with it. None of them had been asked to come into a family lorded over by Burton.

Every day since birth she'd vowed she couldn't bear another day under his cold unblinking eye. Maybe her mother had thought the same from the time of their marriage, but it was hard to believe, at her lying so peacefully in the chair.

The arrow of another cry came down the stairs and into the kitchen, bedding its tip into Mary Ann's heart. At the sound of her feet ascending the narrow wooden stairs Ivy thought that those who suffer most are more punctilious in their obligations to those who put them through it. No one had borne the brunt of him more than Mary Ann, whose loving care for the rest of the family had been the only balm for her endurance. All her married life she had fortified herself by recalling the love that had surrounded her like a halo in those early days.

She had never heard Mary Ann speak a word of complaint against him, as if leaving that to the five daughters and three sons, herself in particular, who always had and always would say what she thought about him, though she'd never done so to his face because, as old as he was, his hand would have been unavoidable.

The framed oleograph above the parlour mantelshelf, a wedding present from Burton's brother George (who had been no angel either) showed a curly-headed debonair youth with a kerchief around his neck, by his sweetheart in a flowered frock. From the couplet beneath it wasn't clear which of the pair was speaking, but Ivy assumed the sentimental thought was shared by both, though it was the young man who offered the bunch of flowers. Mary Ann must often have looked at the picture, and wondered about her life with Burton.

Its mysterious quality had appealed to Ivy even before she could read the words, a scene between two people promising a life of happiness and mutual understanding, and kindness towards any children they would have. She had gazed at it as a little girl, and the bitterness of her intense disillusionment was enough to spoil her life.

Still, the picture had been a strength to Mary Ann, because there was no doubt that in spite of his sins Burton was about to die knowing he had never been loved so much by any other woman. He had loved her, as well, and perhaps he had turned against his children thinking they had formed a barrier between himself and Mary Ann.

Ivy realized that for all Burton's dislike of her, and knowing her hatred of him, he had never threatened to pitch her into the street. He might have thought it often enough – she was sure he had – but he hadn't said it, because having females in the house who daren't answer back was something he couldn't live without. Anyway, the family was the family, and because he had had to put up with the hardships, so must they.

The gate latch clicked, and Oswald came in, tall and ruddy-faced, with the thick hair of Mary Ann's Irish ancestors. He looked worn and raddled, as if caring for Helen rather than his work had tired him out. 'Thomas isn't home yet, but I expect he'll call later,' he said. 'How is Burton?'

'Mother heard him moan, and went up to see what she could do. I don't think he's got long.'

'Everyone has to die sometime.' He recalled how Burton had comforted him after the death of Howard. 'But I do feel a bit upset about it.'

'I suppose you would.'

'Well, he's not dead, is he? He could suddenly recover enough to walk downstairs and be more or less his old self for another five years.'

Ivy's face reddened with horror at the idea. 'No, no he couldn't. He's too far gone.'

He smiled. 'It's been known,' but didn't want to argue with such a sister. 'Has the doctor been?'

'He was in this morning, and just told us to keep him as comfortable as we could. I'm to go and fetch him, if anything happens.'

'I'll do that,' he said. 'Mary Ann will need you here.' He looked out of the window as if to see Burton's soul already lifting across the plot of yard, illuminating the darkness before fading into rest. 'You always think your father's going to last forever, and it comes as a shock to know he won't.'

She disliked his melancholy, so often noticed in Burton. 'Well, he can't.' Arms folded across her bosom, she wanted to say he had lasted too long as it was, but Oswald wouldn't like it, so she didn't. If his sons thought differently it was because they had been quicker at standing up to him and getting out of his way. They found it easier to forgive than women, who'd had more to put up with. 'I don't care what you think. I just wouldn't want somebody like that to last forever.'

'He didn't know any better than to treat us like he did.' Oswald took a spill Burton had made a few days ago, touched a light from the fire for his cigarette. 'I know he was hard, but not all the time with me.' Burton had become easier to get on with in the last few years, and was dying just as he was ready to enjoy life. Maybe the longer two people live together the more they get to be like each other, and being married to Mary Ann for sixty years it was natural that her tolerance should pass onto him – as he'd said to Sabina only last week.

Emily came in, without saying hello, a half-filled basket on her arm. The war had been over more than a year, but times were no easier. You'd be daft to expect it, Ivy thought. Food was still rationed, and all the buildings were shabby and needed a coat of paint.

Emily put the weekly rations in the cupboard. The put-upon aspect of her features that had been there since birth made everyone look on her as a bit touched. It helped to recognize herself in the mirror, which was better than not seeing anything unusual at all.

'I had to queue half an hour. A lot of people jumped in the line just as they saw me coming. Then some pushed in front of me. I wanted to kill 'em, but they pushed and pushed. When I couldn't put up with it any longer I told them to fuck off or I'd blind them.'

'Don't swear.' Ivy remembered her doing so in front of Jane Middleton, who'd been shocked. Tears came at the memory of poor Jane, who'd died of a heart attack two years ago.

Emily gave a wickedly triumphant smile. 'Well, I got my place back, didn't I? And I brought all the groceries home, didn't I? So don't fucking well tell me what to say.' She poured tea, and made a face on tasting it. 'You let it get cold,' glancing at Ivy, who she thought capable of putting ice in it specially for her.

Ivy, knowing better than to argue, was glad to see Sabina and Edith, followed by Thomas. All six crowded the living room, both men still in their working clothes. Sabina kept her coat well-wrapped, looked fearful, as if incapable of tears after her baleful life with Harold. 'How's Dad?'

'The old so-and-so's about to go.' Ivy when in Kent heard Rebecca say she wouldn't bother to come and see Burton when he was ill and looked like kicking the bucket, so everybody was here who should be.

Edith set out cups for the tea Emily was making. 'I know he was a bit of a bogger to me, but I'm sorry he's going.'

Sabina was too miserable to speak. He had been a devil to her as well, though she couldn't forget how he had taken her back into the house after she had run away from home.

Burton shouted, like a much younger man, ordering his sons to start work at the forge: 'Nobody can do a job as well as yourself.' Then he was in the doorway of the house handing out jobs to all and sundry like a sergeant-major. Oliver was walking across the Cherry Orchard towards Robin's Wood, about to vanish in the mist of a warm spring morning. He called for him to come back.

Ivy shook with rage. 'It should be Mary Ann he wants.'

'He loved Oliver more than anybody else except her.' Oswald dried tears with a large white handkerchief, wondering whether

Burton had wept when his father had died. Probably not, because he hadn't been born of a mother like Mary Ann. He stood with Thomas by the bed, the first time they had been in the room while their father was there.

Come to see me go, Burton thought. Mary Ann hadn't slept by his side the night before, which meant that Old Nick was about to have him. Narrow stairs curved upwards, dark and dusty in his waking dream, but he was beyond the effort of climbing.

'What are you doing here?' Oliver stepped from the frame in the parlour, to see him off, or welcome him, his smile no more than a subtle alteration of the lips, as if to start softly whistling, make perfect music to cut himself off from the surrounding tribulations. Burton hoped for love and forgiveness, but Oliver turned like a plaster dummy and walked away.

He shouted, but his son wouldn't listen, had only been happy when by himself as a youth. Burton called again, looked hard and long. 'He's not far off, Mam,' Oswald said, though it took some believing, till he heard Mary Ann crying, poor soul. Impelled by his last strength, Burton sat rigidly upright, the flannel nightshirt buttoned to his neck, a look of inflamed wonder when the velvet patch fell from his skull-like head and revealed the ugly terracotta hole of his dead eye.

He was still for a moment – as if to give traffic on the road outside the chance to stop at his going – until a spark the size he had never imagined spread through his heart and lungs, causing gouts of pink froth to erupt from his open mouth. Blood flowed down his chin, and he saw with a blacksmith's clarity Old Nick coming towards him on a horse. There was shock on his face, and then the eye stopped looking because it could see no more. Never afraid of the dark, he went into it wondering what was there.

Feeling more alone than he ever had, Oswald stepped onto a trolley bus going into town, and paid for an announcement in the *Evening Post* saying that Ernest Burton, blacksmith, was dead. The world would be a different place from now on, and they who had been borne from him would feel themselves different people. He wanted to sit in the Peach Tree over a pint and think about the family's loss but, fearful that something might happen to Helen if he delayed, took the same numbered bus towards home.

One or two men who had worked with Burton at the pit came to Lenton churchyard to see him buried. Many people had heard of his death, but Mary Ann wondered what the dumpy and spectacled woman by the wall, and the tall young man by her side, were doing there.

Old Morgan, thin and upright, was the height of formality in his wing collar and bowler hat, and silver-handled stick pressed firmly to the ground. He stood next to Tom who was dressed equally high and out of fashion, both upright but close together, as if to support whoever might fall, and looking beyond the grave into space they would be entering soon, to find Burton. When the priest had finished his words Tom turned to Morgan: 'There's a dewdrop at the end of your nose, old pal,' and passed the ironed handkerchief from his top pocket.

Morgan snatched it, dabbed, then handed it back. 'Mind your own bloody business. There's one on yours as well.'

Dyslin came to the graveside, and said to Mary Ann: 'My family knew Mr Burton as a young blacksmith in Wales.'

The mention of Burton's youth brought back the days when he had courted her, so she felt momentarily young in her grief. He was the same smart chap who had called at Old Engine Cottages fifteen years ago. 'You mean your mother knew him?'

'Yes. I saw from the paper that he'd died. It's a sad day for me as well.'

He looked like Burton's son, clipped moustache, hard unblinking eyes, a strong line of jaw, tall and spare. Perhaps Burton had fathered more than one child before meeting her.

His laugh made an uncommon noise in the churchyard when she told him. 'In my profession I hear even more outlandish stories. But I must go now. If you ever need anything, you have only to let me know.' He gave her a newer version of the card she had found among the things of Burton he had thought worth keeping.

Oswald saw him walk away under his large umbrella. 'Who was that?'

'He was my captain in the Home Guard,' Thomas put in. 'Wasn't it nice of him to come? I didn't think he thought so much of me. I suppose he found out about it from the *Post*.'

'He was Burton's son,' Mary Ann said. 'Your half-brother, from before Burton married me.' She walked away from their astonishment. A man can scatter children everywhere, she thought when out of the rain and in the car to go home, but if a woman brings one into the house that isn't her husband's, and he finds out, she gets murdered.

Alma, a pale spinster of fifty, hair grey under her rain hat, peered at the ceremony through small gold-rimmed spectacles. The heavy gaberdine mackintosh wasn't quite warm enough to stop her emotional shivers. Thirty-one-year-old Oliver was by her side, both standing well apart from the Burtons. She hardly knew why she was there, except that she had wanted him to see his father buried, but he seemed bored, even irritated.

'I'm sorry I made you lose time from your work,' she said, 'but he was your father. And now you know.'

'It's taken long enough for you to tell me. Up to a few years ago I was burning to know, then found I couldn't care less. Lydia once hinted who it was, but I didn't believe her, thinking it was just another of her stories to amuse me.'

'You played with him once as a child.'

'And I just thought he was some man you'd picked up.'

She was crying. 'He ruined my life, but he made it as well. I never loved any man as much as him.'

He put an arm over her shoulders: better for her to cry, and talk, though how could the stern headmistress of a girls' school allow what happened so many years ago to upset her? 'You let him take me for a walk, I couldn't think why at the time, but the memory kept popping up when I was on those Atlantic convoys, and on the worse ones to Murmansk.' He recalled telling Burton he wanted to see the Amazon, but the Tuloma and the Hudson had been enough. 'I should have known he was my father, because everything about that meeting stayed so vivid.'

'I often wondered whether the past is worth having been lived,' she said, 'but at least I've got you, and your children.'

The last pair to leave the churchyard, he held her arm. By the time they reached the pavement she'd stopped crying. The gate was still open. 'Go back and close it.'

He looked as if thinking her slightly mad. She had brought him up to obedience, though it was a bit much expecting a trained engineer and ex-naval officer to jump to his mother's command. He shut the gate nevertheless.

Mary Ann took a nightdress from her private drawer, folded between sheets of tissue paper and smelling of lavender, every pleat sharply ironed. 'I shall want to be put in this when I die,' she said to Sabina, 'so be sure not to use anything else.'

She had told Sabina to ask Brian to bring some rice back for her from Malaya, so she might not have expected to die as soon as she did. 'They grow it out there, and I know he'll bring it if you let him know it's for me.' She hadn't been able to get any for more than five years, and couldn't understand why it wasn't in the shops now that the war was over, beginning to realize that she and Burton had unwittingly voted for a government that kept people short so that they would know their place. Having imagined such days were over, she wondered now if they ever would be.

She died in her sleep a year after Burton, before Brian could bring the rice. Burton was buried in the same plot as Oliver but Mary Ann wanted to be cremated, which Ivy told Sabina was because she'd had as much of Burton as she could stand during her lifetime, and didn't care to lie in the same grave with him after death.

Sabina replied that Mary Ann asked to be cremated because the grave was full, and she was generous enough to let Burton stay with Oliver. In any case she was frightened of being buried alive in the box.

'Your grandma was timorous,' she said to Brian when he came home, 'but she would stand up to right a wrong whenever she could. She loved Burton from the moment she set eyes on him till the day she died, whatever Ivy might say. And he loved her the same. He thought the world of her. When I went to wake her up on the morning she died I didn't know she was dead, but I saw it as soon as I looked at her lovely peaceful face. She lay on her back, the bedclothes up to her neck as smooth as if she hadn't moved an inch all night. One arm was under the clothes, but the other was outside, her fingers tight together and holding something. I had a job to get the hand open, but when I did I found a two-shilling piece with Queen Victoria's head on it. I'll never know why it was there. Perhaps she thought she'd have to pay her way into heaven when she died, though they'd have welcomed a good soul like her for nothing. It was an old two-bob piece, but the shopkeeper took it, and I don't expect she minded me spending it on groceries.'

THIRTY-TWO

When sirens sounded and the bombers roamed, Helen walked from the house with joyful expectation. To stop her would mean using strength that would hurt, so Oswald let her go. She would come back unharmed, was happy among gunflashes and the shudder of bombs, hoping God would turn sufficiently benevolent to take her to Howard.

After the war, when Oswald's job on the canal came to an end, he had to give up the house as well. Helen didn't want to leave, because Howard had lived there, but Oswald believed a move would be good for her. She would no longer have to walk along the road and pass the place where their son had been struck down.

The air of the council estate was healthier, the aspect more open, but Oswald dreamed of living alone on an island in the middle of a lake, a one-roomed house with bed, table, chair and fireplace, a few trees outside to give shade and fuel. A rowing boat would get him to shore for basic provisions, though a plot of garden (and maybe a chicken coop) would supply much of what was necessary. He wanted solitude and peace, but had to make do with the vision, so as to endure the maelstrom of Helen's moods and needs.

At the new house she wouldn't or couldn't get out of bed without help. She complained of her blighted life, which Oswald considered a good thing because it saved him doing the same, though he wished she had nothing to complain of at all, or could stop herself doing so, then he wouldn't have to think about not doing so, though in that case there'd be nothing to talk about. I'd live in silence, and feel too much like my father, he thought. So he cleaned the house and cooked the meals, carried her up and carried her down, and saw to everything she wanted.

He sometimes thought his heart would burst, a dim explosion in his chest, a jolt, a push from within taking him beneficially down into blackness. He dreaded it because who would then take care of Helen? He thought what a relief it would be to walk away from her eternal lamentations at the hardness of life.

On better days Howard like a true angel receded from her thoughts and let daylight in. After a while this God-given anaesthetic wore away, to be replaced by the pain of realizing that life had no meaning, that she had nothing to live for and, because it was a sin to die, must endure until God (as she put it) took her.

Oswald laid out a bedroom on the ground floor, which opened onto the garden. Every fine day he cradled her to the lawn whose borders he had cultivated into a fresh and colourful display. From his allotment he brought choice blooms, though without expecting much appreciation when she held out a hand for them. Even before taking his boots off in the kitchen he put lettuces in season and small colourful radishes on the table, and then on her plate when he had washed them, all good things gathered so that she would eat. He cared for her as if paying back every woman who throughout the ages had done so for all the Burton men.

He met Edith in town one morning walking along the Ropewalk. He had been to Boots with a prescription for Helen. 'You look like death warmed-up,' she said.

He chose not to worry about the pain that had run across his chest a few weeks ago like a ferret in search of food, since it hadn't come back. Edith put up her umbrella against the rain, and told him she had a house of her own at Beeston now, which her son Gilbert had bought for her who, she said, was doing very well in America. 'But how is Helen getting on?'

'Not too bad.'

'She's got to forget her troubles. It's you who worries me, though, you're too thin. You ought to see a doctor.'

'Who would take care of Helen if he found something wrong? You can't have two people badly in the same house.'

'That's a daft way to look at it. If anything happens to you she won't have anyone to take care of her at all, and then where would she be?'

At such concern he said: 'It's a long time since I gave you a kiss,' and brought her close, not caring what passersby might think. Were her cheeks wet from the rain? Or was she tearful because of him?

She laughed after his kiss. 'The last person who did that to me was a Chinese man last night. There's a caravan in my garden that I let him live in, and I've come downtown to buy some pots and pans so's he can have something decent to cook with. He's a lovely little chap with dark hair. He wears a suit all the time, and makes me a delicious Chinese meal every now and again. We have a little cuddle afterwards. I used to think all men were rotten, but he's not.'

'You always were a devil,' he laughed with her. Once young and flighty, she was now more beautiful than handsome, few wrinkles on her face, and a firm stout figure even after bearing nine children. 'I'm lucky to have such a sister,' he said.

The day was warm, but Helen called for a blanket over her knees while resting in the garden. She lay in a half-sleep, head to one side. When her missal slipped onto the grass Oswald took it to the kitchen. If she lived a hundred years he would look after her in the same way, then happily die in the belief that he had done all he could. A shadow drifted across the doorway, a cool evening breeze bringing the freshness of mown grass and flowers.

She wanted to go in. 'But you must let me walk by myself, Oswald,' she said for the first time. 'I do have two feet, you know.'

'There's no need of that.' She lay with arms by her side, dark eyes glowing from grey curls. 'You don't weigh more than a feather pillow.' His blacksmith's strength would serve for as long as needed, regarding it like Burton as his to command. He carried her with his usual ease to the door.

'This is like the day we were married,' not having reminded him of that before, either. He would get her inside, see that she was comfortable, then make the supper, an omelette for her, and a slice of fat bacon (with potatoes) for him. They would then sit together and watch television, before she went to sleep.

The malign fate which had called his son had kept a blow in

store for him, though not one he would suffer from, except for the second or two of pain which struck across his heart like the cut of a sword. When a neighbour came at Helen's screams it was obvious to anybody except a fool, she said, that he would never get up again.

Helen was cared for in a Catholic nursing home till she was well over eighty. Grief can prolong as well as shorten life, only mysterious and inherited qualities having any say in how long it will be.

The nuns looked after her as if she were their mother, always making sure the framed photograph of Howard stood at the right angle on her bedside table for when she opened her eyes in the morning. One night she went to sleep, and had no further need to look.

Burton had always said that Thomas's marriage to Grace wouldn't last, only wondering whether he would live to see it. He didn't. Grace fell ill from a fatal cocktail of pleurisy, bronchitis and pneumonia. Ivy and Emily took turns nursing her, Thomas rarely at her bedside. He made the excuse of too much overtime, but Ivy said that Grace died because she couldn't take any more of his doing it on her with every woman he set eyes on.

Thomas grieved a little longer than usual, having behaved so badly, then went on with his philandering, having no more to waste thought and energy on alibis which hadn't always been successful.

He didn't find it so easy to get the women he wanted. Times changed. Young women went off with completely unsuitable men (as if they hadn't always) – men, Thomas thought, who were scruffs and runts, or ugly and without any rules of that chivalrous behaviour he had schemed to follow. He was still handsome, tall and well-built, with thick but grey hair, looking fully ahead when out walking, though as Burton had often said, he lacked the ability to see much on either side. Yet he could tell a woman that he loved her (and be believed as often as not) though only so as to get her into bed, and for as long as he himself thought it to be true, which it often wasn't for long, since he hadn't always been convinced in the first place, which drove him to looking for someone else.

When he was sixty-five he met Alice, in her fifties. She had a vinegary tongue, but he settled for her until someone better came along. He made the mistake of moving into her council house at Aspley, such a comfortable place he felt less and less inclined to seek out better prospects. Besides, he no longer had the energy and, being retired, preferred to sit by the fire watching television in winter, and digging around the garden in summer. It wasn't the sort of clover he'd been used to, but the better looking women than Alice, spoken to in pubs or at bus stops, either turned their backs or told him in ripe old Nottingham parlance to fuck off or they'd get their boyfriends to kick him in.

Alice soon lost all liking for this tall man who stood a bit too often before the hearth warming his arse, and in a wavering tenor voice sang a popular ballad from the old days, thinking he was entertaining her in prime television style, like a modern Richard Tauber. Sometimes he would set up a concert of whistling till the sound drove her mad, and she asked the big daft canary to put a sock in it, always much to his surprise at a performance supremely entertaining to himself.

A solo performance started one day, and before she could complain his well-built body rumbled onto the carpet by the living room mirror, such a crash of limbs that in her alarm she knew he couldn't be acting or trying to frighten her.

He gurgled. A foot jerked. She dialled nine-nine-nine and, this being Nottingham, an ambulance came within minutes and took him to the City Hospital, the driver cheerfully telling her (in case she hadn't noticed) that Thomas had had a stroke, and there was no saying when or if he would be home again.

Brian and Derek called at the hospital to see their uncle, tracked him to a small ward whose windows faced well-shaven lawns. Even in a wheelchair they could tell he was a big man. He and half a dozen others were looked after by a black nurse, who told Brian how much liked Thomas was. He couldn't articulate, but when he wanted something he sang it to a popular tune till they understood, which made him a very entertaining patient.

'He sang us *The White Cliffs of Dover* last week,' she said with a sunrise smile. 'We didn't realize there were such good tunes in the olden days.'

Arthur, who came another time, said it was lucky for the nurses that the stroke had put paid to his whistling, otherwise the doctors would have had to cut his windpipe.

Thomas understood all that Brian and Derek said. He took the chocolates, perhaps to woo the nurses with, but didn't want the carton of cigarettes, which Derek gave to a man whose eyes flashed like Eddystone Lighthouse at the sight. They talked about the days at Old Engine Cottages, and at the mention of Burton he showed as much terror as if his father would stride into the room, bang him around the head, and tell him to stop shirking.

Alice, glad of a rest, didn't visit him, having had more than enough of someone complaining about his father yet behaving in ways that showed he was too much like him.

Fit at last to be managed at home, Thomas was packed off in an ambulance. The driver's mate pushed him, clutching a couple of plastic bags of toiletries and a goodwish card from the nurses, along the garden path in a wheelchair. The young woman at the back door put a little more light into Thomas's eyes. Even though she was followed by two kids he wondered whether she would fall in love with him. The ambulance man told her they were bringing him back, duck, about to tip him onto the path whether she claimed him or not. She looked as if they were carting the third prize of a raffle she had long forgotten buying a ticket for, and would certainly no longer want.

She screamed that she had never seen the hopeful yet bemused Thomas before, told them in no uncertain terms to fuck off and take the old man away or she would tip the fucking wheel-chair in the gutter where he'd get run over by a Corporation doubledecker bus and fucking good riddance. Who did they think they were, trying to palm a crippled old-age pensioner off on her, a single mother who was trying to make ends meet in spite of all the fucking council and social services could do to stop her?

'All right, duck, keep your hair on. We must have got the wrong place. We'll go back and check up on it.'

Thomas followed the altercation as if television had come alive at last, and the powers that be had decided to put on something good. The truth was that Alice had found another house, and done such a flit as to be forever unfindable. They weren't married, but she would have gone even if they had been.

Thomas's second stroke six months later finished him off. At eighty Sabina wasn't fit to go to the funeral, and her three sons were so scattered as not to be told in time. Where Thomas's cremated ashes went, nobody knew.

Ivy worked another ten years at the tobacco factory, and retired at sixty-five. She met a pensioner of seventy in the Gregory Hotel, who told her in a sly and dependent way that he had fallen in love with her. He was a cocksure smiler, a trickster, a thin little man with wavy grey hair who wouldn't let her pay for a drink, not yet. His self-assurance and twinkle of malice captivated her, perhaps because he matched her in the shuttlecock and battle-dore game of sarcasm which passed for wit. He asked her to marry him, and in saying yes she made a mistake which was to be her last.

Gerald wanted a house to live in instead of a council flat at the foot of a highrise hencoop where he was threatened nightly, and often during the day, with being kicked in by the local black and white thugs who, when not playing Waterloo among themselves, ran the area.

He brought his few tranklements and moved in with Ivy and Emily, but within weeks Ivy knew she should never have had anything to do with him. Burton must have laughed from the comforting heat of hell's fire on realizing she had more than met her match.

Gerald was spiteful, and a bully. The only good thing for Ivy was that she was too old to complete the disaster by having children. He sat by the fire smoking foul twist in a short black pipe. He would send her for beer from the pub, and she would go so as to avoid the mayhem of a refusal. He wouldn't give any help in the house, not even to change a lightbulb or mend a fuse, and insisted on being served every meal on Mary Ann's best china. Sometimes he would drop a cup or plate to show who was boss of the house, and only stopped when Ivy said how much they would get for it if ever they needed to sell it.

He mocked Emily for her ways, but she was not slow to mock

him back, so he became more wary of her than Ivy. Emily was angry to see that her sister, though capable of knocking him down, was crippled by feelings of stupidity at having brought him into the house.

She should have known better, she told herself over and over again. Even Burton would not have been so heartless as to laugh at what she had done. He would have been angry at her doing something he would never have sanctioned had he been alive. She wouldn't have done it then, of course, but if he had been alive he would have kicked Gerald every inch of the way to the workhouse.

She felt like thumping herself, unable to believe she had let such a thing happen at a time of life when only peace and quiet was needed. She had always vowed, and it was bitter to remind herself, never to marry unless to the right man, and now she knew it had been unwise to marry any man at all. How could an upstanding blacksmith's daughter have attached herself to a type like Gerald? Though a tall strong woman, she couldn't bring herself to throw him out as he deserved.

As years went by, though wizened and close to eighty, it seemed he would live forever. She prayed that God would strike him dead, but it was she who became ill, from Parkinson's disease. When she was being taken out on a stretcher to the hospital Gerald's last words were: 'I hope you don't come back.' Three weeks later only Emily went to her funeral.

Gerald didn't have things all his own way when living with Emily. Ivy was no longer there with the nervously guiding hand to bring her to order. Emily had feared Burton, yet had also loved him, and the space left was gradually filled with utter loathing for the man Ivy had so frivolously brought into the house. Burton's spirit helped her not to put up with his tantrums.

When he tormented her she would, accidentally it seemed, bump into him so forcefully as to send him painfully against the furniture, such hard knocks frightening him more than the thugs from the housing block.

'Say that again.' She fixed him with tight lips and a steady eye. 'Go on, say it once more, just say again what you said just now, you fucking pest. Come on, say it. I'm waiting. But if you do

I'll split your fucking head open and make you clean the rug afterwards.'

She would go out until she was calm enough not to come back and murder him. She would walk down the street and have a talk with Sabina, or make herself useful for an hour at the church hall. Men and women who were not much older smiled as she came around with cakes and cups of tea, laying bets as to whether or not her shaking hands would let go of the tray before she reached them – though they never did.

Most days she would come out of the church hall and go over the road to the Gregory Hotel for half a pint of bitter before facing Gerald at home. He thought himself the most put-upon man in the world, and dreaded the click of the door knob as she came in.

She hung up her coat, and fixed him with her implacable blue-grey eyes, blew smoke over his fragile head from a smouldering Woodbine cadged from Sabina and, though he hadn't spoken, say: 'I know you. I know your sort. I've got you weighed up, I have an' all, mate, so don't think I haven't. Oh yes, I know your game right enough.' Her face went closer. 'You think I don't, don't you? But I do.' She gave a little laugh which to him was no laugh at all. 'I know what you're up to. Right from the start I've known: "Serve me this, and serve me that, get me some ale, and bring me a packet of baccer while you're at it."' She mimicked him perfectly. 'But I'm not Ivy, you know. Ivy was worth a hundred of a rat like you. Well, I won't lift a finger for you anymore.'

She went on so long in her maniacal way as he cringed by the fire not even daring to fill his empty pipe, and hoping her wrath wouldn't explode beyond words. When she cooked a meal she left his part on the gas to turn into mush, or frazzle, and enjoyed seeing him jump up to save it.

Coming out of the church hall one evening she collapsed halfway across the road, and died on the way to hospital. Gerald sat in triumph among his inherited possessions, though Ivy had previously given out Burton's prize horseshoes to the family.

His enjoyment didn't last long. The mangonels of social destruction were moving downhill from the city centre, and he was ordered by the council to quit the place. Whole streets were razed, the space covered by highrise firehazards designed for people's wellbeing by those who would never have to live in them.

His sister in a village near Newark agreed that he could stay with her. He sold every last cup, sheet and artefact of Mary Ann's belongings and, with a fat wallet and pockets rattling, gave his death-mask smile as four suitcases were carried to a taxi to go with him to the station. The only thing left in the house was his marriage certificate to Ivy, screwed into a ball and thrown on the bedroom floor in a delinquent rage, to be found by Sabina's son Derek when he went for a last look at his grandparents' house before it was wiped out.

THIRTY-THREE

A soddened sky, but what else in December? – vegetation ponging like when they were kids, taking Brian back to pulling barrows of rotten potato tops to the compost heap at the Burtons'.

'You'd expect plenty of parking outside a church,' Arthur called. 'There's nothing legal anywhere,' but a touch of anarchy and lateral thinking fitted both cars neatly along a double yellow line: 'If I catch a warden fastening a plastic envelope under the windscreen I'll give him such a pasting he'll crawl back sobbing to his mam for a wank.'

They laughed, always did with Arthur though never at him. The juicy *mot juste*'s got nothing on him, Brian thought. The church was locked and barred, and should you want to get in, a notice on the door said apply to the rectory. Brian had come especially from London, to stay the night at Arthur's. Warm in his countryman's three-quarter woollen overcoat with poacher's pockets, he wore a navy blue suit, a white collarless Jermyn Street silk shirt buttoned to the neck. 'It's Sunday morning, and in any case the doors should be open for sanctuary. You might be an asylum-seeker, or the cops could be after you. I suppose they're afraid of the Nottingham Lambs kicking the altar down.'

'If it did get kicked down they'd build a mosque in its place,' Derek said.

Arthur adjusted his Rohan garment from a car-boot sale, spruced up and reconditioned for a few quid to look new. 'The yobs would burn that down as well. Nothing's sacred. They'll turn on the town hall one day. Somebody ripped up a Belisha beacon in town the other day and slung it through a shop window. A naked dummy clutched it to her tits like a big lollipop, everybody pissing themselves going by.'

Derek's Gortex jacket had seen much service in the Pennines, and kept the rain off as he opened the cemetery gate. 'It must have been as wet as this in 1946, and at Oliver's funeral as well. They were buried about the same time of year.'

Brian carried flowers, and champagne in a plastic bag. 'Don't drop it,' Arthur said, 'or Burton will jump out of his grave and thump you.'

He lifted the bottle. 'He'll like the idea of us celebrating the anniversary of his death with Moët et Chandon. Shame he can't come up for a sup.' Grass was long and rank around the multitude of graves, grownover pathways knitting into each other, half-covering fallen or slanting stones. Brian paced the back wall of the church, made a right angle, and trod over the long dead to where the grave should be.

'Too far,' Arthur called. 'Go a bit left. Then on from there.'

Brian cursed the uncertainty of his bifocals. Green mould streaked the names. 'Can't read a thing.'

'You're right next to it, so watch where you put your great clodhoppers. Me and Avril cleaned the grave up a year ago.'

The sacred plot was rectangled by indestructible marble, and under Oliver's inscription was chiselled: ALSO ERNEST BURTON, FATHER OF THE ABOVE, DIED DEC. 8TH, 1946. AGED 80.

Derek lifted a vase from the next grave, filled it at the tap, and set their flowers by the scroll with its embossed horseshoe. 'At least we're remembering him.'

'He'll appreciate it,' Arthur said. 'If you can't remember, you're dead from the neck up.'

'Fifty years ago to the day.' Brian laid three plastic cups along the ledge. 'He lived thirty-two years after the death of his favourite son. It must have been pain all the way.'

'It don't bear thinking about.' Arthur righted a cup tilted in the breeze. 'We should have brought proper glasses. Burton won't like plastic.' A hand to his mouth, he leaned over the beige stalks. 'We're drinking to you with champagne, Grandad! If it's too hot down there, come up and have a swig.'

The cork curved out onto the grass, no sound in the heavy air. Arthur steadied the spout, three beakers filled without spilling.

They took off their caps and stood at the head of the grave. 'Here's to Burton! If *he* can't hear us down there, nobody can.'

Derek waved at a man in a Sikh turban framing the back window of one of the houses. 'He thinks we're nicking tombstones to make a garden path.' A shade of consideration passed over his features on turning back to his brothers. 'We'll spare a thought for Oliver. He deserves it just as much.'

They agreed, and drank to him. 'Here's to the South Nottinghamshire Hussars as well.'

Brian tipped the rest of the drink out in shares as equal as any could gauge. 'Burton should feel happy at three of his grand-sons drinking to his memory.' A cloud over the church tower spat rain as he put cups and bottle in the bag. 'When we cel-ebrate his sixtieth anniversary I expect it'll still be pissing down.'

Arthur put his cap on, and turned towards the gate. 'How many of us will be alive in ten years? But if we live that long we'll bring half a dozen bottles and have a party, and come by taxi.'

'And bring our Zimmer frames as well,' Derek said.

A thought lit Arthur's grey eyes. 'Mine'll have a built-in pocket for Viagra.'

They embraced, one-time members of the unkillable poor. Brian shared Arthur's Peugeot, and Derek got into his sleek Volvo Estate saying: 'See you at the Five Ways tonight.'

Arthur fingered his jar. 'Our mother was the last of the Burtons.'

Derek gentled tobacco into his pipe to be sure of a smooth draw. '*We* haven't gone yet.'

'We soon might be. I'm sixty-two, and Brian's sixty-eight. You're the baby, at fifty-seven.'

'I saw Burton in a dream a few nights ago.' Brian came from behind his cloud of Antico Toscano cigar. 'He was smartly dressed, as usual. "I was something else before I was a blacksmith," he said. I was going to ask what, but he walked away, keeping the secret to himself. I don't normally remember dreams.' Why should I? Dreams were only dreams, could mean anything, or nothing. You'd never get to the botton of them, and they were your own affair anyway. 'I've got one of his prize horseshoes, that Mother passed on to me from Ivy. It was made to fit a lame horse, which is right for me. The other day I cleaned it till I could see my face. Then I saw Burton looking at me.'

'What did he say?' Derek asked.

'I know.' Arthur put on Burton's commanding tone. '"Shine it up a bit more. It's not good enough."'

'I wonder what he'd think of things if he came back to life?' Brian said.

Derek turned his glass in a circle. 'He wouldn't recognize the place.'

'He'd know us,' Arthur said, 'and we'd know him. He was a family man, and I can't think of him without seeing Mary Ann as well, so let's drink to her. As long as we're alive they will be.'

Brian lifted his glass. 'You're only immortal as long as somebody remembers you. Then you fade into the billions already dead. We'll drink to her, then. She's in heaven, but I'm sure Burton's allowed to go and see her now and again.'

Three glasses tapped wood on coming down at the same second. Derek smiled. 'There's a lot of him left in us. Arthur's got all his prejudices, for a start.'

'Now then, that's slander,' Arthur said. 'I'll get my lawyer on the blower.' He drank the rest of his jar, arm at ninety degrees to give himself space, proving the truth of his brother's remark. Arthur's height and stance indisputably resembled Burton's, and apart from his gardening he had worked all his life in heavy industry. He retorted that Brian reminded *him* of Burton, in the way he wore his cap, and stood with fingers in the pockets of his waistcoat crossed by watch and chain.

'What a right pair you are,' Derek said, 'to believe in such things.'

'You're like him as well,' Arthur said, 'in not believing anything anybody says. But nobody these days has to work as hard as Burton did. A blacksmith would have ear-muffs, and leather gauntlets to prevent scars on his arms, and a visor to stop sparks blinding him. When we fired Brens and threw grenades in the army we didn't have anything to protect our ears, but I'll bet swaddies have them today. I can just imagine them going over the top with ear-muffs to keep out the noise.'

At the gaffer calling 'Time!' Derek went for three more pints, knowing the towels wouldn't go on till such favoured clients stood to leave. When he got back Arthur was saying: 'If Burton had a permit from hell to take a look at the modern world he'd have to sink a dozen pints to get the cinders out of his throat. But he'd be amazed how easy life is, and how soft people are. If I took him a walk around town he'd be glad in some way but not in others. He wouldn't think much of the highrise hencoops, and I don't suppose he'd think much of all the fat guts walking about the streets. As for a beggar tapping him for a quid, he'd push him aside, and anybody trying to mug him would get the worst pasting of his life, while a police car went by and took no notice. Imagine him though, if you can, going into Yates's Wine Lodge on Saturday night, and after talking to one of the gorgeous young girls, getting her outside behind a wall to give her a bit of you-know-what, and finding a button in her cunt! It wouldn't stop him, but what a surprise.

'As for what's called ale, he'd think it was brewed out of suds at the Raleigh, and he wouldn't touch the grub in any pub or restaurant because apart from it being like shit he'd find everything overpriced to what it had been in his day, even allowing for inflation. He'd notice the rabbit hutches in place of the cosy little houses in Woodhouse, but the railway bridge is still there, and a bit of the lane leading to where Old Engine Cottages used to be. The pub's doing good trade at the top of Radford Bridge Road, where Oswald's wife Helen used to go for her stout after Howard died, though the traffic's murder if you want to get to it. Neither Lenton nor Radford stations exist anymore, and though Wollaton Hall no longer belongs to Lord Middleton it still looks as good as ever on its hill. Nottingham's spread as far west as the motorway, and he'd have to look out for cars, buses, vans, lorries and motorbikes speeding all the time like Dinky toys gone mad. He'd soon get used to looking both ways before crossing a one-way street. The supermarkets and legal bookies would surprise him, but there'd be no corner-shops or beer-offs for Mary Ann to gossip in or play the one-armed bandits. Maybe in heaven there's a special arcade for her to pass an hour in, and they give her endless pennies to keep her happy.

'Burton on his way to town would wonder where all the pedestrians were, nobody on the pavements to say hello as he went by, till he realized they were all in their motorcars, and if they waved it would only be to laugh at him for using Shanks's pony, and for being togged up in a suit and wearing a hat, and not in trainers and a bomber jacket. He'd wish himself back in hell rather than among such sloppy dressers, though he'd be glad to see the White Hart looking the same, at least from the outside, with the row of cottages opposite where he set off from for Wales on his twenty-first birthday. He met Mary Ann there, but wouldn't recognize the inside because the walls have been ripped out to make more piss-up space. If he went in and got jostled too much at the bar he'd think it time to nip back to Old Nick's taproom, because there's no sabbath in hell, and he'd have his own special place, the only member of the club not forced to stand in a queue when the ale's given out. In a place like that the Big Wheel's always turning, and old tunes he liked are played whenever he feels like hearing them, so it can't be as hard as the world when he was in it. He'll be in hell as long as anybody thinks it exists. It'll be a shame that after we've snuffed it there'll be nobody to remember him, though the more we drink to him the better, because I see the landlord's getting twitchy to put the towels on, so we'd better look sharp and sup up. When Burton's decided his leave from hell is over he'll walk away saying: "It was nice to see you chaps again, but when Old Nick calls time for the three of you you'll know where to find me. I'll be waiting."'

P.S.

Ideas,
interviews
& features . . .

Interview with Alan Sillitoe

by Travis Elborough

ON ILKESTON ROAD IN Radford, there is a student accommodation complex named in honour of the author of *The Loneliness of the Long Distance Runner*. All buildings, and their names for that matter, are transient (the old Raleigh factory where Alan Sillitoe worked as a teenager was bulldozed to make way for housing and this extension of Nottingham University's campus) but for the time being Sillitoe Court fixes the writer into the official topography of a landscape that he has charted for nearly half a century. An antique map of the city – dark green, streets marked out like veins in an oak leaf – hangs on the study wall in Sillitoe's West London home. Waving his pipe at a bay of bookshelves laden with tomes, he says, 'All those are about Nottingham, just so I get it right. Nottingham,' he adds, the pipe hovering by the corner of his mouth, poised for re-entry, 'is only half of my output.'

To consult the 'Also by Alan Sillitoe' page amidst the reams of paper celebrating the endeavours of typesetters in Stirlingshire and printers in Cornwall at the front of this novel (itself by no means a complete list) is to be reminded of his range and prolificness – the Sillitoe oeuvre encompasses novels, short stories, film scripts, poetry, travelogues, plays, essays and children's books. 'I often imagine myself as basically a lazy person, who has to disprove the fact that I am lazy. I think with me it is more an obsession than an occupation. I don't write every day, but I do in that I write my diary, write letters, correct typescripts.' Sillitoe has stated elsewhere that when he first told his family that he was going to have a novel published, his father replied, 'That's bloody good. You'll never have to work again.' 'He was quite right, of course. You sit here scribbling. I am very diffident about regarding it as work.' Idleness, you will recall, is something Ernest Burton cannot abide; and call it work or not, Sillitoe can hardly be described as idle. His workroom, with its orderly rows of box files, tidy stacks of maps and charts, compasses and instruments, radio set and large oak desk, has the air of a military campaign centre, a den in which the compact and spry author – the Napoleon of Notting Hill – plots his next strategy. Everything Sillitoe writes is initially drafted in pen, typed up and then 'saturated in corrections, re-typed and then *that* saturated in corrections again'. *Saturday Night and Sunday Morning* may have been set in Nottingham but it's worth noting that it was written, with the encouragement of Robert Graves, 'in the autumn of 1956, sitting under an orange tree' in Majorca.

Before the age of thirty Sillitoe spent eight years outside England, six of them on the continent, mastering his craft, with his wife, the American poet Ruth Fainlight. Fainlight, who pops into the room to discuss parking arrangements for guests expected from France, is today busy translating Mexican poetry in another part of the flat, although bronchitis is hindering her efforts. While Sillitoe goes off to prepare coffee for us all ▶

> ❝ I often imagine myself as basically a lazy person, who has to disprove the fact that I am lazy. I think with me it is more an obsession than an occupation. ❞

LIFE AT A GLANCE

BORN

4 March 1928.

EDUCATION

Till 14, but it was enough.

CAREER

Labouring – working on a capstan lathe. Air traffic control, wireless operator in the RAF (which taught me how to stand up for three hours, which later was good for cocktail parties), then writer.

Interview with Alan Sillitoe (continued)

◄ ('Alan makes wonderful coffee,' she says with pride, and a dry cough or two), we chat about M.F.K. Fisher and Aix-en-Provence, where the Sillitoes lived for a time. And when Sillitoe reappears bearing what is indeed wonderful coffee and our conversation returns to the eleven or so Nottingham/ Seaton novels, it is Balzac, rather than D.H. Lawrence, that is his first point of comparison. 'Well, looking back over the books I've written, what I've tried to do – only half consciously, I suppose – is to make a *comédie humaine* of novels all to do with Nottingham people set in Nottingham.'

Later on, when I do raise Lawrence, Sillitoe finds the idea that, other than their shared profession and geographical background, there is much common ground between them slightly bemusing. 'I didn't start to read, really read, until I was twenty, and I came across *The Rainbow* and I saw he had made something of the local landscape, or at least a landscape that I knew well, so that was interesting for me, apart from which it's a very good novel. Otherwise there's no more connection between him and me. The books that he wrote later, often in anger, well ... they were rotten. Certain parts of them were wonderful writing, of course, but take *The Plumed Serpent* or *Kangaroo*. Just ghastly. And as for *Lady Chatterley's Lover*, it's awful, actually. But the early books – *Sons and Lovers*, *The Rainbow* – wonderful books, absolutely; they give him his place.'

A Man of His Time he maintains probably brings his Balzacian sequence to a close. 'What I do have are short stories, they are still in my notebooks, and I am not sure if I'll use them; I am just feeling my way, really.' There's always been a strong autobiographical element to this particular fictional cycle, with, for those interested in such things, numerous parallels between the Seaton and Sillitoe clans. Burton, first mentioned, if obliquely, in *Saturday Night and Sunday Morning,* is, as he willingly admits, closely based on his grandfather, a tyrannical illiterate blacksmith (Sillitoe's father was also illiterate). A non-fiction portrait of the 'real' Ernest Burton appears in *Raw Material* (1972), Sillitoe's 'part novel, part autobiography'. But as a character in Philip Roth's *The Counterlife* observes, 'it's the distance between the writer's life and his novel that is the most intriguing aspect of his imagination'. Sillitoe, an admirer of Roth ('A great writer, a truly great writer'), concurs. 'Using your family, using things you know about, it's just classic stuff, but the fact is it's fiction and your imagination is working on these people all the time. You don't want them to be historically real people, you just want to make a novel.'

Novels for Sillitoe, as his essay *Her Victory: A Novel Born or Made* confirms, often have a long gestation and sometimes emerge from the idea of a single character or occasionally even an occupation. 'I do think that what people do in life has great implications for what kind of character they are, and *vice versa*.' He tells me he spent twenty-five years mulling over a novel about a wireless operator until a story clicked into place and he wrote *The Lost Flying Boat*. 'Often, though, it's someone you've never met before; you'll pass them on the street and ▶

❛Looking back over the books I've written, what I've tried to do is to make a *comédie humaine* of novels all to do with Nottingham people. ❜

Interview with Alan Sillitoe *(continued)*

◄ there's a spark and from that point on you have to build up everything. But at least you've got their face and you drive ahead fitting all the pieces together. You see, I've always thought Burton was worthy of more than a few pages, such as there were in *Raw Material*. You just think you are going to live for ever and you are going to do it in your own time and if twenty years go by, so what? About ten, twelve years ago, I finally went back to Burton and wrote a film script about him. But nothing came of it, so I just put it aside. Some eight years later I had a look at it and thought, I am not going to waste this, I am going to make it into a novel. And by then I had lots more information which had been bubbling about in my mind.'

Sillitoe shows me a prize-winning shoe his grandfather fashioned for a lame horse; a crescent of chromed iron, it lies on a cabinet beside his desk. From a neat pile of papers he then retrieves a modern copy of an old sepia photograph; a tall, elderly gent, dapper in an oversized cloth cap, three-piece suit, watch-chain and bow tie, is placed before me. A caterpillar moustache spans his top lip. It's Ernest Burton. 'The whole Wales thing in the book is based on one line, which my aunt said to me when I was a kid: "Your grandfather once worked in Wales." That's all it came from. But from the original of another photograph of him – the one I describe in the novel – I managed to track it down to Pontllanfraith. So I went down there, with my two brothers, and we went all over the place and checked it out and tried to find the forge where he'd worked. In the end we did find it, we went there twice. It was semi-derelict and surrounded by barbed wire.'

In the indomitable Burton, many reviewers spied something of Sillitoe's own creative past: Arthur Seaton as he appeared in *Saturday Night and Sunday Morning*. 'Well, I've always written about people who are independent-minded, who aren't interested in "improving themselves". I think it's more interesting to create characters who are below that line, who don't have that kind of political awareness. I do tend to write about those members of society who are not too well known about, I think. But yes, it's very attractive, that sort of continuity. You sometimes try to think it exists, but it may not, clearly. There are characteristics that flow through families, though. There's always this thing: is it heredity that forms a person? Or is it circumstance? I've always thought it's predominantly heredity. Circumstances shape you to a certain point because they give you opportunities to exploit what is positive from your genes. You either take it, or not. Below all this, there's this enormous continuity with the past.'

John Updike has written that ancestors 'lived that we may live. We reverence them because they participate in the mystery of our being.' Sillitoe, too, believes that there is something essentially human in 'the craving, the desire, to recreate memories that fix us to the past so we can think about the future', as he puts it. 'In a sense, I can appreciate the Chinese because they worship their ancestors. I don't think we should worship them – I have absolutely no religion – but we should ▶

Q & A

What is your idea of perfect happiness?
No such thing, but I'm happy enough at having peace and leisure to write.

What is your greatest fear?
I fear nothing, but there are things I don't like, such as fundamentalist terrorism; or anything which might make travelling more dangerous.

What objects do you always carry with you?
Generally a map, and binoculars if I am in the countryside.

Where do you go for inspiration?
Into myself.

What are you writing at the moment?
Stories.

Interview with Alan Sillitoe *(continued)*

◄ certainly think about them. You are only immortal as long as people remember you. When we brothers die, Burton will have faded away; nobody will be alive who knew him so he'll be gone.' Burton the fiction, however, is destined to endure, joining Smith from *The Loneliness of the Long Distance Runner* and Arthur in *Saturday Night and Sunday Morning* among the ranks of Alan Sillitoe's and, for that matter, English literature's finest creations. ■

❛Using your family, using things you know about, it's just classic stuff, but the fact is it's fiction and your imagination is working on these people all the time. ❜

Sillitoe and the Smith

by Travis Elborough

> 'Zillah also gave birth to Tubal Cain, the forger of every cutting instrument of brass and iron.' Genesis 4:22

A WRITER, ALAN SILLITOE has observed, works with words as a 'blacksmith uses the tools of his strong and often subtle art'. The comparison is not unusual. In the Romany language, to which we owe such words as *busk* and *tramp*, the concept of the *'lavengro'* or 'wordsmith' has an ancient-ish pedigree; the nineteenth-century 'Gypsy-philologist' George Borrow, who popularized the term in England, maintained that there was 'something highly poetical about a forge'. But there is an added poignancy in this instance, nonetheless. For while Sillitoe's blacksmith grandfather Ernest Burton may have been illiterate, it was at his grandparents' home as a small boy that the author regularly encountered books outside the classroom. Sillitoe 'spent most weekends and school holidays at their cottage, a mile or so in the country'. A glass-fronted case in their parlour housed a collection of 'sober volumes' that the Burton children had received as Sunday school prizes. 'I had,' Sillitoe confesses in *Mountains and Caverns*, 'never seen so many books in one home.' His grandmother Mary Ann, who later encouraged him to sit (without success) a scholarship exam for the grammar school, gave him the odd book from this store 'to take home and keep'. Burton, it is plain, was tolerant of his bookish grandson. In *Raw Material*, Sillitoe writes that he was 'treated well by Burton because, apart from being able and ▶

> **❝** A writer works with words as a "blacksmith uses the tools of his strong and often subtle art". **❞**

9

Sillitoe and the Smith *(continued)*

◄ willing to labour physically, I also bothered myself industriously with books and writing paper . . . reading or drawing maps, and I know that he looked at me strongly now and again because he had not seen the like of it before.'

Such scenes have their fictional counterparts in *A Man of His Time* – Burton looks benignly over Brian reading on the rug and Mary Ann likes to see the boy take books from the bookcase in the parlour because it reminds her of Oliver – and, earlier, in *Key to the Door*: 'At home there were no books, but he found a store at the Nook, ancient dust-covered Sunday-school prizes with the names of his uncles and aunts inscribed in impeccable writing within the front covers.' Arthur Seaton in *Saturday Night and Sunday Morning* remembers 'his grandfather who had been a blacksmith, and had a house and forge at Wollaston village . . . and its memory was a fixed picture in Arthur's mind'. And in Sillitoe's children's book *Big Jim and the Stars*, the smith takes on a magical aspect; Jim is 'a blacksmith with a fiery red beard' who lights up the night sky. ■

> ❝While Sillitoe's blacksmith grandfather Ernest Burton may have been illiterate, it was at his grandparents' home as a small boy that the author regularly encountered books outside the classroom. ❞

Sillitoe on Screen

A MAN OF HIS TIME began life as a film script; the project unfortunately (or fortunately, since we have the novel instead) failed to take off. Intriguingly, following the recent box office success of Walter Salles's *The Motorcycle Diaries*, another of Sillitoe's unrealized screen treatments is a script about the life of Ernesto 'Che' Guevara that he wrote in 1968, at the behest of Tony Richardson who directed his screenplay of *The Loneliness of the Long Distance Runner*. Of Sillitoe's published works *The Ragman's Daughter* and *The General* also made the transition from page to screen. However, the latter, filmed without the author's involvement as *Counterpoint* (1968), and starring Charlton Heston, Maximilian Schell and Leslie Nielsen, bears only a nodding resemblance to Sillitoe's original novel.

The author's involvement in film dates back to his own highly successful adaptation of *Saturday Night and Sunday Morning*. When the American producer Harry Salzman acquired the film rights for the book for Woodall Films, the company Richardson and John Osborne formed to bring *Look Back in Anger* to the screen, he had insufficient funds to pay a named screenwriter and so asked Sillitoe to oblige. Sillitoe was initially surprised. As he told Alexander Walker (the long-standing film critic of the *Evening Standard*) in 1972, 'I'd been to very few films in my life ... To me at the time, a film was likely to mean an Ealing comedy.' (Both the British Lion and the Rank Organisation, previously offered the film, turned it down.) But having, as he believed, 'written a novel without experience', he set about honing his story into a script, a ▶

> ❝Having "written a novel without experience", he set about honing his story into a script, a process that took him around nine months and four drafts. ❞

11

Sillitoe on Screen *(continued)*

◄ process that took him around nine months and four drafts. The film censor later also intervened, demanding various cuts and rewrites; Brenda's gin-in-the-bath abortion, a success in the novel, is a failure in the movie. (Such nips and tucks didn't prevent the film, when it went on general release, being banned by Warwickshire County Council.)

Sillitoe worked closely with the Czech-born director Karel Reisz throughout. To prepare for the film, Reisz – a leading force, along with Lindsay Anderson and Richardson, in the British socio-realist Free Cinema movement – travelled to Nottingham with Sillitoe and the pair collaborated on a documentary about a local miners' welfare centre for the Central Office of Information. Much of the finished film was shot on location, with the Raleigh factory and Sillitoe's mother's house providing the backdrop in a number of scenes. To this day, Sillitoe admits he found it hard to imagine Albert Finney as Arthur Seaton. Harder still is to picture Peter O'Toole in the role – he, apparently, expressed serious interest – even conceding that the Yorkshire-born actor would have had little trouble mastering the scenes where Arthur imbibes an ocean of black-and-tan, and staggers about drunkenly. Finney's performance as the truculent lathe-operator Seaton, wolfing down bacon and eggs after bedding his workmate's wife, made him a star. In its aftermath, it was Albert Finney that David Lean wanted for *Lawrence of Arabia*. British cinema was never quite the same again. ■

To this day, Sillitoe admits he found it hard to imagine Albert Finney as Arthur Seaton.

Alan Sillitoe on Reading

'AS A READER I want a bit of veracity and I
prefer, if I can, to read about people I don't
know very much about, because that's also
what I write. If I read about ten pages and I
don't find anything in it stylistically, I stop. I
love stories, of course – the Bible and
Shakespeare I couldn't be without. I read the
Bible all the while I was writing *Saturday
Night and Sunday Morning*.

'One of the modern writers I like is John
King. I thought *The Football Factory*, which
they've made into a film, was excellent; he's a
very fine writer. I tend to read a lot of writers
from Israel – David Grossman, Amos Oz –
there's plenty of good stuff at the moment.
I've just come to the end of a long novel by
Oz, a story of life and death, that's simply
wonderful, but I'd recommend his
autobiography, *A Tale of Love and Darkness*;
it's translated by Nicholas de Lange, who is
first rate.'

The Nottingham Books

A MAN OF HIS TIME concludes a series of Sillitoe's novels and stories – beginning with *Saturday Night and Sunday Morning* – that feature various members of the Seaton family. Below is a complete list of Sillitoe's Nottingham books.

1. *Saturday Night and Sunday Morning* (1958)
2. *Key to the Door* (1961)
3. *Raw Material* (1972)
4. *The Storyteller* (1979)
5. *Down from the Hill* (1984)
6. *The Open Door* (1989)
7. *Leonard's War* (1991)
8. *The Broken Chariot* (1998)
9. *Birthday* (2001)
10. *New and Collected Stories* (2003)
11. *A Man of His Time* (2004)

For anyone wanting to discover more about the man who inspired the fictional Ernest Burton, Sillitoe's novelistic memoir *Raw Material* (1972) and his compelling and beautifully written autobiography *Life Without Armour* (1995) are well worth seeking out.

Have You Read?

Other titles by Alan Sillitoe

Saturday Night and Sunday Morning (1958)
Working all day at a lathe leaves Arthur Seaton
with energy to spare in the evenings. A hard-
drinking, hard-fighting young rebel of a man,
he knows what he wants and he's sharp enough
to get it. And before long, his carryings-on with
a couple of married women are local gossip.
But then one evening he meets a young girl in a
pub, and Arthur's life begins to look less simple.

Alan Sillitoe's classic novel of the 1950s is a
story of timeless significance.

'A novel of today with a freshness and raw
fury that makes *Room at the Top* look like a
vicarage tea party'

Daily Telegraph

'His writing has real experience in it and an
instinctive accuracy that never loses its touch.
His book has a glow about it as though he had
plugged it into some basic source of the
working-class spirit'

Guardian

'Brilliant ... if he never writes anything more,
he has assured himself a place in the history of
the English novel'

New Yorker

**The Loneliness of the Long
Distance Runner** (1959)
Smith is an incorrigible and defiant young
rebel, inhabiting a no-man's land of
institutionalized Borstal. Watched over by an
indifferent sunlight, as his steady jog-trot
rhythm transports him over an ▶

◄ unrelenting, frostbitten earth, he wonders why, for whom and for what he is running.

'Graphic, tough, outspoken, informal'

The Times

'A beautiful piece of work, confirming Sillitoe as a writer of unusual spirit and great promise'

Guardian

The Broken Chariot (1998)

When Herbert Thurgarton-Strang was seven, his parents – as loving, as doting as any parents of their generation – took him away from India and left him in a boarding school in England.

Through the years which follow, Herbert is held together by his desire for revenge on those loving parents, and by the knowledge that, out there, a new world beckons.

And when he's seventeen, he steals away from school and becomes a different person.

'Sillitoe's sheer narrative drive manages to suspend most of the reader's disbelief. This is an old-fashioned novel – technically conventional, pulling off the usual tricks of character and motivation – but oddly alive in a way that a great deal of modern fiction, written by those as yet unborn when Sillitoe began his career, patently is not'

Mail on Sunday

'*The Broken Chariot* explores familiar themes for Sillitoe: working in factories, drinking in pubs and chasing women in post-war Nottingham. But the writer has found a fresh, new approach to his specialist subject; one that again allows him to tackle the issue of class in a way that is often surprising and always entertaining'

Yorkshire Post

Birthday (2001)
Birthday is the long-awaited sequel to *Saturday Night and Sunday Morning*. Four decades on from the novel which was at the forefront of the new wave of British literature, we rediscover the Seaton brothers: older, certainly; wiser – possibly not.

'Sequels are seldom better than the original but this one is'

Allan Massie

'There are parallels here with Kingsley Amis's *The Old Devils* – another old man's book about old age. But it is well worth reading, both for its evocation of a vanished way of working-class life, and for its steadfast depiction of the horrors of old age and the valour and comradeship that can, in part at least, redeem it'

Daily Telegraph

The Web Detective

http://www.nottinghamcity.gov.uk
The city's official site.

http://www.thisisnottingham.co.uk
Notttingham news engine.

http://www.cressbrook.co.uk/matlock.htm
Tourist information site for Matlock.

http://www.raleighbikes.com/home.html
Raleigh Bikes of Nottingham's website – although the cycle factory on Triumph Road has now been demolished.

http://www.nottinghamgallery.co.uk
This site offers a photographic survey of Nottingham past and present.